Shadows

Jamie stared into his father's eyes and saw only a dark unyielding obsession.

Jamie knows what to expect if he doesn't win: his father is obsessed with the idea that Jamie will become a world squash champion, and succeed where he had not. But Jamie doesn't share his father's single-minded ambition and is desperate to escape from the verbal and physical abuse that will follow when he fails.

Then he finds the girl hiding in his shed, and in helping her to escape from her past and the danger that is pursuing her, he is able to put his own problems into perspective. He realizes that he can't run away for ever—he must come out of the shadows and face up to his father, however painful the process might be.

TIM BOWLER was born and brought up in Leigh-on-Sea, Essex, the setting of his first novel, *Midget*, and still visits there regularly.. Since leaving university, where he received an honours degree in Swedish and Scandinavian Studies, he has worked in a variety of fields including forestry and the timber trade and as a teacher of modern languages. He now works as a freelance writer and translator of Scandinavian languages and lives in Devon. *Shadows* is his fourth novel for Oxford University Press. He won the Carnegie Medal for his third novel, *River Boy*.

SHADOWS

Other books by Tim Bowler

Midget
Dragon's Rock
River Boy

SHADOWS

Tim Bowler

Oxford University Press
Oxford New York Toronto

OXFORD

UNIVERSITY PRESS

Great Clarendon Street, Oxford OX2 6DP

Oxford University Press is a department of the University of Oxford.
It furthers the University's objective of excellence in research, scholarship,
and education by publishing worldwide in

Oxford New York

Athens Auckland Bangkok Bogotá Buenos Aires Calcutta
Cape Town Chennai Dar es Salaam Delhi Florence Hong Kong Istanbul
Karachi Kuala Lumpur Madrid Melbourne Mexico City Mumbai
Nairobi Paris São Paulo Singapore Taipei Tokyo Toronto Warsaw

and associated companies in Berlin Ibadan

Oxford is a registered trade mark of Oxford University Press
in the UK and in certain other countries

First published 1999
First published in paperback edition 2000

British Library Cataloguing in Publication Data available

ISBN 0 19 275062 3

Typeset by AFS Image Setters Ltd, Glasgow
Printed in Great Britain by Cox & Wyman Ltd, Reading, Berks

For Ivan and Elizabeth
with love

'Kinship is healing; we are physicians to each other.'

Oliver Sachs

1

Jamie tried to ignore the shouts from the spectators, the urging, the willing, the madness. Across the squash court, Danny glared back at him. But there was an element of triumph in the boy's face. His cockiness was gone—the first two games had at least wiped that from him—but having fought back with characteristic aggression to two games all, he clearly felt he was in with a chance of taking the match.

Jamie tried to focus his mind and energy. He knew the pressure was on him now. He had had a two–love lead and thrown it away. He had never beaten Danny in the twelve months since the boy had moved down from the north, and though this was meant to be a minor affair, the semi-final of the Under 19 Knockout in the 'friendly' atmosphere of their own club, it was obvious that everyone saw it as a taster for the Regional Championships in two weeks' time.

He glanced up at the faces in the gallery. They were all there: Andy, Joe, the bar crowd, and, of course, Bob Powell blustering on with pride every time Danny won a rally, as though his son were a god and not the arrogant poser that he was. But there was only one face up there Jamie was bothered about. And right now he did not dare to look at it.

'Fifth and final game,' called Geoff. 'Love–all.'

The shouts from the gallery died away and he forced his mind back to the match. Danny walked over to the right service box, glanced his way for a second, and served.

A floater, hanging high. Jamie drove the ball down the backhand side wall and took up the T position midcourt. Danny powered it back across court, too close to the far wall for him to cut it off. He scuttled back and played a boast off the side wall, hoping the ball would catch the nick where the wall met the floor and give him an outright winner. But Danny scooped it up and played a cross-court drop.

Jamie dived forward. Earlier in the match he would have reached this one but now, with his energy almost spent, he stopped, knowing it was out of reach, anxious to save what strength he had left.

There was clapping from the gallery, then Powell's voice bellowed out.

'Good boy, Danny, good boy! He's finished!'

He heard disapproving noises from Joe who, as owner of the club, always tried to curb Powell's open hostility towards his son's opponents. It never did any good.

'One–love,' called Geoff.

The next serve came, another floater, higher this time and dropping close to the back wall. Somehow he managed to volley it before it dipped into the dead spot at the back of the court, but it was a poor return. He was out of position and Danny had already moved to the front of the court for the drop shot. Another simple point.

'Two–love,' called Geoff.

He was playing like a fool, giving away rallies like a beginner. He glanced back to the gallery and this time forced himself to look at the figure in the top right corner. The face was impassive, like hewn marble. There was no expression in the eyes. But the mouth was tight.

The next serve came, another curler, but not so close to the side wall this time. He struck out, aiming across court, but Danny cut it off and volleyed towards the backhand nick. He struggled to the front of the court and just managed to flick it back. It was meant to be a lob but it was too low. Danny leapt, drove it down the forehand side and buried it at the back of the court.

'That's the one!' shouted Powell. 'Kill him!'

He glared up and saw Joe trying to calm Powell again. But Powell had eyes for Danny alone. From the top right corner of the gallery there was only stillness.

'Three–love,' called Geoff.

He turned back to the court, determined to fight back but now desperately jaded. It seemed to him suddenly that he'd been on a squash court every waking moment of his sixteen years. And before the next service came, he just had time to reflect that this wasn't far from the truth. No wonder these walls had come to feel like a cell; and it was a cell of tension, tempered by moments of jubilation, but dominated for the most part by an ambition he sensed he would never fulfil.

The serve came, again a high curler. He struck out early, this time down the side wall, a better length than he had managed for a while but still short. Danny raced across and drove it the same way. Jamie followed suit and soon they were locked in a duel down the side wall, each aiming for the perfect width and the perfect length to make the ball cling to the side wall and die in the nick at the back.

Keep it tight, he told himself. Keep a good length. Keep plugging it down the side wall. Make him go for the risky winner.

And there it was. Danny had driven the ball in short, aiming for the forehand nick, but it was loose. Jamie reached it and played a drop to the same part of the court. Danny lunged and barged against him. The ball rolled along the floor, dead.

Danny turned expectantly to Geoff.

'Let, please.'

Jamie looked away. He knew Danny was not entitled to a let but he didn't expect a problem. Geoff was not a person to be fazed by anyone, not even Danny or his father.

'No let,' said Geoff.

'Oh, come on,' said Danny. 'He was just standing there. How am I supposed to get to the ball if he won't move out of the way?'

Jamie turned quietly to the side wall. He had heard this sort of dialogue so many times from Danny and, if it went on long enough, which it usually did, Bob Powell was bound to chime in.

'You were out of position,' said Geoff. 'You couldn't have reached the ball. I'm sorry. No let.'

'But he's been standing in the way all through the match.'

Jamie picked up the ball with his racket and moved to the right-hand service box, ready to start. The accusation was unfounded but there was no point in saying anything. Danny was still glaring at Geoff.

'Tell me how I'm supposed to reach the ball with him plonked in the way.'

'I've given my decision. Play on, please.'

Sure enough, Bob Powell broke in.

'Pathetic. I've never seen such marking in all my life. The kid was blocking the way. Anyone could see it.'

Jamie said nothing and continued to wait, ball in hand. In a strange way, he was grateful for this interruption. It gave him a moment to catch his breath. But not for long. Geoff leaned on the rail and fixed his eyes on Danny.

'Danny, play on, please, or I'll award a penalty point.'

There were murmurs round the gallery as Danny, with a final glare, sloped into position to continue the match. Jamie served at once, hoping the incident would have unsettled Danny's rhythm.

But Danny was now fired up. The ball came back like a bullet. Jamie raced to the back and returned it down the side wall. Danny was onto it at once and cut it short across court.

Jamie lunged and sent the ball down the side wall. Danny cut it off and drove it across court. Jamie raced after it, caught it before it died and sent a back-wall boast flying over their heads to the front wall. Danny took it early, before it touched the floor, and sent it cutely into the forehand nick.

'That's the boy!' roared Powell.

4

Jamie glanced up and saw him flushed and jubilant, as though vindicated after a great injustice. But there was no time to think of that. Danny was already in the service box, chafing to finish the match. Jamie felt the spectre of defeat over him.

The serve came, a hard one this time, and aimed straight at him. He jumped to the side, too sluggishly—and the ball clipped the edge of his shorts. There was a gasp from above, then more cheers from Powell. Jamie looked down, ashamed.

He couldn't believe he'd let Danny catch him out like that.

'Four–love!' called Geoff.

Danny served from the left-hand box, another hard one straight at him. This time he was ready. He jumped to the side and drove the ball back. He desperately needed a point now to restore his confidence. But first he had to regain the serve.

Danny, however, seemed bent on denying him everything. The shots came back more crisply than ever and the pace and power which were Danny's trademark had returned. To Jamie, the next four points seemed to fly past in a maze of drives, volleys, and smashes that forced him back, yanked him forward, played with him like a toy. He knew then that he could not beat Danny. Not today. Perhaps not ever. Danny was too strong.

'Eight–love!' called Geoff. 'Game and match ball!'

Match ball. It seemed only moments ago that Geoff had called love–all in the first game of the match. He sensed the tension up in the gallery.

The serve came from the right-hand box, the first lob serve Danny had sent him for several rallies. Jamie stretched out and feebly tried to play a volley, though he had now ceased to care about the destiny of the restless little ball and wanted only to be free of it.

His wish was soon granted.

The ball climbed over his racket, dipped into the back corner and achieved what for him was the ultimate shame.

An ace.

He looked up at the gallery, searching the top right corner. And this time saw an empty space.

Joe and Andy clapped him on the back, told him he'd done well, that it was a terrific match. He didn't listen. He knew where he was meant to be and hurried on. Best to get it over with straight away. He hoped there would be no one in the changing room. Somehow it was always worse when they had to go to the back of the car park.

The changing room was empty. He walked to the centre of the room and waited, then the door opened behind him.

He stiffened and turned.

The hand flew out and struck him in the side of the face. His head flicked back, despite his efforts to keep it still. He cursed himself silently. He had told himself on the way here that this time he must not flinch. He forced his head forward, ready for the next one.

It came, the same cheek, but harder. There were no words, not yet. Later there would be words. There were always words, plenty of words. But not now.

His muscles tightened. There would be one more. One for every game he'd lost today. The usual deal. And the last was always the hardest.

The hand lashed out; and this time he yelped. He looked down, breathing hard, then made himself straighten up.

But his father had already left the room.

2

Ashingford seemed quiet for a Saturday evening and the December chill made it seem an even more lonely place. He trudged through the town centre, shifting the weight of his squash bag from one hand to the other and wishing he'd had the foresight to bring his coat. He should have known from bitter experience that Dad would make him walk home if he lost, with his kit, of course.

The punishments were predictable enough after all these years, as were the rewards. It was all a question of pass or fail, and the degree of effort involved, in Dad's eyes. A pass—in other words a win—meant money. Not as much as Danny would be getting from Bob Powell tonight in the usual ostentatious hand-out in the bar, but money nevertheless, and sometimes even words of praise, though, in keeping with Dad's relentlessly unforgiving standards, these were always tempered with exhortations to train harder, aim higher.

But a fail—that was different. A fail where Dad felt there was some effort involved meant extra workouts. A fail where he thought there was no effort meant . . .

He rubbed the side of his face and walked on, pushing the thoughts from his mind. The sprawling town centre fell away at last and the estates opened up on either side of him. He left the clock tower behind him, wandered past the lane that ran down to the school and on as far as the station, then cut down the alleyway that tracked the railway line and came out at the bottom of their garden. He liked this way home, detached from the streets. It left him alone to think and he liked to come up to the back of his house through the allotments.

Suddenly he stopped.

Two men blocked his path a few feet away, one tall, the other slightly shorter and stockier. The darkness obscured their faces somewhat and he had little time to study them before they turned and moved to the side to let him pass. He did so, quickly, and hurried on, sensing their attention still upon him.

He didn't know why he felt uneasy. They hadn't challenged him but there was something about them he didn't trust. He knew this way home was not one his mother approved of. She worried about the more rowdy elements in the town and thought he shouldn't walk in places where he could be exposed to danger. But he had never felt danger here before.

He strode on a few more feet, then glanced over his shoulder.

They had not followed. But he had been right. Even in the darkness he sensed them watching.

He hurried on and didn't slow down until he saw the sheds dotted about the allotments on his left, and, to his right, the back gardens of the houses in his street. The wall of the alleyway came to an end and he started to relax a little. He liked this spot. Very few people came here and, with the allotments on one side and the gardens on the other, he could almost pretend he was in the country, though it took a good deal of pretending.

He reached their own patch of ground and gazed with some affection at the little shed at the bottom. It had become a kind of refuge. Dad wasn't keen on gardening and the allotment had always been Mum's special passion, but for some reason she seemed to have lost interest in it over the last year and since the shed was now rarely used, except to store sticks and plant pots and other gardening junk, he'd found it an excellent place to escape to when he wanted privacy. They never seemed to think of looking for him there. He'd had a duplicate key cut, secretly, and had left an old blanket and a tatty cushion there, hidden inside a bin bag and stuffed under some plant pots.

It was tempting to walk down there now, even in this cold weather.

But that would only make things worse later.

He wandered up to the back gate of the house and stopped. Upstairs he could see a light on in Dad's study, and downstairs, Mum busy in the kitchen. He took a deep breath, tramped up to the house and opened the back door.

Mum looked round as he entered the kitchen.

'Darling, where have you been? I was expecting you ages ago.'

He frowned. 'I had to walk home.'

She looked at him for a moment, as though she wanted to say something, then leaned forward and gave him a hurried kiss.

'Well, never mind, you're here now and . . .' She put on her oven gloves and opened the oven door. 'The food will probably . . .'

She was doing it again: starting sentences and not finishing them. She'd only begun doing that recently. He stared at her, wondering whether Dad had hit her, too, tonight.

'Sit down, darling,' she said. She was smiling, but it was a distracted smile, a smile that barely had the energy to reach him. He sat down at the table, feeling numb and confused. An overdone lasagne appeared before him, followed by overdone carrots and overdone potatoes. He ate in silence.

Mum didn't ask about the squash.

Dad remained upstairs.

After supper he took the basketball, wandered out to the garden and threw the ball up at the basket on the wall. He often found it relaxing to come out here and throw a basketball and there was always the chance that the sound would bring Spider out from next door and they could talk.

But there was no light at his friend's window. Suddenly he heard footsteps at the bottom of the garden. He whirled round, thinking of Spider.

But it was not Spider.

It was a figure moving past the gate. The face turned for an instant and Jamie drew breath. It was one of the men he had seen earlier, the taller one. There was no mistaking him, even in the darkness. Their eyes met, briefly, then the man passed from view.

Jamie stood there, still holding the basketball and wondering why he felt so nervous. There was no reason why this person shouldn't be walking round here at nine o'clock at night. But he wondered where the other man was.

Then he saw him.

Down among the sheds at the foot of the allotments was the shorter, stockier figure, also unmistakable. A few moments later the tall man joined him and the two stood there for several minutes, seemingly in conversation, though Jamie caught no words.

Then, with a glance in his direction, they turned and were gone.

3

'I've come to a decision,' said Dad over breakfast. 'I'm stopping your money.'

Jamie stared at him, then at Mum. But she was avoiding both their eyes. He sensed that she and Dad had already argued over this; and he would have come off best as usual.

'You're not winning,' Dad went on. 'I don't know why. You should be. Your last six opponents—apart from Danny—were all worse players than you. And you should have taken Danny apart in that third game, like you did in the first and second. I don't know what's got into you.'

Jamie looked away. He hated the money side of squash. But Dad wasn't talking about the win bonuses, as he liked to call them.

'I'm talking about your pocket money. It's time you started winning again so the win bonuses stay. But no pocket money. You're on commission only.'

'That's not fair. You know it's not.'

'It's perfectly fair and that's the way it'll be. When you start playing the way you should, I'll reinstate the pocket money.'

'So I'm to get nothing at all. Unless I go out and get a job.'

'You've already got a job—to improve your squash and start playing to your potential.'

'And what do I do if I want to go and see a film with Spider?'

'You shouldn't be wasting your time with that boy anyway. He's a loser. He's going nowhere.'

'Well, somebody else, then?'

Dad merely shrugged. 'You'll just have to start winning matches again.'

Jamie felt anger rise within him. He had to have money. The win bonuses were useful but even after a string of losses, he had always had the lifeline of pocket money.

Dad stood up from the table.

'I know you think this is hard. But you're not going to get where you want to go without making some sacrifices. You'll thank me for this one day.' He looked at his watch. 'You'd better get ready. We're behind already this morning.'

Half an hour later, he and Dad were driving in through the school gates.

Years ago, in the days when he'd enjoyed squash, he had thought it a good thing that his school had its own squash court, grotty though it was. And Dad being Chairman of Governors as well as a former squash celebrity and a highly successful writer of motivational books, not to mention a close personal friend of Mr Talbot, the headmaster, himself a squash fanatic, meant that they had their own key and could use the court whenever they liked.

Especially since Dad had said publicly on numerous occasions that his son would one day turn professional and become world champion. Big words, and they always made Jamie cringe when he heard them, but Dad believed in talking that way. For him, everything came down to visualizing the goal, affirming that it's going to happen, then working hard to achieve it.

World Champion. It seemed a crazy ambition but Dad kept telling him he could make it. And sometimes, when he played, and the game went well, he almost felt he could do it. He knew he was good. But what frightened him was how much each match now cost him.

They pulled up outside the squash court. Dad switched off the engine and swivelled round in the seat. Jamie looked at him and knew what was coming. Sure enough, it was smile-time.

'You think I'm being hard on you, don't you?' said Dad.
Jamie said nothing. Dad put an arm round him.

'You've got to understand, I don't hit you because I like it. I hit you because it'll help you. One of these days you'll be a father and you'll know what I'm talking about. There'll be times when you can see your boy's going wrong and the only way to correct it is with a short, sharp shock.'

And Mum? he thought. Does she need a short, sharp shock every time you hit her? But he said nothing, knowing what the response would be. Dad squeezed him.

'I know it's hard for you to understand what I'm aiming at. But you've just got to trust my judgement. When I was your age, I had no one to help me. I had to find my own way. There were lots of times when I . . . are you listening to this?'

Jamie started at the sudden change of tone. Having heard these words so many times, his mind had drifted to thoughts of the two men and, more importantly, his worries about money. He quickly managed a half-smile.

'Sorry.'

Dad looked hard at him for a moment and Jamie wondered what was in his mind. He wished he could be close to his father, like Spider was with his. Dad squeezed him again.

'Let's get started.'

They climbed out of the car and Jamie went round to the boot to fetch the gear while Dad unlocked the court. The little building looked drab, especially on this miserable December morning, and there was an air of depression about the place. But at least it was never cold. The heating system that fed the court was so antiquated that it could not be properly regulated. When it was on, it was uncomfortably hot but since he never played matches here, it didn't matter too much. And in cold weather like this he was grateful for the warmth.

He picked up his racket and fiddled with the strings, unwilling to get started.

'Never mind the racket,' said Dad. 'Get on with your stretching exercises while I warm the ball up.'

He went through the stretching routine, glancing now and then at his father driving the ball rhythmically against the front wall. Even now Dad looked immaculate on court, though well past his prime and with his body broken by the over-training of his youth, not to mention the knee injury that prematurely cut short his brilliant playing career. All his shots were grooved, precise, economical. There were no frills. His body position was always perfect, though he moved sluggishly now.

Like greased lightning, he used to be, Mum always said, and Jamie wondered how he would have fared in a match with his father, had Dad been sixteen now. He finished his exercises and stepped forward, unable to put things off any longer. Dad said nothing and merely hit the ball to him, and for a few minutes they warmed up together, neither speaking as they drove the ball across court to each other.

'Change,' muttered Dad after a few minutes, and he moved across and they repeated the procedure on the other side. This was usually the silent time. They would warm up slowly, then it would be boasts and drives followed by the rest of the practice routines and finally ghosting—simulated squash without the ball—which he hated.

Dad grunted, the signal to start the boasts and drives, and Jamie went forward. Having spent so much time on court together, they hardly needed to speak now and Dad didn't usually bother to announce the next thing. They both knew the sequence so well.

He started the routine, driving the ball down the forehand side wall, moving back to the T position, forward to the backhand wall to pick up the shot his father had boasted to him from the back of the court, then driving it hard down that side, and so on, ad nauseam; though, in reality, he quite liked this routine. The only thing that stopped it being properly enjoyable was the thought of all the more torturous routines to come.

Yet even as he ran and hit and sweated and lunged, he found his thoughts wandering again. To the problem of money.

And the two strange men.

Spider opened the front door and looked him over in his quizzical way.

'And what do you want, disturbing me on a Sunday afternoon?'

Jamie managed a smile. 'Fancy a walk into town?'

'To see the tourist attractions?'

'What tourist attractions?'

'Well, give me a couple of hours and I'll come up with something. Suppose your dad's out or he'd never approve of this.'

Jamie felt himself flush. It always made him uncomfortable when Spider commented on Dad's disapproval, not that his friend was the slightest bit bothered whether anyone approved of him or not. That was one of the refreshing things about him.

Spider shrugged.

'I suppose I can put up with you for a couple of hours, as long as you don't get too paranoid and moody. Got any money?'

Jamie looked down. 'No.'

'What a surprise. Well, come in, anyway. It's freezing.'

He entered the house and Spider closed the door behind him.

'So did you win?'

Jamie shook his head.

'Oh, dear,' said Spider. 'I've got to be nice to you. What was the score?'

'What do you care? You hate squash.'

'I don't hate squash. I'm just bored by it. There's a difference. Boredom doesn't require effort. Hatred does. Can't stand effort.'

'I had noticed.'

15

'Good God, humour. There's hope for you yet. What was the score?'

'Three–two to him.'

'And who's him?'

'Boy called Danny. You wouldn't know him. He doesn't go to our school.'

'Is that the one who acts the prima donna on court?'

'There are lots of people who do that.'

'But he's the one who beat you three–nil last time, right?'

'Three–love.'

'Three–love. You told me about it. He messed about during the match and accused you of gamesmanship or something.'

Jamie nodded. 'That was him.'

'Have you ever beaten him?'

'No. I've come close lots of times. People keep telling me if I could just be more aggressive on court, I'd take him apart.'

'And would you?'

'Maybe.' Jamie paused. 'I just . . . can't work up aggression that easily. And if you're too aggressive, your strokes and tactics can go to pieces. I usually manage to get fired up for a couple of games and, when I do, things go pretty well. But I can't keep it going. I seem to bottle out when it really counts.'

'Oh, well. Beat him next time. When are you playing him again?'

'Two weeks. The Regional Championships. Of all the coincidences.'

'What do you mean?'

'Well, since we've both had our birthdays, we no longer qualify as under sixteens. We've had to join the under nineteens.'

'What's wrong with that?'

'Nothing. It's just that when we were under sixteens, he was seeded one in the county and I was seeded two.'

'I thought you were number one.'

'I was number one until Danny moved down here.'

Jamie paused again, thinking of the things Dad had said to him on the day he lost the number one spot; and the things he had said since. 'Anyway,' he went on, 'because of the way we were seeded, we usually met in the final at the Regional Championships. But now that we've joined the under nineteens, where the standard's much higher and you're up against the likes of Andy Bailey—'

'Who's he?'

'Boy at the squash club. Eighteen. Brilliant player.'

'Another prima donna?'

'No, he's OK. I like him. But because there are more players like Andy around, Danny and I are now seeded lower and it was about a one in God-knows-how-many chance for us to be drawn to meet in the first round of this year's Regionals. And guess what's happened?'

Spider reached for his coat.

'Well, you'll just have to beat him, then, won't you? Are these Regional Championships important?'

'Fairly. And they're a sort of warm up for January.'

'January?'

'The Junior Open. The World Championships.'

Spider looked at him in silence for a moment.

'All these tournaments you go to. You're always off somewhere.'

Jamie frowned. Spider was right. There were so many tournaments about the country and Dad dragged him round most of them. It was supposed to improve his ranking, his match play, his temperament, but he knew that in reality it did none of those things. For him, at least. All that happened was that he played and lost.

They walked through to the front room where he heard sounds of laughter.

'What's going on?' he said.

'The twins were ten yesterday. We've been eating the leftovers of the party.'

Jamie entered the front room and saw Mr and Mrs Dean on the floor with Amy and Becky, plates and bottles and plastic cups all around them. He loved coming here. It was so unlike the atmosphere in his own

17

house where everything was obsessively neat and life was geared only to squash. The Deans, by contrast, seemed to live in a state of permanent chaos and took people and events as they came, no questions asked and no judgements made.

'Jamie!' shouted Mr Dean. 'How are you?'

'He's not very happy,' said Spider.

'Why not?'

'He lost.'

'Lost what?'

Spider looked at Jamie and laughed.

'Sorry, but squash isn't top priority in this household.'

'Squash?' Mr Dean looked across. 'You lost at squash?'

'Yes,' said Jamie.

Mrs Dean stood up.

'Never mind, Jamie. Would you like some cake?'

'He hasn't got time for cake,' said Spider. 'We're walking into Ashingford.'

Mrs Dean cuffed Spider, then looked back at Jamie.

'We'll just rewind and try that again. Jamie, would you like some cake?'

'No, thanks.'

'Don't take any notice of Spider. He's above himself because he's gone and got another job.' She frowned. 'Yet another. Don't ask me how he's going to fit his homework in round all the things he's doing.'

Jamie looked at Spider.

'So what's this one?'

'It's only part-time. Saturdays and after school some days.'

'But what is it?'

'Stock replenishment executive.'

'What?'

'Stock replenishment executive.'

Jamie stared at him. 'Is that what I think it is?'

Mrs Dean pushed Spider to the side and took Jamie by the arm.

'He's a shelf-stacker at the supermarket. As if he

hasn't earned enough money already towards this wretched car.'

'That's just the point,' said Spider. 'I haven't earned enough. I want to save up more to put towards lessons when I'm seventeen, and any repair bills and stuff like that.'

Mr Dean snorted.

'Why's it got to be a sports car? What's wrong with an old banger? That was always good enough for me.'

'It shows,' said Spider.

Jamie chuckled, having heard variations of this discussion so many times. Spider had been single-mindedly saving since he was twelve towards the dream car he intended to buy in time for his seventeenth birthday and had had a succession of jobs over the years, often two or three at the same time. He made no secret to Jamie or anyone else of how much he had saved, and it was now a considerable amount of money. It often amused—and sometimes irritated—Jamie that his friend's dry and laid-back manner caused so many people—especially Dad—to misjudge him and think he had no motivation.

Not that Spider cared.

'He's obsessed with money,' said Mr Dean. 'I think he's trying to become a magnate.'

'What's a magnate?' said Amy, her mouth full of cake.

Becky looked round at her. 'You pick up metal with it.'

Mrs Dean laughed.

'He's transferred all his money from the building society into his bank account so that he's got it ready the moment he wants to make an offer, and he's actually started going out looking at some of the cars he's interested in, which means his dad has to go with him, or I do, so that someone can drive the car. Then he's not happy because he doesn't think we're giving the car a proper test run.'

'What's a proper test run?' said Jamie.

'A fast test run,' said Mr Dean. 'I can't work out how a boy who takes three hours to get dressed in the mornings wants a car that screams out of the blocks like a bat out of hell. Thank God he hasn't found the one he wants yet.'

Mrs Dean chuckled.

'Anyway, Jamie—tea?'

He glanced at Spider.

'No, thanks. We were . . . going into town.'

'There won't be much open this afternoon.'

'The fast food's open,' said Spider. 'We can get a milk shake or something.'

Mr Dean pointed a chocolate finger biscuit at Jamie.

'Well, make sure Spider pays for something. Becky, don't do that with the jelly.'

Spider took him by the arm. 'Come on, let's get out of here.'

4

They walked down the road, burying their chins in their scarves. The cold snap that had set in since the beginning of December seemed set to continue and, if anything, was growing worse.

'Not sure this is a good idea,' said Spider. 'Think I'll go for a hot chocolate instead of a milk shake. If we make it there without turning back.'

They made their way towards the town centre.

'So, this Danny,' said Spider. 'Where does he go to school?'

'Fairways.'

'Oh, *Fair-ways*!' Spider twitched up his nose. 'No wonder we haven't seen him at our school. His folks must be well off.'

'His dad's loaded.'

'He'd have to be. So what's he like? Apart from being a pain on court.'

'I don't know him that well. I just see him up at the club or on the playing circuit. I don't know where he lives or what kind of family he's got. They came down from up north a year ago. I know his dad. He comes to watch everything.'

'And what's he like?'

'Obnoxious. He and my dad hate each other.'

'I wonder why,' said Spider, his face deadpan. 'Still, just as well you don't know the rest of the family. They're probably obnoxious, too.'

'If there are any others. I told you, I don't know anything about them. Don't particularly want to.'

They passed the clock tower and turned down the main street, walking faster as they grew colder. The

21

traffic was heavier here, even on a Sunday, and there were cars parked on both sides of the road. Spider broke into a trot.

'Come on, I can't stand any more of this.'

And they ran the last few hundred yards.

Rossi's Burger Bonanza was not the most up-market of establishments but on a day as cold as this, they were grateful for it. Spider hurried up to the counter, took off his gloves and looked round at him.

'So you haven't got any money?'

'Sorry.'

'What do you want, then?'

'Just a hot chocolate. Thanks.'

'Don't you want any chips?'

'No, thanks.'

'I'm having some.'

'You've just been eating cake and jelly.'

'What's that got to do with it?' He looked at the assistant. 'Two hot chocolates and two large chips, please. To eat here.'

Jamie looked at him. 'But I said—'

Spider stopped him with a glance. 'Your stomach said something else. Do something useful and look for a table.'

Jamie found one upstairs overlooking the street and stood by it for a moment, thinking. He hated being bailed out by Spider, who, despite Mr Dean's jokes, was always generous with his money. But he knew he couldn't go on like this. There had to be a way of getting money of his own—and not from playing squash. Suddenly he stiffened.

The two men had appeared in the street below. He recognized them at once, even though he had only seen them in the darkness before. He moved back from the window but kept his eyes upon them.

Spider appeared with a tray.

'There you go,' he said, holding out one of the cartons of chips.

'Thanks.' Jamie took the chips absentmindedly, his eyes still on the street.

'What are you looking at?' said Spider.

Jamie snapped out of his reverie.

'Oh, nothing. Just . . . looking.' He sat down quickly. 'So, what's this job like, then?'

'Pretty boring. Just a means to an end. But we have some fun, too. And there's some nice girls there. Not that you'd be interested, being married to squash.'

'Very funny.'

He looked away, feeling awkward again. He wished he could be like Spider. Spider always seemed so comfortable in his own skin. He was never fazed by anything and seemed to coast through life, unaffected by all the worries he himself felt burdened with. No wonder Spider had lots of friends while he had only one. And that was Spider.

He stiffened again.

The men had appeared downstairs and were standing at the counter, talking to one of the assistants. He could just see them through the gap where the stairway twisted round. They didn't seem to be ordering food.

'What's up?' said Spider.

Jamie glanced at him, then back at the two men.

'Nothing, I just . . .' He made up his mind. 'I've just got to go to the loo.'

'OK.'

He jumped to his feet and made his way downstairs, trying not to look hurried. Crazy though it was, he knew he had to get close to these men, without making them aware of him. He didn't want them to recognize him from yesterday, yet he had to satisfy his curiosity and hear what they were saying.

He joined the back of the nearest queue and studied them surreptitiously. They certainly weren't short of money, judging from the stylish clothing, and the watches and rings they both sported. The taller one seemed about twenty-five and stood out more, not merely by virtue of his height but by a certain air and swarthy good looks. The shorter man seemed older, perhaps because he was balding; but Jamie disliked him more.

23

He knew this suspicion was probably unfounded, yet something about the men still disturbed him. He leaned forward, trying to catch some of their words while holding himself in readiness to turn his back if they looked round. But they were already at the end of their conversation.

'OK,' said the tall one to the assistant. 'Well, let us know if you do. The phone number's on the card.'

And, a moment later, they had walked past him and were gone.

He watched them for a while as they sauntered off down the street, then he hurried back upstairs. Spider's eyes were bright with amusement.

'You losing your marbles?'

'What?'

'You walked right past the loo.'

'Oh.' He tried to look unconcerned. 'Yeah, I forgot.'

'So aren't you going?'

'No, I can't be bothered. Let's just eat.'

Spider raised an eyebrow but said no more.

It was six o'clock when he arrived home and he knew at once that something was wrong. Dad was standing before him in the hall, scowling.

'Why did you take the money from your mother's purse?'

Jamie stared at him. Somewhere upstairs he heard Mum crying.

'I . . . I didn't take any money.'

'So why is there money missing?'

'I don't know.'

Dad took a step forward.

'There were three notes in your mother's purse. They're all gone.'

Jamie moved back towards the door. He knew why suspicion fell on him but this was too much. His father's hand lashed out. Jamie ducked, just in time, and raced out into the street.

He knew this would do him no good but he couldn't stop himself. To be denied money was bad enough; to be unjustly accused of stealing it was worse. He ran to the end of the road and cut back towards the alleyway behind the houses. There was only one refuge he knew of, cold though it would be.

He reached the allotments, slowed down and padded between the sheds until he reached their own. It looked chilly and uninviting in the darkness but he knew of no other sanctuary right now. He lifted the stone under which he hid his duplicate key, then gave a start.

The padlock was lying on the ground close by and beside it a small iron bar. He straightened up and stared at the latch. It had been forced. Cautiously he opened the door and peeped in.

There was no one there. But in the corner where he liked to sit, he could see the old blanket and tatty cushion on the floor. And he distinctly remembered leaving them in the bin bag last time he was here.

But he couldn't think about that now. He closed the door behind him and stood there for a moment, enveloped in blackness, trying to calm his racing thoughts; then he wrapped the blanket round him, propped the cushion under his head, and lay back in the dark.

5

In the night he heard voices. He lay as still as he could, though he was shivering uncontrollably now and desperately anxious to go back to the house. But there was a coldness there he feared even more than this.

The voices came closer, then, to his relief, faded away.

He thought of Mum crying and wondered what had happened. But it was easy enough to guess. Dad would have first accused her of losing the money. Then he would have hit her. And finally, having presumably decided she was telling the truth, he would have jumped to the next conclusion.

Mum would receive flowers in the morning, of course, and the usual note saying how wonderful she was. As for himself . . .

He bit his lip and pulled his coat more tightly around him. It was no use trying to think about the future when the present demanded all his attention. Suddenly he heard a new sound.

Footsteps.

He held himself rigid, wondering who it could be. A few seconds later, a hand fiddled with the latch.

He sat up, trying to keep quiet. The door opened a fraction and he sensed a dark form there. He thought of the blanket and cushion that had been moved. If this were a tramp returning, there could be trouble. Tramps might be violent if they found a squat taken over. The door opened wider and moonlight fell upon the figure. He gasped.

It was a girl.

He must have moved or made some sound, as she turned at once and rushed away. He jumped to his feet, startled, and plunged out into the chill of the night. She was stumbling off across the allotments, running awkwardly as though in pain.

'Wait!' He called out, as loudly as he dared, not wanting to draw attention from the house. She did not stop. He hurried after her and caught her up. 'Please wait. I don't mean you any harm.'

She stopped and turned round. 'What makes you think I'm scared of you?'

He stared at her, unsure what to say. 'Well, you're . . . I mean, you're running away.'

She looked him over scornfully. 'Don't flatter yourself I'm bothered about you.'

He frowned, unsure whether to turn and leave her. She obviously wanted nothing to do with him, and he had enough problems of his own. He studied her, warily.

She seemed about his age and he wondered what she was doing wandering about this place on a cold December night. She was wearing a short jacket, which didn't look as though it afforded her much warmth, a longish skirt and a thick pullover, and high boots. Her hair was straight and ran down as far as her shoulders and she had a woollen hat on that made her look somewhat mischievous. Her face, with its small mouth, impish nose and bright eyes, would normally have been attractive to him, in a wild kind of way, had there not been so much defiance in it. She was carrying a battered-looking holdall.

She turned to walk on and he caught her profile. He drew breath.

She was pregnant.

Heavily pregnant, too, by the look of it. He knew little enough about such things but even he could tell that this girl could not have long to wait before she gave birth.

He spoke again.

'Listen, I'm sorry I startled you. If you've been using the shed, that's OK. I was just . . . I mean . . . if you want to have it back for a while—'

27

'What were you doing there?' she said.

He looked away. He wasn't sure he wanted to give any explanations to a strange girl. But he didn't have to tell her he lived close by.

'I've fallen out with my dad,' he said.

She said nothing but started to walk back towards the shed. He followed her, still wondering whether to leave or stay. But he didn't know where else he could go now. All he knew was that he couldn't go back home, not as things stood. He glanced at the house and saw a light on in his room. They were still up, though there was no one at the window. He glanced at his watch and saw it was two o'clock.

Two in the morning and here he was, tired, hungry, cold, following some vagrant girl towards an allotment shed. She didn't slow down for him to catch her up but she wasn't looking over her shoulder so he assumed she trusted him a little. She reached the shed first and walked straight in without a backward glance.

Maybe this was how things were for those sleeping rough. You took what you could while it was there. If someone else took your doss, you fought them for it or found another place. Or came back later and reclaimed it.

He entered the shed and looked towards the corner. She didn't seem afraid of him; indeed, she appeared hardly to notice him now. She had pulled an old blanket from her bag and, together with his own blanket and the cushion, was awkwardly trying to make herself comfortable. She didn't look towards him as he stood in the doorway.

Then, to his surprise, she spoke. 'Thanks for giving up your place.'

It wasn't a soft voice—but it wasn't a hard voice, either. It was a tired voice, a voice that spoke of pain. He thought for a moment, then, remembering the other voices he had heard, answered her.

'Listen, I'm going to close the door to keep out the chill, all right? That's all I'm doing it for.'

She said nothing and he took that as consent.

He closed the door and blackness fell once more on the inside of the shed. He sat down on the wooden floor, close to the door. It was cold and there was a steady draught that ran over his back. He shifted to try and avoid it, but without success. She spoke again.

'You can move round this side if you want.'

He looked over towards her. There was precious little room for two people where she was but he needed no further persuasion to get away from the draught. He crawled slowly towards her, trying not to startle her by making any sudden movements. She reached out and pushed some of the plant pots to the side to clear a space. He sat down on the floor, his back against the same wall as her, and stretched his legs out alongside hers.

He still felt cold but it was a little better. She didn't speak and neither did he. He desperately needed to think. He couldn't stay here indefinitely. Sooner or later he would have to go and face his father and sort out the business with the money, and make sure Mum was OK.

Yet, strangely, he also felt he had to do something to help this girl.

He knew it was stupid even to think of getting involved. She probably couldn't wait to see the back of him. He found himself wondering about the baby and stole a glance at her. She was staring up at the roof of the shed, seemingly lost in thought. He hesitated.

'Shouldn't you . . . I mean . . . shouldn't you be in hospital or something?'

'Shouldn't you be minding your own business or something?'

The response came back as sharp as a knife. And he understood well enough. No questions, then. And that was fair enough. He didn't want to talk about himself, either. At least, not much. But one question was surely OK.

'Can I ask your name?'

'You can ask.'

He looked away.

No names either, then. He thought for a moment, wondering whether to give his own name, anyway. But he said nothing and she remained silent, too. He was shivering more and more now and wondering whether he would be able to stick the night out like this. The thought of going back to the house sickened him. It would be like defeat. But if he didn't stop shivering soon, he would have to consider it, whatever the consequences.

She spoke suddenly. 'You'd better share this a bit.'

She was spreading the blankets his way. He tried to wrap himself up in them but still felt freezing and imagined she did, too, though she said nothing and simply lay on her back, staring as before up at the roof of the shed. Even so, he sensed she was keeping a furtive eye on him.

He tried to settle himself to sleep, but it was no good. The chill seemed to cut through body and mind. Suddenly he realized she had turned to face him.

'Listen,' she said abruptly, 'we'll get through this better if we lean our bodies together.'

'OK.'

'But I'm telling you, if you start—'

'It's OK. You don't need to worry.'

'I might be pregnant but I can take care of myself.'

'I told you—it's OK. We don't have to lie together at all if you don't want to.'

He wasn't sure he wanted to now, though he knew she was right. It was probably the only way they would get through tonight. She eyed him a moment longer, then moved slowly towards him.

'Just remember what I said,' she muttered.

He didn't answer but moved cautiously closer, keeping his arms at his sides. Their bodies touched, arm to arm first, then, after some hesitant shuffling, hip to hip, leg to leg. He held himself rigidly still, aware of her softness, even as he felt the tension in her and realized, with relief, that, for all her talk, she was as wary of him as he was of her.

He didn't know whether she was dangerous. Perhaps she was. She might have a knife hidden somewhere but, whatever the case, he didn't imagine she would be looking for trouble in her present state. Whatever she said, she must surely feel vulnerable.

They lay rigidly still for some minutes, neither talking, neither moving. Her body did indeed take away some of the chill, as did the blankets, but he was still horribly cold. After a while, he felt her stir.

'Put your arm round me,' she said. 'And remember, don't—'

'Yeah, yeah.'

He pulled his arm up from his side, reached carefully over her shoulder and let it rest down the other side of her body, but without touching her. She seemed reassured by this and moved her head into the crook of his arm, then, after a few more minutes, onto his chest. He felt her hair brush against his nose and moved his head back to stop it tickling. She moved no more and neither did he. For some reason he found himself strangely aware of the bulge in her belly, though he could not see it and did not touch it.

She was right. They were warmer together. Parts of him were still very cold but he did not dare bring his body fully round against hers, though he wanted to. She, clearly, had no such intention, either. They lay there, in silence, and somehow, against all the odds, he fell asleep.

6

When he awoke, the girl was gone. And he saw daylight under the door.

He was still cold, hungry, upset. He stretched and felt a crick in his neck, then sat up and tried to think. He was not ready to face Dad. While part of him yearned to stride into the house and find out if Mum was all right, not to mention attack the contents of the fridge, a greater part still boiled with anger and hurt.

He pressed the light-button on his watch. Ten to nine. It didn't seem possible that he'd managed to sleep through the cold. He thought of Spider. His friend wouldn't have waited for him this morning and he certainly wouldn't have called at the house, knowing he was unpopular with Dad.

Jamie yawned. There was only one place to go, though it was no solution and would only postpone the moment of reckoning a little bit. But at least he would be warm there.

He stood up, walked over to the door and peeped out, then, seeing no one, slipped out and hurried away across the allotment.

He arrived at school at half-past nine and made his way straight to room eleven. He knew he should have reported to the office but he no longer cared about rules. He needed to sit down, he needed to be somewhere warm, he needed to see Spider. He wanted his friend by him, at least for a few minutes, before Dad caught up with him.

He stopped outside room eleven and listened to Mrs

Campbell's voice. He hated German, not just because he was no good at it but because Mrs Campbell seemed to whine at him all the time. But then, lots of the teachers had started whining at him over the past year. And it was only recently that he had noticed that their whining coincided with the increase in training Dad had been demanding of him. But there was no point in dwelling on that now.

He took a deep breath and opened the door.

Faces turned towards him as he entered the room. Mrs Campbell looked him over.

'You're very late, Jamie. I presume you have a reason?'

'Yes, miss.' He couldn't be bothered to invent one. All he wanted to do was sit down and be left to himself. He saw Spider watching him from the corner. Mrs Campbell spoke again.

'And what is the reason?'

He tried to clear the dullness from his mind.

'I . . . I had to go home and change my clothes,' he said finally. 'I fell in a puddle.'

It was a ridiculous excuse, and he knew it, but he couldn't think of anything better. And at least it gave him some kind of a reason for not being in school uniform. He heard titters round the class. Mrs Campbell frowned.

'Have you reported to the office?'

'Yes, miss.'

'And where are your books and things?'

'I forgot them.'

She pursed her lips.

'Well, you'd better join us, now you're here, but I'm not very impressed, Jamie. I don't know what's happening to you these days.'

He didn't know either, but there was no point telling Mrs Campbell that. He sat down in his usual place next to Spider and pretended to study the text book his friend had pushed towards him. To his relief, Mrs Campbell turned to the blackboard and started writing. Spider leaned across and whispered.

'Are you OK?'

Jamie stared at him for a moment, then shook his head. Spider leaned closer.

'Mr Talbot came in just after the lesson started and asked if you were here.'

Jamie shrugged. He'd expected the Head to be involved, as Dad's bosom buddy. His father would have rung him first thing this morning at home.

'What did he do when he saw I wasn't here?' he murmured.

'Just went out again.' Spider glanced at Mrs Campbell, who had turned back to the class, and said no more; but Jamie sensed his support.

The lesson dragged on and somehow Jamie managed to stay awake, though he was aching to lower his head to the desk. And he was so hungry now, so desperate for some hot food and a hot drink. Even here, close to the radiator, he felt cold, as though the chill of the shed still clung to him. And the confusion of the night was starting to overwhelm him. He was worrying about Dad, and Mum, and money, and the two men; and now, most of all, the girl.

'Well, Jamie?'

He looked up with a start, realizing Mrs Campbell had asked him a question.

'Yes, miss?'

'The accusative case is for what?'

'The direct object of the sentence,' he said mechanically, just remembering her words a few minutes earlier.

'And the direct object is what?'

He said nothing.

'Jamie?' She had that edge back in her voice. 'The direct object is what?'

Luckily Tanya put up a hand.

'Yes, Tanya.'

'It's, like, the person or thing that gets something done to it. I mean, like, if the dog bites the man, it's the man that's the object.'

'The direct object, Tanya.'

'Yes, miss.'

Jamie looked at Tanya gratefully and wanted to smile at her; but Mrs Campbell's eyes had fastened upon him again.

'I was hoping you might explain it to us, Jamie. And when else is the accusative case used?'

He didn't know and he didn't care. His thoughts were now fixed on a strange girl who had entered his life and then left it again.

'Jamie?'

'I don't know.'

'Well, perhaps if you'd been paying attention rather than staring out of the window for the last ten minutes, you would know.'

Tanya's hand went up again.

'Yes, Tanya.'

'It's, like, used after certain prepositions.'

'Exactly. And Jamie can copy out the list of them, together with the rest of the section on the accusative case on page 31. Jamie, I'll speak to you afterwards.'

But this was not to be. The door opened and Mr Talbot entered the room.

'Excuse me again, Mrs Campbell. Ah, Jamie, you're here. A word with you in my office, please.'

Jamie stood up, trying to ignore the looks from the rest of the class. He felt a soft pat from Spider as he left the desk and walked over to Mr Talbot. The headmaster led the way down the corridor and didn't speak until they were in his office.

'Sit down, Jamie. Now, what's going on?'

Jamie tried to think of the right thing to say. He knew he couldn't tell Mr Talbot too much, not because he didn't like him or trust him—which he did—but because he knew the headmaster would only see Dad's point of view.

'I had a sort of bust up with my dad,' he said eventually.

'So I gather.' Mr Talbot took his place behind the desk and picked up the phone. 'Ron? It's Jim. Yes, he's here. In my office. Do you want to speak to him? You'll come over. OK, fine. See you in a few minutes. Bye.'

Jamie pictured his father's face and the image frightened him. And he wondered about Mum. Where she was, what she was doing, what she was feeling. Mr Talbot's voice broke in upon him.

'Are you set for the Regional Championships?'

Jamie stared at him. The Regional Championships? As if he cared about the Regional Championships. Strange how Mr Talbot assumed that the boy in front of him was as mad about squash as his father and headmaster were. He tried to drag some kind of response out of himself.

'Yes, sir. I've . . . I've been training hard.'

'And how's it going?'

'OK.' He wished they could stop this conversation but the Head was obviously trying to be pleasant.

'Is that other boy going to be playing in the Regionals? What's his name? Ron did mention it. The boy who moved down here last year.'

'Danny Powell.' He remembered Danny punching the air after their last encounter; Bob Powell crowing with jubilation; Dad lashing out in the changing room. He took a slow breath. 'I'm playing him in the first round,' he said.

The Head stroked his chin.

'Danny Powell. That's the one. Good player, I gather. Is he above you in the national rankings?'

'Yes, sir.'

'Well, I'm sure you'll catch him up. I believe he goes to Fairways?'

'Yes, sir.'

Mr Talbot thought for a moment, then chuckled.

'Well, I suppose it's not quite politically correct to say this but I do hope you beat him. It would be so nice to get one over on the public school sector. But don't quote me on that or you'll get me into trouble.'

There was something surreal about all this. Mr Talbot was clearly trying to be friendly and talk about something he thought they were both interested in; yet it was obvious he didn't know whether to be pleasant to his friend's son or tear him off a strip. He certainly looked as though he'd be glad when Dad turned up.

If so, he was in luck. Jamie could already see the car through the window as it pulled into the school car park. It hadn't taken long; the Head must have contacted Dad on his car-phone. Which meant his father must have been driving around looking for him. Jamie wondered for how long.

Dad climbed out of the car and walked in the main entrance. A moment later there was a knock at the door.

'Come in,' said Mr Talbot.

The Head's secretary appeared.

'Mr Williams is here, headmaster.'

'Thank you, Mrs Beatty.' Mr Talbot stood up. 'Come in, Ron.'

Dad came in and shook hands with Mr Talbot. But his eyes were on Jamie. Jamie shuffled in the chair, wondering how the two men would handle this. How Dad would handle things when they were alone he knew well enough. But for now his father was all smiles.

'Sorry about the inconvenience, Jim. It's just a family misunderstanding. Nothing serious. We'll give Jamie the day off school today—with your agreement—and get him home and shove some food inside him. He looks like he needs it.'

'And a good wash,' said Mr Talbot, also smiling.

So everyone was pretending they were happy. Except him. He could pretend nothing. And even now, in the midst of these charades, he found the face of that girl pressing itself into his mind again.

Dad put an arm round his shoulders.

'Right, Jamie, let's get you home.'

'Keep in touch,' said Mr Talbot.

'No problem.'

Dad led the way out of the office and Jamie followed, wearily, unsure what to make of anything right now. Lack of sleep, lack of food, lack of warmth were nothing

to the anguish spreading through his mind. He walked
to the car, opened the passenger door and took his place,
strangely unconcerned about what he knew was to
follow.

'We'll talk later,' Dad said.

And without another word, he started the car and
drove them out of the school gate.

Jamie was silent, too, but not now from tiredness or
confusion. For in that instant both had vanished. He
twisted in his seat and stared as the car sped away.

Standing by the gate, gazing towards the school, were
the two men.

7

He sat on his bed, staring out of the window with distaste as drizzle discoloured the morning. Somehow it seemed to match the colour of his thoughts; the colour of his life.

He hated being beaten by his father. It wasn't just the pain, which was always bad, since Dad was a strong man and didn't believe in moderation—it was also the indignity, and the knowledge that he should have the guts to stand up to his father.

Especially as he had not deserved this beating.

He reached behind the bookcase, pulled out his secret book from its hidden place and started writing.

'One day he won't hit me and I'll have a real relationship with him, like Spider does with his dad. I want him to respect me. I know he doesn't respect me. I don't know why. I respect him. And I want to love him but I can't because he won't let me. I know he was a great squash player, better than I'll ever be. I never saw him play but Mum says he was brilliant, and I've read the reports so he must have been good. And he learnt his squash in Australia and Australia is supposed to breed top squash players, so he keeps telling me. But we don't live in Australia.'

He was rambling now and he knew it. He skimmed through the entries he had written over the last few months since he had started keeping the book and found he had written much the same way each time. He was turning into a writing machine; a machine with only one story to tell.

He heard footsteps on the stairs. It would be Mum with tea and toast or some offering. He thrust the book under his pillow. There was a knock at the door.

'Come in,' he called.

Mum entered, as expected with a tray. He watched her, trying to gauge her feelings from the expression on her face, but it was always difficult to know what she was thinking. He wished he could break through the mask of correctness she always seemed to have.

She put the tray on the desk and sat next to him on the bed.

'Jamie—'

'I know. He still loves me. Even though I'm a failure.'

'You're not a failure, darling. And yes, he does love you. Just like I do. You mustn't forget that everything your father says and does is to help you. It's for your own good. No one ever got anywhere without self-discipline. And if someone is struggling to achieve that, he needs someone else to impose that discipline for him. Until he can manage to do it himself.'

Straight out of the manual. It might have been his father speaking or a passage from one of his books. He wished so much that Mum would speak her own mind. But it was always locked behind a façade of perfect behaviour. And despite being knocked about and driven to tears on so many occasions, her loyalty to Dad and her belief that he knew best never seemed to waver.

He took the cup of tea she offered him and sipped at it, unsure what to say. She stiffened suddenly.

'What's that book under your pillow?'

He looked round and saw to his horror the corner of his secret book protruding.

'Oh, it's . . . just an exercise book. Something for school.'

'Shouldn't it be in your school bag?'

'Probably, yeah. I'll put it there later.'

She was still looking at it.

'It's a funny place to put an exercise book. Under your pillow.'

'Yeah, well, it's—' He pulled the book out as casually

as he could, took it over to his school bag and thrust it in. Mum watched him as he came back to the bed.

'You're being a bit secretive,' she said.

He shrugged, trying to think of a way of deflecting further questions. She spoke again.

'I thought maybe you were writing secret letters to a girlfriend.'

It was meant to be a joke, though a slightly probing one. But it gave him a chance to change the subject.

'When have I got time for a girlfriend with all the training he makes me do?'

Sure enough, she immediately forgot the book in the need to defend Dad.

'Jamie, when your father was your age, he had nothing. His parents had had nothing and had to fight for everything they could get. And when they died, it was even worse for him. But he vowed he would never be poor like they had been and he'd only ever be a winner.'

'I've heard this story. You've told me. He's told me.'

A thousand times. A million times.

But she went on, following the script, which he felt he could recite word for word without her. He knew about his father's struggles: parentless at five, brought up by his uncle and aunt in Australia before they dumped him at fifteen to make his own way. And how he fought back, at school, at work; and especially at squash.

'Especially at squash,' he heard Mum say, her lecture keeping pace with his thoughts. 'Think of what he had to do. He was fifteen when he started, not three, like you were. Think of the advantages you've had which he didn't have. And he had to travel miles just to play, and he had to finance himself for it. He couldn't afford more than one trip a week to the courts so he—'

'Painted markings on the walls of an old garage and practised by hitting the ball against them. I know all this.'

'Well, don't be ungrateful, then, and show a little understanding. He's only tough on the world because the world's been tough on him. He's been through a lot. He knows what it's like to fight and he doesn't like to see you throwing your opportunities away.'

After she had gone, he retrieved the secret book from his school bag and replaced it behind the bookcase. Then he sat back on the bed and stared out of the window once more. The allotment was now dull with rain and it was growing cold again.

In the evening the rain stopped. Dad drove him to the school squash court and they did some stroke practice, then went outside to the rugby field for some fitness training. On the way home an idea occurred to him.

After supper he helped Mum with the washing up, while Dad went up to his study to work. At nine o'clock she went in to the sitting room to watch the news.

He waited for a moment to make sure no one was coming back, then grabbed three of the rolls Mum had bought that afternoon, thrust them inside a polythene bag and hurried out of the back door and down to the allotment. The shed loomed before him, dark and silent. He opened the door, cautiously.

There was no one there.

He stole in, left the bag by the old blanket and hurried back to the house.

8

In the morning the rolls were gone. And there was no sign of the girl.

He stared down at the space where they had been, listening all the while for sounds of his parents calling or, worse still, walking down to the shed. But he had chosen his moment carefully, with Dad still shaving and Mum drying after the shower.

He knelt down and checked the blanket. It was flattened where someone—the girl, presumably—had sat on it. He studied it more closely and saw crumbs from the rolls. She must have taken the bag away with her. Then he saw it stuffed behind a plant pot.

He took a slow breath, feeling strangely reassured that she had returned, though he didn't know why. He wondered whether she had been thinking about him as much as he had been thinking about her.

Probably not. She no doubt had far more pressing things to worry about. Just as he had. He hurried back to the house to find Mum already in the kitchen. She looked at him, startled.

'Jamie? Where have you been?'

He had his answer ready. 'I wanted to check the brakes on my bike.'

'Aren't they working properly?'

'They felt a bit funny last time I went out.'

'Do you want your father to look at them?'

He shook his head quickly.

'No, there was just something caught in them. They're OK now.'

She hesitated, then spoke again. 'Darling, have you

been at the bread bin? I bought some rolls yesterday but some of them seem to have vanished.'

He was ready for this, too.

'Yeah, sorry, I meant to tell you. I was hungry late last night and came down and ate them.' He had a sudden idea. 'They were really nice. Could I take some for lunch today?'

'Of course, darling. How many can you eat?'

'Er . . . all of them.'

'There's ten, Jamie. Ten big rolls. I think that's pushing it, even by your standards.'

'No, I could definitely eat ten. I think I need more carbohydrates at the moment. I'm sure that's why I flagged on court the other day.'

He despised himself for this lie; but it didn't work anyway.

'Jamie, you know you're not short of carbohydrates. Your father's been through your diet with you enough times.'

He tried a second lie.

'But I always get hungry about break time and have to go and buy crisps and chocolate and stuff.'

This one worked immediately.

'Jamie!' Mum stared at him. 'I'm horrified. You shouldn't be eating things like that. I had no idea. You'd better not tell your father.' She looked at him, frowning. 'I'll do you seven and we'll see how many you bring back this afternoon.'

'I won't bring any back. I'll eat them all.'

'We'll see about that. What do you want in them? Cheese, salad, peanut butter?'

'Some with cheese, some with salad, please.'

He looked away, uncomfortable at how easy it was to deceive her.

Dad came down, sat at the table without a word and started to read the paper. Jamie glanced at him but there was no response. He frowned. His father had become so much moodier over the last year. Since the squash had started going badly.

Mum hesitated.

'Ron, don't forget the Talbots are coming over for a drink tonight.'

Dad said nothing and simply went on reading the paper.

Jamie looked at her but she turned away, went over to the bread bin and started to prepare the rolls. He sat down at the table and began to eat. He knew he was out of favour and wouldn't be in favour again until he started winning matches like he used to. But all he wanted to do now was give up squash. He had thought about it a lot.

But somehow he would have to tell his father.

And survive the response.

Mum finished the rolls, packed them up and put them in Jamie's school bag. Jamie watched, forgetting squash now and trying to decide the best way to put his new idea into effect. But he needed to be left alone.

Suddenly Dad pushed his cereal bowl to the side of the table. Mum looked at him.

'There's toast coming.'

'I don't want any.' Dad stood up. 'I've got to get on. Where's that new shirt? I couldn't find it anywhere.'

'In the wardrobe. Hanging up on the left. I did tell you, darling.'

'Well, I couldn't see it.'

'I did put it there.' Mum put the toast on the table in front of Jamie, then looked back at Dad. 'Come on. I bet I'll put my hand straight on it.'

And she led him upstairs.

Jamie waited until they had gone, then jumped to his feet, retrieved the rolls and hurried towards the back door. Then another idea occurred to him.

But he would have to be quick. And very quiet.

He crept to the foot of the stairs and listened. Mum was talking to Dad in the bedroom and he could hear the sound of hangers being pushed along the wardrobe rail. He tiptoed up the stairs as far as the airing cupboard, opened it and took out the big hairy blanket

45

they never used, then slipped back downstairs as quietly as he could.

There was no sound of them returning but they would be back in an instant.

He opened the back door, raced down to the shed with the blanket and rolls, dumped them inside in the corner, and sped back to the house.

Spider kept off awkward questions on the way to school and Jamie was grateful for that. He knew his friend must be buzzing with curiosity about what had happened. But Spider—for all his gentle mockery—could always be trusted not to push things. When he spoke, it was on a safe subject.

'I suppose you're playing squash after school. Or training or something.'

'I'm playing. Dad's picking me up and bringing my kit. So don't hang about for me.'

'Who are you playing? Not that . . . Danny boy?'

They stopped and looked at each other, and the joke seemed to register with them both at the same time. The next moment they had burst into song.

'*Oh, Danny Boy, the pipes, the pipes are calling . . .*'

An elderly lady looked quizzically at them from the other side of the road. They broke off, chuckling, and walked on.

'Can't remember the next line,' said Spider.

'Neither can I.'

'So is it this Danny?'

'No, it's Andy Bailey.'

'You said he's good, didn't you?'

'He's not good. He's brilliant.'

'So you're going to get stuffed.'

'That's putting it politely.'

Spider thought for a moment.

'So if you don't mind my asking, what's the point of playing him?'

Jamie looked away. What was the point of playing

anyone? He was getting no pleasure from squash now, no matter who the opponent was. He shrugged.

'It's supposed to raise my game.'

'And does it?'

'I don't know.'

They walked on in silence towards the town centre. Suddenly he stopped. Spider looked round at him and stopped, too.

'What's up?'

Jamie nodded forward. It was the two men again, this time approaching down the street. Spider glanced round at them, then back at him.

'What's the problem?'

'Those men. Do you know them?'

'No. Do you?'

'No.'

'So what's the fuss?'

Jamie tried to look casual.

'No fuss.'

Spider shook his head. 'You really are getting paranoid.'

They walked on and the two men drew nearer. Jamie lowered his head but found himself sneaking glances at them even so. Spider stepped to the side to let them pass. But the men stopped and the taller one spoke.

'Excuse me, lads. You got a second?'

It was a high, strangely thin voice, and the accent sounded foreign, though Jamie couldn't place it. He found himself avoiding the eyes of both men. Spider simply looked back at them, confident and unconcerned.

The shorter man pulled something from his pocket.

'Sorry to hold you boys up. I'm sure you're dying to get to school.' He gave a laugh, then held out a photograph. 'Just wondered if you've seen this girl in the area.'

Spider took the photograph, glanced at it and shook his head.

'No.' He held it out to Jamie. 'You seen her?'

Jamie felt his hand tremble as he reached out. The men's eyes, and Spider's, all fixed upon him. He took the photo, knowing what he would see there; and, sure enough, it was her.

He swallowed hard, then shook his head.

'Sorry.'

'Ah, well.' The shorter man took back the photo and smiled. 'Worth a try. We're from a missing persons' bureau and she's been spotted in the area. If you do see anything, can you give this number a call?'

He pulled out a card from his pocket and scribbled a telephone number on it.

'Do two,' said the taller man. 'One for each lad.'

'Don't bother,' said Spider. 'I'll only lose it. Give it to Jamie. He's more organized than I am. If I see anything, I'll get the number from him.'

'Fair enough.' The taller man smiled, then looked at Jamie. 'Think I've seen you around. Haven't you got a house down by the allotments?'

Jamie took the card from the man's companion.

'Yes.'

'Thought so.' The taller man was still smiling, but Jamie had the feeling he was being quietly assessed. 'They're nice houses down there. You've got the one with the basketball ring, right?'

'Yeah.' Jamie shifted from one foot to the other, wishing the men would move on. The taller man looked him over a moment longer, then winked.

'Well, we mustn't hold you two up any longer. Don't want to get you in trouble at school. Thanks for your time.'

And the men moved on.

Spider looked at him.

'What were you so edgy with those men for?'

'I don't know. They just look shifty. Do you reckon they're really from a missing persons' bureau?'

'Why not? People go missing. And other people make a living out of finding them.'

'But those two . . . I mean . . .' Jamie stopped and examined the card. 'Look, he's just written on a blank card. No name, nothing. If that man was genuine, he'd have had a proper card, you know, with his name and company or whatever. This is just a card with a telephone number. And that's not a local number either.'

Spider glanced at it.

'Probably a mobile phone number. Look, you're worrying about nothing. You haven't seen the girl, so you don't need to have any more contact with those men if you don't like the look of them.' Spider paused. 'You haven't seen the girl, have you?'

Jamie walked quickly on.

''Course I haven't,' he said.

After school, Dad dropped him off at the squash club and drove into Ashingford to buy a new suit. Jamie watched him go, relieved to know that he could disgrace himself on court without worrying about Dad's watchful eye in the gallery above, yet also glad that his father was coming back to give him a lift home. Forty minutes with Andy Bailey were so exhausting they felt like eighty minutes with anybody else.

Yet he liked Andy and was grateful that the older boy was prepared to give up time playing someone he could beat so easily. But halfway through the first game Andy stopped and looked round at him.

'What's bugging you, Jamie? You're playing crap.'

Jamie thought of the two men, and the girl, and his father, and the money, and the almost overwhelming desire to break his racket. But it wasn't fair to burden Andy with his problems.

'I don't know,' he said. 'I just . . . can't keep my mind on the game at the moment.'

He heard a booming voice from one of the other courts.

'Come on, Danny, work it, work it!'

Chris Welland. The voice was unmistakable. Danny was going to be even better now that Powell had forked out for the best coach in the area. He saw Andy looking at him.

'Jamie?'

'What?'

'You're a better player than Danny.'

Jamie looked away. 'I don't know about that.'

'I do. He only knows one way to play and he plays it very well but when it doesn't work and he gets into trouble, all he's got left is gamesmanship and arguing with the marker. He'll never go all the way to the top, no matter how much he trains with Welland. Do you know why?'

'Why?'

'Because at heart he's just a bully, like his dad. He likes being aggressive on court and playing people like you who always fold up against him. When you play him, you go into your shell and start playing cautious. You can't do that with Danny. It's like with any other bully, if you go in aggressive and stay aggressive, you'll faze him out. You can't do that against a clever opponent, someone with a bit of court craft, because he'll use your aggression against you. But Danny won't. He hasn't got the tactical sense. He'll go to pieces. Take it from me.'

'How do you know?'

'Because I've done it to him. Lots of times. He never plays me now, except when he has to in a tournament.'

'Yeah, but you're . . . I mean . . . you're a fantastic player.'

Andy looked at him impatiently.

'So are you, for God's sake. You just forgot it somewhere along the way. Come on. Pretend I'm Danny. Get angry and start treating me like dirt.'

They played on and he felt himself loosen up a little. It was hard to tell whether he was playing better or Andy was just going easy on him. The booming voice from the other court intruded upon his mind as they played out the rallies. But by the end of the game he was feeling a little better.

Though he was well beaten.

And his father was looking down from the gallery.

9

He wasn't sure what to think that evening when the Talbots turned up for a drink. He'd always been uncomfortable about Dad's friendship with the Head. Somehow it made him feel he was always under Dad's eyes, even at school, and that whatever he did there would somehow get back.

And for the Talbots to come round on a Tuesday was unusual. They often came for dinner or a drink, but it was generally at the weekend. He couldn't imagine they wanted to talk school business. It was more likely to be squash.

And so it proved.

The conversation ranged from tournament to tournament, player to player, match to match, and inevitably to him. He looked round and imagined for a moment the effect if he chose this precise time to announce his desire to give up the game. And for a crazy moment it seemed almost a good idea. Dad couldn't possibly hit him in front of all these people.

But the reaction later would be terrible; more so for the public embarrassment caused. No, this was not the moment. And besides, he had another thing on his mind. He fumbled for an excuse to leave the room.

Fortunately there was one that none of them could disapprove of.

'I've got some homework to get on with.'

'Good lad,' said Mr Talbot. 'Nice to see you back in school today, by the way.'

Jamie nodded at him uneasily. Then he saw Mrs Talbot smiling at him.

'What is it tonight, Jamie? Maths? French?'

'English. We've got an essay on *Macbeth*.'

She raised an eyebrow.

'And very appropriate on a dark, chilly night like this. Ideal conditions for meeting witches on the heath.'

'Except there isn't a heath,' said Mr Talbot.

She shrugged.

'Well, the allotment out the back's a bit on the wild side. With a little poetic licence, you could almost imagine meeting strange people there. I'm sure Jamie knows what I mean.'

He smiled at her, warily, unsure whether anything lay behind her words. But it was unlikely. She was too direct. He'd always liked Mrs Talbot. Dad laughed.

'I know we've neglected the allotment but I think describing it as a meeting-place for witches is a bit excessive.'

The others chuckled. Dad turned to Jamie.

'All right, lad, off you go.'

He left the room gratefully and hurried upstairs. He had done what he could of the *Macbeth* essay during the lunch hour, mostly with Spider's help, since he hadn't read the scenes he was supposed to have studied. It wasn't a good essay but he didn't care. He was only interested in one thing right now.

He gazed out of his bedroom window towards the allotment.

It was hard to see anything clearly so he turned off the light, opened the window and stared again, waiting for his eyes to grow used to the darkness.

Gradually the outline of the sheds came to him, then their own, slightly apart from the rest. The door was closed and there was nothing to indicate whether anyone was or had been there. He stayed by the window, watching, despite the chill of the night that now seeped in through the window.

Downstairs he heard the Talbots laughing, and Dad offering more drinks. And he suddenly realized how quiet Mum was. She had said little while he was with them and since he had come upstairs, he had hardly heard her voice at all. There was a strange remoteness about her.

The Talbots didn't stay late and when Mum and Dad looked in on their way to bed, he was ready at his desk with books spread all around him.

'I thought you'd be changed for bed,' said Mum.

'I've been busy with the essay.'

He looked at her, trying to gauge what was wrong. She came over and kissed him.

'I think it's time to sleep now, darling. You must have finished it, surely.'

'Yes, I was just going to get undressed.'

'All right. Goodnight, darling.'

'Goodnight.'

She left the room but Dad remained in the doorway. His face looked a little florid as though he had drunk more than usual. He nodded to Jamie.

'Difficult essay?'

'Yes.'

'But you managed it all right.'

'Yes.'

'Good.'

And his father turned and left.

Jamie undid his shirt to make it look as though he were getting undressed, then sat on the bed and waited. Fortunately, they didn't take long in the bathroom and he soon heard the click of their door, then silence.

He left it a good while to make sure, then fastened his shirt buttons again and pulled on his thick pullover. Then he slipped out on to the landing as quietly as he could and listened.

There was no sound from his parents' room so he crept downstairs to the hall, took his coat from the peg and the torch from the cabinet, and stole through to the kitchen.

This was the first risky part, but he had decided it was essential. He filled the kettle, switched it on, then listened again. But the house remained silent and there was no sound of movement upstairs. He left the lights off and stood there in the darkness, staring at the little power-light on the kettle as the water heated up.

Still there were no sounds from upstairs. He fetched the big thermos flask from the bottom cupboard, washed it out and spooned in some coffee granules, and a little sugar.

The sound of the kettle seemed horribly loud now and he was sure his parents must hear it, even with the door shut. But still there were no voices, no footsteps on the stair.

The kettle switched itself off with a loud click, then silence fell once more.

He listened again, then poured the hot water into the thermos, added a little milk, and screwed on the top. Then he glanced around the kitchen.

Mum had bought some more rolls but he didn't dare take any this time. He hunted round, opening cupboards, looking in the fridge, and before long had a carrier bag stuffed with pieces of cake, slices of bread, apples, bananas, a bar of chocolate, and some crisps.

He tiptoed to the back door, opened it as softly as he could, and crept out into the night.

There was a deep stillness around him, though now and then he heard the drone of cars from the town centre. He clutched the bag to him, slipped down to the gate at the bottom of the garden, and made his way down to the allotment.

The sheds rose about him like dusky fingers pointing at the sky. He found he was shivering already, and very nervous. Suddenly he stopped.

A light was approaching from the far end of the allotment, a small moving beam from a torch darting across the ground. It was a couple of hundred yards away but drawing closer even as he watched. He slid behind the nearest shed and waited, trying to decide what to do.

He could nip back to the house. Or just walk back. After all, he wasn't doing anything wrong. But whoever was coming would probably be near enough now to see him, and which house he went into.

He clenched his hand tight round the handle of the bag. It shouldn't matter, he told himself. He wasn't doing anything illegal. He had every right to be out here. There was no reason why he shouldn't just walk back to the house.

But he did not move. He knew he could not.

The light vanished behind one of the sheds and he heard the sound of someone trying the door. Then the light reappeared, flickering around the top end of the allotment as it lit up the dark soil before vanishing again. It was drawing closer. Soon it would be upon him.

There was no hiding place here. He pressed himself against the wall of the shed, tensed, ready to run. He wondered about the girl. Somehow he had dismissed from his mind the possibility that this could be her. He did not remember her having a torch and, even if she had one, he felt sure she would not use it now. She had been here before, and she wouldn't want to draw attention to herself. It was more likely to be the two men. Or someone else.

He heard footsteps, then the sound of another door being tried, one of the smaller sheds up to the left. Then more footsteps. The beam flashed to his right and he heard another door being tried, still not his shed, but they were close now. They would try his one soon. He prayed that the girl would not be here. But even if they didn't find her here, they would surely see the blanket and know someone had been there.

They.

He wondered why he assumed it was more than one person. He had seen nobody, only the torchlight. But he sensed it was the two men.

Suddenly, about thirty yards away, two figures appeared. They were walking to the left of him to check the sheds up by the houses, and he saw them for a moment before they disappeared from view.

It was them. There was no doubt about it. But there was no time to ponder this. The beam was already approaching as they made their way down towards his parents' shed. After that they would check here.

Unless they found the girl first.

He clenched his fists. He couldn't stay here but he also knew he couldn't abandon her. If she were in the shed and they found her, he would have to do something. The light flashed upon his parents' shed; then he heard the door open and they went in.

He waited, listening for words, or sounds of violence. There were none.

But he heard them rummaging about.

He knew it was now or never. In a trice he was hurrying back towards the house, expecting the beam to fall over him any second, or a voice to call out. But nothing checked him. A moment later he was behind the gate, holding it just open so he could peep through the gap.

The figures came out and lingered by the shed, talking in low voices. It was obvious they hadn't found her, but they would have seen the blanket and the cushion. He wondered what they would do next.

To his relief, they seemed to be leaving. Presumably they were satisfied with what they had found, or had just had enough. They didn't bother to look at the remaining sheds. He watched them go and even stepped out of the gate again to watch their forms disappear completely from view.

He looked down at the bag he had packed for the girl and wondered what to do with it. It would certainly be risky taking it down there now. The shed was not a safe place for her and the last thing he wanted to do was encourage her to come back here.

He decided to leave her a note. He would go back to the kitchen, write her an anonymous warning note and leave it in the shed, in case she returned.

But there was no time for that.

At the far end of the allotment a new figure had appeared.

10

He slipped back inside the gate and watched again, keeping as still as he could. It was hard to see the face of this new person and there was now no torchlight to give him a clue. But it had to be the girl. How many more people could there be, wandering about this place in the chill of night?

But if it were the girl, she was surely in danger, and he must tell her so.

He continued to watch. The figure reached the shed, opened the door and disappeared inside.

It had to be her. He clutched the bag to himself and made his way down towards the shed. A few feet away he stopped and looked about him for signs of the men. There were none. He tiptoed up to the door, eased it a fraction ajar and peered through.

Suddenly it flew open.

The edge drove into his face with a thud. He jumped back, momentarily blinded, and dropped the bag to the ground. The next moment, he felt hands clawing at his eyes.

'Get off!' he muttered, twisting his face away.

A knee drove into his groin.

'Ah!' He doubled up but somehow managed to stumble a few steps away from the shed. But his attacker had drawn back.

He turned, feeling his groin gingerly, and stared towards the shed.

The girl was standing there, watching him. She seemed ill-at-ease, as though unsure how to react to him. But after a while she spoke.

'Sorry.'

She glanced down at the bag he had dropped. He took a step forward—then stopped, seeing her stiffen.

'It's for you,' he said. 'I brought it in case you needed it.'

She reached awkwardly down and picked it up, keeping her eyes on him as though she still didn't fully trust him. Then she glanced inside it.

'You brought this for me?'

'Yeah.'

She thought for a moment. 'Did you leave those rolls, too?'

'Yeah.'

She stared at him for a moment.

'Thanks,' she said eventually. She glanced round the allotment. 'I thought you were somebody else.'

'I know.' He saw a questioning look on her face and went on. 'There's two men looking for you. They're asking questions. They stopped me and my friend in the street today and showed us your photo.' He saw the alarm on her face and quickly added: 'It's OK. I said I hadn't seen you.'

'Does your friend know about me?'

'No. I haven't told anyone about you.' He paused. 'The men said they were from a missing persons' agency.'

She said nothing but he noticed the scorn in her face.

'They were here a few minutes ago,' he said. 'I came out to leave this stuff for you and nearly got caught by them. They were looking in the sheds. They'll have seen the blanket and cushion.' He studied her face. 'Are you all right?'

She had started breathing heavily and had a hand on her stomach.

He took a step forward. 'Is it . . . I mean, can I . . . ?'

But she waved him away, struggled with the bag back to the shed and disappeared inside, without closing the door. He stood there, unsure what to do. She was clearly not well and the exertion of fighting him couldn't have helped.

Perhaps he should just leave her now. He had given her the food and the coffee, warned her about the men. She hadn't asked him to hang around.

He stared at the open door of the shed, then slowly walked over to it and looked in.

She was slumped against the wall in the corner on the thick hairy blanket he had left here earlier, the cushion stuffed behind her back. And she was eating.

Ravenously.

Never in his life had he seen anyone eat that way. She attacked the food like a starving dog, biting off chunks and swallowing almost without chewing.

He wished now that he had brought more. He stayed by the entrance, unsure whether to come in and sit down. She took no notice of him at first and seemed intent only on the food; then she glanced up at him.

'You'd better close the door if those men are around.'

He did as she said and darkness fell upon them. But he saw her form huddled in the corner as she went on devouring the food. She had not touched the coffee yet. All she wanted was bulk. He wondered again whether he should go.

Then she moved.

It was only a small thing, just a shift of her body to the side and a glance towards him, before she turned back to the food. But it was enough for him to recognize an invitation.

He hesitated, then stepped forward and sat down next to her. The under-blanket had moved to the side with her, and he felt only the damp boards of the shed against his trousers, but she seemed aware of this and stopped eating again to pull the blanket back for him. Then, without a word, she draped the other blankets over their legs.

'Thanks,' he said.

She said nothing and continued attacking the food.

He leaned back against the wall of the shed, thinking about Dad and Mum, and squash, and all that was wrong with his life. It didn't seem sensible to get mixed up in this girl's life, especially with those men involved.

He stole a glance at her in the darkness and saw she had finished the food and was unscrewing the thermos flask. Suddenly she turned to him.

'Why are you doing all this for me?'

He felt the intensity in her eyes and wanted to look away.

'I don't know. I just—'

'I can't give you anything back.' She gave him a defiant look. 'I won't give you anything back. So if you're expecting—'

'I'm not expecting anything. I don't want anything from you.'

They stared at each other in the darkness. After a moment she looked away, poured some coffee from the flask and took a sip; then, to his surprise, offered the cup to him.

He thought for a moment, wondering whether to refuse and show her he had some pride of his own; but he was thirsty, and perhaps it would be good to share something small between them. He took the cup, blew on the coffee and sipped a little, then handed it back.

'You drink the rest. I can have as much coffee as I like. I only live a few yards away.'

She gave a start. 'Which house?'

He frowned. He hadn't intended to tell her where he lived. But now that he'd blurted this much out, he might as well tell her the rest.

'The one with the big brown gate at the bottom and—'

'The basketball ring.'

'Yes.'

She looked slightly sheepish for a moment, then reached into a pocket and thrust some coins into his hand.

'It's all I've got left.'

He stared at her. 'What's this for?'

'It's from your house. I'm sorry. I wouldn't have

taken it if I'd known you were going to help me. But your mother left the back door unlocked and her handbag in view of the window so what did she expect?'

He looked away, unsure what to say.

'I didn't take anything else,' she said.

There was something in her voice, something more conciliatory than before, as though she felt she owed him something now—but not too much. They sat in silence for a few minutes, the girl sipping more coffee. Then she spoke again.

'How long are you staying here for?'

'I don't know. I suppose—'

'Only it's getting cold and if you're staying, we'd better lie together again.'

He detected the tension in her voice and quickly tried to reassure her.

'It's OK. You can have the blankets to yourself. I won't be stopping. I'll go back to the house in a minute. But I'm still worried about you out here on your own. Those men might come back tonight. They—'

He stopped, aware that she was watching him intently. Then she spoke.

'Don't get mixed up in my life.'

It didn't sound like a threat; more like a warning. He sensed she wanted him to drop the subject. But he knew he could not.

'So what are you going to do tomorrow night? It'll be risky coming back here. Even if the men don't come back tonight, they're bound to come back some time soon.'

'You don't need to bother about that. I can take care of myself.'

'But you need somewhere to go.'

'I told you. You don't need to bother. I'll look after myself.'

There was a finality in her voice that told him it was time to shut up. And he knew he should. This was, after all, her business. But he had had an idea and, at the risk of annoying her, he knew he had to express it.

'Listen, I don't want to interfere—OK?—but if you get stuck tomorrow night and you need a place to doss down, I could probably find you somewhere. Not here, I mean. Somewhere else where you should be safe for the night.'

She said nothing and it was hard to tell whether she was angry with him or not. He waited for a moment, then, with a slight hesitation, handed her back the money.

'Keep this. And just leave the thermos flask and stuff here. I'll pick them up in the morning. And if you . . . I mean . . . if you do need somewhere, meet me tomorrow night about half twelve in the town centre. Next to the health food shop there's a small alleyway. People often park motorbikes in there. It doesn't lead very far and—'

'I know it.' The voice was flat; neither approving nor disapproving.

'Well, I'll come down about half twelve. Or it might be later. It depends when my parents go to bed. But they usually go to bed early and I can—'

'There's no point in coming. I won't be there.'

Her voice was sharper this time and he knew he had said enough. He saw her face soften slightly, as though she felt she needed to offer him something. She spoke again.

'I know you mean well. But I told you, don't get involved in my life.'

He absolutely must go now. She was trying to be kind to him, in a strange, bruising kind of way and he shouldn't try to push things further. He stood up and, against all his reasoning, added one last thing.

'It's no problem if you've got somewhere else to go. But I'll be there about twelve-thirty just in case. And I'll bring more food.'

And before she could answer, he stepped out of the shed and hurried back to the house.

11

It was at breakfast that he knew for certain something was wrong with Mum.

She would not meet his eyes.

He sat at the table, asking himself whether lack of sleep made him see things that weren't there. She had spoken to him willingly enough, albeit about mundane things like sandwiches for school and what he wanted for breakfast. He glanced at her again and tried to catch her eye.

She looked away once more.

Dad seemed to notice none of this and simply read the paper in silence. Jamie started his cereal, feeling more and more anxious. Maybe Mum and Dad had had a row and Dad had hit her again.

No, this was something different. He sensed it. It was between Mum and himself.

Dad stirred suddenly and glanced across at him.

'I might be a few minutes late picking you up for the gym this afternoon. I've got to go into Ashingford. Just wait by the school gate.'

'OK.'

Dad was silent for a moment but Jamie knew something was waiting to be said; and finally it came.

'I want much more effort from you with the weights, Jamie. Most of your problems are down to your poor mental attitude in matches, but I've noticed your fitness levels aren't what they should be either. I want to see something good from you this afternoon.'

Jamie frowned. He hated weight training, especially as he sometimes bumped into Danny and Bob Powell at the gym. And he did try hard.

'I do my best,' he said eventually, his mind still on Mum as she stood at the cooker. Dad shook his head.

'Your best'll have to be far better than what I'm seeing. You just don't push yourself. You'll really have to sharpen up if you're going to get past Danny in the Regionals.'

Mum was hovering by the table, ready to take away Dad's bowl. Jamie looked straight at her and tried again to catch her eye. She looked at him this time, somewhat warily, and seemed to be trying to smile. Then her eyes moved away. Dad handed her his bowl; she took it over to the sink, then returned to the table and put a plate of scrambled eggs in front of him.

'Jamie?' she said. 'Scrambled eggs for you?'

Her voice sounded as though it would break any moment.

'Yes, please,' he said. 'Mum, are you—?'

'Do you want some mushrooms with them?'

'Er . . . yes, please.'

She turned quickly back to the cooker. Dad swivelled round in his chair to look at her.

'I thought you were doing me some mushrooms.'

She whirled round. 'Oh, darling, I'm sorry. I forgot. I'll do them now.'

'No, leave it. I haven't got time.'

'I'm sorry, darling. I just . . .'

Her sentence trailed away. Dad said no more and ate his scrambled eggs. Jamie sat watching Mum cook, wondering whether to try and speak to her again. But she clearly did not want to talk. She put his own scrambled eggs in front of him. There were no mushrooms for him either. But he said nothing.

Dad finished his breakfast and left the room. Jamie glanced at Mum again. She was standing by the sink, her back towards him.

'Mum,' he said, 'is there—?'

'Can you pass me your plate, darling?'

He stood up, took his plate and walked slowly over to her. Perhaps he should force this. Make her give him a direct answer. But if she really didn't want to talk, it didn't seem right. He held out his plate.

'Mum . . .'

But she merely took the plate from him and turned back to the sink.

'You'd better hurry up, darling. You'll be late for school.'

Spider was beaming as they walked to school.

'Call me a genius. I've found it.'

'Found what?'

'Wake up. What's the one thing I've been looking for lately?'

'Even more girlfriends than you've already got?'

'My dream car, thicko. Dad's found a guy at work who's got exactly the one I want. Even the right colour. His wife's decided he looks stupid in a young man's car and says it's too thirsty on juice.'

'It will be when you start driving it.'

'It's not absolutely settled. I haven't paid anything yet. We had a look at it last night but didn't have time for a spin 'cause Dad had a meeting at the bridge club, so we just checked the engine over and hunted for rust and things like that. Couldn't find a thing wrong. The man's a fanatic. I reckon he's spent more time cleaning it than driving it. I suppose I'll have to do the same until I'm seventeen. Still, I can live with that.'

Spider's face was flushed with pleasure. Jamie felt happy for him. At least one of them had something to celebrate. Spider glanced round.

'No sign today, then.'

'No sign of what?'

'Those two men asking about the missing girl.'

'Oh.' Jamie tried not to sound interested, though his eyes had been searching for them, too.

'Wonder if they found her,' said Spider.

'Don't suppose we'll ever know.'

'I tell you what, I think you're right. There's no way they're from a missing persons' agency. I wonder who they are.'

Jamie looked away. He didn't want to know who they were. And he certainly didn't want to see them again.

But he did see them again. Straight after school.

They were sauntering up the lane towards the school gate where he stood, waiting for Dad to arrive to take him to the gym. He pulled the hood up on his jacket to conceal his face and turned to look into the playground. A girls' netball match was in progress and he watched it, keeping his back to the lane and hoping the men would pass without noticing him.

'Jamie!'

He turned reluctantly and saw them standing a few feet away. The taller man was smiling at him.

'Thought it was you.'

Jamie looked at him suspiciously. 'How do you know my name?'

'Your friend mentioned it when we met you in the street.'

'Oh.'

'So, how are you? Cold, obviously.'

'What?'

'You've got your hood up.' The man still smiled. 'And I was just saying to my friend here that I thought today was slightly warmer than yesterday. Still chilly, though, isn't it? Too cold to be hanging around. Waiting for your mate?'

'No.'

He didn't see why he should tell them what he was doing. The shorter man's eyes wandered over to the playground and rested on the netball players for a moment, then fixed on Jamie again.

'No sign of our girl, then?' He made to produce the photograph but Jamie waved it away.

'I don't need to see it. I can remember it.'

'So have you seen her?'

'No.'

The man's eyes seemed to search his for a few moments. There was something chilling about both men but this shorter man seemed somehow even more frightening. The taller man spoke.

'Jamie, if you see anything or know anything, you will get in touch with us, won't you? It's urgent. We're very worried about her. We know she's in the area. She's been seen by several people.'

'What's she done?' he said, and cursed himself at once. The more he showed interest, the more they would hang around and maybe even suspect he knew something. He mustn't give them any clues. But the question had been asked.

The taller man answered it.

'You'll appreciate, Jamie, we can't divulge any precise information. We're bound by confidentiality. But we can tell you she's in danger. If you do know where she might be, or if you've seen her somewhere, you'll be doing her a favour by letting us know. And you'll be doing yourself a favour. There's money in it for you.'

Both men were watching him keenly now. The shouts of the girls in the playground, the sound of the whistle, all seemed suddenly distant. Pupils were still coming out of the school and he saw faces turn towards him and the two men. But the men's eyes remained on him.

'I haven't seen her,' he said finally.

Still they watched him, and he had the feeling they suspected he was lying. Then the taller man smiled.

'Well, I'll give you our telephone number again. I expect you've lost the card we gave you.' He reached into his pocket.

'Don't bother. I've still got it.'

The man checked himself, then smiled again. 'All right, Jamie. We'll see you around.'

And they walked on up the lane.

Jamie watched them go, feeling more uneasy about them than ever. A few moments later a car horn sounded behind him.

It was Dad.

Jamie frowned as the problem of the men faded and the problem of squash returned.

12

Somehow he had to tell his father, no matter what it cost.

He climbed in the car, clipped on the safety belt and went over in his head the things he had to say. Dad turned the car in the lane and drove back to the main road.

'Dad . . .' he began.

'Damn!' His father scowled as they locked into a traffic queue. 'We should have gone the other way.'

Jamie said nothing for a few moments, then nodded ahead.

'It's moving.'

Dad eased the car forward a few yards before they had to stop again.

'We'll never get there at this rate.' He looked round suddenly. 'Well?'

'Well what?'

'What happened at school today?'

'Just lessons.'

'What lessons?'

'Science, German, English, Maths.'

'And?'

'And what?'

'And how did they go?'

'OK.'

The traffic started moving again. Dad drove on, saying nothing, and Jamie sat there, silent too, aware that yet again he could not bring himself to confront his father over squash.

Ten minutes later they were at the gym.

Jamie didn't like the gym but he did like its owner.

Greg Mason was in his early thirties and dedicated to physical fitness, but he was also his own man and didn't kowtow to anyone. His gym was popular and the numbers of men in particular were increasing, especially since the appointment of Stephanie for physiotherapy and massage.

But Greg was far more than just a meat-loaf pumping iron. He'd had a great deal to do with Andy's startlingly improved level of fitness this season, and now he was helping Danny on a regular basis, which, Jamie thought, was probably the reason why Dad had now taken over his own weight-training programme.

Whatever the reason, it was no coincidence that Jamie's gym sessions were scheduled at different times to Danny's. It was rare for them to meet here.

But today was to be one of those occasions. To his dismay, he found Danny and Bob standing in the entrance, talking to Greg. Dad nodded to Powell and they exchanged the briskest of courtesies.

'Bob.'

'Ron.'

Greg was not favoured with a word of greeting, but Dad always acted strangely with people who weren't intimidated by him. Jamie caught Danny's eye. Neither spoke.

Dad turned round.

'Right, Jamie. Go and get changed.'

He hurried to the changing room, glad to be free of the tension for a moment, but Danny soon appeared, and the two boys started changing. He wondered whether he should try and say something. But Danny did not speak and, as the minutes passed, the silence seemed only to deepen.

Danny finished changing first and walked through to the weights room. Jamie took his time, glad to be alone for a moment, then, unable to put things off any longer, made his way through as well.

Surprisingly, there were no other members there. Dad was standing stiffly to one side of the room, Powell equally stiffly on the other. He went through the warm up, secretly watching Danny doing the same, then made his way over to the exercise bike. Danny was already astride the other bike but hadn't started yet as Greg was adjusting the settings.

Dad came over.

'Right, Jamie. On you go.'

Jamie climbed on the bike and glanced to his right. But Danny was staring straight ahead. Greg straightened up and looked at Danny.

'Right, try it on that setting but don't push it. It's more than you've been doing. If you find it a struggle, put it back on the old setting.'

'OK,' said Danny.

'Good boy. How are you doing, Jamie?'

'Fine.' Jamie wished the others would go away and leave him to train in peace. And he wished Danny weren't here. He started to adjust the setting on his own bike.

But Dad leaned forward. 'I'll do it.'

Jamie gasped as he saw his father raise the setting to the same level as Danny's.

He looked away, unsure what to do. Greg would have prepared Danny for this setting but Jamie wasn't ready for it, and he knew it. Ever since Dad had discarded Greg's services and taken over the weight training himself, things had been far less systematic.

He had to resist this. But now here was Powell getting involved.

'Right, boys. Let's see who's got the gas!'

Danny made to start pedalling and instinctively Jamie found himself doing the same. But Greg reached out a hand to each of them and they stopped.

'You,' he said, looking at Danny, 'are here to train, not compete.' He turned to Powell. 'And you're here to watch, not egg him on. Save the rivalry for the squash court.' His eyes fixed on Jamie. 'And you're not ready for this setting.' He leaned across to adjust it.

Dad reached forward and stopped him.

'Leave it. He's managed that setting before. He's used to it.'

'He's not ready.'

'He is. Ask him yourself.'

Jamie felt Greg's eyes burn into him. But his father's eyes burned deeper still. And in spite of himself, the answer stuttered out.

'It's . . . it's fine. I'm . . . I'm OK with it.'

Greg looked at him hard.

'Jamie, people who come to my gym do things right or they don't do them at all. They're out.' He paused. 'You can try that setting for a bit, but if it's too much, you stop and lower it. Is that clear?'

'Yes.'

Dad tapped Greg on the shoulder.

'I told you. He's fine on this setting. There's no need to interfere. We know what we're doing.'

Greg looked round.

'If someone's doing something wrong in my gym, I'll tell them about it. If they take no notice, then they're out. Simple as that. I don't have room for lawsuits with people who hurt themselves because they ignore my advice.'

Dad stiffened. 'Jamie's training under my direction. Any mistakes will be my responsibility.'

Greg narrowed his eyes. 'They certainly will be.'

He nodded to Jamie and Danny. 'I'll be keeping an eye on the pair of you.' He glanced at Dad and Powell, and Jamie sensed that the words applied just as much to them.

Stephanie appeared at the door. 'Greg. Phone.'

'All right. I'm coming.'

And, with a last look round, he hurried out.

'Thank God for that,' muttered Dad.

Powell looked at him and Jamie detected an ominous agreement between them, though no words were spoken. Dad turned back to Jamie.

'Right, get started.' Then he leaned forward and whispered. 'And I don't want Danny upstaging you. You don't stop before he does. Understand?'

Jamie stared down at the floor, wishing he could climb off and run away from all this. But he heard Danny start pedalling and before he knew what was happening, he was pedalling, too.

At once he felt the resistance of the higher setting and he knew at once that he would not be able to keep going long. Danny was driving the pedals hard, and as Jamie struggled to do the same, he became aware of Powell and his father moving closer.

Watching.

Soon the strain in his legs was starting to tell. He lowered his head and forced himself to drive his legs down, down, down. Already he yearned to stop, and they had only been going a short time.

Danny must be hurting, too. He surely couldn't keep this up either. But the whirr of the pedals went on next to him. Then the talking started. Dad first.

'Come on, boy, don't ease up.'

And Powell.

'Go on, Danny, go on.'

Jamie scowled at the two men. They just couldn't resist, despite what Greg had said. He wondered what Danny was feeling and whether he, too, wanted to make a contest out of this. He looked at Danny and the glance that came back told him all.

It was war.

'Push it, Jamie!'

'Come on, Danny!'

He noticed, with contempt, that both men were keeping their voices low so as not to attract Greg. Powell started to pace up and down in front of the bikes.

'Come on, Danny. He's weakening.'

Dad looked round at him in disgust.

'Weakening? Are you out of your mind? Danny's the one who's slowing down. Look, he's trying to save energy by not pedalling so hard.'

Danny shot him a venomous glance and put on speed. Powell scoffed.

'That's rubbish. Your boy's the one who's slowing down. Look at him. He's knackered.'

'He'll outlast your boy.'

'No way.'

'Fifty quid?'

'Done.'

Jamie stared at his father in disbelief. But Dad's eyes merely grew fiercer.

'Go on, Jamie. Give it your best.'

Powell laughed.

'If that's the best he's got, it won't take him very far.'

'Shut your mouth,' said Dad.

But Powell only laughed again.

Jamie dipped his head and tried to focus on the pedals. But his thoughts were confused now. They told him to stop because this was wrong. They told him not to stop because of what Dad would do to him if he lost.

But he was losing. He knew it.

He stole a glance to the side. Danny showed no signs of weakening and, if anything, seemed boosted by the element of competition. His mouth was open, gulping air, the sweat was vivid on his face; but he was clearly determined not to stop first.

If only Greg would come back. But there was still no sign of him.

The pain was almost unendurable now. He knew his face betrayed it. Like Danny, he was gulping in air but, unlike Danny, he was showing all his despair. Powell watched him for a few moments with an air of satisfaction, then threw a triumphant glance at Dad.

'Make it cash.'

Dad's answer came straight back, low and dangerous. 'Raise it.'

Powell stared at him. 'Are you out of your mind?'

'Raise it. Unless you're scared to.'

'For Christ's sake, just look at the kid. He's keeling over.'

Dad paused for a moment.

'A hundred,' he said, still not looking at Powell.

'You're crazy.'

'A hundred.'

'Look, I'm not doing this. I don't need your money that much.'

'So you are scared. I always knew you were.'

Jamie broke in, despite his exhaustion.

'Listen . . . I . . .'

Both men looked at him, and Danny, too, though he kept on pedalling. Jamie stared into his father's eyes and saw only a dark, unyielding obsession. And he could say no more.

Powell spoke again. 'I'm not raising the stakes. It's taking candy from a baby.'

Dad snorted. 'There's only one baby round here. And it's not Jamie.'

Powell's face darkened at once. 'All right. A hundred quid. And I'll see you damned.'

'Done. Excuse me if I don't shake hands.'

The two men turned back to the bikes.

But the contest was already over.

Jamie was falling. He remembered hearing them closing the bet and turning to look at him. He remembered the terror of not being able to breathe, of feeling his legs numb and useless, his will spent, his balance gone. He remembered the floor, walls, ceiling slipping out of alignment, the handlebars moving closer. He remembered Greg running forward.

He remembered Dad's face.

Then nothing more.

13

He was roused by the touch of fingers in his back. He opened his eyes to find himself lying on his stomach on the massage table in the treatment room. He didn't need to look round to see whose hands they were. But he twisted his head to see who else was here.

'Relax,' said Stephanie.

But he had seen all he needed. Dad wasn't here. That was all that mattered. He heard the door open, then Greg's voice.

'Finished, Steph?'

'Just about.' Stephanie bent down so that Jamie could see her without moving his head. 'You're so tensed up. Your body's like a spring. Even when you were asleep it was all knotted. It's better than it was when we started but you need a lot more of this. And a lot less of whatever's causing the problem.'

Greg drew up a chair and sat down where Jamie could see him.

'And we know what that is, don't we, Jamie?' He glanced at Stephanie. 'Haven't you got to pick up your kids? I thought they had a play rehearsal or something.'

'It's OK. Pete's picking them up.' She ruffled the top of Jamie's head. 'So I've got time to look after some of the bigger kids.'

Greg frowned.

'The really big kids have gone. But they're past helping anyway.'

Jamie stirred. 'You mean—?'

'I mean your dad's gone home. And the Powells.' He glanced up again. 'Go on, Steph. You've stayed on long enough. I'll get Jamie in the shower and take him home.'

She stood back from the table.

'OK. He's about as good as I'm going to get him today.' She leaned down again and smiled. 'Jamie, don't give us any more scares like that, OK?'

Jamie sighed. 'I'll try.' He paused, then: 'Thank you.'

'No problem. I'll see you around. Bye, Greg.'

'Bye, Steph. Thanks.'

Jamie breathed slowly, weary beyond anything he had ever known; and now desperately confused.

'What did my father say?'

Greg didn't try to hide his disgust.

'He said you're to walk home. Thought it would do you good, settle you down. But we both know that's not the reason, don't we?'

Jamie said nothing. Greg watched him for a moment.

'Listen, Jamie, it's none of my business and my mouth's got me into enough trouble over the years as it is, but I'm going to say this anyway. You're not enjoying training, you're not enjoying squash, you're not enjoying anything right now as far as I can see. I'm not going to say why because that's stating the obvious, but I'll tell you one thing. You're never going to be happy until you decide for yourself what you want in life and go after it in your own way.'

He paused for a moment.

'I'm afraid to say it'll probably mean getting into conflict while you assert yourself, and that'll hurt. Maybe a hell of a lot. But if you don't start taking steps to live your own life the way you want, you're going to end up getting hurt even more.'

Jamie rolled over onto his back and stared up at the ceiling, unsure what to say. Greg gave him a pat on the stomach.

'Right, end of lecture. Shower time. You should have had one earlier but we didn't have much choice over the order of events.'

'What happened?'

'You collapsed. We hoicked you in here and you came to, then fell asleep for the last half hour. The Powells packed up for the day and left without finishing the programme. Your dad hung around just long enough for Steph to look you over and tell him you weren't going to die, then he cleared off. I saw money changing hands between him and Bob. I didn't ask any questions and I don't want any answers. Right, let's get you on your feet.'

'I'm OK. It's all right.' Jamie stood up, awkwardly.

'You look a bit dizzy.'

'It's OK. I can manage.'

Greg walked with him to the changing room and switched on the shower for him. Jamie took off his clothes and climbed under. The sluicing water felt good but he was still desperately tired.

Greg leaned against the wall outside the shower, his body blurred through the opaque glass of the door.

'I worry about you, Jamie. Haven't heard you laugh for a long time. What do you do when you're not training or playing squash?'

'Nothing much.'

'You got a girlfriend?'

'No.'

'But you've got mates?'

'I've got one. My father doesn't approve of him.'

He saw Greg shift his position outside.

'Jamie, like I say, you're going to have to sort out what you really want. If it's to be a squash champion, that's fine. Squash is a great game. But don't deceive yourself. If you're not enjoying it any more, then it's time to stop or ease up. And try and find space in your life for something other than squash, like meeting more people, for example, preferably people who aren't interested in squash.'

'Spider's like that.'

'Who?'

'My friend.'

'Is that his name?'

'It's a nickname. Everyone calls him Spider. He thinks squash is a stupid game. He's more interested in deciding which girl to go out with on a Friday night.'

'Well, he sounds the kind of boy you want to see more of. When you've done showering and got dressed, come to my office and I'll run you home.'

But Jamie no longer knew where home was.

He stood outside his house, shivering in the chilly air, and stared at it through the darkness. All the curtains were drawn but the lights were on in the sitting room and his parents' bedroom. He waited until Greg's car had gone, then walked up to the front door, put the key in the lock and turned it.

Inside the hall he paused for a moment and listened, the door still open behind him. From the sitting room came the noise of the television, but he also heard sounds upstairs, the heavy footsteps of his father moving about the bedroom. He closed the door quietly and hurried through to the sitting room.

Mum was sitting on the sofa when he entered but she stood up at once.

'Darling, what's happened?'

He looked at her, wondering what to say. Dad would have given her his version of things already, and that would no doubt be the one that would count for her. But her eyes held no accusation. And he could tell that the tension she had shown at breakfast was still there. If anything, it was worse.

He tried to keep his mind on what he had to do.

'I had a problem at the gym. There's something I've got to talk to Dad about.'

'He said you weren't feeling well.'

'More than that.'

She stared at him. 'What do you mean?'

'Didn't he tell you?'

He studied her face and saw a conflict of emotions. It was some moments before she answered.

'He . . . told me you were on the exercise bike and . . . Danny was there and you . . . you didn't feel very well so you stopped. And he agreed with you that it would be best for you to walk home because you needed some fresh air. And Mr Mason was looking after you.'

Jamie looked away, trying to control the anger that now flooded through him. Somehow he kept his voice calm.

'Do you want to know what really happened? I'll tell you.'

But at that moment Dad entered the room.

Jamie stiffened and tried to marshal his thoughts into words. But Dad spoke first.

'Are you feeling better?'

The question took him by surprise. He had expected some kind of reprimand. He sensed Mum close by, rigidly still. He looked at Dad.

'I'm . . . OK. Now.'

'Good.'

'But I'm tired. I'm really tired. And I . . .' He took a deep breath, his thoughts racing. He had to say this now, before his will wavered. 'I've decided—'

'You'd better get some food inside you. Your mum's got something for you in the oven, I think.' Dad glanced at Mum, clearly expecting her to go and attend to that. But she took a step towards him.

'What happened at the gym?'

Dad frowned. 'I told you what happened.'

'Something else happened. Something you haven't told me.'

Jamie stared at her. She never questioned Dad like this. Dad still frowned.

'I've told you everything that happened,' he said. 'And what needs to happen now is for Jamie to get some food inside him.'

Mum hesitated, then looked round at Jamie.

'There is some food. I'll . . . I'll put it out for you on the kitchen table. It'll be a few minutes because I want to do some peas. But I . . .' She glanced at Dad. 'I . . . I still want to know—'

Dad cut her off. 'There's nothing more to tell. You're worrying about nothing.'

She stared at him, her face clouded with confusion, then she bit her lip and left the room.

Jamie clenched his fists. Her resistance had ended so quickly. But now his had to start.

'I've . . . I've come to a decision.'

Dad said nothing. Jamie dropped his eyes.

'I've come to a decision. I . . . I want to stop.'

'Stop what?'

Jamie forced himself to look up.

'I want to stop squash.'

'I presume that's a joke.'

'It's not a joke.'

'Then I'll overlook it because you're tired.'

'I am tired but it's not . . . because I'm tired. I've thought about this and I've . . . I've decided. I want to stop.'

Dad's face darkened.

'Are you out of your mind? You've spent your life training to be a champion. You've spent hours in the gym, hours on the running track, hours on court and so have I. I've put all my effort and not a little expense into turning you into a future winner, and all you can say, after an evening at the gym that didn't go too well and which—incidentally—cost me a hundred quid, is that you're giving up. Well, you can wipe that idea out of your mind right now. I'm not listening to any of it.'

'I—'

'I'm not listening to any of it, do you understand?' Dad's voice rose. 'What hurts me most is your ingratitude. I've given up practically all my waking hours to your success. You'd be nowhere without the time and money I've invested in you. You were born with talent and you've got everything going for you. And you want to throw it all away.'

Jamie looked down again. This wasn't how he'd intended it. But then, he'd known his father would argue with him. He swallowed hard.

'I just . . . I just—'

'I'm disappointed in you, Jamie. I'm so disappointed. I came back tonight determined to give you a second chance after you made a fool of me in front of Bob Powell. I'm prepared to let that go and—'

'I collapsed. Are you saying that was my fault?'

'Of course it was your fault. Who else's fault was it? If you'd been putting the right amount of effort into your training, you'd have been able to stick it out on the exercise bike. Danny managed it. So why couldn't you?'

Jamie felt himself tremble. It was no good. He would never get through to his father.

'Look, I can't take any more of this. I'm going.'

He took a step towards the door. But Dad caught him by the arm.

'I haven't finished speaking to you, yet.'

Jamie stared at him for a moment, then tried again to walk on. Dad gripped his arm more tightly.

'I said I haven't finished speaking.'

Jamie looked once more into the dark, unyielding eyes, and they scared him.

'I want to go,' he said, and tried to pull his arm away.

But Dad thrust him back against the wall and pinned him there.

'I've worked all my life for what I've got. I've struggled in ways you'll never know. And all I've ever wanted was for you to have the chances I never had. And now I've given you those chances, you—'

Jamie saw what was coming and ducked. Too late. Dad's hand struck him hard in the side of the face. He struggled to free himself but the hand swung in again, and again, and again, Dad spitting out words with each blow.

'Ungrateful . . . little . . . shit . . . bloody . . . little . . . shit.'

Jamie fell back, breaking from Dad's grasp. His foot caught the poker standing by the fire and sent it clattering over the hearthstones. He grabbed the edge of the mantelpiece and clung to it, trying to keep his balance. Dad seized him by the scruff of the neck and pulled him up until their faces were inches apart.

'If you ever do this to me again, I'll really teach you what discipline means.'

In the darkness, he made his way past his parents' room and down to the hall. There he stopped and listened.

The house was still. He crept through to the kitchen, loaded his rucksack, and checked his watch.

Midnight.

He thought of Mum again and in his mind saw her face as she stood in the doorway after Dad had left him, and watched in silence, before retreating to the bedroom.

He tiptoed to the back door, opened it as quietly as he could and closed it after him. Then he shouldered the rucksack, slipped out of the back gate and hurried away towards the town.

14

There was no sign of the girl in the alleyway by the health food shop but he wasn't surprised. This was the last place he'd have wanted to go to alone, now that he thought about it, and he felt sure that even if she had considered coming to meet him, she would probably have taken one look at the dark entrance and changed her mind. He should have thought of a better meeting-place.

He looked around him uneasily. There had been several muggings in this part of town and all kinds of violent episodes after dark. The pubs had emptied some time ago but there was no knowing what kind of people might be lurking round here.

A car beam cut through the darkness, catching the side of the shops as it fanned down towards him. He stepped back inside the entrance to the alley and hid himself in the shadows. A few moments later, a police car swept past. And silence fell.

Then he heard a voice.

'You're late.'

He whirled round, startled, but saw nothing.

'Here.'

The voice came from further down the alley. He walked to where the passageway twisted round at the end and saw the girl slumped on the ground, her back against the wall, her holdall beside her.

'Have you got any food?' she said bluntly.

He looked at her for a moment, then started to undo the rucksack. She spoke again, slightly less abruptly.

'Sorry. Being hungry takes away your manners.'

'It's OK.'

He handed her one of the sandwiches he'd made up in the kitchen. She took it without a word and started wolfing it down with the same intensity as the last time he had seen her eat. He let her finish the sandwich, then spoke again.

'Are you cold?'

'What do you think?'

'Only . . .' He paused. 'I've thought of a way of getting you warm tonight.'

She looked at him suspiciously.

'It's all right,' he said. 'You can trust me. I promise.'

She held his gaze for a few more seconds, then sniffed and looked away.

'Sorry. I know you're trying to help.'

'I didn't think you'd be here.'

'Neither did I.'

'So what made you—?' He broke off, sensing a slight embarrassment in her. 'Come on,' he said. 'I can find a warmer place than this.'

He stood up and waited to see if she would move, too. She started to struggle to her feet. He hesitated, having momentarily forgotten she was pregnant, then reached out a hand. She took it at once and he pulled.

Her hand felt cold but she was soon on her feet and let go of his hand at once. He picked up his rucksack.

'Let's go.'

'Wait,' she said.

He turned. 'What's up?'

'Those men you told me about. Have you seen them tonight?'

'No.'

'Only . . . I don't want to bump into them.'

'Neither do I. So that's not a problem.'

'You don't understand. This . . .' She looked at him hard. 'This . . . isn't a game. It could be dangerous. I told you before. You shouldn't get involved in my life. There's nothing I can give you except trouble.'

He looked down.

'I don't want anything from you. You don't owe me

anything. You've got your troubles and you don't need to tell me about them if you don't want to. Anyway, I've . . . I've got troubles of my own. I won't burden you with them, but I . . .' He took a deep breath. 'I've left home. I'm going to have people looking for me from tomorrow morning. Police, probably, and my parents, and maybe other people. People who know me. But . . .'

He looked up again and saw her eyes fixed on his. He went on.

'I won't be going home again. I need to get away, somewhere, anywhere, away from Ashingford. There'll be too many people who recognize me. I don't know what I'm going to do. I haven't got any money. I haven't got any food apart from what I've stuffed in my rucksack, and that was meant for you anyway. I haven't got any plan of what I'm going to do. I . . .' He looked down again. 'I'm a mess. A complete bloody mess.'

She said nothing and he didn't look up. He felt sure, now that he'd told her all this, that she would walk on and leave him. With all that she had on her mind, the last thing she would want now was a lame duck on her hands. But she spoke to him.

'So we're both shadows.'

He looked up. 'What?'

'Shadows. I thought it was just me. But you're the same, aren't you? Maybe we need each other for a little while.'

'But why shadows?'

She looked hard at him.

'When you live in the shadows long enough, you become one.'

They walked down the main street, keeping close to the buildings.

'Don't walk so fast,' she said. 'I can't keep up. And if you see those men, tell me. If necessary, we split, right? And meet again later.'

'Where?'

'Back in the alleyway. But with any luck, it won't happen.'

'I haven't seen them around tonight.'

'I have. One's in a car. The other's walking the streets. They keep in touch by mobile phone.'

Jamie frowned. 'These men . . . I mean . . . who—?'

'I don't want to talk about them,' she said. 'Just tell me if you see them, OK?'

She fell silent and he could tell from the set of her face that she didn't want him to probe further.

'Which way to this place of yours?' she said.

'I'll show you.'

He led her past the clock tower and away from the town centre, a feeling of unreality creeping over him as he walked through the streets with this strange vagrant girl.

He stopped suddenly.

'What's up?' she said, stopping, too.

'I don't even know your name.'

She looked at him. 'Shadows don't have names.'

They walked on for a few minutes in silence. Then she spoke.

'Listen, we need to have an understanding. You don't tell me anything you don't want and I don't tell you anything I don't want, OK?'

'OK.'

'You've got your life and I've got mine. We don't need to know anything else. We're just two people sticking together for a little while and then we'll go our separate ways.'

He dug his chin into the top of his coat.

'OK.'

'How much further?'

'Just up this lane.'

'But there's only a school up there.'

'I know.'

Again he saw suspicion on her face. But he could understand that. The school lane was a lonely place at night.

'It's OK,' he said. He thought for a moment. 'I'm not going to do you any harm.'

She shrugged. 'Well, let's get a move on. I'm freezing.'

He led her down the lane, gazing ahead at the sombre outlines of the buildings and the trees around the playing field. A few minutes later they reached the school gate.

'Now what?' she said.

'Bit further,' he said and walked on past the gate. She followed, lagging behind now and clearly very tired. Finally he reached the gap in the fence and stopped. She caught up with him and examined the opening.

'Through this?'

'Yes.'

'You first.'

He bent down and squeezed through, wondering as he did so whether she would follow. Somehow he felt their alliance hung on the most slender of threads, one which could break at any moment. But when he straightened up on the other side, she was still there, watching him.

'Where are we going after this?' she said.

'I'll show you when you get through.' He saw her hesitate and added: 'I promise you it's very warm.'

She seemed to come to a decision, bent down and started to squeeze herself through. For her it was more of a struggle. The fence opening, loosened and worked by countless hands on countless occasions, was only prepared to give so much. She reached out a hand.

'Help me.'

He took it and pulled, and a moment later they were standing together on the soggy playing field. She let go his hand.

'Where to now?'

'Not far.'

He led the way across the playing field, keeping his eyes alert for movements around them. But all seemed still. He heard her shiver behind him and glanced over his shoulder.

'How have you been keeping warm at nights? When you weren't in my shed, I mean.'

She said nothing for a while and he thought back to what she had said about not talking about themselves if they didn't want to. But she answered him.

'Depends on where I was. I spent one night standing in a public loo, pressing the hand-drier to keep warm.' She paused. 'You need to think hard before you take on this kind of life.'

He frowned and walked on across the field. At last they were there. He stopped and turned to her. 'This is it.'

She stared up at the building before them. 'What's this place?'

'The squash court. Come on.'

He started to make his way round to the door. But she caught his arm.

'What is it?' he said.

'Ssh!'

She tightened her grip and he stood still, wondering what was wrong. Then he heard it, too. The sound of a car, far down the lane. He turned and saw headlights approaching.

She tugged at his arm. 'Quick! Get behind the building.'

They hurried round the side of the squash court and stopped by the door. Jamie threw the rucksack to the ground and fumbled with the catch.

'What are you doing?' she said.

'Looking for the key.'

'The what?'

'The key. To the squash court.'

The loom of the lights was growing brighter as the car drew nearer. In a moment it would be level with them and they would be visible through the fence. He found the key, turned it in the lock and pulled open the door.

'Get in!'

She didn't hesitate but hurried inside. He jumped after her, closed the door and locked it from the inside, then took out the key. They stared at each other in the darkness, both breathing hard.

The sound of the engine grew louder, then, as the car drew level with the building, the tone changed to a tick-over. He saw the alarm in her face.

'They're stopping,' she whispered.

He tried to think of something to say to reassure her.

'They might not have seen us. And it might—'

'Keep your voice low,' she hissed.

He took a deep breath and went on, whispering as she had done.

'It might not be those men. It might just be a police patrol. Or a couple of lovers or something.'

She leaned back against the wall and stared ahead of her.

'It's them. I recognized the car.'

He, too, leaned against the wall, and they both listened. The engine fell silent, then one of the car doors opened and shut, and, a moment later, the other door. He clenched his fists. They must have been spotted. And here they were, trapped in this cage. He glanced at the girl. And stiffened.

Never in his life had he seen a face like that. It was racked with fear. He knew then that whatever part these men had played so far in this girl's life, it was a terrible one.

He reached out a hand.

She didn't see it, didn't look his way when she felt it; but she held it, tight, so tight that he was on the point of asking her to relax her grip—when he heard a new sound.

Footsteps.

They must have climbed over the fence or slipped through the hole.

The girl's hand tightened still further. He tried desperately to think. The door was locked—that was one thing—and it was the only way in. They would have to break it down to get at them. That would make a fair bit of noise, though it was doubtful anyone would hear them. There was no one around the school buildings at this time of night.

Or perhaps they would pick the lock.

The door-knob twisted suddenly.

He felt his hand squeezed again, so sharply that he nearly yelped.

The door did not open. The knob twisted back and was still. He looked at the girl in the darkness and tried to give her a reassuring glance. But all he saw in her face was terror.

The door-knob twisted once more, then flicked back to its normal position.

A moment later, he heard feet tramping away. He breathed out and opened his mouth to whisper. She squeezed his hand at once and he saw her eyes fixed on him with fierce intensity. Her finger was at her lips. He nodded to reassure her, and said nothing.

She still watched him but seemed relieved now that she knew he wasn't going to speak. She let go his hand, and it seemed to him a sign that she was regaining control of herself. He thought of the tension he had felt in that hand, and looked away, feeling strangely vulnerable himself now that it was gone.

He listened, yearning for the sound of car doors and the engine revving up again. But those sounds did not come. Somewhere outside, the men were still roaming.

He heard a sharp click in the direction of the main buildings. It sounded as though they were trying the door to one of the prefab classrooms. If so, there might yet be hope. The men might not have seen them enter the squash court after all.

Silence fell once again, then there was another click, further to the left. That sounded like the PE storeroom. He strained his ears and listened for more sounds. They tried another door, then another, then footsteps approached again. He tensed, certain they would try the squash court door once more.

But they went straight past, back towards the fence. He looked at the girl. She was staring ahead, her face taut as she listened for the sounds they both longed to hear.

At last they came. One car door opened and closed, then the other. The engine started and revved up, then they heard the car turn in the lane and motor off towards the town.

The girl gave a sigh. 'That was close.'

He stared at her.

'I can't work out what made them come here. I didn't see them following us. And I thought they'd be hanging around the shed tonight. But they must have seen us somehow. Why would they go to all the trouble of coming out here if there wasn't good reason?'

She glanced at him.

'There was good reason. I dossed at the school one night, before I found your shed.'

'What, not in here?'

She shook her head.

'Wish I could have done. You're right. It's warm. No, I used the girls' loo by the PE hut. There was no problem getting in there. It was freezing but it seemed a safer place than the streets. I didn't think they'd look for me inside a school.'

'But how did you get in?'

'You're not the only one who knows about the hole in the fence.'

'But have they actually seen you here?'

She thought for a moment.

'Don't think so. But lots of other people saw me in the lane and if the men have been asking questions in town, it's possible someone might have said they've seen me here.' She shrugged. 'Well, hopefully it'll all be over soon. Have you got any more food?'

'Sure.'

'And is there a changing room in here somewhere? I've got to sit down. I don't feel too good.'

He looked at her.

'What . . . you mean . . . ?'

'Yeah. The baby.'

'Is it due soon?'

'Never mind that. I want to sit down.'

He nodded to the right.

'There's a girls' changing room down that end. It's got a loo and I think there's a radiator in there. There's one in the boys' changing room anyway.' He nodded to the left. 'Up there.'

'Which is more comfortable?'

'Don't know. I never go in the girls' changing room. The boys' is a bit primitive.'

She walked down to the girls' changing room and glanced round the door, but didn't switch on the light. A moment later she came back.

'Let's try your changing room.'

He led the way past the open door to the squash court, a curious symbol now of a life that seemed to belong to someone else, and entered the boys' changing room.

She followed and sat straight down on the bench nearest the radiator. He joined her, rummaged in the rucksack for the sandwiches and handed her one. She took it and leaned back against the wall.

'Thanks.'

He watched her for a moment as she ate with that same desperate urgency, then leaned back, too, fighting his own hunger.

'Aren't you going to eat?' she said.

'No. I had a big meal before I came out. The sandwiches are all for you.'

She did not seem to detect the lie and went on eating. After a while she closed her eyes and dozed.

But Jamie did not even try to doze. He knew his thoughts would not let him. Instead, as she slept, he stared out at the dark cell of the room and wondered about the future.

She only slept for about an hour, and her sleep was fitful and jerky. Then she woke and asked for another sandwich. He handed her one and leaned back again, watching her.

She finished the sandwich in silence, then suddenly looked round at him.

'Those men, they're . . .' She paused. 'Listen, I don't want any questions about things I don't want to tell you, OK?'

'We've already agreed that.'

'So don't push me.'

'I'm not going to.'

She paused again, as though waiting for him to say more. But he remained silent. She went on.

'I'm in serious trouble. You must have worked that out already. I'm not from round here—you've maybe worked that out, too—but I had to come to try and sort something out.'

She breathed hard.

'Those two men . . . I owe them money. A lot of money. Much more money than I can lay my hands on. And they want it badly. Not just that, they want revenge. I haven't got a bean on me and I'm terrified of what they'll do to me if they catch me. And I'm frightened for the baby.'

Something in her manner seemed to soften as she uttered the last word. She'd thrown out the other words all at once, as though to rid herself of them as quickly as possible. But the mention of the baby changed her completely.

He sat up. 'How much money do you owe them?'

'You don't want to know. But it's a lot. Several thousand.'

'How many thousand?'

She looked down and spoke, in such a low voice that he barely caught the answer. But he heard; and it made him whistle.

'How the hell did you get that much in debt?'

There was a long silence, and he realized he had just broken the rule of not asking questions. Sure enough, she wasn't prepared to tell him.

'I don't want to talk about it. But they're dangerous, OK? You're best off not associating with me.'

He hesitated.

'This money, did you, I mean . . . ?'

'Did I steal it?' She almost snarled at him. 'No, I didn't. I'm not a criminal. I might have taken money from your house but this money was legitimate so if you bloody well think—'

'I don't, I don't.' He held out a hand. 'I don't think anything. Please don't get angry. I'm not accusing you of anything.'

She had sat bolt upright but quickly slumped back on the bench again. He cursed himself silently for overstepping the mark, especially when there was no need. He had already worked out who the enemy was. He looked at her and spoke as gently as he could.

'Those men, would they leave you alone if you paid them the money?'

'What difference does it make? I can't pay them anyway. Not now.'

'What do you mean, not now?'

She glanced across at him and again he sensed her reluctance to talk.

'Listen,' he said. 'I know there are things you don't want to tell me. That's fine. There are things I don't want to tell you. But let me ask you things and if I ask you something you don't want to talk about, don't bite my head off. Just say you don't want to talk about it, and that's no problem.'

She seemed to relax slightly; and after a moment's thought, she answered him.

'I came here to try and get the money to pay them off. I know someone who I thought . . . might give me the money and I could somehow send it to them, without having to meet them. But . . . well, I can't get the money from him.'

He studied her face. The darkness had softened it and it seemed strangely childlike. It occurred to him with a slight shock that they had never actually seen each other in the daylight. Perhaps she was right. They were shadows after all.

'But just for argument's sake,' he said, 'if you did pay them off, would they leave you alone then?'

She pulled her coat round her shoulders.

'Maybe, maybe not. They're not the men to forgive. They'd probably take the money, then sort me.'

He looked at her. 'You mean . . . ?'

'I mean they'd kill me. At the very least, they'd make sure I never win any beauty contests.'

She looked down suddenly.

'Why the hell are you getting involved? It's nothing to do with you, all this. You don't owe me anything. Nobody owes me anything.' She shook her head. 'You're nice and I know you mean well but you should be thinking about your own problems and leave me to sort out mine. I told you, I can't give you anything back.'

'I don't want anything back. Listen—' He looked down again. 'My life's in a mess, too, and maybe, I don't know, maybe I just . . . need a friend for a little while, just like you need a friend, for a little while. That's all. No strings attached. Just a couple of shadows, like you said, sticking together, until we can go our separate ways.'

She didn't speak and he kept his eyes riveted to the floor, but he sensed her watching him in the darkness. He spoke again, his voice small and tense.

'I'm really scared. Not scared like you were just now

when the men were outside. I know my problem's nothing compared with yours. But I'm still scared. I don't know what's happened to my life. I don't know where I'm going or what I'm doing. I don't know anything about tomorrow.'

To his surprise, he felt her hand touch his. He took it and held it, glad for it, until embarrassment seemed to master them both, and their hands slid apart once more.

He looked round at her. 'You said earlier that all this would hopefully be over soon. What did you mean?'

'I'm leaving Ashingford tomorrow. I told you, I came down to try and borrow the money to pay them off but . . . well, anyway, I couldn't do it. So I'll just have to go to ground and keep looking over my shoulder.'

She yawned.

'I've got an address in Cumbria, friends of a friend. They'll hide me, help with the baby, keep me out of the way for a bit until I can move on. If I can slip away from here without being spotted.'

'Will these people pay the men off?'

'No. It's just a sanctuary, for me and the baby, when it comes. I was going to go straight there but I decided to come here first and try to get the money.'

She yawned again.

'Better get a bit more rest. I'll have to set off before daylight. It's too dangerous for me to move around when it's light. I should be heading for the motorway now but I'm too tired. I'll just have to get through another day lying low and start hitching in the evening.' She looked at him suddenly. 'We'll have to split after we leave this building.'

Jamie leaned closer.

'Listen, I won't get in your way. I won't do anything that causes you problems but . . . can I come with you? To Cumbria, I mean. Just to make sure you get to your sanctuary. I won't stay, not long. But I want to help you and, like I said, I . . . I need a friend myself. Just for a bit.'

97

She seemed to ponder his words for a long time. Then she shrugged.

'OK.'

They didn't sleep. They tried to doze, lying on the benches, then sitting up, backs against the wall, and finally, without a word between them, moved to the corner of the room, where two benches joined, and stretched out, lying in opposite directions, his head in the crook of her shoulder, hers in the crook of his.

After about an hour, she sat up. 'We should be going. I can't sleep anyway.'

He sat up, too. 'OK. When do you want to start hitching tonight?'

'When it looks safe. We've got to get across Ashingford to the roundabout on the ring road where the motorway starts. That'll take a while. I can't walk very fast.'

He thought for a moment about the idea that had been growing in his mind.

'Listen,' he said. 'There's something I've got to do. Something I've got to sort out. Can we split when we get out of here and meet up this evening?'

'You walking out on me already?'

'No, it's not that.'

'I'm not bothered if you do.'

'No, OK, but . . . I mean . . . I'm not. I've just got some things to sort out, too. So what time do you want to meet at the roundabout?'

'I won't wait for you. If you're not there, tough.'

'Fair enough. But what time?'

She thought for a moment. 'Call it six o'clock tomorrow evening.'

'This evening. Not tomorrow evening.'

She shrugged. 'Whatever. But I told you, I'm not waiting for you.'

'I'll be there.'

She looked at him for a moment. 'OK. But don't meet

me at the roundabout itself. It's too exposed. Anyone can see you.'

'So where shall we meet?'

'Get to the roundabout, OK?'

'Right.'

'Take the slip-road that goes up towards the motorway, then look up to your right. There are some slabs of concrete supporting the motorway, where the flyover meets the verge. If you climb up inside them, they make a kind of room underneath the carriageway. It's not a very good doss but once you're in there, you can't be seen from the road.'

She grimaced suddenly and clutched her stomach.

He reached out and held her by the arm.

'Is it—?'

'Of course it is.' She reached out with her other hand and held on to one of the locker handles. 'God, if this baby comes early . . . I don't think I can handle that on top of everything else. It's not due for another two weeks. I'd been . . . counting on having it up north where these people can help me.'

'Are you sure you're fit to move?'

She looked at him.

'What choice have I got?' She stiffened and lurched towards the door. 'Come on. Let's get out of here.'

She was breathing hard and didn't look well enough to move but he said nothing and followed her to the door of the building. They both listened for sounds outside.

All was quiet.

'Have you got a watch?' she said.

'Yeah.' He looked down at it. 'Half-past four.'

'It's about the right time to move, while there's still darkness. I just wish it wasn't so cold.'

He unlocked the door, opened it and stepped out. The coldness of the night air struck him at once. She joined him outside the building and shivered.

'Wish we could have stayed a bit longer,' he said, locking the door again.

Suddenly she gripped his arm.

'What is it?' he said.

'Be quiet.'

He looked around them yet he could see nothing threatening, only the outlines of the school buildings and further down, across the field, the outer fence which ran alongside the lane. She leaned closer, still gripping his arm.

'Is there another way out of this school?'

He nodded towards the main buildings.

'If you go round the side of the main block and past the library building, you come to the gym. On the other side of that there's another fence. But you'd have to climb over. There's no hole. We're better off going the way we came in.'

He winced suddenly as she squeezed his arm tight.

And then he understood.

From the other side of the playing field two figures were racing towards the squash court.

16

'Quick!' said Jamie. 'Towards the main buildings.'

He dropped the rucksack and started to run. The girl struggled with him, clutching her bag, her face screwed up with fear. But she could not go fast and he knew they wouldn't get far like this.

He glanced back at the two men. They must have worked out that he and the girl were still somewhere on the school grounds and had hung around waiting. They were still a few hundred yards away but there was no chance of outrunning them. He could get away easily but the girl wouldn't. They would have to hide. And there was only one place he could think of.

'Hurry!' he said. 'Round the side of the main building.'

They stumbled round the corner and he ran ahead to the big dustbins at the back of the school kitchen. The first one was full, the second almost empty. The girl caught him up, breathlessly.

'Get in!' he said.

She didn't argue and tried to lift herself over the side of the bin.

'I can't do it,' she said. 'It's too high.'

He heard the panic in her voice.

'Easy, easy,' he said. He pulled over a small wooden crate. 'Stand on that.'

It broke under her weight the moment she stepped on it.

He looked frantically towards the corner of the building. The men would be here any moment. Beside him the girl was trembling uncontrollably. Maybe they should run, look for somewhere else to hide.

But he knew of nowhere. And the seconds were running out. It had to be the bin.

'Come on. I'll give you a leg up.'

He locked his fingers together and made a support. She placed her foot in the cradle of his hands and somehow climbed in. He handed her the holdall and the broken crate, then made to close the lid.

She looked out at him, her face small and petrified.

'Don't leave me! Please don't leave me!'

He knew he dare not linger. If the men saw him by the bins, all would be lost. But he had to comfort her somehow.

'Just stay as quiet as you can with the lid down. I'll try and lead the men away from here somehow. We'll meet where we said, at the motorway.'

'But—'

'There's no time. I've got to go.'

He closed the lid before she could answer. Then, on an impulse, opened it again.

'I won't desert you. I promise.'

He closed the lid again and raced down towards the science huts. Somehow he had to make them see him and think she was with him. He reached the corner of the Physics lab, stopped and looked back.

The men appeared round the side of the main building and stopped, looking around them. They had not spotted him yet. The taller one walked forward to the bin in which the girl was hiding and put his hand on the lid.

Jamie stepped into view, as though he had just come from behind the Physics lab.

'There!' shouted the other man, pointing towards him.

Both men started running towards him. He turned towards the Physics lab and shouted as if to someone behind it. 'Go on! Go on!'

He didn't know if they were taken in by this but at least they had left the bins.

He ran down the side of the lab and cut through the

other prefab huts in the science area. Footsteps sounded hard on his heels.

He called out again, as if to the girl. 'Go that way! Through the hole in the fence by the gym!'

He listened again for their footsteps but suddenly there were none. He stopped, anxious not to give his position away, and strained to hear them.

There was not a sound but he did not doubt they were moving close by. He stared round at the huts, searching for movement.

Somehow he had to get away. He crept to the edge of the Chemistry lab. There was no sign of the men but that made him warier still. Down to his left were the tennis courts and gym. There was no hole in the fence there but it was just possible the men had heard him and gone to check it out. He looked about him, saw nothing, and started to run towards the Home Economics huts.

The next moment, a hand seized him by the shoulder.

The taller man had him by the scruff of the neck. He felt himself pushed back against the side of the building. Then the shorter man appeared.

Jamie looked from one to the other. There was no chance of escape but he might still do some good.

'Run for it!' he shouted in the direction of the gym. 'Run for it!'

He hoped the girl would not hear him from inside the bin and think he meant her to climb out. But there was no time to think of that now. The taller man pulled out a knife, then glanced round at his companion.

'You go after the girl. She won't get far the way she's moving. I'll just settle up with young Jamie.'

'Which way?' said the other man.

'The way our friend just told us. Go on, quick. Before she finds a place to hide. I'll be along in a minute.'

'Well, don't hang about. Put the body in one of the bins.'

The shorter man ran off towards the gym. The tall man turned his attention back to Jamie.

103

'Well, boy, you've not been straight with us. I don't like that.'

Jamie gulped and tried to think. The plan he had formed back in the squash court could still be used. But he would have to change it. And quickly.

'Money,' he blurted. 'I—'

'I don't want your money. You haven't got any money. At least, not the kind of money I might be interested in.'

'Money for the girl. The . . . the money she owes you.'

The man looked him over. 'What about it?'

'I've got it. I . . . I was going to come and find you tomorrow and tell you. I've . . . I've . . . got it saved up . . . for her . . . I mean and . . . I could . . . get it for you and give it to you and . . .'

The hand at his neck tightened and he choked. The man snarled at him.

'You haven't got any money. Why should I listen to you? I haven't got time for this.' He glanced at the knife fondly. Jamie spluttered on frantically.

'I . . . inherited it. And I've been saving. It was for something else. But I met the girl and she . . . she told me she owed you some money—'

'A lot of money. A hell of a lot of money.'

'Yes and . . . and I decided to help her and pay you off so you'd . . . you'd leave her alone again.'

The grip on his neck eased slightly. Jamie studied the face before him, praying that the man's greed would overcome his desire to kill. There was a sound of footsteps and the shorter man reappeared.

'There's no sign of her,' he said. 'And there's no hole in the fence by the gym either.' He glanced at Jamie, then back at his companion. 'Haven't you done him yet?'

The taller man still looked at Jamie.

'Not yet,' he said quietly. 'But I'm going to lose my patience pretty quick if he doesn't tell us where the girl is now.'

Thoughts rushed through Jamie's mind. He knew his

life depended on the answers he gave these men. And the girl's life, too, perhaps. He kept his eyes on the taller man.

'I made it up about the hole in the fence by the gym. To distract you. To give her time to get away. She'll be gone by now.'

'Which way?'

'There's a hole in the fence just along from the main gate.' He felt the grip round his neck tighten and hurried on, choking. 'No, there . . . there really is a hole. I'll show you if you like. I . . . I wanted to give her time to get away. She'll have . . . escaped by now.'

The grip eased once more. The taller man stood back, then, without warning, flung the knife. Jamie gasped—but the knife was not aimed at him. It flew past his face and thudded into the door of the lab, where it quivered and then was still.

The man watched it for a moment, then went on.

'Well, Jamie, it looks like you'll have to pay the price yourself. We want the girl and we want the money. Instead, we've got you and you've got the money. So let's start with the money. You say you've got it. Well, the first thing you can do is give it to us.'

'I haven't got it on me.'

'I wasn't thinking you had it on you.' The man leaned closer. 'It's a lot of money. Little boys don't carry that kind of money around with them. But I expect you to get it by tonight. Now, just so we understand each other.'

The man's hand swung out. Jamie felt the fist smash into the side of his face. He fell backwards against the building. Another fist drove into his stomach, forcing out the breath. He doubled up, gasping for air.

Another blow came, to the side of his head, knocking him down, then a boot crashed into the small of his back. He writhed over the ground, moaning with pain. A hand seized him by the hair and twisted his head round. He looked up into the tall man's eyes, as chilly as the night sky that shrouded them. The voice that spoke was chillier still.

'I don't like people who cross me, Jamie. So I make sure they understand what's what. Now, today you're going to get hold of this money, and you're going to bring it to me in my car. The money will be in cash inside an envelope. Of course, you won't be stupid enough to phone the police or tell anyone because you've probably realized by now that I'm not a very nice person and we wouldn't like to see a series of unfortunate accidents, starting with your mother, and then your father, and maybe that nice boy you walk to school with. And perhaps he's got some brothers and sisters. And then, of course, the girl, not to mention yourself.'

He paused.

'Don't forget yourself. Because there won't be any escape, Jamie. And don't think getting us caught will solve any problems for you because it won't. Firstly, we won't both be in the car, so my friend here will be free to hunt you down, and secondly, even if we did get caught and go to prison, we've got plenty of friends who'll be happy to do jobs for us on the outside. You'd be watching your back every minute of the day and night. Am I making myself clear?'

Jamie looked at him dumbly, too shocked to speak.

The hand whipped out again and smacked into his cheek.

'Am I making myself clear?'

'Yes.' Jamie swallowed hard. 'Yes. Where . . . where do I meet you?'

The man thought for a moment.

'You go to the roundabout where the ring road joins up with the motorway. Just down from it, there's a lay-by. I'll be pulled in there. You come on your own. At six o'clock.'

Jamie stiffened. Of all the places to meet, of all the times to meet.

'I . . . I'm not sure I can get out there by six o'clock. Couldn't I meet you in town somewhere? Maybe at—'

'You meet me at the lay-by. Six o'clock. And don't be late.'

106

Jamie opened his mouth to speak again but there was no time for further protestation. He felt himself lifted from the ground and thrown against the side of the lab. The man advanced, pulled the knife from the door, and seized him by the hair again.

'Don't let me down, Jamie.'

'I'll . . . I'll be there. And if I give you the money, will you . . . will you leave the girl alone after that?'

The man's eyes bore into him like darts.

'We'll think about that when we've seen the money.'

The fist flew out again and Jamie remembered no more.

When he came to, the men had gone. He was lying on the ground beside the Chemistry lab, shivering in the cold, his head aching where the blows had struck. He felt his cheeks and nose. Nothing seemed to be broken though he was badly bruised. But he knew he'd been lucky. Their first plan had been to kill him.

He struggled to his feet and looked about him. It was still dark and the men seemed to have gone but he was wary now. They had clearly not been fooled earlier when he and the girl had been inside the squash court. They must have parked the car down the lane, walked back and climbed the fence or used the gap, and waited for them to appear again.

He looked at his watch. Five o'clock. A couple more hours and his parents would be waking. Waking to find him gone. But they seemed like inhabitants of another world now.

He stumbled towards the main building, still watching for signs of the men. The bins came into view and he walked slowly towards them, trying not to show any interest in them, in case he was being watched. He stopped by the one in which he had left the girl, and looked about him again.

Still he saw no one.

He made up his mind and pulled up the lid.

She was not there.

He closed it again and leaned on the bin, unsure whether to feel relieved or concerned. He knew he had to find her at the roundabout before the men did. But there was much to do first. And despite the pain, hunger and cold, he somehow had to will himself into action.

He wandered down to the squash court, found his rucksack still lying on the ground and wearily picked it up. Then he crossed the playing field, squeezed through the hole in the fence and made his way slowly and painfully down the lane.

17

If it had been anyone else but Spider, the sight of a figure climbing in through his bedroom window and leaning over the bed might have provoked at least a gasp. But he merely stared in silence for a moment, then murmured, 'What the hell are you doing here?'

Jamie sat on the bed, trying to calm himself. He was so tense now he felt his nerves would snap. Spider sat up in bed and switched on the lamp.

'Christ, what happened to you? Who did that to your face?'

Jamie looked away, unable to speak. Spider started to climb out of bed.

'I'll get Mum and Dad.'

'No.' Jamie reached out and held his arm. 'Please. They mustn't know anything. You see, I've . . .' He stopped, breathing hard.

'Take your time,' said Spider.

'I've . . . I've left home.'

'You've what?'

'I've left home.' The words tumbled out, now that he had started. 'I left last night. My parents probably don't know yet, unless they've already woken up. But they never wake before seven. And I didn't see a light on. So they . . . they probably don't know anything yet.' He looked away towards the window. 'They didn't hear me put the ladder up against your wall.' He laughed nervously. 'You must be the only person in the country who sleeps with the window ajar when it's as cold as this.'

He knew he was talking aimlessly but his thoughts were no longer his own. Spider spoke at last.

'But why? I mean, I know things are difficult. But running away's surely a bit drastic. Did you have a bust up or something?'

Jamie frowned. There was so much Spider didn't know and it was unfair to get him involved in all this without telling him everything. But the less he knew, the better. Then, if he was asked questions, he couldn't give anything away. Yet something had to be said, especially in view of what Jamie was about to ask him.

'I did have a bust up with my dad. He knocked me about and . . . well, anyway, I've just got to get away. So I'm hitching up north this evening—with a friend.'

'Who?'

'Don't ask me.' He saw the concern on Spider's face and hurried on. 'Please don't ask me. The less you know, the better.'

'But you're in trouble. Anyone can see that. Can you at least tell me who did that to your face? Was it your dad?'

'No. It was . . . someone else.'

Jamie sighed. If he mentioned the two men, Spider would put two and two together and connect him with the girl. He remembered what the taller man had said about hurting Spider's family, and the thought of Amy and Becky in the hands of those men decided him. He shook his head.

'It's best you don't know anything. Please don't try and force me. If anyone asks, you haven't seen me, right? And you mustn't call the police. You don't know anything. It's for your own good.' He took a deep breath. 'But there's something else. I . . . I need your help. I need it really badly.'

Spider drew his knees up to his chest.

'What do you want me to do?'

Jamie studied his friend's face in the glow of the lamp. It was so still, so composed, so strong. He had been dreading this moment.

'I don't know how to ask you this. But there's no one else I can turn to. I can't turn to my dad or my mum.

But this . . . .' He hesitated, anxious to give no clues about the girl. 'This friend of mine's in much bigger trouble than I am. If I don't do something, this . . . person . . . could get killed.'

He paused again, waiting for Spider to speak. But his friend was silent. He looked down and went on.

'I need . . . money. A lot of money. It's not for myself. It's for my friend. It's to pay off the . . . the people who are after my friend.'

He stopped, still looking down at the bed. Spider spoke.

'How much do you need?'

Jamie looked up at him, desperately trying to think of something to say other than what he had to say. But there was nothing else.

'I need . . . as much as it costs to buy a good sports car.'

Spider held his eyes for a long time, then leant back against the head of the bed.

'When do you need it?'

'I'll pay you back. Somehow. It'll take time but—'

'When do you need it?'

Spider's voice was quiet, almost detached. Jamie took another deep breath.

'Today.'

Spider's eyes flickered away for a moment, then back.

'I can't get it to you until after school. And it might be a bit difficult reaching you without someone spotting us. I mean, your parents will call the police the moment they find you're missing. And it'll get round the school, and other people will be looking out for you. And people are bound to ask me questions and watch what I'm doing. Where will I find you?'

Jamie tried to think. At the moment he was still stunned at the calm, unquestioning attitude of his friend. It seemed inconceivable that Spider could face the prospect of losing everything he had worked so hard for without some show of anger. Jamie almost wanted him to be angry. He touched his friend on the arm.

111

'I'm so sorry. I'm so sorry. I'll—'

'Never mind that. Where will I find you?'

He forced himself to think. He certainly should keep Spider away from the roundabout by the ring road. Then he thought of the obvious place.

'You know the little alleyway by the health food shop? Can you meet me in there? I'll be right at the end, where it bends round out of sight.'

'Are you sure you want to meet there? You get a lot of drifters hanging about that place.'

Jamie frowned. 'Shadows,' he murmured.

'What?' said Spider.

But Jamie shook his head. 'It doesn't matter. I'll meet you in the alleyway. I'll be all right.'

'I won't be able to get the money to you before about five.'

'That's OK. I can meet you at five.'

'I suppose it's got to be in cash?'

Jamie stared at him, again feeling the enormity of what he was asking.

'Yeah. In an envelope. Christ, I'm so sorry. What will you say when people ask you if you've seen me?'

'I'll just say I haven't.'

'What about the money?'

'What about it?'

'Aren't you mad at me?'

'Yep.'

There was no anger in Spider's voice. But Jamie knew what the loss of this money would mean to his friend.

'What about the car you were going to buy? What'll you tell your parents?'

'I'll tell them it's not quite what I want after all and that I'm not going to rush into buying anything.'

Jamie looked down. 'I feel a bastard.'

'You're not a bastard. You're just a pain.' Spider swung himself out of bed. 'Have you eaten anything?'

'Not much.'

'Have you got any food on you?'

'No.'

'Money?'

'No.'

Spider's face softened.

'You'd better stay here while I sneak downstairs. I'll see what I can rustle up.'

Spider slipped out of the room and closed the door behind him. Jamie waited, listening for sounds from his own house next door, but there were none. After what seemed a long while the door opened again and Spider entered with a plastic bag. He closed the door behind him and sat on the bed.

'Get these inside you.'

He pushed some sandwiches into Jamie's hand and Jamie attacked them gratefully. Spider watched him for a moment, then went on.

'Listen, I haven't taken too much food, just some rolls and cake, and some apples. If I take too much, Mum and Dad'll notice and when I'm asked questions, it'll be obvious I've seen you and helped you. It'd be far better if you could buy yourself something.' Spider reached into the drawer of his bedside cabinet. 'Here's some money. It's not much but it'll get you and your friend enough food for a day or two. And I'll bring you more tonight.'

Jamie looked up from the sandwich, guilt flooding over him once more.

'Take it,' said Spider, then, when Jamie still hesitated, reached out and pushed the notes into Jamie's pocket. 'Listen, buy the food early today, before the news really gets out about you. And don't go anywhere where people know you. Try somewhere where you can slip in, buy the food and slip out quickly. What about that mini-market just past the bus station? Do you ever go in there?'

'No.'

'Well, try there. With any luck, the only person you'll see will be some sleepy cashier. Where are you going to hang out today?'

'I don't know.'

'Well, you need to make sure no one sees you. No one at all, if possible, not just police and people who know you. You don't want some do-gooder seeing your boyish, youthful appearance and asking why you're not in school. Not that you look very boyish and youthful right now. Hang on.'

Spider crept out of the room again but quickly returned.

'Lean forward,' he said.

'What's that stuff?'

'Arnica cream. Mum swears by it. We only have to bang an elbow and she's slapping it all over us.'

He squeezed some cream from the tube and reached out. The touch of his finger on the bruises made Jamie wince, but he said nothing and continued eating the sandwiches. Spider went over all the bruises, then leant back.

'It's the best I can do. Here, take the cream and put some more on later.'

'Thanks.'

Spider glanced at the bedside clock, then back. And for some moments simply watched him eat. Then he spoke again.

'Are you sure there's no other way out of this?'

And Jamie looked back at him; and shook his head.

'I wish there was,' he said.

Spider was right about the mini-market. The only person who took any notice of him was the girl at the check-out and she merely asked him for the money. He had already decided that his best place to hide was the alleyway itself. Uncomfortable though it was, and too close to the town centre for comfort, there seemed little point in moving about from place to place. The more he moved, the more likely he was to be spotted.

It was cold, though, and damp as he huddled against the wall. He was not left to himself. A stream of motorbike riders came and went as usual, parking their bikes under the sheltered part of the alley, but only a few came far enough down to see him at the end and none approached him. He looked away when they appeared.

There were tramps, too, who ambled down the alleyway, seeking to rest there perhaps, but they retreated at the sight of him. Only one person bothered him, an old drunk who lurched over him, spitting and moaning, before stumbling away back to the street.

There was no sign of the police, nor any pursuit. Eventually darkness fell and it grew colder. And with the cold came the greater chill of fear.

Just after five, he heard footsteps in the passageway.

It was Spider.

His friend dropped a carrier bag on the ground.

'I can't stay long. There's a big hue and cry about you and everybody's suspicious of me. I don't think I was followed but I'm sure Mum and Dad think I know something. We had your dad on the doorstep first thing this morning, asking if I'd seen you.'

Jamie shifted restlessly. It would be touch and go to reach the roundabout by six and he was anxious to be moving—but he had to know more.

'What was he . . . what was he like?'

'Your dad? Bit rude when he turned up this morning. He was more civil after school but he looked nervous. The police were no problem to deal with.'

'The police?'

Spider looked at him. 'What did you expect? They've been in school, asking questions.'

'Have you . . .' He hesitated. 'Have you seen my mum?'

Spider shook his head. 'Your dad looked bad enough so I expect she's worse. You didn't leave a note, your dad said, so for all they know, you could be dead.'

'I should have written them one. I wish I had now.'

Spider reached inside his bag.

'I thought you might say that so I brought you some paper and an envelope. I'll post it. I'm not putting it through the letter box—I might be spotted. I've put a stamp on it. If you send it from here, they might think from the postmark that you're still in the area.'

Jamie looked at him gratefully. Spider had been so practical, so unselfish.

'I'll make this up to you,' he said.

'You certainly will,' said Spider. 'Go on. Write the thing and get moving. I can't stay long.'

'What excuse did you give your parents for slipping out?'

'I didn't give an excuse. They're at the supermarket with the twins but they'll all be back soon so hurry up. And here's the money. I had a couple of hundred left in the account so I shoved that in, too. Hope it helps.'

Without ceremony, Spider pushed an envelope towards him. Jamie stared at it.

'Go on,' said Spider. 'Take it.'

Jamie took the envelope and thrust it inside his rucksack. Spider handed him a piece of paper, a pen, and an envelope with a stamp on it.

'Use my back,' he said, and turned round.

Jamie rested the paper against Spider's back and tried to think of what to write. But it was difficult. He wanted to tell them he wasn't dead, so that they didn't start a murder hunt, but he also wanted to say something that would make Mum feel better.

He wasn't sure he had anything to say to Dad.

'Hurry up,' said Spider. 'I've really got to be moving. I don't want to have to tell more lies to Mum and Dad. And don't print the letters. You need to make sure your parents recognize the handwriting.'

Jamie started to scribble. He didn't say much, partly because there wasn't time, partly because the point of the pen kept pushing through the paper; but mostly because he really didn't know what to say.

He wasn't happy with the result and it seemed a little melodramatic but it was the best he could do.

I'm OK. Don't worry about me. But I can't see you any more. I'm going away to live my own life. Please don't try to find me. I won't come back.

I'm sorry.

Jamie.

'Finished?' said Spider.

'Yes.' He sealed the note inside the envelope.

Spider turned round.

'If you address the envelope, I'll post it on the way back.' Spider glanced at his watch. 'Quarter-past five. I'll drop it through the box at the depot in King Street. It'll catch the last post and your parents should get it in the morning.'

'Can you turn round again?'

Spider turned round and Jamie wrote the address on the envelope.

'OK.'

Spider turned back and took the envelope.

'I bought some more food for you on the way here. It's in the bag.'

Jamie looked at him.

'Thanks. Thanks for everything. I'll never forget what you've done for me.'

And Spider looked back, the familiar half-smile on his face; then, without a word, he reached out, cuffed Jamie lightly over the head, and left.

Jamie watched him go, his mind in a turmoil of guilt and fear. But it was time to act. He stuffed the food that Spider had brought inside his rucksack along with the food he had bought himself. Then he noticed the envelope.

He pulled it out, looked warily about him, and opened it.

It was all there, including the two hundred pounds extra as Spider had said. He stared at it all. Thousands of pounds, each note a fragment of his friend's dream, now gone.

But perhaps they would save a girl's life.

He separated the two hundred pounds, put them in his pocket and counted the rest again to make sure the amount was right. Then he replaced the notes in the envelope, pushed it inside his rucksack and fastened the catch, and set off towards the street.

He had planned his route during the hours of waiting.

118

Down the main street—that couldn't be avoided—then along Litchfield Avenue as far as the traffic lights where it should be possible to cut through one of the lanes that straggled up to the ring road. But he would have to hurry. He was really late now.

He forced himself to walk down the main street but kept to the side and hugged the shops. The town was crowded with people flooding out of work, not to mention pupils from the school, and he knew this was the most risky stretch. He kept his head down and pulled his hood up.

He reached Litchfield Avenue safely and turned down it, relieved to be away from the main street, but now self-control deserted him. He started to run, the rucksack thumping up and down on his back. He had to get away from this part of the town. He knew so many pupils who lived round here.

He reached the traffic lights at the bottom and waited for the signal to cross. To his right, he sensed someone's presence beside him. He turned away and readjusted his hood.

'Too cold to be standing around,' said a voice.

He pretended not to hear. It wasn't a voice he recognized but that meant nothing. It might still be someone who knew him. Or a policeman. The voice spoke again.

'Murphy's law, isn't it? They're always on red when you want them on green.'

He made himself glance round and saw an elderly man standing there. The man caught his eye and winked.

'Running away from home?'

'What?'

The man nodded at Jamie's rucksack.

'That's fairly bulging. You look like you're stocked up for a long trip or maybe you've just got the Crown Jewels in there.'

Jamie looked at him suspiciously and said nothing. The man smiled.

'It's time.'

'What?'

The man smiled again, apparently unconcerned at the abrupt response he was getting.

'The lights.'

'Oh.'

They crossed together and parted company on the other side. Jamie forced himself not to run straight away but let the man disappear in the direction of the sweet shop, then he sped off again.

He had a choice of lanes before him, all leading the way he wanted to go. Frantically he ran his mind over the people he knew who lived round here, but there were so many, it scarcely made any difference.

He cut through Parkhurst Lane into Compton Drive and on to the parade of shops at the end. So far, so good. There were only a few people on the streets here and none of them seemed interested in him as he ghosted by in the darkness. He gave the shops plenty of room and skirted round the other side of the street as far as the entrance to Channock Hill.

Still no one called his name; no car pulled over. He ran up Channock Hill and turned down Pendle Lane towards the ring road. Now, far ahead, he could see the lights of the traffic moving along the ring road towards the motorway junction. Nearly ten to six. He might just make it but it was going to be close.

He raced on, keeping his eyes alert. The garden centre appeared on his left, then, a hundred yards on, the playing fields opened up to the right, and beyond them, raised on the embankment, the ring road itself, cluttered with lorries and cars.

He ran to where Pendle Lane crossed under the ring road, climbed over the fence and scampered up the bank to the top. This was the next dangerous moment. The road was so much used that anyone might see him and recognize him. And if there had been reports on the news about him, even strangers might guess who he was.

But he had to take that risk.

He plunged on down the road, the traffic thundering past him. He felt exhausted now, and it was still nearly half a mile to the lay-by at the motorway junction. Somehow he drove himself on, cursing the weight of the rucksack, and starting to panic about the man he was to face.

The road started to bend to the right and now, as he drew closer, he could see the roundabout ahead and the motorway running over it, and there, too, the flyover under which the girl was waiting, he hoped, hidden in a forest of stone.

But his eyes did not linger on this. They were scanning the road ahead. And there, just a short distance from him, was the lay-by.

In it was a car.

He stopped and caught his breath. The man mustn't see him running—if it was the man. It was hard to tell. He strained his eyes to see as the headlights from passing vehicles brushed over the car, but it was no good.

He walked slowly forward, trying to think of some way to give himself a chance of safety. And suddenly an idea came. It wasn't a very good one—indeed, it might misfire by arousing the man's anger—but it was all he could think of right now.

A lorry rumbled past and threw its beam over the car in the lay-by.

And in that moment Jamie caught the outline of the man he feared.

19

He didn't knock at the window but stood there, a few feet back from the passenger door. The man saw him and a moment later the automatic window slid down.

'Get in.'

Jamie didn't move.

'Get in.'

Jamie looked at the face, remembering what the man could do. He also wondered where the shorter man was hidden. There was no sign of him here but that meant nothing. He opened the passenger door and leaned down.

The man glanced at him.

'I'm not talking to you standing out there.'

Jamie took a deep breath, climbed slowly into the car and closed the door behind him. Without a word, the man started the engine.

Jamie forced himself to speak as confidently as he could.

'If you drive me anywhere, you won't see the money.'

The man looked him over coldly.

'What?'

Jamie clenched his fists. He knew he must not let the man drive him away. All his instincts told him that any journey with this man would be the last he ever made.

'If you drive me anywhere, you won't see the money.'

'Don't play games with me, boy.'

'I'm not . . . playing games. But . . .' Jamie moved back slightly, aware of the anger building in the man's eyes. 'I haven't got all the money on me here. I left half of it just down the road. It's only a few yards away. I'll tell you where it is when you promise me you'll leave the girl alone and let me out of the car safely.'

The man studied his face for a few moments, his features dark and threatening, then, without switching off the engine, held out his hand.

'Money.'

Jamie felt his hands tremble but somehow managed to look the man squarely in the face.

'When you've promised to leave the girl alone. And me.'

The man raised an eyebrow, reached forward and turned off the engine. Then, with startling suddenness, he seized Jamie by the throat and thrust his head back against the window of the door.

'Ah!' Jamie cried out with the pain. The man jerked him forward by the hair, then rammed his head back against the window. Jamie squirmed in the seat, trying to shake his head free, but the man was too strong. Again and again his head was yanked forward, then driven back against the window.

Suddenly he was released but the man's face moved closer.

'Now listen, Jamie.' The voice seemed to breathe venom. 'You're not in a position to make conditions. And let's be honest about this—how do you know I'd keep any promise I might make? Much as I'm flattered to have your trust, I'm not sure I'd even trust myself. No, Jamie, the problem you've got is that I might just get angry and kill you here, instead of where I was planning, take what money you've got on you, go and look for the rest and, even if I find it, keep on looking for the girl until I find her and kill her, too. She won't get very far. Her trail's warm enough. Besides, even if you could trust me to keep my word, you haven't thought of my mate. Now he really is a nasty piece of work. I wouldn't bet on him honouring a pledge.'

The man looked him over in silence for a moment, then gave a chilly smile.

'So we'll look at what money you've got and then we'll talk again.'

Jamie knew it was foolish to resist. And what this man

said was true: his word would count for nothing. There was little else for it but to pay up and hope.

'I'll give you what I've got,' he said.

The man leaned back but stayed close enough to make Jamie feel uncomfortable. Jamie hesitated, then opened his rucksack and drew out the notes.

Once more the enormity of what he was doing overwhelmed him. Spider's hard-earned money given away to a man like this, who might well take it and still go on hunting the girl. But there was just a hope that the money would take away the lust for blood. He had to cling to that.

He held out the notes.

The man took them and counted them.

'So where's the rest?'

'Let me get out of the car first.'

The man eyed him in silence, and seemed to be pondering what to do. Clearly he was unwilling to lose Jamie and wanted him dead, but he must want the rest of the money, too. Jamie tried to think of some way of putting pressure on him.

'If you let me out of the car and don't bother me or the girl again, I'll tell you where the rest of the money is and . . . and I won't tell the police about the video.'

The man frowned. 'What video?'

'The video of you and your mate.'

The man sneered at him.

'You haven't got any video.'

'It's not mine,' said Jamie, thinking hard. 'It was taken by the parent of one of the girls at my school.'

The man looked at him, disbelieving yet suspicious. Jamie hurried on.

'When you talked to me outside the school gate that time, there was a netball match going on. One of the parents took some video film of his daughter playing. He told me about it because he said I was in the picture, talking to two men. I haven't seen it but you'll be on it.'

He knew this was a tissue of lies but he prayed the

124

man would not suspect it. More ideas rushed into his head and he blurted them out.

'And the headmaster saw you. He came out after you'd gone and asked me who you were. He'd been watching you through the window of his office. He said he thought you looked suspicious. And people in town have been talking about you asking them about the girl and giving them a phone number to ring and saying you'll pay them money and stuff.'

'None of that incriminates me.'

Jamie tried to think. He knew this was not evidence but it was just possible that he'd said enough to make the man feel it would be best to take the money and clear out. He bit his lip and spoke again.

'If you leave me and the girl alone, I promise I won't mention you to anyone or say anything about all this.' He paused, then added: 'And unlike you and your mate, I do keep my word.'

The man looked him over in silence. Jamie tried to stare boldly back, but it was hard. The eyes frightened him so much. There was no mistaking how dangerous this man could be.

Suddenly he spoke. 'Get out of the car.'

Jamie needed no second invitation. He opened the door and jumped out, pulling the rucksack after him. The thunder of the traffic broke upon his ears again but it was a welcome sound. The man jumped out of the driver's door.

'Where's the rest of the money?'

Jamie pointed back down the carriageway.

'About fifty yards down that way. Just back from the road where the fence posts get taller there's a gate with a big stone nearby. I put the money under the stone. It's in an envelope.'

The man pointed a finger at him. 'You wait here till I get back.'

'The money's there.'

'It better be.'

The man's face had changed suddenly. All the coolness

was gone; in its place was the flame of greed. Jamie said nothing. He knew he should run—he wanted desperately to run—but he knew, too, that he had to wait, not because he'd been told to but because he had to see this man drive away, with the money.

The man hurried off down the carriageway.

Jamie moved back from the car to give himself more room to escape but there was no need. The man was soon back in the driver's seat, counting the rest of the money.

The next moment, the car was gone.

Jamie waited for a few minutes to see if it reappeared but there was no sign of it or the other man. He looked about him a few more times, then crossed the carriageway, made his way to the other side of the roundabout, and walked towards the flyover.

20

The noise of the traffic seemed even louder here. He stood by the slip-road to the motorway, checked around him one more time for signs of danger, then climbed up the verge.

It was just as she had said. The road fell away below him and as he drew closer to the underside of the motorway, he could see that the concrete supports created a kind of flat pocket, bordered by slabs. He reached the outer slab, a low horizontal wall, and looked over it into the dark space within.

At the far end was a figure, bent over the opposite side.

He heard a moan, just audible over the roar of the traffic, then the figure moved and he caught the profile of the girl. Suddenly she fell against the slab.

He clambered into the little space, hurried up behind her and put a hand on her shoulder. She jumped.

'Easy,' he said. 'It's me.'

She turned towards him and he saw her face twisted with pain. He shook his head in despair.

'What have they done to you? How did they get to you?'

She stared at him for a moment, then grimaced and clutched her stomach.

'Don't be stupid. I'm . . . having a bloody baby, you idiot.' She moaned again. 'God, two weeks early. Why couldn't it wait till I got to Cumbria? I started to . . . feel funny this morning, then it . . . cleared a bit so I . . . came out here about twelve to rest and wait for you and . . . and suddenly it started.'

He took a step back.

'I'm going for an ambulance.'

'No!' She gripped his arm. 'Please don't go.'

'But—'

'Please.' Her face was pleading, desperate, her hand still tight round his arm. 'It's going to come soon and . . . I'm really scared.'

'But you need a doctor. I don't know what to do.'

She held him tighter still. 'Don't leave me alone here.'

He saw the fear in her face and knew he could not go. She had already endured six hours of solitary labour in this miserable place but now, with darkness fallen and the worst part surely to come, he knew he had to stay and try to help her. If he could master his own fear.

He took her hand. 'I'll stay.'

He saw the gratitude in her eyes but there was no time for her to answer as her body tensed in another spasm. She bent over the slab, groaning. He let go her hand and put his arm round her shoulder.

'It'll be OK,' he said.

She didn't answer and merely went on groaning, then, after a while, the pain seemed to ease. She slumped to the ground, her back against the wall, her eyes fixed ahead of her.

'Are you cold?' he said.

'Yes.'

'Have you still got that blanket you were carrying with you?'

'In my holdall.'

He fetched the blanket and draped it over her shoulders. She looked up at him, shivering. She seemed so vulnerable, yet somehow so beautiful. The spasms soon started once more and the cycle of pain and relief went on, the contractions growing steadily more stressful.

An hour passed. The contractions grew stronger, more frequent, the girl shifting position constantly as she tried to ease her discomfort. Jamie watched, mopping her brow with his handkerchief and trying to offer words of encouragement, but feeling increasingly helpless. Suddenly she gave a moan, struggled into a squatting position and gripped him by the shoulders.

'Help . . . me!' she said.

He put his hands on her waist and held her steady.

'Come on,' he said. 'You're nearly there.'

She started to scream, her hands digging into his shoulders so hard he wanted to cry out, too. He watched in horror, remembering stories he'd heard of women who died in childbirth. Then he looked down.

The top of the head had appeared.

'It's coming,' he said. 'It's coming.'

The girl didn't look down and merely gripped him as before, breathing hard.

'Come on,' he said. 'Push!'

And she pushed, screaming as before and gripping him more tightly than ever. Suddenly, with a gasp of relief, she slumped against him.

He held her for a while, then slowly leaned back enough to glance down.

The head was out now but not the body. He looked back at the girl. She was still breathing hard and her head now rested on his shoulder, as though she wanted to sleep.

'Come on,' he said. 'One more effort.'

And sure enough, with the next contraction, the body eased out.

He reached down and put a hand under it. It felt slippery and strange; tiny, yet somehow immense. And it was crying.

The girl seemed unable to speak, unable to move. He looked back at her.

'I've got the baby. It's OK.'

She said nothing and simply clung to him, gulping in air as the baby went on crying. He waited, wondering why she hadn't reached down to take the child. Then, suddenly, she gave a moan.

And he felt the baby slip free.

He moved back, still holding it, then recoiled at the sight of what had come out with it. The girl spoke at last, her voice so weary he could barely hear it.

'It's the afterbirth. We'll sort it out later. Just give me my baby.'

He lifted the baby towards her, his eyes still on the unpleasant-looking jelly at the end of the umbilical cord. The girl took the child in her arms and cradled it, making soothing noises as it cried. Then she looked at Jamie.

'Didn't you check?'

He stared at her, then realized what she meant. She gave a tired laugh.

'I've got a little boy. I've always wanted a little boy.'

She undid her shirt and put the baby's mouth to her breast.

'He won't get any milk just yet. Dear little boy.'

He said nothing, feeling strangely redundant and still uneasy about the afterbirth. The girl slumped back against the slab, holding the baby to her.

She was spent.

Jamie watched her for a moment, trying to think of something he could do. Then he saw that the blanket had slipped to the ground. He picked it up and draped it over her again.

'Thanks,' she said, wrapping it quickly round the baby, too.

Her eyes were glazed with weariness but at least the baby was now silent and seemed to be trying to suckle. Jamie moved closer.

'What do we do now?' he said.

She took a long time answering, as though it were a struggle even to speak.

'We've got to clean him and dress him before he freezes to death. And we've got to get rid of the umbilical cord and the afterbirth.'

Jamie looked down at it again. 'How do we do that?'

She took some deep breaths, then slowly sat up straight.

'I know what some peasant women do. I've read about it. But I don't know if I can—' She stopped, still breathing hard. 'Can you pass me my holdall? I've got some things in there I've been collecting for the baby.'

130

'What, like nappies?'

'And baby clothes.'

He handed her the holdall and she pulled out some string. Then she looked round at him.

'I'd . . . rather do this bit on my own. If I can bring myself to.'

'Are you sure?'

'Yeah, I think so. Anyway, I need to . . . clean myself up a bit.'

She looked at him somewhat shyly but he understood well enough. He jumped to his feet.

'I'll be over there. Just shout if you want me.'

He walked over to the outer slab and gazed down at the roundabout, blowing his hands in the cold air. Below him cars passed in the darkness like weird anonymous lights, some heading for the motorway, others along the ring road, some back towards Ashingford. And he found his mind running with them, to Mum, to Dad, to what he had left behind.

He gave the girl plenty of time, then cautiously looked round. She had straightened her clothing and was now lying with her back to the far wall, the baby still wrapped up inside the blanket and held to her breast.

He walked over to her and knelt beside her. 'Are you OK?'

She looked up. 'I'm . . . not very comfortable, but I'll be all right. We must get the baby dressed before the cold gets to him. Can you help me?'

'Sure.'

He edged closer. 'Did you . . . get rid of the afterbirth?'

'Yes.'

He hesitated. 'What did you do?'

'I bit through the cord and tied the end with string.'

He stared at her, slightly shocked. 'So where's—?'

'I've thrown it away.'

Jamie frowned. 'Didn't it hurt him?'

She looked down and he saw this was not the time to throw questions at her. He quickly forced a laugh.

'Well, he looks fine, anyway, just like his mum. Come on. Let's get him dressed.'

The girl paused for a moment, as though she were having to will herself to move, then she reached inside the holdall, pulled out some wipes and some cotton wool, and started to clean the baby.

'I'll get his clothes out,' said Jamie.

He poked inside the holdall and found a little baby suit with mittens, trousers and hood, and some boots, socks, a vest, a shirt, and a tiny hat. The girl pulled a nappy from the holdall, then suddenly stopped.

'Are you all right?' said Jamie.

She didn't answer, didn't look up. Her face was dark with fatigue. He reached out and took the nappy from her.

'Come on,' he said. 'I've seen the way they do this.'

But she took the nappy back again.

'I'll do it,' she said.

In the end they both did it, with considerable fumbling, first the nappy, then the clothes. The girl leaned back against the wall, holding the baby to her, wrapped once again inside the blanket. Jamie watched her for a moment, then rummaged in his rucksack for the sandwiches he had bought and handed her one. She took it with a nod of thanks, still holding the baby, and they lay back together against the slab and ate in silence.

He waited until she had finished eating before he spoke.

'I paid the men.'

She looked round at him. 'What?'

'I paid the men. At least, I paid the taller one. Just before I turned up here. I got caught by them after I left you in the bin at school. They—'

She gripped his arm, stopping him.

'What did they do to you?'

'It's OK. I'm all right.'

'But what happened?'

'The tall guy beat me up. But I told them I'd give them the money if they promised to leave you alone. I know a promise from them isn't worth much but I thought it might make a difference.'

'But you didn't give them any money?' A look of incredulity passed over her face. He thought of Spider and frowned.

'I've got a friend.' He bit his lip. 'A bloody good friend. He's been saving up for—' He stopped. There was no point going into details. It would only make the girl feel guilty and he didn't want that. 'He lent me the money. Enough to pay off the men. I met the tall guy just down the road from here and gave it to him.'

'Where was the other man?'

'I don't know. Didn't see him. I just gave the tall man the money and he drove off.'

She stared at him for some time, not speaking. Then he realized she was crying.

He hesitated, then slid an arm round her shoulder, ready to pull it back the moment she gave any sign that she didn't want it; but she moved forward, as if to help him, and he pulled her gently towards him. She leaned her head into the crook of his neck, still clasping the baby to her.

'I'm sorry . . . I don't mean to . . .' She sniffed. 'It's just that . . . no one's ever shown me so much . . .'

He stroked her arm.

'It's OK. Don't worry. We're in this together. I help you. You help me.'

'I don't help you. How do I help you?'

He thought for a moment, anxious not to say the wrong thing. There was so much that she gave him, so much that he knew he could not express, partly because he didn't understand it very well himself. He knew he was captivated by the warmth and softness of her body, the tickle of her hair under his nose, her scent, her voice; but much more than all this, he was drawn to the enigma of what she was.

He fumbled for words that would not offend her.

'You help me because . . . because I'm on my own, like you, and I . . . don't know what I'm going to do or where I'm going to go. And you've become a . . . kind of a friend.' He turned his head away but still felt hers against him. 'I really . . . care about you.'

He was making a complete mess of this. He fell silent, feeling useless and clumsy, and certain that he had now spoiled the tender atmosphere they had had a moment ago.

But she moved her head towards him, making him turn and look at her, then leaned forward and kissed him softly on the mouth.

'Thank you,' she said.

And she turned back to the baby once more.

Somehow they slept, despite the cold, the girl rolled over on her side, hugging the baby to her, Jamie lying against her back, his arm flopped over them both; and the blanket draped over them all.

Some time later he woke to the sound of the baby crying. Darkness was still around them and so was the sound of the traffic, though it was intermittent now. The cold was growing worse.

He felt the girl stir and start to unbutton her shirt. His arm was still over her and she made no effort to push it away, but he pulled it back and spoke.

'How are you feeling?'

'I've been warmer.'

Jamie looked over at the baby. 'What about him?'

She pulled the baby to her breast. 'I think he just wants a bit of this.'

Gradually the crying ceased. Jamie watched, feeling slightly embarrassed, then he thought of something.

'What are you going to call him?'

The girl was silent for a while. Then she turned and looked at him. 'What's your name?'

He stared at her, remembering what they had agreed about questions. But so much had changed now.

'Jamie,' he said.

She turned back to the baby and kissed it. 'We'll call him Jamie, then.'

His mouth fell open. She had said it in such a matter-of-fact way it took him by surprise. It was some moments before he realized he should be flattered. But there was another gift he wanted from her. And one he now felt he was owed.

'What's your name?'

She was still looking at the baby. But she answered at once. 'Abby.'

And that was all. No more details, no more questions.

But it was a name. And the knowledge of it now seemed the most precious thing he had.

21

At around three in the morning, she spoke again. 'I can't sleep in this cold and I'm worried about little Jamie. We're better off moving.'

He stretched and rubbed his eyes.

'Whereabouts in Cumbria is it we've got to go?'

'A few miles from . . . I think it's called Cartmel Fell. I've got the address somewhere.'

'And these people . . .'

'I've never met them. I told you, they're friends of a friend. But they've been told I'm coming and they said I can stay.' She seemed to sense his anxiety. 'I'm sure they won't turn you away. Not if you've come that far with me. But I can't ask them until we get there because they're not on the phone.'

He looked away, thinking over the other anxieties that were now preying upon him. She seemed to sense those, too.

'Listen, you don't have to come with me. If you want to go back home and sort out whatever's wrong—'

He shook his head firmly.

'I'm coming to Cumbria. I want to. Anyway, I'm not leaving you after you've just had a baby.'

She looked at him for a moment, then smiled. 'Let's go, then.'

They emptied out the rucksack and stuffed the contents into the holdall, then Abby changed the baby's nappy, wrapped him in the blanket again and placed him upright inside the rucksack; then, keeping a hand under his neck for support, she slid her arms—first one, then the other—through the straps and pulled the rucksack into her body so that the baby was facing her chest, her hand still behind his neck; and they set off down to the slip-road that led up to the motorway.

Jamie watched her closely. She was walking very gingerly, her face set with determination, and she clearly didn't want him fussing over her, but he could see she was in great discomfort.

They reached the slip-road and Jamie turned to face the traffic, his hand held out to start hitch-hiking. Abby came up to him.

'I'll do it,' she said. 'They're more likely to stop if they just see a girl on her own. You go and sit over there with the baby. And try and keep well back so the headlights don't pick you up so easily.'

'But you should be sitting down, not me.'

'I can't help that. I've got to stand so they see me.' She looked at him. 'Go on, Jamie, just do it. I'll sit down if I get really tired.' She moved closer so that he could take the rucksack. 'And keep a hand under his neck. Don't take it away, whatever you do. He's got to have something supporting his head.'

Reluctantly, he took the baby from her and, holding the rucksack as she had done, moved back from the road. A tense hour went by as he sat on the verge, the baby—mercifully still sleeping—close against his chest, and watched Abby standing by the roadside, her arm outstretched. He noticed her body swaying as she fought with exhaustion. At last a transit van pulled over.

She opened the door and started talking to the driver.

Jamie hurried over with the baby. Inside the van was a dumpy man with a somewhat bleary expression, who looked at him with some surprise.

'Oh, there's two of you. Didn't see.'

'Is that OK?' said Abby.

The man didn't look too happy but he shrugged.

'I can't take you all the way but I can give you a start and drop you off at a motorway exit or a service station.'

'That's fine,' said Abby and made to get in.

Jamie stepped forward.

'I'll go in the middle. Here, take the rucksack.'

He didn't know why he was being cautious. This man looked no threat but for some reason he didn't want Abby sitting next to him. Abby said nothing but took the rucksack and let him climb in first.

'It's a bit of a mess,' said the man. 'Just kick those bits of piping out of the way or shove them behind you.'

Jamie climbed in and pushed the piping to the side. Abby sat down beside him, placed the rucksack carefully on her lap, one arm over it, the other under the baby's head, then leaned wearily against him. The driver watched uneasily.

'You didn't say you had a baby.'

'Sorry,' said Abby.

The man now looked distinctly uncomfortable, as though he'd bitten off more than he'd intended to chew in picking them up, but he started to drive on.

'Hope it's not a noisy baby.'

'He'll be quiet,' said Abby. 'He's very sleepy.'

'I know the feeling. I'm Alan, by the way.'

'I'm Sarah,' said Abby. 'This is Tom.'

'What's the baby called?'

'Steven.'

Jamie looked at Abby and saw she was fighting to keep awake. He hoped the driver wouldn't ask too many questions; but the man spoke again at once.

'So what do you do, Tom?'

Jamie didn't answer, forgetting for the moment who he was meant to be. Then he felt Abby nudge him.

'Er . . . I'm . . . a student.'

'What are you studying?'

'I'm . . . sort of . . . between courses.'

'What does that mean?'

Abby looked round at the man. 'He's dropped out. To marry me.'

The man guffawed. 'Oh, I get it.' He glanced at the baby again. 'Shotgun wedding. So you're married?'

'We're getting married,' she said.

'You look a bit young. How old are you both?'

'Eighteen.'

The man yawned suddenly.

'Well, I wish you well. I got married when I was twenty and I thought that was young but I suppose I didn't have a kid to think about then.' He shook his head. 'I've had four of them to think about since.' He yawned again. 'Don't mind me rambling on. I picked you up to stop me falling asleep. I've been driving all night and I've got to keep going for another few hours so if you can talk to me, it'll help.'

So they talked to him, or rather Jamie talked. He knew Abby was aching for sleep and, tired though he was and anxious in case he said something that might give them away, he knew he had to give her the chance to rest.

And so, while she rested, he forced himself into conversation, mostly probing the man with questions about his life and family, and, when questioned himself, inventing a fantasy life that included Abby and the baby. And, as he talked, he found himself wishing it were true.

But the life he was describing—that pleasant, dream life—was not his life, nor was it hers. Their lives still hung in the balance of uncertainty. And one thing was growing in his mind as the miles passed behind them.

He was running away. Running from a problem he had not resolved to a future that could not resolve it.

Finally, it seemed, the man fell silent. Jamie looked round at Abby. She was slumped against him, her head on his shoulder, her arms cradling the rucksack with the baby inside, sleeping as soundly as his mother. Jamie closed his eyes and dozed, too.

Some time later he heard a voice. It was the radio.

'The news at six o'clock. Police are still looking for a sixteen-year-old boy who has disappeared from his home in Ashingford. Jamie Williams was last seen . . .'

He opened his eyes and looked towards Abby but she was still sleeping, and so was the baby. He glanced to the right.

The man seemed uninterested in the news bulletin and soon fiddled with the radio until he found some music. Jamie yawned and tried to sleep again.

But his thoughts were racing now, not northwards to where his body travelled, but back, always back, to the spectre of his former life.

The man dropped them at a motorway service station and they used some of Spider's money to buy breakfast. Abby seemed only slightly refreshed from her sleep and was still walking uncomfortably, but she was eager to push on. They changed the baby's nappy and made their way to the motorway slip-road.

An hour later they were moving again, this time with a lorry driver who also wanted conversation and who received from Jamie much the same story as the previous driver. But this man only took them forty miles. They waited again and soon picked up a lift with some students in a camper van who shared food with them, asked no questions at all, and took them another twenty miles.

More waits, more lifts. Rain started, stopped, started, stopped. By ten in the evening they were heading through the lanes of Cumbria with a forester and his son in a battered Land Rover. By midnight they were standing at a deserted country crossroads.

Abby was exhausted.

Jamie looked at her. He, too, was tired but he knew his weariness was nothing compared with hers. And they would surely have to walk now, with little chance of picking up any more lifts out here.

He glanced down at the baby, asleep in the rucksack he was now cradling to his chest. It felt so strange to be carrying a child. He walked over to Abby and reached down for the holdall she had dropped to the ground.

'Let me take that,' he said.

She looked up at him. 'Jamie, I don't know if I can go any further.'

'How far is it from here?'

She pulled a slip of paper from her jacket pocket and

squinted at it in the darkness, then peered up at the signpost.

'About eight miles from here. We go down this road for five miles, then take a right fork and after a while we should come to a farm and then a lane that takes us to the house.' She leaned wearily against the signpost. 'But I don't know how much energy I've got left.'

He put his arm round her.

'Listen, we'll take it really slowly and we'll stop for rests whenever we want, but we've got to make it. And we're going to make it. For the baby's sake.'

She took a deep breath. 'So are you up to a hike?' she said.

He looked at her, trying to hide his dread at the prospect of an eight-mile walk, and even managed a smile.

'I didn't have any other plans for tonight.'

22

The walk through the night seemed endless. They spoke little, just a few words now and then, and mostly to ask if the other was all right.

He offered to carry the baby and the holdall but Abby refused and insisted on taking the baby, which soon started to cry. They stopped and changed his nappy by the side of the lane, then trudged on through the night.

As the hours passed, the air grew colder.

Jamie looked at Abby. Her head was down and she was moving more and more slowly, as though every step were a struggle. But at last they reached the fork.

Jamie looked round at her.

'Turn right here?'

'Yes.'

'How far is it to the lane that leads to the house?'

'Don't know. Just hope it's not too far.'

But an hour later they still had not reached it. They forced themselves on for another half an hour, then finally saw a cluster of barns to the right.

'If that's the farm,' she said, 'the lane should be just past it.'

'Has it got a name, this farm?'

'Yes, but I can't remember it.' She stared at the slip of paper. 'Can't read this. It's too dark.'

'Let me have a look.'

She handed him the paper and he studied it.

'Looks like . . . Beck . . . Beck . . .'

'Beckside Farm. I remember it now.'

'Well, let's see if it is.'

They wandered past the barns and saw more buildings and what looked like the entrance to the farm.

A dog started barking within. Jamie went over to the gate and peered at the notice.

'Beckside Farm. That's it. Come on, let's move on before they think we're burglars.'

They left the farm behind them and walked on. Half a mile down the road was a small notice pointing down a lane.

Abby walked over and read the words aloud. 'To Mill Dam Lodge.'

'Is that the place?'

She nodded.

'OK,' said Jamie. 'One last haul and we're there.'

But the last haul was the toughest of the night, and by the time they came to the end of the lane and saw the huge house with its barns and outbuildings, Jamie was carrying both the baby and the holdall and it was five o'clock in the morning.

There were no lights on in the house.

Abby leaned against the door.

'Doesn't seem right to wake them at this hour but I can't stand up any longer.'

And she pressed the bell.

It seemed to make no sound and Jamie wondered for a moment whether it was working. Then, through the glass panel in the door, he saw a light go on inside the house and, a moment later, the outline of a figure descending the stairs.

The front door opened and a woman appeared in a night-dress.

She looked about fifty and was tall and well-built, with strong, capable hands. She studied them calmly, as though being woken at five in the morning were the most natural thing in the world.

'Can I help you?'

It was a pleasing voice, Jamie decided, certainly not the voice of an enemy, but he let Abby do the talking.

'I've been given your address. I'm sorry we've turned up at this time of the morning.'

The woman shrugged. 'Happens all the time.'

Suddenly she looked hard at Abby. 'You wouldn't by any chance be . . . Jude's friend?'

'Yes.'

'Abby?'

'Yes.'

The woman smiled. 'We've been expecting you for days. We were getting worried something had happened to you. But we thought you were on your own.'

'This is Jamie.'

'Hello, Jamie.'

'Hello.'

The woman's eyes looked him over in the same calm way. He had the impression that there was very little that could startle this woman. Her eyes left him and moved to the rucksack he was holding to his chest.

'So that's . . .' She peeped over the top at the baby, who was sleeping soundly inside. 'That's three of you. Are there any other members of the party I need to know about?'

'I'm sorry,' said Abby. 'I would have warned you but you're not on the phone, are you?'

The woman smiled again. 'Fortunately not. We're not very keen on telephones here. Anyway, my name's Savita. Come inside.'

She led the way into the house, switching on lights as she walked through the rooms. Jamie looked about him, too dazed to take much in, but he saw that everything was clean and simple, and there was a pleasant air of comfort about the place.

Savita entered the kitchen and turned to face them. 'Right. Food, wash, or sleep first?'

Jamie looked at Abby and they spoke in unison. 'Food, please.'

'OK.' Savita glanced at the baby who was still fast asleep inside the rucksack. 'No point in taking him out of there just yet. He looks so comfortable. But let's put some cushions under him.'

She found some cushions and made a kind of bed at the end of the kitchen table. Jamie laid the baby carefully down, then slumped into a chair. Abby did the same and they sat there in silence.

Savita started cooking and before long a smell of toast, mushrooms, and baked beans was wafting towards them. Soon they were eating ravenously. Savita put two mugs of tea on the table.

'I'll go and fix your room,' she said, and disappeared.

Jamie glanced at Abby. 'The room . . . she thinks we're . . .'

Abby looked up. 'Don't leave me, Jamie.'

She held his gaze, as though seeking reassurance. He felt slightly embarrassed, but managed a smile.

'Of course I won't leave you. Not if you don't want me to.'

She smiled back, but it was a tired smile, a vulnerable smile.

Savita soon returned.

'The room's ready. More food for anyone?'

They shook their heads.

'Right,' said Savita. 'Let's go, then.'

She led the way out of the kitchen and up the stairs. Abby carried the sleeping baby and Jamie came last, wondering about this place. Clearly it was some kind of sanctuary, as Abby had said, but they would surely have to pay to stay here.

They reached the first floor, made their way along a corridor and up more stairs to the second floor, then along another corridor to the end and into a large bedroom.

'There's a basin over there,' said Savita. 'The loo's down the corridor and the bathroom next to it. If you need me, I'm in the first room at the top of the stairs on the first floor. Sleep as long as you want.'

And, with a brief smile, she left them.

Jamie looked around the room, still feeling awkward about the sleeping arrangements. There were two single beds but he noticed they had been pushed together and made up as one. He wondered whether he should offer to move them apart again.

But Abby seemed unconcerned about this. She placed the baby on the bed, then simply pulled off her jacket, jumper, shirt, skirt, and socks and dropped them to the floor. Then she eased the baby out of the rucksack and, cradling him in her arms, climbed into bed.

'Put the light out, Jamie. Hurry up.'

Somewhat flustered he switched off the light and stripped down to his underpants in the darkness, then felt his way round to the other side of the bed. At least the room was warm. He would have no need of pyjamas. He found the other side of the bed, pulled back the sheet and climbed in.

Abby had turned towards him, the baby held close to her so that he was lying between them, and she already seemed to be drifting into sleep. But she murmured: 'Goodnight.'

'Goodnight,' he said.

Tired though he was, he did not find sleep mastering him at once. He found this strange, considering how much he had yearned for sleep throughout the course of the day, especially during the long walk through the night. But now all he could think of was the closeness of Abby and her child.

Both were sleeping, the little boy turned inward to his mother's breast, while she . . .

He studied her face in the darkness.

It seemed full of mystery. And there was a scent about her, not the scent of the road, which she no doubt couldn't wait to wash off, but another scent: a scent so intimately part of her that he yearned just to lie here and drink it like wine. She had never been so beautiful to him as she was now.

In that thought, he finally slipped into sleep.

Some time later, he felt her hand on his. He woke and saw light breaking through the windows of the room, though it was only the pale light of early morning. She had not opened her eyes, had not shifted her position, and the baby was still tucked in between them. But she pulled his hand gently towards her and placed it over her shoulder, then let go.

She did not speak, did not look at him, seemed still deep in sleep. He moved a little closer to her, to make himself more comfortable now that his arm was outstretched. She shifted, too, just a little towards him. He breathed hard, drinking in the scent of her again, enjoying the softness of her skin under his hand. The little baby was close against his chest and he found himself curiously captivated by it.

And they slept on, all three.

23

The next time he woke was to the sound of the baby crying. He opened his eyes to see broad daylight at the window and Abby sitting in the chair, putting the baby to her breast. Her hair was wet and she had a towel wrapped round it. To his surprise, she was wearing different clothes: a navy-blue skirt and a pale blue shirt.

He sat up in bed and she looked round at him.

'Hi,' she said. 'Savita gave me the clothes and she said she'll try and get hold of some men's things for you if you want. These don't quite fit but it's the first time I've worn anything else for ages. What do you think?'

'They look great.'

'It feels so good to have a shower and a hair-wash. Why don't you have one? There's shampoo and soap in the bathroom which Savita said we could use, and she's given us a couple of new toothbrushes and some towels.' Abby turned and murmured to the baby. 'And she's got lots of nice things for you, too, hasn't she? Yes, she has. Yes, she has.' She kissed the top of the baby's head.

Jamie watched, a little uncomfortable at the baby talk and still feeling self-conscious about being dressed only in his underpants and sharing a bed with Abby. But he needed a shower and couldn't lie here for ever. He pulled back the top-sheet, hoping Abby would continue to watch the baby. But she looked round again.

'I've had a long chat with Savita. She said Savita's not her real name.'

'What is?'

'I don't know. She didn't tell me. She said she changed her name to symbolize her break with the past. All the women here have got a past.'

'Is it only women here?'

She nodded. 'Apart from you. Who's a lucky boy, then?'

He frowned, thinking not of this but of his own past, which was now reaching out to him again.

Abby chuckled. 'Don't worry. You're not going to be thrown out. Savita's accepted us as an item. She thinks you're Jamie's father.'

'What else did she tell you?'

'She just said her old life was so painful she'd decided to start again. So she gave herself a new name and came here. She inherited a lot of money and bought the house and land outright, and decided to use it as a refuge for women in trouble.'

'When did she come here?'

'Twenty years ago.'

'And the women . . . I mean, do they live here all the time?'

Abby shook her head.

'Only a few of them. Most are just passing through like me. It's not an official home or anything. It's a kind of commune. Savita's made it her life's work. She lets people stay for a while, until they can get back on their feet, then they move on and others take their place. They don't have to pay anything but they're asked to make a donation if they can and everyone's expected to muck in and work. They've got animals and they grow their own vegetables and stuff.'

He looked down. 'So you'll . . . you'll have to move on, too.'

'I always knew I would.'

He thought once more of his own life, and the mess he had still not resolved; and then of his feelings for Abby. Feelings he had never had before; feelings that bound him to this place.

She came round, still holding the baby to her, and sat next to him on the bed.

'Don't stay just because of me, Jamie. If you've got to go back, I understand. When I ran away from home, I

149

thought I was escaping, but all I was doing was running away from myself. I should have stayed and fought my corner.'

He looked at her. 'Are you saying it's always wrong to run away?'

'No, not always. Everybody's situation's different. Some people are in danger if they stay, and they have to run.'

'What happened to you? I mean—'

He stopped, remembering what they had said about not forcing questions. But, to his surprise, she started to talk.

'I ran away to get away from my dad. I just couldn't handle things any more. I took as much money as I could find from his wallet and Mum's purse and walked out of the house in the middle of the night.'

'How old were you?'

'Fourteen.' She sighed. 'I was a total mess. I didn't know what to do, where to go. All I knew was I didn't want to go back home. So I left the area and wandered about, sleeping rough, getting hungry, cold. Then I met Angelo.'

'Angelo?'

A look of pain crossed her face.

'The taller one.'

Somehow he'd guessed and he was starting to guess the rest, though he hoped he'd be wrong. She studied his face for a moment with an air of concern, as though anxious not to hurt him.

'Go on,' he said. 'Please. If you can bring yourself to tell me.'

She glanced at the baby for a moment, then kissed its head and looked back.

'He found me when I was at my most vulnerable. I had no money, no food, nowhere to live. He took me in, looked after me. He was good to me in the beginning. And he was a real charmer. I fell for him hook, line, and sinker. I thought he loved me. I can't believe I was so stupid.'

She frowned. 'He didn't love me. He just wanted me for one thing and when he got bored with that, he decided to use me for something else.'

Jamie drew breath. 'You mean . . . ?'

She narrowed her eyes. 'Some men make money honourably and some get other people to make it for them. You understand?'

He saw anger in her eyes, as though all the pain of her past had flooded back in this confession of her life. His own life slipped into focus, and he saw it for what it was. And it was nothing compared to this.

He spoke as gently as he could. 'And . . . the baby?'

'It's his,' she said bluntly.

He stared at her, and the defiance and hurt in her face made him lower his eyes.

'And the money he wanted from you?'

'It was money I'd earned for him, and it was only part of what I made for him. He didn't want to lose me. He threatened me. Told me if I ran away, he'd always find me and make sure I never worked again, not for him or anyone else. And he said he'd make sure no man ever found me attractive again. He meant it, too.' She shuddered. 'I saw what he did to Jude and some of the other girls.'

She fell silent again and looked down at the baby, as though she drew strength from it. Jamie waited for a moment, unwilling to press for further confidences. She looked up again.

'The money wasn't for me. It was for Jude. To help her get away.'

'What happened?'

'He beat her up so badly. I knew I had to help her and try to escape myself. Angelo kept lots of cash at his house so he didn't have to declare it, but I knew where he hid it so I broke in and took it. Gave most of it to Jude so she could get away to Canada and start a new life. She's got people out there she knows.'

'Why didn't you go with her?'

'I had some stupid idea I wanted to sort things out with my family.'

'So who's the other man? The stockier one.'

Abby's face curled up in disgust.

'That's Vittorio, Angelo's brother. They're half-Italian, half-English. Vittorio's even more dangerous than Angelo. They're always at each other's throats. Neither trusts the other. They're always fighting about something.'

'But what made you come to my part of the country?'

'To see my dad. We're from Leeds originally. But after I ran away from home, I found out from a friend that my family had moved down to Ashingford. When I ran away from Angelo, I was desperate. I'd only kept a little bit of money for myself because I wanted Jude to have a good chance of making it, and what I had I soon spent on food and stuff. I thought about going straight to Cumbria but I knew Angelo would be after me, and Vittorio would be with him to make sure his brother didn't get the money and then pretend he'd never seen me, so I decided to swallow my pride and go home and ask Dad to help me pay off Angelo.'

She looked down.

'I watched the house for days, trying to pluck up courage to ring the doorbell, and getting more and more scared because by this time I'd seen Angelo and Vittorio in town.'

'So what happened?'

'I forced myself to call at the house.' She looked up at him. 'The day we met in the alleyway by the health food shop.'

'And what did your dad say?'

'He wouldn't even look at me. I stood on the doorstep and tried to speak to him. He just stared past me, said he didn't have a daughter any more because I'd walked out, told me my brother was carrying the family's hopes, said if I'd got into trouble, that was my fault and I'd have to sort it out myself.'

'Bastard. Sorry, I mean—'

'It's OK. You're right. He is a bastard. I'll never see him again now.'

'But what about your mum?'

'She wasn't there when I called but she wouldn't have made a fuss. She never argues with my dad.'

Jamie frowned, disturbed at the echoes from his own life. He looked at her.

'Abby—look, don't answer this if you don't want to, but—what did your father do to you to make you want to run away?'

She looked away.

'He ignored me.' She wiped the corner of her eyes. 'He ignored me from the day I was born. It was like I didn't exist. I tried to make him love me but he took no notice of me because he was so busy loving my brother.'

Jamie stared at her. 'How old's your brother?'

'Same age as me. He's my twin.'

'But why did your father love him and not you?'

'Because I'm not a winner at anything. My dad only likes winners.'

He reached out and touched her arm.

'Abby, you are a winner. As far as I'm concerned.'

'Thanks.' She smiled at him. 'But my dad wouldn't agree with you.'

Jamie frowned. 'So . . . what is it your brother's a winner at?'

Abby looked down and kissed the baby. 'Danny's big thing has always been squash.'

24

Over the next few days Jamie tried to come to terms with what Abby had told him, but all he felt was anger.

Not at Abby. Never that. She was dearer to him than ever now. His anger had other targets and he knew what he had to do.

He did not speak of this to Abby or tell her of his own life and his encounters with her brother and father. She needed to grow strong again, not carry his emotions on top of hers. And she was growing stronger. Day by day the healing effect of Savita and the others was starting to show.

He was glad for her.

There was a bond between the women that he knew he could not share but it didn't matter. All that mattered was Abby. So he peeled potatoes and washed up and chopped wood, and spoke when others spoke to him, and wandered round the farm, thinking, waiting; and at night he lay down with Abby, and they talked together, and then slept, the baby now beside the bed in a little makeshift cot.

The week drew on. It was growing colder again and the days were short. It was hard to believe Christmas was so close. On the Thursday evening after supper he wandered into the fields alone and gazed up at the night sky, and stayed there until it was late.

When he returned to their room, the light was off and Abby was already in bed, the baby asleep in the cot. He walked round to his side of the bed, stripped down to his underpants, and climbed in.

Abby lay still, but he knew she was not sleeping. After a while she spoke.

'You're leaving in the morning, aren't you?'

He rolled over and looked at her. She was lying on her back, staring up at the ceiling and did not turn his way. She spoke again.

'I know you've got to go back to sort out what's wrong. Whatever it is.'

'I don't want to. I want to stay with you.'

'I want you to stay with me. But . . .' She turned to face him, her eyes bright, in spite of the darkness. 'I can feel your restlessness.' She watched him for a moment. 'We've got different paths, Jamie. I've got to stay here for a while, if Savita will let me, then I'll have to move on, too.'

'Back to your family?'

'No, never. That's over.'

She was silent for a long time. Then she spoke once more.

'Jamie?'

'Yes?'

'Hold me.'

He reached out his arm and stretched it over her shoulder and down her back. And, to his surprise, felt only bare skin. She moved towards him and lay against him, her head against his chest.

He tensed slightly, embarrassed by her nakedness and his feelings of arousal. She reached over his side and stroked his back. He turned his head to look down at her and found her looking up at him.

They kissed, softly, on the mouth, and drew back; then kissed again, a longer kiss but still soft, still hesitant; then a third kiss, longer still, but always soft, always hesitant, as though each were asking permission of the other. Suddenly she drew back and he saw she was crying.

'Abby, what is it?'

She dipped her head into his chest and went on crying.

'Abby, please. Is it something I've done?'

She shook her head, but still wouldn't look up.

155

He stroked her hair, feeling desperately confused and somehow guilty. Then Abby looked up.

'It's not you, Jamie. It's me. Don't you see? I've . . . I've been damaged. I can't . . . make love with you or anything. It's not that I don't want you. It's just that I've . . . I've been messed with so much I don't know if I'm—' She gulped. 'I haven't got any protection and even if I did, I'd never forgive myself if I gave you—'

'Abby—'

'I mean, I'm going to get myself checked out as soon as I can, and little Jamie, obviously, in case he's picked up any . . . you know . . .'

'Abby, it's OK.'

'But it's not just that. I mean, I can't even . . . kiss you without feeling . . . kind of . . . screwed up inside. And now you'll think I'm playing with your feelings and you'll hate me and—'

'Sssh, Abby. It's OK. I'm never going to hate you.' He kissed the top of her head as she went on crying against his chest. 'We don't have to do anything. We can just lie here. I never thought we were going to make love.' He tried to sound self-mocking. 'I don't suppose I'd be much good at it anyway. I'd probably stick the wrong thing in the wrong place.'

She didn't speak, but she was still crying, though more softly. He went on, still stroking her hair.

'We don't have to do anything. It's good just . . . just to hold you. I've never held anyone before. Not someone naked, I mean. And your body's so beautiful.'

'No one's ever told me my body's beautiful, no one who meant it, anyway. Angelo used to say I was sexy.'

'You are sexy.'

'But he was just flattering me to make me do what he wanted. He didn't really mean it.'

'I mean it.'

'I'm glad you do.'

They lay in silence for a moment. Then Jamie looked down at her.

'Abby?'

'Yes?'

'I understand about you not wanting to make love. But why does it make you feel funny to kiss me?' He tried the self-mocking tone again. 'But break it to me gently. I know I'm not much of an expert in that department.'

She turned her face towards him, her eyes close to his, and he saw a look of tenderness there.

'Jamie, you should have more confidence in yourself. There's nothing wrong with you in that or any other department.' She shook her head. 'It's not you. It's just that . . .' She thought for a moment. 'When you kiss someone, mouth to mouth, it's one of the most intimate things you can do with them. It opens you up to them. That's not a problem if you're together in yourself but if you're screwed up, it really—'

She broke off, still staring into his eyes. He thought she was about to cry again and reached out a hand to stroke her cheek.

'Abby,' he murmured. 'Abby.'

And she leaned forward and kissed him again, on the mouth, still softly as before, and he kissed her back, as gently as he could, frightened lest he kiss too hard and cause her pain, but her own kiss grew stronger and she slid her hand round the back of his neck and pulled him to her. He felt her body tight against his, her breasts moving softly against his chest. Then, slowly, she pulled back, and looked into his face again, and he saw she was crying once more.

'Abby, I'm sorry. I didn't mean to—'

But she reached out and put a finger on his lips. 'It's OK. I promise it's not you.'

She wiped her eyes with the back of her arm. He watched for a moment, then reached out a hand and with a finger smoothed away the moisture from her cheeks. She took the hand in hers, then, still holding it, twisted over on to her side, and pulled his arm over her so that he was snuggling into her back; and they lay there together in the darkness.

'Jamie?'

'Um?'

'Thanks.'

'There's nothing to thank me for. I should be thanking you.'

'What for? What have I done for you?'

He thought for a moment, anxious not to say the wrong thing, but also anxious not to think too long in case she thought he was having to make something up.

'You've made me believe in myself again,' he said finally.

He felt her squeeze his hand. Silence fell once more, a long silence this time, and he thought for a moment she was drifting into sleep. Then . . .

'Jamie?'

'Um?'

'When you leave . . . don't say goodbye.'

He drew back to look at her but she spoke at once.

'Don't pull back. Hold me.'

He leaned closer again and pressed his face into her hair. 'No goodbyes?'

'No. Just go.'

'Like a shadow?'

She breathed slowly in; and slowly out again. 'Yes. Like a shadow.'

He thought for a moment. 'And is that all we'll be now? Shadows?'

She twisted her face round and peered at him in the darkness.

'Whenever you see your shadow, Jamie, just remember you're looking at me.'

25

Mum and Dad were nowhere to be found.

He walked down the hall and checked the sitting room, then made his way through to the kitchen, and then upstairs, and back down again.

The house was empty.

And there was something eerie about it.

It was immaculately tidy. There was no rubbish in the bins; nothing was out of place. Surfaces had been scrubbed or polished or waxed; taps gleamed; ornaments had been dusted and replaced. The books in the shelves had been rearranged into near-perfect symmetry.

It was as though no one lived here.

Not that tidiness was unusual. Mum was fastidious and had always kept things neat and clean. But this was different. And why the house should be empty at half-past seven in the morning he could not understand.

He sat down at the kitchen table and thought back over the last twenty-four hours. It had been a tough journey, walking, waiting, picking up lifts where he could; then getting stuck at midnight for three hours until the lorry driver picked him up and brought him the last of the way.

He had pictured so many variations of this homecoming and all of them involved confrontation with Dad, yet here he was, sitting in an empty house.

No matter. There were other confrontations he had returned for and they would not wait.

But first he had to eat.

He pulled open the fridge. Here, at least, were signs that someone lived here. It was full to bursting. Mum must have gone shopping last night. Out of curiosity, he opened the freezer.

That, too, was full-up, and he noticed Mum had left lots of her own ready-made meals, each one neatly labelled.

The hunger that had nagged him all the way home now overwhelmed him. He closed the freezer door, opened the bread bin—also stocked full—and pulled out some rolls. The pantry, unsurprisingly, was also full of provisions. He took a jar of honey and was soon eating voraciously.

When he had finished, he walked upstairs to his room and found the things he needed, then left the house by the back door and made his way into Ashingford.

His entry to the squash club felt unreal. He had been prepared to parry questions but in the end he found the reception area unmanned and was able to slip in unnoticed and walk straight to the changing room.

There was no one there. He changed quickly, then walked with his rackets into the loo area and locked himself in one of the cubicles. He looked at his watch.

Nine o'clock. There would be some time to wait. He sat there, thinking of Abby. And as he thought of her and what had happened to her, he found the anger boiling up again.

Gradually people started to enter the changing room. He heard them talking and laughing, and recognized most of the voices. But he stayed where he was, his anger still bubbling as he focused his mind on the objects of his rage, and what he had come to do.

More people entered the changing room. He heard Andy speaking, and Joe, then more voices, and finally, the two he had been listening for.

He stiffened. They were here at last. Only a few feet from him. He listened, clenching his fists. They talked for a while, loudly, confidently, then came into the loo and finally left. Others followed and soon the changing room was silent again.

Jamie looked at his watch and stood up.

The Regional Championships were ready to start.

He unlocked the cubicle, walked out of the changing room and straight over to the tournament registration desk. Faces turned his way and he heard his name muttered all around him. But he took no notice. Brent Marrick was behind the desk.

'Jamie, what the—?'

'What court am I on?'

'Jamie, I thought . . . we all thought . . .'

'What court?'

'Court four. But look, is everything—?'

But Jamie turned away, ignoring all glances and attempts to speak to him, and made his way down to the courts.

There was no one on court four, and no one looking down from the gallery; but that was no surprise. Everyone would have been expecting a bye for Danny in the first round.

Jamie wasn't bothered. He no longer cared what anyone thought, except Abby, and this was for her. He did some stretching exercises, then started to hit the ball against the wall.

'Jamie!' A voice called down from the gallery.

He stopped and looked up to see Andy staring down at him.

'Jamie, I thought you . . . I mean—'

'I'm here,' Jamie said flatly. He meant no unpleasantness to Andy, no more than he had done to Brent, but right now he was not disposed to be sociable to anyone. He thought for a moment, then, feeling he had to offer Andy something, said: 'Good luck in the tournament.' He paused, then added: 'I hope you win it.'

And he turned back to the front wall and started driving the ball against it again. Soon he heard more voices in the gallery. He did not turn round—he decided he would not turn round again—but he could hear it filling up rapidly, and people gabbling excitedly at the strange reappearance of someone they perhaps had thought dead.

He resolutely ignored them, even Joe who called down to ask where he'd been hiding himself. He kept his eyes on the little ball thudding down against the front wall and drove all his hatred into that.

The noise in the gallery was swelling to huge proportions. More voices called down to him, some joking, others serious, then a strange silence fell, as though the watchers had suddenly realized he was not going to turn and explain to them what had happened, was not going to acknowledge them; or perhaps they had simply been quelled by the strange, focused anger he felt as he struck the little ball, and thought of Abby, and how she had cried in his arms.

In that silence, he heard the door of the court open and shut. He turned and saw Danny walk forward. They looked at each other and the cockiness that he usually saw in the other boy was absent. In its place was confusion.

Danny held out another ball.

'The match ball. Joe just gave it to me.'

Jamie said nothing and merely took the ball, put his own in his pocket, and started to hit the new ball against the wall. Danny, looking somewhat edgy, took up his position on the other side of the court, and they went through the knock-up, neither speaking.

Above them, Jamie heard more voices, and now he spared a brief glance up there. It was crowded to capacity. He didn't suppose anyone was watching any of the other games. And for once—for the only time he could remember—his own father was not there.

He let his gaze rest on Bob Powell and made sure as their eyes met that the man caught every drop of the hatred intended for him.

'Change sides,' called the marker.

They changed sides and he practised on the backhand. It felt strange to be holding a racket again after so many

162

days; more days without practice than he could ever remember. He had no plan, no tactics, no concern for himself. He was not playing for himself. He was not playing for his father.

He was playing for Abby.

And the mere sight of Danny and Bob Powell was making him angrier by the second.

'Spin, please,' called the marker.

Danny came over, still watching warily as though he found Jamie's manner unnerving. Jamie did nothing to make him feel better and simply stared back. Danny spun his racket and Jamie called.

'My serve,' said Danny, holding out the racket to show him.

But Jamie ignored him and simply turned to the backhand side of the court to receive serve. A hush fell over the gallery.

'Danny to serve,' said the marker. 'Love–all. Play.'

And the first serve came at him. He drove it back hard, far harder than he normally hit the ball, and harder than he needed to hit the ball. But the strange focus he felt, and the anger, and the communion he sensed with Abby, all seemed to favour him. He knew from that first shot that today was to be different.

He drove Danny to the back of the court and set up a series of drives that sent the boy scuttling from one side to the other. A few strokes later, he had regained the serve and never lost it again in that game.

'One–love.'

'Two–love.'

'Three–love.'

And so it went on, as he played like a man possessed. He had only one shot today, the lashing drive that sent Danny chasing from one corner to the other. Even at the front of the court he found he could not play a drop shot. His anger was too great; all he could do was drive the ball hard towards the nicks.

Usually for a winner.

When it wasn't a winner, his energy and his rage were

163

so great that he was more than able to retrieve whatever Danny threw at him in return. Between points he saw the panic on the other boy's face. Danny's game was usually pacy. His own game was the more pedestrian. But the aggression Andy had told him he needed had come of its own volition. It would probably never come again.

'Nine–love. Game to Jamie.'

He turned without a word and walked off the court to fetch the towel from his bag. He heard murmurs up in the gallery, but shut his mind to them. He didn't care about their excitement. He didn't care about Danny's confusion. He didn't care about Bob Powell's shouts of exhortation, which had started towards the end of the last game once it became evident that Danny was being run off his feet.

Danny came off court, too, reached for his own towel and mopped his face.

'You're playing well,' he said, self-consciously.

Jamie stood up and stared at him; then, without a word, walked back on court, took the ball and started driving it against the wall again.

'Ease up on the ball, Jamie,' someone shouted up in the gallery. 'It's got to last for the rest of the match.'

He heard laughter from above, the kind of laughter that is a release from tension, but when he simply continued driving the ball without a backward glance or any response at all, the laughter fell away and the murmuring returned.

The door closed again and he saw Danny take up his position to receive serve. The boy's face looked pinched. He hadn't scored a point yet and he must be worrying not just about losing the match but being given the ultimate disgrace of a twenty-seven–love whitewash. Perhaps there would be tantrums in this game. There usually were.

Jamie shrugged. It would make no difference now.

'One game to love to Jamie,' called the marker. 'Love–all.'

He served, again a hard driving serve, and the pattern of the game continued. He drove and drove. When the ball came hard at him, he drove it hard back. When it came high, he smashed. When it was short to the front, he drove it hard down the line, or across court, or into the nicks.

All the shots he usually played, the lobs and boasts and drops, were gone today. He knew he could not play them. He had only anger. Sooner or later, he supposed, it would wear out, but he knew it was deep enough for what he had to do today.

It was not supposed to win matches. By all standards of logic, he knew he should not be playing as well as this. He was out of his mind with anger and, as the game progressed, he found that—far from subsiding—it was growing deeper. He was so incensed when Danny finally won his first point, that he smashed his backhand return of serve straight into the nick for an outright winner to regain the serve, then won the remaining three points of the game in a breathless succession of nicks and kills that sent the gallery into mad applause.

'Game to Jamie, nine–one,' he heard the marker say, as he walked off court again.

Now, as he towelled his face outside the court, he heard the noise in the gallery rising to a roar. Danny came off court, scowling, and this time avoided all attempts at small talk.

Jamie didn't bother glancing at him. Yet strangely, even in his fury, he was starting to feel a curious sympathy for Danny. He knew now that Danny was no more than the creation of another man's will. Something he himself might have been.

He turned back to the court, picked up the ball and, once again, started to pound it against the wall. A moment later he heard the door of the court close once more, as Danny entered. And this time, as he turned to look at his opponent, he caught a new face up in the gallery.

Dad.

So someone had contacted him. Brent probably or Joe. He turned and struck the ball hard against the wall again. It didn't matter. He had expected this. And nothing would change what he had come here to do.

'Jamie leads two games to love,' called the marker. 'Love–all.'

Silence fell once more. He glanced at Danny and saw his face etched with tension. Then he served, hard as usual, the only shot he knew today. Danny powered it back and the rally started. This time Jamie felt the desperate energy of his opponent. He knew Danny would throw everything he could into this game to try and salvage the match.

But the match was beyond salvage. Jamie knew it and he sensed, after he had weathered the onslaught, that Danny felt it too. Today was going to be his. He had summoned a whirlwind that would probably never visit him again. And somehow he hoped it would not. It was starting to frighten him.

At five–love ahead, he felt Danny's spirit drop. Up in the gallery he heard Powell bellowing encouragement. There was tension in that voice, too, just as there was in Danny's face; tension, embarrassment, even a touch of fear. To lose was one thing; to be annihilated was another.

And this was annihilation.

He heard the cheers, too, the cheers that had resounded throughout the match, yet they had been oddly muted cheers, as though everyone had been touched by the strangeness of this experience.

'Hand out. Love–seven.'

So Danny was making a last-ditch fight and had regained the serve for the first time in ages. Jamie stared across at his opponent and almost snarled at him. It was so easy to summon the energy he needed: he only had to think of Abby, and Powell up there blustering in the gallery; and this boy here.

He drove the return of serve down the line. Danny raced after it and tried to play a cross-court, but it was a tired shot and Jamie barely needed to move to cut it off and smash it into the nick.

'Hand out. Seven–love.'

He took the ball and decided to serve from the left-hand box. Up in the gallery he sensed the tension mounting, even as it was down on court. No one spoke. He felt the eyes of everyone upon him. He stared at the little ball, then served, hard to the forehand.

Danny struck back, this time aiming down the line, and the ball clipped the top of the tin. Another tired shot. There was a gasp from the gallery.

Jamie picked up the ball and walked across to the right-hand service box.

'Eight–love,' called the marker. 'Game and match ball.'

He glanced at Danny. The boy was finished. The job was done. He made to serve hard as usual, then checked himself and played a lob serve. The only lob he had played in the whole match.

The ball climbed high, so high he feared it would come down out of court, but it fell just inside the red line and dropped beyond Danny's racket into the nick at the back of the court.

Jamie's mind raced back to the last shot of the last game they had played; and it seemed an appropriate irony that this match, too, should end on an ace.

'Game and match to Jamie, nine–love, nine–one, nine–love.'

Cheering and clapping broke out in the gallery. Jamie shook Danny briefly by the hand and strode away from the court without a word, leaving his rackets and bag behind. He had one more thing to do and he was going to do it now.

He ran up to the gallery. They cheered as he entered and hands clapped him on the back. Dad walked towards him.

But Jamie pushed straight past him.

'Bob, look out!' someone shouted.

Powell ducked, seeing what was coming, but he was not quick enough. Jamie threw himself on him, wrestled him to the ground and rained blows upon his face.

'Stop him!' Joe shouted.

Jamie felt hands seize him from all sides and drag him, struggling, from on top of Powell. Powell rolled to the side, wiping blood from his nose.

'What the . . . bloody hell are you playing at?'

Jamie still fought to get at him but several people were holding him now. Then Dad stepped forward.

'Let him go. I'll take care of this.' He turned to Powell. 'I'm terribly sorry. I'll—'

'He'll pay for that.' Powell glared at Dad. 'You'll pay for that. I'll make sure your boy never—'

But Jamie didn't wait to hear the rest. He broke free and ran for the changing room, people stepping aside to let him pass. Behind him he heard a confusion of voices.

He stormed into the changing room. It was empty but he knew it would not be for long. He turned and waited, still bristling with anger. Then Dad stepped in.

They stared at each other in silence for a moment, then his father stepped forward.

Jamie pointed a finger at him and snarled, 'If you hit me *once*, I'll walk out of your life forever.'

Dad stopped. Then started forward again.

'I *mean* it!' snapped Jamie.

Dad stopped a second time, and they stared at each other again in silence. And now, as Jamie studied his father's face, he saw that it was unshaven, and seemed old and tired and sad.

But that was still not enough to quench his defiance.

'I'm only staying if you're going to be a proper father, and I'm giving up squash for a while. Maybe for ever. It'll be my decision.' He clenched his fists. 'I can live at home or I can live somewhere else. I don't have to stay at home but I'm telling you, if you try and push me around any more, or if you hit me or anything, then I'm off. For good.'

Dad watched him for a moment, his face dark and still. Then he looked down.

'Your mother's dead, Jamie.'

Jamie sat alone in the car in the squash club car park. He was still in his kit, his anger now spent, and he was filled with a sick confusion. After a while Dad appeared at the door of the club, carrying the squash bag he had left behind, and walked towards him.

Gone was the confident stride. This was an old man's walk. His father opened the door, climbed in and pulled the door to. They sat in silence for a moment.

'What happened?' Jamie said.

His father stared at the windscreen.

'I don't know if I've sorted it with Powell.' The voice was jaded, almost empty of expression. 'I've pulled you out of the tournament, obviously. They'd have disqualified you anyway. I apologized to Powell, said you'd been through a tough time. I don't know if he's going to press charges but Joe's calmed him down a bit.'

He frowned.

'I phoned the police while I was in there, told them you'd been found. They may want to come round and speak to you.'

Jamie said nothing. His question had not been about Powell or the tournament or the police, but Dad answered it now.

'She thought she was never going to see you again after she read your note. She rounded on me, accused me of destroying you, taking you away from her. Then she went into her shell and never came out of it again. Wouldn't look at me, wouldn't speak to me. It was like living with a mute. She spent every minute of the day busy round the house. I couldn't stop her. She was manic. She cleaned everything, made up stacks of meals and shoved them in the freezer, sent off the last of the Christmas cards.' He shook his head. 'The house is spotless now. Spotless and empty. But I guess you saw that when you collected your kit.'

Jamie bit his lip, unable to speak. Dad went on.

'Then yesterday she went to the hairdresser in the morning and came back and cooked me my lunch, and washed up all the things, and dried them and put them away. She wouldn't leave anything in the rack. Every single thing had to be put away.' He took a slow breath. 'I had to go out in the afternoon. When I got back, I found her lying on the bed. She'd made herself up, put on her best dress, and taken an overdose.' He looked down. 'There was nothing I could do.'

Jamie gripped the edge of the seat, too stunned to speak. Dad took another slow breath.

'They took the body away yesterday and I've . . . I've been walking ever since. I just . . . walked all night. I don't know where I've been. I only got back about ten and then Joe rang to say you were here.' Dad stopped, breathing hard, then reached across to the glove compartment and took something out. 'I found this on the bed beside her.'

Jamie stared.

It was his secret book.

He screwed up his eyes, racked with guilt at the thought that he had come home just a few hours too late. He could picture it all now. Mum must have found his book before he ran away. No wonder she'd been acting strangely. If only she'd confronted him about it. And then after he'd gone . . .

All the cleaning and tidying and cooking and shopping. It was the way Mum would have acted. Making sure the house was as right as it could be—before taking herself off to die.

He heard his father crying and looked across. This was something he had never seen before. His felt his own tears start but checked them, somehow. There had to be something he could say. They both needed help now.

'Dad,' he said. 'Dad, listen . . .'

His father stared at him, his face warped with grief.

'Dad, we'll . . . pull through this somehow.'

His father still stared at him, his eyes so wild that Jamie thought for a moment he had not been heard. Then Dad reached out and put a hand on his shoulder.

And that was all.

Late in the afternoon he walked with Spider down to the playing fields at the end of the road. His friend already knew about Mum.

'Christ, Jamie, I'm so sorry. I don't know what to say.'

Jamie looked down. 'Who told you about it?' he said, though he didn't really care.

'Mrs Sanderson down the road. Don't know how she got to hear of it.'

Jamie frowned. If Mrs Sanderson knew about it, half of Ashingford would have heard about it by now. He shrugged. People had to find out some time.

'When's the funeral?' said Spider.

'Don't know yet. Dad's fixing it.'

They stopped by the swings in the children's playground and Spider spoke again.

'So what did you tell your dad about where you've been? And where have you been, by the way? If you don't mind my asking.'

Jamie thought back to Abby and all that had happened. Dad had not asked for explanations. No doubt he would later, as Spider was doing now.

But Jamie had already decided that he would never tell anyone about Abby, not even Spider. Abby was his own secret, the one part of his life he was proud of, and he wanted to keep it that way. Besides, she deserved as much privacy as possible if she was to start a new life for herself.

He reached out to the nearest swing and pushed it gently.

'I just drifted for a few days. Dossed about, got cold, hungry, came home again.'

'What about your mate?'

'Eh?'

'Your mate. The one I gave you the money for. Did you get him out of trouble?'

Jamie thought of Abby again, her beautiful face, her beautiful body, her mystery; the way she had needed him, for that short time.

'Yes,' he said, still seeing her in his mind. 'I got him out of trouble. He's OK now.'

'Good. Did you hear about those men? The ones who asked us about that girl they were looking for?'

Jamie pushed the swing again and tried not to sound interested.

'What about them?'

'The taller one's been stabbed to death and the other one's charged with his murder. There was a thing about it on the news.'

Jamie said nothing.

'It was a bit gruesome,' Spider went on. 'Apparently they were brothers and people saw a car pulled over at the side of the motorway with both doors open and these two fighting by the verge. There were lots of witnesses. The big guy was seen running away with blood streaming down his face, and the smaller guy caught him up and started stabbing him. Some men in a van pulled over and went to help but it was too late. Just as well we didn't bump into them again.'

Jamie looked away. So Angelo was dead. No doubt he'd told Vittorio the boy hadn't delivered the money so he could keep it for himself, and his brother hadn't believed him. It didn't matter now. What mattered was that they weren't going to bother Abby again.

Spider went on.

'I got loads of questions while you were away. It was bad enough with the police and Mum and Dad and half the street, but everybody at school was pumping me about you as well. Teachers, pupils, dinner ladies. Old

Man Talbot had me in his office. Wanted to know if I'd seen you.'

'What did you tell him?'

'I told him what I said to everybody. I hadn't seen you and I didn't know where you were. The hardest questions were the ones about your state of mind.'

'Eh?'

'Some of them asked me if I thought you were depressed or suicidal or anything.'

'What did you say?'

'It was difficult. I mean, I've always said you were off your trolley anyway.' Spider checked himself. 'Sorry, mate. It's not the right time for jokes, is it?'

Jamie looked down.

'It's OK, but . . . you'll have to be patient with me.'

Spider put an arm round him.

'I told them you'd seemed a little worried lately. That was the truth. I said I didn't know the reason. That wasn't. But I told them you had a squash tournament coming up and maybe that was part of it. I didn't give anything away. I hope I did the right thing.'

Jamie looked up again. He couldn't manage a smile but he did his best.

'You did all the right things. Thanks. You've been the best friend I could ever have had.'

He pulled the swing to him and sat on it.

'Careful,' said Spider. 'You're a bit big for that now. You're not a kid any more.'

Jamie gripped the chains and stared up at the grey sky.

No, he wasn't a kid any more. Indeed, it seemed to him now that he had suddenly grown very old. He wondered whether he would ever be able to grow young again.

27

He found his father in the sitting room, in the chair Mum used to like. There was no light on and at first Jamie thought the room was empty; then he saw the figure sitting there, caught in the light from the hall.

He walked in and Dad turned to look at him. They faced each other in silence, not a hostile silence, but a silence in which Jamie felt they were each struggling to master a new language; a language they would have to learn quickly if they were to have a future together.

He knew his father was broken, just as he, too, was broken. Somehow, they had to build something on the ruins of what was left. Much that was bad seemed to have gone.

But the price had been terrible.

Dad stirred. 'Do you want something to eat?'

Jamie shook his head. His father reached over and flicked on the side light, and Jamie stared at the face now illuminated before him.

It was full of pain.

'Sit down, Jamie.' The voice was weary. It did not command; it did not hector. It almost asked permission. Jamie sat down in the chair opposite; and Dad went on, in the same tired voice.

'I don't really know where we go from here. You're mixed up. I'm mixed up. I've . . .' He frowned. 'I've read what you said about me. I . . . I suppose I must deserve it. I've always wanted the best for you. I've . . . tried to give you the advantages I never had and push you, and . . .' He stopped again, and his eyes slanted away towards the far wall.

Jamie watched, helplessly. And he realized suddenly

that this man before him, now skewered with sorrow, was a man he had never known before; a man who had never known him; and who only now, it seemed, was starting to know himself.

He thought back to the man he had once feared.

But that man was gone.

Dad spoke again. 'I meant the best, Jamie. I meant the best but I've . . . I've made mistakes. And, my God, they've cost me dear.'

Jamie saw tears in Dad's eyes again and made to get up, but his father waved him back.

'Don't. I'll be all right. I'm more concerned about . . . getting you right again. I'm a fighter. I'll always pull through somehow. But—'

'I'm a fighter, too, Dad,' said Jamie, looking hard at him.

His father's face softened for a moment.

'Yes, Jamie. I know you are.' Dad leaned back in the chair, breathing slowly. 'Can you tell me where you went?'

Jamie looked away and Dad quickly spoke again.

'You don't have to tell me. I'm not going to push you. Just as long as you didn't get into any trouble.'

Jamie thought for a moment, then made up his mind.

'I ran away because I was mixed up about you, and Mum, and myself. But I also . . .' He hesitated. 'I also had to borrow some money, a hell of a lot of money. For a good cause, I promise you. Don't ask me what it was for because I'll never tell you.' He bit his lip, anxious not to compromise Spider. 'So I . . . borrowed it from a friend of mine who gave up all his savings to help me.'

'Spider.'

Jamie frowned, desperate not to put his friend in trouble. Dad spoke again.

'It's all right. I won't tell anybody. I won't tell him or his parents that I know. If he helped you like that, and it was for a good cause, like you say, then I admire him for it. I've obviously been wrong about him, like I have about everything else. How much do you owe him?'

'I'm . . . too embarrassed to say. It's such a lot of money. Several thousand.'

'Well, whatever it is, I'll give you the money and you can pay him back. You don't have to tell him it came from me. Leave it a few weeks, then tell him you inherited it or something or . . .' But Dad stopped again. Self-control was deserting him again. He clenched his fists over the arm of the chair. 'I'm sorry, Jamie. I seem to have done so much wrong. I just . . . hope I can put some of it right.'

His body started to shake. Jamie hesitated, then stood up and walked over.

And this time his father did not wave him back.

In the night, he tossed in his bed, his mind wakeful with grief. Yet even in misery there seemed to be some kind of hope. His father had embraced him, said he was sorry, shown his own vulnerability, for the first time ever.

Perhaps it would never happen again. The fighter who had won all those squash tournaments in Australia back in the old days would surely set himself to the task of starting life all over again.

He did not know whether they had a future. He hoped so. But healing, if it came, would take time. Perhaps a whole life. As for himself . . .

He had to start again, too.

He rolled over, thinking of Mum, and how peaceful her face had looked when Dad had taken him to the undertaker's. His own tears had started then, and he was glad. He needed to weep.

Somehow he fell asleep, but soon woke again. It was dark and the house was still, the street silent. The clock on the bedside table said half-past one.

And he found himself thinking of Abby.

On an impulse, he slid out of bed and dressed, then went downstairs and found the big lamp from the cupboard, and softly unlocked the back door, and walked out into the night.

The stars were out, it was a full moon, and there was a sharp chill in the air. He did not switch on the lamp, but walked to the gate, opened it as quietly as he could, and wandered down to the little shed where he had first seen the person who had changed his life.

He opened the door and looked in. There, in the corner, even without the lamp on, he could see the blankets they had used, and the old cushion, and, after a moment, even the spare cup that went with the thermos flask. He must have left that behind.

He went over to the corner, tidied the blankets, and lay down, listening to the silence, and his own feverish breathing. Then he switched on the lamp and shone it against himself.

And there on the timbered wall close by, as though lying with him, was his shadow.

Abby's words came back to him.

'Whenever you see your shadow, Jamie, just remember you're looking at me.'

And in the silence of the night the shadow moved as he moved, and breathed as he breathed, and wept as he wept.

And then was gone.

Also by Tim Bowler

River Boy
ISBN 0 19 271756 1
Also in mass-market paperback ISBN 0 19 275035 6
Winner of the Carnegie Medal

Standing at the top of the fall, framed against the sky, was the figure of a boy. At least, it looked like a boy, though he was quite tall and it was hard to make out his features against the glare of the sun. She watched and waited, uncertain what to do, and whether she had been seen.

When Jess's grandfather has a serious heart attack, surely their planned trip to his boyhood home will have to be cancelled? But Grandpa insists on going so that he can finish his final painting, 'River Boy'. As Jess helps her ailing grandfather with his work, she becomes entranced by the scene he is painting. And then she becomes aware of a strange presence in the river, the figure of a boy, asking her for help and issuing a challenge that will stretch her swimming talents to the limits. But can she take up the challenge before it is too late for Grandpa . . . and the River Boy?

'A moving rite-of-passage novel which skilfully blends fantasy and reality.'

The Library Association

'an accomplished, crafted book'
The Times Educational Supplement

'all the hallmarks of a classic . . . You are not the same person at the end of this book.'

Carnegie Medal judges

Now in mass-market paperback

Dragon's Rock
ISBN 0 19 275036 4

That day it came for him again.

Benjamin remembered leaning back and resting, and rocking to the motion of the train. And closing his eyes.

The next moment it was upon him, racing like an angry fire through the landscape of his sleep. He ran, gasping for air in the stifling heat of its breath, but it was no good. He could feel it drawing closer, roaring its fury after him. Any moment now he would have to face it and suffer for the wrong he sensed he had done it . . .

He closed his eyes once more, but this time resisted sleep. Sleep had become a place of fear, a place where the dragon hunted him. But now he had a chance to go back, back to Dragon's Rock and put things right. And perhaps then the dragon would leave him alone.

'most likely to appeal to confident readers who enjoy a blend of fantasy and realism.'

School Librarian

'a nightmarish chiller which blends the flavour of *Twin Peaks* with Alan Garner.'

The Times Educational Supplement

Now in mass-market paperback

Midget
ISBN 0 19 275037 2

'*Midget the Mumbler. Fifteen years old. And he still can't master his speech impediment.*' '*Midget the Moron. Can't read the simplest word or write his own name.*' '*Midget the Mess. Acne all over. And three feet tall.*' '*Midget the Mistake. My pathetic little brother.*'

Locked in himself, locked in the body he hates, Midget still keeps thinking of the dream. The dream that they told him he could never have—the boat with the sail bent on the boom, the boat plunging out through the water with Midget at the helm, away from the shore, away from the darkness and the pain.

'*Midget* makes compulsive reading.'
> *Leigh Times*

'a masterly handling of suspense and cold trickling horror.'
> *Sunday Telegraph*

'the style is the perfect accompaniment to an extremely disturbing story, focusing on this occasion on fraternal hatred, developing into murderous intent.'
> *Irish Times*

KU-417-872

'An engaging and timely critique . . . that will . . . help us to heal our divided societies' Matthew Goodwin, *Sunday Times*

'Original, lively and no mere critique: unlike many others who have written on the "sorting" of society into winners and losers, Sandel produces a persuasive argument about the kind of community we should seek . . . an important work, makes a profound point that our leaders would do well to understand' Nick Timothy, *Daily Telegraph*

'An existentially important book for the left, by the world's most influential living philosopher. Its concept of "contributive justice" challenges the prevailing shrivelled view of society as composed merely of individuals with rights and the state with obligations' Paul Collier, *New Statesman*, Books of the Year

'A blueprint for a brighter future' Sean Smith, *Independent*

'A lucid, learned, closely reasoned book . . . Like its unfailingly civil author, the book is temperate in tone but radical in implications' George F. Will, *The Washington Post*

'Rich in moral exhortation – the kind that does your soul good' Polly Toynbee

'Credentialism is the last acceptable prejudice . . . blends fact, analysis and opinion in eminently readable non-fiction' Rana Foroohar, *Financial Times*

'Well-argued, clear, and nicely timed to appeal to the growing disillusionment with meritocracy' Simon Kuper, *New Statesman*

'What stands out is his approach – he allows people to reach their own conclusions, guided and challenged by the art of Michael Sandel's own methods of enquiry and challenge. His is the most effective method I've ever come across to help us think afresh and maybe change our minds – the hardest thing to do in these times. He sets an example to us all of how political discourse should and could be carried out. The book is a masterclass in the art of gentle persuasion' Andy Haldane, Chief Economist at the Bank of England

'Resets the political vocabulary and is awash with possibilities for the future' John Cruddas MP

'We live in a meritocracy, we are told, where hard work and talent are rewarded with success. Only, the game is rigged. All the stats show that the wealthier your parents, the more likely you are to "succeed" – which is to say, enjoy a top job or high wage. In *The Tyranny of Merit*, Michael J. Sandel takes apart the myth of meritocracy and examines its corrosiveness' Andrew Johnson, *i newspaper*, Books of the Year

'He is good at dismantling the cheap language of recent politics . . . compelling, too, in diagnosing the growing use of discriminatory language' Julian Glover, *Evening Standard*

'Many of us need what [Sandel] does so well: help us grapple with the unexpected and uncomfortable questions that history delivers us . . . Now's a good time for both sides to sit down for a very serious talk, with *The Tyranny of Merit* required reading for all' Arlie Hochschild, *New York Times Book Review*

'The latest salvo in Sandel's lifelong intellectual struggle against a creeping individualism that, since the Reagan and Thatcher era, has become pervasive in western democracies . . . The implicit claim is that vulnerability and mutual recognition can become the basis of a renewed sense of belonging and community. It is a vision of society that is the very opposite of what came to be known as Thatcherism, with its emphasis on self-reliance as a principal virtue' Julian Coman, *Observer*

'In a much talked-about new book, *The Tyranny of Merit* . . . Sandel argues that the polarized politics of our time, and the resentments that fuel it, arise, paradoxically, from a seemingly attractive ideal – the meritocratic promise that if you work hard and go to college, you will rise' Thomas L. Friedman, *The New York Times*

'It's the same critique my father made of meritocracy when he coined the word in 1958 and Sandel sees the populist uprisings of 2016, with Brexit and Trump triumphing at the ballot box, as a foretaste of the bloody revolution my father predicted would occur in 2034' Toby Young, *Spectator*

'Sandel shows . . . how the very conception of life as a relentless competitive race unjustly denigrates the losers, produces a cynical and arrogant elite, corrupts institutions of higher education, and replaces democracy with technocracy. Unwittingly, it thereby creates populist backlash' Elizabeth Anderson, *The Nation*

'A brilliant book, *The Tyranny of Merit* . . . gets at this all-important question of humiliation, and its relationship to populism and democracy' Anand Giridharadas, *The.Ink*

ABOUT THE AUTHOR

Michael J. Sandel teaches political philosophy at Harvard University. His books *What Money Can't Buy: The Moral Limits of Markets*, and *Justice: What's the Right Thing to Do?* were international best sellers and have been translated into thirty languages. Sandel's legendary course 'Justice' was the first Harvard course to be made freely available online and on television and has been viewed by tens of millions of people. His BBC series *The Global Philosopher* explores the philosophical ideas lying behind the headlines with participants from around the world.

Sandel has been a visiting professor at the Sorbonne, delivered the Tanner Lectures on Human Values at Oxford and the Reith Lectures for the BBC, and is a member of the American Academy of Arts and Sciences. His lecture tours have taken him across five continents and packed such venues as St Paul's Cathedral (London), the Sydney Opera House (Australia), and an outdoor stadium in Seoul (S. Korea), where 14,000 people came to hear him speak.

THE TYRANNY
OF MERIT

What's Become of
the Common Good?

MICHAEL J. SANDEL

PENGUIN BOOKS

PENGUIN BOOKS

UK | USA | Canada | Ireland | Australia
India | New Zealand | South Africa

Penguin Books is part of the Penguin Random House group of companies
whose addresses can be found at global.penguinrandomhouse.com.

First published in the USA by Farrar, Straus and Giroux 2020
First published in Great Britain by Allen Lane 2020
Published in Penguin Books with a new Prologue 2021

005

Printed and bound in Great Britain by Clays Ltd, Elcograf S.p.A.

The authorized representative in the EEA is Penguin Random House Ireland,
Morrison Chambers, 32 Nassau Street, Dublin D02 YH68

A CIP catalogue record for this book is available from the British Library

ISBN: 978-0-141-99117-7

www.greenpenguin.co.uk

For Kiku, with love

CONTENTS

THE TYRANNY
OF MERIT

PROLOGUE TO THE
PAPERBACK EDITION

When the coronavirus pandemic hit in 2020, the United States, like many other countries, was unprepared. Despite warnings the previous year from public health experts about the risk of a global viral contagion, and even as China contended with its outbreak in January, the United States lacked the ability to conduct the widespread testing that might have contained the disease. As the contagion spread, the wealthiest country in the world found itself unable to provide even the medical masks and other protective gear that health care providers needed to treat the flood of infected patients.

Beyond its lack of logistical preparedness, the country was not morally prepared for the pandemic. The years leading up to the crisis were a time of deep division—economically, culturally, politically. Decades of rising inequality and cultural resentment had brought an angry populist backlash in 2016, resulting in the election of Donald Trump. The partisan divide persisted as the crisis unfolded. Few Republicans (only 7 percent) trusted the news media to provide reliable information on coronavirus; few Democrats (4 percent) trusted the information Trump provided.[1]

Amid the partisan rancor and mistrust came a plague that demanded the kind of solidarity few societies can summon except in times of war.

People throughout the world were implored, and in many cases required, to observe social distancing, to abandon work, and to stay at home. Those unable to work remotely faced lost wages and disappearing jobs, or else jobs that required them to risk their health and lives by working in places where the virus was hard to avoid.

Morally, the pandemic reminded us of our vulnerability, of our mutual dependence: "We are all in this together." Public officials and advertisers reached instinctively for this slogan. But this upbeat mantra soon rang hollow. It did not describe a sense of community embodied in an ongoing practice of mutual obligation and shared sacrifice. The pandemic made this clear. COVID-19 bore down most heavily on people of color, who disproportionately held jobs that exposed workers to greatest risk. The Latino death rate was 22 percent higher than that of whites; among Black Americans, the COVID death rate was 40 percent higher than among white Americans.[2]

These grim tallies of death reflected pre-existing conditions of privilege and privation. The same market-driven globalization project that had left the United States without access to the domestic production of surgical masks and medications had deepened inequalities and deprived many working people of well-paying jobs and social esteem.

Meanwhile, those who reaped the economic bounty of global markets, supply chains, and capital flows had come to rely less and less on their fellow citizens, as producers or as consumers. Their economic prospects and identities were no longer dependent on local or national communities. As the winners of globalization pulled away from the losers, they practiced their own kind of social distancing.

The political divide that mattered, the winners explained, was no longer left versus right but open versus closed. In an open world, success depends on education, on equipping yourself to compete and win in a global economy. This means that national governments must ensure that everyone has an equal chance to get the education on which success depends. But it also means that those who land on top come to believe they deserve their success. And, if opportunities are truly equal, it means that those who are left behind deserve their fate as well.

This way of thinking about success makes it hard to believe that "we are all in this together." It invites credentialed elites to consider their success their own doing, and many working people to feel that those on top look down with disdain. It helps explain why those left behind by globalization would become angry and resentful, and why they would be drawn to authoritarian populists who rail against elites and promise to reassert national borders with a vengeance.

When Joe Biden won the Democratic nomination in 2020, he became the first Democratic nominee for president in thirty-six years without a degree from an Ivy League university. This may have helped him connect with the blue-collar workers his party has struggled to attract in recent years. But this novel aspect of his candidacy should prompt us to reflect on the credentialist prejudice we have come to take for granted in our public life. This prejudice not only constrains the choice of candidates for national office. It also shapes the way mainstream politicians across the political spectrum have responded to the inequality and wage stagnation of recent decades—by telling workers to get a college degree.

The bluntest critique of the credentialist impulse in contemporary politics was offered by Representative James Clyburn of South Carolina, the highest-ranking African American in Congress. Clyburn, whose endorsement of Biden in the South Carolina primary rescued Biden's struggling candidacy and set him on the road to the nomination, saw Biden as representing an alternative to the relentless credentialism that had alienated working people from the Democratic party. "Our problem," Clyburn said, "is too many candidates spend time trying to let people know how smart they are, rather than trying to connect with people." He thought Democrats had put too much emphasis on college education. What does it mean "when a candidate says, you need to be able to send your kids to college? Now how many times have you heard that? I hate to hear that . . . I don't need to hear that. Because we've got people who want to be electricians, they want to be plumbers, they want to be barbers."[3] Although he did not put it quite this way, Clyburn was pushing back against the meritocratic political project that had unwittingly disparaged working-class voters and opened the way to Trump.

Assuming office after a violent siege of the U.S. Capitol by Trump supporters hoping to overturn the election result, Biden promised to bring the country together. It would not be easy. Trump had been defeated but not repudiated. Even after watching him bungle the pandemic, inflame racial tensions, and flout constitutional norms, 74 million Americans had voted for him. Some were traditional, well-off Republicans who liked his tax cuts. But many rural and working-class voters were drawn to his politics of grievance. His animus against political and cultural elites spoke to their resentment, their sense of humiliation. His policies did little to help them, but they felt he was on their side. To be sure, Trump's animus was entangled with racism, and white supremacists heeded his call. But his politics of grievance resonated for reasons beyond race. For decades, the divide between winners and losers had been deepening, poisoning our politics, pulling us apart.

As Biden took office, the country was polarized in ways that a restoration presidency would not heal. To dissipate the rancor, the mainstream parties, like their counterparts around the world, would need to rethink their mission and purpose. They would need to see how the market-driven, meritocratic ethic they championed had fueled resentment and prompted the backlash. Any hope of renewing our moral and civic life depends on understanding how, over the past four decades, our social bonds and respect for one another came unraveled. This book seeks to explain how this happened, and to consider how we might find our way to a politics of the common good.

February 2021
Brookline, Massachusetts

INTRODUCTION:

GETTING IN

In March 2019, as high school students awaited the results of their college applications, federal prosecutors made a stunning announcement. They charged thirty-three wealthy parents with engaging in an elaborate cheating scheme to get their children admitted to elite universities, including Yale, Stanford, Georgetown, and the University of Southern California.[1]

At the heart of the scam was an unscrupulous college-counseling consultant named William Singer, who ran a business that catered to anxious, affluent parents. Singer's company specialized in gaming the intensely competitive college admissions system that had in recent decades become the primary gateway to prosperity and prestige. For students lacking the stellar academic credentials top colleges required, Singer devised corrupt workarounds—paying proctors of standardized tests such as the SAT and ACT to boost students' scores by correcting their answer sheets, and bribing coaches to designate applicants as recruited athletes, even if the students did not play the sport. He even provided fake athletic credentials, photoshopping applicants' faces onto action photos of real athletes.

Singer's illicit admissions service did not come cheap. The chairman of a prestigious law firm paid $75,000 for his daughter to take a college entrance exam at a test center supervised by a proctor paid by Singer to ensure the student received the score she needed. One family paid Singer $1.2 million to get their daughter admitted to Yale as a soccer recruit, despite the fact that she did not play soccer. Singer used $400,000 of the payment to bribe the obliging Yale soccer coach, who was also indicted. A television actress and her husband, a fashion designer, paid Singer $500,000 to get their two daughters admitted to USC as bogus recruits to the crew team. Another celebrity, the actress Felicity Huffman, known for her role in the television series *Desperate Housewives*, somehow got a bargain rate; for only $15,000, Singer put in the fix for her daughter's SAT.[2]

In all, Singer took in $25 million over eight years running his college admissions scam.

The admissions scandal provoked universal outrage. In a polarized time, when Americans could scarcely agree on anything, it drew massive coverage and condemnation across the political spectrum—on Fox News and MSNBC, in *The Wall Street Journal* and *The New York Times*. Everyone agreed that bribing and cheating to gain admission to elite colleges was reprehensible. But the outrage expressed something deeper than anger at privileged parents using illicit means to help their kids get into prestigious colleges. In ways that people struggled to articulate, it was an emblematic scandal, one that raised larger questions about who gets ahead, and why.

Inevitably, the expressions of outrage were politically inflected. Surrogates for President Trump took to Twitter and Fox News to taunt the Hollywood liberals ensnared in the scam. "Look at who these people are," Lara Trump, the president's daughter-in-law, said on Fox. "The Hollywood elites, the liberal elites who were always talking about equality for all, and everyone should get a fair shot, when here is the biggest hypocrisy of all: That they're writing checks to cheat and get their kids into these schools—when the spots really should've gone to kids that were actually deserving of them."[3]

For their part, liberals agreed that the scam deprived qualified kids of the places they deserved. But they saw the scandal as a blatant instance of a more pervasive injustice: the role of wealth and privilege in college admission, even where no illegality was involved. In announcing the indictment, the U.S. Attorney declared what he took to be the principle at stake:

"There can be no separate college admissions system for the wealthy."[4] But editorial and opinion writers were quick to point out that money routinely plays a role in admissions, most explicitly in the special consideration many American universities accord children of alumni and generous donors.

Responding to Trump supporters' attempts to blame liberal elites for the admissions scandal, liberals cited published reports that Jared Kushner, the president's son-in-law, had been admitted to Harvard despite a modest academic record after his father, a wealthy real estate developer, had donated $2.5 million to the university. Trump himself reportedly gave $1.5 million to the Wharton School of the University of Pennsylvania around the time his children Donald Jr. and Ivanka attended the school.[5]

THE ETHICS OF ADMISSION

Singer, the mastermind of the admissions scam, acknowledged that a big gift sometimes gets marginally qualified applicants admitted through the "back door." But he pitched his own technique, which he called the "side door," as a cost-effective alternative. He told clients that the standard "back door" approach was "ten times as much money" as his cheating scheme, and less certain. A major gift to the college offered no guarantee of admission, while his "side door" of bribes and fake test scores did. "My families want a guarantee," he explained.[6]

Although money buys access in both "back door" and "side door" admissions, these modes of entry are not morally identical. For one thing, the back door is legal, while the side door is not. The U.S. Attorney made this clear: "We are not talking about donating a building so that a school is more likely to take your son or daughter. We are talking about deception and fraud, fake test scores, fake athletic credentials, fake photographs, bribed college officials."[7]

In prosecuting Singer, his clients, and the bribe-taking coaches, the feds were not telling colleges they could not sell seats in the freshman class; they were simply cracking down on a fraudulent scheme. Legality aside, the back door and the side door differ in this respect: When parents buy their child's admission through a big donation, the money goes to the college, which can use it to improve the education it offers all students. With Singer's scheme, the money goes to third parties, and so does little or nothing to help the college itself. (At least one of the coaches Singer bribed, the sailing coach at Stanford, apparently used the bribe to support the sailing program. Others pocketed the money.)

From the standpoint of fairness, however, it is hard to distinguish between the "back door" and the "side door." Both give an edge to children of wealthy parents who are admitted instead of better-qualified applicants. Both allow money to override merit.

Admission based on merit defines entry through the "front door." As Singer put it, the front door "means you get in on your own." This mode of entry is what most people consider fair; applicants should be admitted based on their own merit, not their parents' money.

In practice, of course, it is not that simple. Money hovers over the front door as well as the back. Measures of merit are hard to disentangle from economic advantage. Standardized tests such as the SAT purport to measure merit on its own, so that students from modest backgrounds can demonstrate intellectual promise. In practice, however, SAT scores closely track family income. The richer a student's family, the higher the score he or she is likely to receive.[8]

Not only do wealthy parents enroll their children in SAT prep courses; they hire private admissions counselors to burnish their college applications, enroll them in dance and music lessons, and train them in elite sports such as fencing, squash, golf, tennis, crew, lacrosse, and sailing, the better to qualify for recruitment to college teams. These are among the costly means by which affluent, striving parents equip their progeny to compete for admission.

And then there is tuition. At all but the handful of colleges wealthy enough to admit students without regard for their ability to pay, those who do not need financial aid are more likely than their needy counterparts to get in.[9]

Given all this, it is not surprising that more than two-thirds of students at Ivy League schools come from the top 20 percent of the income scale; at

Princeton and Yale, more students come from the top 1 percent than from the entire bottom 60 percent of the country.[10] This staggering inequality of access is due partly to legacy admissions and donor appreciation (the back door), but also to advantages that propel children from well-off families through the front door.

Critics point to this inequality as evidence that higher education is not the meritocracy it claims to be. From this point of view, the college admissions scandal is an egregious instance of the broader, pervasive unfairness that prevents higher education from living up to the meritocratic principle it professes.

Despite their disagreements, those who consider the cheating scandal a shocking departure from standard admissions practices and those who consider it an extreme example of tendencies already prevalent in college admissions share a common premise: Students should be admitted to college based on their own abilities and talents, not based on factors beyond their control. They agree, in other words, that admission should be based on merit. They also agree, implicitly at least, that those who get in based on merit have earned their admission and therefore deserve the benefits that flow from it.

If this familiar view is right, then the problem with meritocracy is not with the principle but with our failure to live up to it. Political argument between conservatives and liberals bears this out. Our public debates are not about meritocracy itself but about how to achieve it. Conservatives argue, for example, that affirmative action policies that consider race and ethnicity as factors in admission amount to a betrayal of merit-based admission; liberals defend affirmative action as a way of remedying persisting unfairness and argue that a true meritocracy can be achieved only by leveling the playing field between the privileged and the disadvantaged.

But this debate overlooks the possibility that the problem with meritocracy runs deeper.

Consider again the admissions scandal. Most of the outrage focused on the cheating, and the unfairness of it. Equally troubling, however, are the attitudes that fueled the cheating. Lying in the background of the scandal was the assumption, now so familiar that it is scarcely noticed, that admission to an elite university is a highly sought prize. The scandal was attention-grabbing not only because it implicated celebrities and private equity moguls but also because the access they tried to buy was so widely desired, the object of fevered striving.

Why is this so? Why has admission to prestigious universities become so fiercely sought that privileged parents commit fraud to get their kids in? Or, short of fraud, spend tens of thousands of dollars on private admissions consultants and test prep courses to boost their children's chances, turning their high school years into a stress-strewn gauntlet of AP classes, résumé building, and pressure-packed striving? Why has admission to elite colleges come to loom so large in our society that the FBI would devote massive law enforcement resources to ferreting out the scam, and that news of the scandal would command headlines and public attention for months, from the indictment to the sentencing of the perpetrators?

The admissions obsession has its origins in the growing inequality of recent decades. It reflects the fact that more is at stake in who gets in where. As the wealthiest 10 percent pulled away from the rest, the stakes of attending a prestigious college increased. Fifty years ago, applying to college was less fraught. Fewer than one in five Americans went to a four-year college, and those who did tended to enroll in places close to home. College rankings mattered less than they do today.[11]

But as inequality increased, and as the earnings gap between those with and those without a college degree widened, college mattered more. So did college choice. Today, students commonly seek out the most selective college that will admit them.[12] Parenting styles have also changed, especially among the professional classes. As the income gap grows, so does the fear of falling. Seeking to avert this danger, parents became intensely involved with their children's lives—managing their time, monitoring their grades, directing their activities, curating their college qualifications.[13]

This epidemic of overbearing, helicopter parenting did not come from nowhere. It is an anxious but understandable response to rising inequality and the desire of affluent parents to spare their progeny the precarity of middle-class life. A degree from a name-brand university has come to be seen as the primary vehicle of upward mobility for those seeking to rise and the surest bulwark against downward mobility for those hoping to remain ensconced in the comfortable classes. This is the mentality that led panicky, privileged parents to sign up for the college admissions scam.

But economic anxiety is not the whole story. More than a hedge against downward mobility, Singer's clients were buying something else, something less tangible but more valuable. In securing a place for their kids in prestigious universities, they were buying the borrowed luster of merit.

BIDDING FOR MERIT

In an unequal society, those who land on top want to believe their success is morally justified. In a meritocratic society, this means the winners must believe they have earned their success through their own talent and hard work.

Paradoxically, this is the gift the cheating parents wanted to give their kids. If all they really cared about was enabling their children to live in affluence, they could have given them trust funds. But they wanted something else—the meritocratic cachet that admission to elite colleges confers.

Singer understood this when he explained that the front door means "you get in on your own." His cheating scheme was the next best thing. Of course, being admitted on the basis of a rigged SAT or phony athletic credentials is not making it on your own. This is why most of the parents hid their machinations from their kids. Admission through the side door carries the same meritocratic honor as admission through the front door only if the illicit mode of entry is concealed. No one takes pride in announcing, "I've been admitted to Stanford because my parents bribed the sailing coach."

The contrast with admission based on merit seems obvious. Those admitted with sparkling, legitimate credentials take pride in their achievement, and consider that they got in on their own. But this is, in a way, misleading. While it is true that their admission reflects dedication and hard work, it cannot really be said that it is solely their own doing. What about the parents and teachers who helped them on their way? What about talents and gifts not wholly of their making? What about the good fortune to live in a society that cultivates and rewards the talents they happen to have?

Those who, by dint of effort and talent, prevail in a competitive meritocracy are indebted in ways the competition obscures. As the meritocracy intensifies, the striving so absorbs us that our indebtedness recedes from view. In this way, even a fair meritocracy, one without cheating or bribery or special privileges for the wealthy, induces a mistaken impression—that we have made it on our own. The years of strenuous effort demanded of applicants to elite universities almost forces them to believe that their success is their own doing, and that if they fall short, they have no one to blame but themselves.

This is a heavy burden for young people to bear. It is also corrosive of civic sensibilities. For the more we think of ourselves as self-made and self-sufficient, the harder it is to learn gratitude and humility. And without these sentiments, it is hard to care for the common good.

College admission is not the only occasion for arguments about merit. Debates about who deserves what abound in contemporary politics. On the surface, these debates are about fairness: Does everyone have a truly equal opportunity to compete for desirable goods and social positions?

But our disagreements about merit are not only about fairness. They are also about how we define success and failure, winning and losing—and about the attitudes the winners should hold toward those less successful than themselves. These are highly charged questions, and we try to avoid them until they force themselves upon us.

Finding our way beyond the polarized politics of our time requires a reckoning with merit. How has the meaning of merit been recast in recent decades, in ways that erode the dignity of work and leave many people feeling that elites look down on them? Are the winners of globalization justified in the belief that they have earned and therefore deserve their success, or is this a matter of meritocratic hubris?

At a time when anger against elites has brought democracy to the brink, the question of merit takes on a special urgency. We need to ask whether the solution to our fractious politics is to live more faithfully by the principle of merit, or to seek a common good beyond the sorting and the striving.

WINNERS AND LOSERS

These are dangerous times for democracy. The danger can be seen in rising xenophobia and growing public support for autocratic figures who test the limits of democratic norms. These trends are troubling in themselves. Equally alarming is the fact that mainstream parties and politicians display little understanding of the discontent that is roiling politics around the world.

Some denounce the upsurge of populist nationalism as little more than a racist, xenophobic reaction against immigrants and multiculturalism. Others see it mainly in economic terms, as a protest against job losses brought about by global trade and new technologies.

But it is a mistake to see only the bigotry in populist protest, or to view it only as an economic complaint. Like the triumph of Brexit in the United Kingdom, the election of Donald Trump in 2016 was an angry verdict on decades of rising inequality and a version of globalization that benefits those at the top but leaves ordinary citizens feeling disempowered. It was also a rebuke for a technocratic approach to politics that is tone-deaf to the resentments of people who feel the economy and the culture have left them behind.

The hard reality is that Trump was elected by tapping a wellspring of anxieties, frustrations, and legitimate grievances to which the mainstream parties had no compelling answer. A similar predicament afflicts European democracies. Before they can hope to win back public support, these parties must rethink their mission and purpose. To do so, they should learn from the populist protest that has displaced them—not by replicating its xenophobia and strident nationalism, but by taking seriously the legitimate grievances with which these ugly sentiments are entangled.

Such thinking should begin with the recognition that these grievances are not only economic but also moral and cultural; they are not only about wages and jobs but also about social esteem.

The mainstream parties and governing elites who find themselves the target of populist protest struggle to make sense of it. They typically diagnose the discontent in one of two ways: As animus against immigrants and racial and ethnic minorities or as anxiety in the face of globalization and technological change. Both diagnoses miss something important.

DIAGNOSING POPULIST DISCONTENT

The first diagnosis sees populist anger against elites mainly as a backlash against growing racial, ethnic, and gender diversity. Accustomed to dominating the social hierarchy, the white male working-class voters who supported Trump feel threatened by the prospect of becoming a minority within "their" country, "strangers in their own land." They feel that they, more than women or racial minorities, are the victims of discrimination; and they feel oppressed by the demands of "politically correct" public discourse. This diagnosis of injured social status highlights the ugly features of populist sentiment—the nativism, misogyny, and racism voiced by Trump and other nationalistic populists.

The second diagnosis attributes working-class resentment to bewilderment and dislocation wrought by the rapid pace of change in an age of globalization and technology. In the new economic order, the notion of work tied to a lifelong career is over; what matters now are innovation, flexibility, entrepreneurialism, and a constant willingness to learn new skills. But, according to this account, many workers bridle at the demand to reinvent themselves as the jobs they once held are outsourced to low-wage countries or assigned to robots. They hanker, as if nostalgically, for the stable communities and careers of the past. Feeling dislocated in the face of the inexorable forces of globalization and technology, such workers lash out against immigrants, free trade, and governing elites. But their fury is misdirected, for they fail to realize that they are railing against forces as unalterable as the weather. Their anxieties are best addressed by job-training programs and other measures to help them adapt to the imperatives of global and technological change.

Each of these diagnoses contains an element of truth. But neither gives populism its due. Construing populist protest as either malevolent or misdirected absolves governing elites of responsibility for creating the conditions that have eroded the dignity of work and left many feeling disrespected and disempowered. The diminished economic and cultural status of working people in recent decades is not the result of inexorable forces; it is the result of the way mainstream political parties and elites have governed.

Those elites are now alarmed, and rightly so, at the threat to democratic norms posed by Trump and other populist-backed autocrats. But they fail to acknowledge their role in prompting the resentment that led to the populist backlash. They do not see that the upheavals we are witnessing are a political response to a political failure of historic proportions.

TECHNOCRACY AND MARKET-FRIENDLY GLOBALIZATION

At the heart of this failure is the way mainstream parties conceived and carried out the project of globalization over the past four decades. Two aspects of this project gave rise to the conditions that fuel populist protest. One is its technocratic way of conceiving the public good; the other is its meritocratic way of defining winners and losers.

The technocratic conception of politics is bound up with a faith in markets—not necessarily unfettered, laissez-faire capitalism, but the broader belief that market mechanisms are the primary instruments for achieving the public good. This way of thinking about politics is technocratic in the sense that it drains public discourse of substantive moral argument and treats ideologically contestable questions as if they were matters of economic efficiency, the province of experts.

It is not difficult to see how the technocratic faith in markets set the stage for populist discontent. The market-driven version of globalization brought growing inequality. It also devalued national identities and allegiances. As goods and capital flowed freely across national borders, those who stood astride the global economy valorized cosmopolitan identities as a progressive, enlightened alternative to the narrow, parochial ways of protectionism, tribalism, and conflict. The real political divide, they argued, was no longer left versus right but open versus closed. This implied that critics of outsourcing, free-trade agreements, and unrestricted capital flows were closed-minded rather than open-minded, tribal rather than global.[1]

Meanwhile, the technocratic approach to governance treated many public questions as matters of technical expertise beyond the reach of ordinary citizens. This narrowed the scope of democratic argument, hollowed out the terms of public discourse, and produced a growing sense of disempowerment.

The market-friendly, technocratic conception of globalization was embraced by mainstream parties of the left and the right. But it was the embrace of market thinking and market values by center-left parties that proved most consequential—for the globalization project itself and for the populist protest that followed. By the time of Trump's election, the Democratic Party had become a party of technocratic liberalism more congenial to the professional classes than to the blue-collar and middle-class voters who once constituted its base. The same was true of Britain's Labour Party at the time of Brexit, and the social democratic parties of Europe.

This transformation had its origins in the 1980s.[2] Ronald Reagan and Margaret Thatcher had argued that government was the problem and that markets were the solution. When they passed from the political scene, the center-left politicians who succeeded them—Bill Clinton in the U.S., Tony

Blair in Britain, Gerhard Schröder in Germany—moderated but consolidated the market faith. They softened the harsh edges of unfettered markets but did not challenge the central premise of the Reagan-Thatcher era—that market mechanisms are the primary instruments for achieving the public good. In line with this faith, they embraced a market-friendly version of globalization and welcomed the growing financialization of the economy.

In the 1990s, the Clinton administration joined with Republicans in promoting global trade agreements and deregulating the financial industry. The benefits of these policies flowed mostly to those at the top, but Democrats did little to address the deepening inequality and the growing power of money in politics. Having strayed from its traditional mission of taming capitalism and holding economic power to democratic account, liberalism lost its capacity to inspire.

All that seemed to change when Barack Obama appeared on the political scene. In his 2008 presidential campaign, he offered a stirring alternative to the managerial, technocratic language that had come to characterize liberal public discourse. He showed that progressive politics could speak a language of moral and spiritual purpose.

But the moral energy and civic idealism he inspired as a candidate did not carry over into his presidency. Assuming office in the midst of the financial crisis, he appointed economic advisors who had promoted financial deregulation during the Clinton years. With their encouragement, he bailed out the banks on terms that did not hold them to account for the behavior that led to the crisis and offered little help for those who had lost their homes.

His moral voice muted, Obama placated rather than articulated the seething public anger toward Wall Street. Lingering anger over the bailout cast a shadow over the Obama presidency and ultimately fueled a mood of populist protest that reached across the political spectrum—on the left, the Occupy movement and the candidacy of Bernie Sanders; on the right, the Tea Party movement and the election of Trump.

The populist uprising in the United States, Great Britain, and Europe is a backlash directed generally against elites, but its most conspicuous casualties have been liberal and center-left political parties—the Democratic

Party in the U.S., the Labour Party in Britain, the Social Democratic Party (SPD) in Germany (whose share of the vote reached a historic low in the 2017 federal election), Italy's Democratic Party (whose vote share dropped to less than 20 percent), and the Socialist Party in France (whose presidential nominee won only 6 percent of the vote in the first round of the 2017 election).

Before they can hope to win back public support, these parties need to reconsider their market-oriented, technocratic approach to governing. They need also to rethink something subtler but no less consequential—the attitudes toward success and failure that have accompanied the growing inequality of recent decades. They need to ask why those who have not flourished in the new economy feel that the winners look down with disdain.

THE RHETORIC OF RISING

What, then, has incited the resentment against elites felt by many working-class and middle-class voters? The answer begins with the rising inequality of recent decades but does not end there. It has ultimately to do with the changing terms of social recognition and esteem.

The age of globalization has bestowed its rewards unevenly, to say the least. In the United States, most of the nation's income gains since the late 1970s have gone to the top 10 percent, while the bottom half received virtually none. In real terms, the median income for working-age men, about $36,000, is less than it was four decades ago. Today, the richest 1 percent of Americans make more than the bottom half combined.[3]

But even this explosion of inequality is not the primary source of populist anger. Americans have long tolerated inequalities of income and wealth, believing that, whatever one's starting point in life, it is possible to rise from rags to riches. This faith in the possibility of upward mobility is at the heart of the American dream.

In line with this faith, mainstream parties and politicians have responded to growing inequality by calling for greater equality of opportunity—

retraining workers whose jobs have disappeared due to globalization and technology; improving access to higher education; and removing barriers of race, ethnicity, and gender. This rhetoric of opportunity is summed up in the slogan that those who work hard and play by the rules should be able to rise "as far as their talents will take them."

In recent years, politicians of both parties have reiterated this slogan to the point of incantation. Ronald Reagan, George W. Bush, and Marco Rubio among Republicans, and Bill Clinton, Barack Obama, and Hillary Clinton among Democrats, all invoked it. Obama was fond of a variation of this theme, drawn from a pop song: "You can make it if you try." During his presidency, he used this line in speeches and public statements more than 140 times.[4]

But the rhetoric of rising now rings hollow. In today's economy, it is not easy to rise. Americans born to poor parents tend to stay poor as adults. Of those born in the bottom fifth of the income scale, only about one in twenty will make it to the top fifth; most will not even rise to the middle class.[5] It is easier to rise from poverty in Canada or Germany, Denmark, and other European countries than it is in the United States.[6]

This is at odds with the long-standing faith that mobility is America's answer to inequality. The United States, we tell ourselves, can afford to worry less about inequality than the class-bound societies of Europe because here, it is possible to rise. Seventy percent of Americans believe the poor can make it out of poverty on their own, while only 35 percent of Europeans think so. This faith in mobility may explain why the U.S. has a less-generous welfare state than most major European countries.[7]

But today, the countries with the highest mobility tend to be those with the greatest equality. The ability to rise, it seems, depends less on the spur of poverty than on access to education, health care, and other resources that equip people to succeed in the world of work.

The explosion of inequality in recent decades has not quickened upward mobility but, to the contrary, has enabled those on top to consolidate their advantages and pass them on to their children. Over the past half century, elite colleges and universities dismantled barriers of race, religion, gender, and ethnicity that once restricted admission to the sons of the privileged. The

Scholastic Aptitude Test (SAT) was born of the promise to admit students based on academic merit rather than class and family pedigree. But today's meritocracy has hardened into a hereditary aristocracy.

Two-thirds of the students at Harvard and Stanford come from the top fifth of the income scale. Despite generous financial aid policies, fewer than 4 percent of Ivy League students come from the bottom fifth. At Harvard and other Ivy League colleges, there are more students from families in the top *1 percent* (income of more than $630,000 per year) than there are students from all the families in the bottom half of the income distribution combined.[8]

The American faith that, with hard work and talent, anyone can rise no longer fits the facts on the ground. This may explain why the rhetoric of opportunity fails to inspire as it once did. Mobility can no longer compensate for inequality. Any serious response to the gap between rich and poor must reckon directly with inequalities of power and wealth, rather than rest content with the project of helping people scramble up a ladder whose rungs grow farther and farther apart.

THE MERITOCRATIC ETHIC

The problem with meritocracy is not only that the practice falls short of the ideal. If that were the problem, the solution would consist in perfecting equality of opportunity, in seeking a society in which people could, whatever their starting point in life, truly rise as far as their efforts and talents would take them. But it is doubtful that even a perfect meritocracy would be satisfying, either morally or politically.

Morally, it is unclear why the talented deserve the outsize rewards that market-driven societies lavish on the successful. Central to the case for the meritocratic ethic is the idea that we do not deserve to be rewarded, or held back, based on factors beyond our control. But is having (or lacking) certain talents really our own doing? If not, it is hard to see why those who rise thanks to their talents deserve greater rewards than those who may be equally hardworking but less endowed with the gifts a market society happens to prize.

Those who celebrate the meritocratic ideal and make it the center of their political project overlook this moral question. They also ignore something more politically potent: the morally unattractive attitudes the meritocratic ethic promotes, among the winners and also among the losers. Among the winners, it generates hubris; among the losers, humiliation and resentment. These moral sentiments are at the heart of the populist uprising against elites. More than a protest against immigrants and outsourcing, the populist complaint is about the tyranny of merit. And the complaint is justified.

The relentless emphasis on creating a fair meritocracy, in which social positions reflect effort and talent, has a corrosive effect on the way we interpret our success (or the lack of it). The notion that the system rewards talent and hard work encourages the winners to consider their success their own doing, a measure of their virtue—and to look down upon those less fortunate than themselves.

Meritocratic hubris reflects the tendency of winners to inhale too deeply of their success, to forget the luck and good fortune that helped them on their way. It is the smug conviction of those who land on top that they deserve their fate, and that those on the bottom deserve theirs, too. This attitude is the moral companion of technocratic politics.

A lively sense of the contingency of our lot conduces to a certain humility: "There, but for the grace of God, or the accident of fortune, go I." But a perfect meritocracy banishes all sense of gift or grace. It diminishes our capacity to see ourselves as sharing a common fate. It leaves little room for the solidarity that can arise when we reflect on the contingency of our talents and fortunes. This is what makes merit a kind of tyranny, or unjust rule.

THE POLITICS OF HUMILIATION

Seen from below, the hubris of elites is galling. No one likes to be looked down upon. But the meritocratic faith adds insult to injury. The notion that your fate is in your hands, that "you can make it if you try," is a double-edged sword, inspiring in one way but invidious in another. It congratulates the winners but denigrates the losers, even in their own eyes. For those who can't find work or make ends meet, it is hard to escape the demoralizing thought that their failure is their own doing, that they simply lack the talent and drive to succeed.

The politics of humiliation differs in this respect from the politics of injustice. Protest against injustice looks outward; it complains that the system is rigged, that the winners have cheated or manipulated their way to the top. Protest against humiliation is psychologically more freighted. It combines resentment of the winners with nagging self-doubt: perhaps the rich are rich because they are more deserving than the poor; maybe the losers are complicit in their misfortune after all.

This feature of the politics of humiliation makes it more combustible than other political sentiments. It is a potent ingredient in the volatile brew of anger and resentment that fuels populist protest. Though himself a billionaire, Donald Trump understood and exploited this resentment. Unlike Barack Obama and Hillary Clinton, who spoke constantly of "opportunity," Trump scarcely mentioned the word. Instead, he offered blunt talk of winners and losers. (Interestingly, Bernie Sanders, a social democratic populist, also rarely speaks of opportunity and mobility, focusing instead on inequalities of power and wealth.)

Elites have so valorized a college degree—both as an avenue for advancement and as the basis for social esteem—that they have difficulty understanding the hubris a meritocracy can generate, and the harsh judgment it imposes on those who have not gone to college. Such attitudes are at the heart of the populist backlash and Trump's victory.

One of the deepest political divides in American politics today is between those with and those without a college degree. In the 2016 election, Trump won two-thirds of white voters without a college degree, while Hillary Clinton won decisively among voters with advanced degrees. A similar divide appeared in Britain's Brexit referendum. Voters with no college education voted overwhelming for Brexit, while the vast majority of those with a postgraduate degree voted to remain.[9]

Reflecting on her presidential campaign a year and a half later, Hillary Clinton displayed the meritocratic hubris that contributed to her defeat. "I won the places that represent two-thirds of America's gross domestic product," she told a conference in Mumbai, India, in 2018. "So I won the places that are optimistic, diverse, dynamic, moving forward." By contrast, Trump drew his support from those who "didn't like black people getting rights" and "didn't like women . . . getting jobs." She had won the votes of the winners of globalization, while Trump had won among the losers.[10]

The Democratic Party had once stood for farmers and working people against the privileged. Now, in a meritocratic age, its defeated standard bearer boasted that the prosperous, enlightened parts of the country had voted for her.

Donald Trump was keenly alive to the politics of humiliation. From the standpoint of economic fairness, his populism was fake, a kind of plutocratic populism. He proposed a health plan that would have cut health care for many of his working-class supporters and enacted a tax bill that heaped tax cuts on the wealthy. But to focus solely on the hypocrisy misses the point.

When he withdrew the United States from the Paris climate change agreement, Trump argued, implausibly, that he was doing so to protect American jobs. But the real point of his decision, its political rationale, was contained in this seemingly stray remark: "At what point does America get demeaned? At what point do they start laughing at us as a country? . . . We don't want other leaders and other countries laughing at us anymore."[11]

Liberating the United States from the supposed burdens of the climate change agreement was not really about jobs or about global warming. It was, in Trump's political imagination, about averting humiliation. This resonated with Trump voters, even those who cared about climate change.

TECHNOCRATIC MERIT AND MORAL JUDGMENT

Taken by itself, the notion that the meritorious should govern is not distinctive to our time. In ancient China, Confucius taught that those who excelled in virtue and ability should govern. In ancient Greece, Plato imagined a society led by a philosopher-king supported by a public-spirited class of guardians. Aristotle rejected Plato's philosopher-king, but he, too, argued that the meritorious should have the greatest influence in public affairs. For him the merit relevant to governing was not wealth or noble birth, but excellence in civic virtue and *phronesis*, the practical wisdom to reason well about the common good.[12]

The founders of the American republic called themselves "Men of Merit," and hoped virtuous, knowledgeable people like themselves would be elected to office. They opposed hereditary aristocracy, but were not keen on direct democracy, which they feared could bring demagogues to power. They sought to design institutions, such as the indirect election of the U.S. Senate and the president, that would enable the meritorious to govern. Thomas Jefferson favored a "natural aristocracy" based on "virtue and talents" rather than an "artificial aristocracy founded on wealth and birth." "That form of government is the best," he wrote, which provides "for a pure selection of these natural aristoi into the offices of government."[13]

Despite their differences, these traditional versions of political meritocracy—from the Confucian to the Platonic to the republican—share the notion that the merits relevant to governing include moral and civic virtue. This is because all agree that the common good consists, at least in part, in the moral education of citizens.

Our technocratic version of meritocracy severs the link between merit and moral judgment. In the domain of the economy, it simply assumes that the common good is defined by GDP, and that the value of people's contributions consists in the market value of the goods or services they sell. In the domain of government, it assumes that merit means technocratic expertise.

This can be seen in the growing role of economists as policy advisors, the increasing reliance on market mechanisms to define and achieve the public good, and the failure of public discourse to address the large moral and civic questions that should be at the center of political debate: What should we do about rising inequality? What is the moral significance of national borders? What makes for the dignity of work? What do we owe one another as citizens?

This morally blinkered way of conceiving merit and the public good has weakened democratic societies in several ways. The first is the most

28

obvious: Over the past four decades, meritocratic elites have not governed very well. The elites who governed the United States from 1940 to 1980 were far more successful. They won World War II, helped rebuild Europe and Japan, strengthened the welfare state, dismantled segregation, and presided over four decades of economic growth that flowed to rich and poor alike. By contrast, the elites who have governed since have brought us four decades of stagnant wages for most workers, inequalities of income and wealth not seen since the 1920s, the Iraq War, a nineteen-year, inconclusive war in Afghanistan, financial deregulation, the financial crisis of 2008, a decaying infrastructure, the highest incarceration rate in the world, and a system of campaign finance and gerrymandered congressional districts that makes a mockery of democracy.

Not only has technocratic merit failed as a mode of governance; it has also narrowed the civic project. Today, the common good is understood mainly in economic terms. It is less about cultivating solidarity or deepening the bonds of citizenship than about satisfying consumer preferences as measured by the gross domestic product. This makes for an impoverished public discourse.

What passes for political argument these days consists either of narrow, managerial, technocratic talk, which inspires no one; or else shouting matches, in which partisans talk past one another, without really listening. Citizens across the political spectrum find this empty public discourse frustrating and disempowering. They rightly sense that the absence of robust public debate does not mean that no policies are being decided. It simply means they are being decided elsewhere, out of public view—by administrative agencies (often captured by the industries they regulate), by central banks and bond markets, by corporate lobbyists whose campaign contributions buy influence with public officials.

But that's not all. Beyond hollowing out public discourse, the reign of technocratic merit has reconfigured the terms of social recognition in ways that elevate the prestige of the credentialed, professional classes and depreciate the contributions of most workers, eroding their social standing and esteem. It is this aspect of technocratic merit that contributes most directly to the angry, polarized politics of our time.

THE POPULIST UPRISING

Six decades ago, a British sociologist named Michael Young anticipated the hubris and resentment to which meritocracy gives rise. In fact, it was he who coined the term. In a book called *The Rise of the Meritocracy* (1958), he asked what would happen if, one day, class barriers were overcome, so that everyone had a truly equal opportunity to rise based solely on his or her own merit.[14]

In one respect, this would be something to celebrate; the children of the working class would at last compete fairly, side by side with the children of the privileged. But it would not, Young thought, be an unmitigated triumph; for it was bound to foster hubris in the winners and humiliation among the losers. The winners would consider their success a "just reward for their own capacity, for their own efforts, for their own undeniable achievement," and would therefore look down on those less successful than themselves. Those who failed to rise would feel they had no one to blame but themselves.[15]

For Young, meritocracy was not an ideal to aim at but a recipe for social discord. He glimpsed, decades ago, the harsh meritocratic logic that now poisons our politics and animates populist anger. For those who feel aggrieved by the tyranny of merit, the problem is not only stagnant wages but also the loss of social esteem.

The loss of jobs to technology and outsourcing has coincided with a sense that society accords less respect to the kind of work the working class does. As economic activity has shifted from making things to managing money, as society has lavished outsize rewards on hedge fund managers, Wall Street bankers, and the professional classes, the esteem accorded work in the traditional sense has become fragile and uncertain.

Mainstream parties and elites miss this dimension of politics. They think the problem with market-driven globalization is simply a matter of distributive justice; those who have gained from global trade, new technologies, and the financialization of the economy have not adequately compensated those who have lost out.

But this misunderstands the populist complaint. It also reflects a defect in the technocratic approach to governing. Conducting our public discourse as if it were possible to outsource moral and political judgment to markets, or to experts and technocrats, has emptied democratic argument of meaning and purpose. Such vacuums of public meaning are invariably filled by harsh, authoritarian forms of identity and belonging—whether in the form of religious fundamentalism or strident nationalism.

That is what we are witnessing today. Four decades of market-driven globalization have hollowed out public discourse, disempowered ordinary citizens, and prompted a populist backlash that seeks to clothe the naked public square with an intolerant, vengeful nationalism.

To reinvigorate democratic politics, we need to find our way to a morally more robust public discourse, one that takes seriously the corrosive effect of meritocratic striving on the social bonds that constitute our common life.

"GREAT BECAUSE GOOD":

A BRIEF MORAL HISTORY

OF MERIT

There is nothing wrong with hiring people based on merit. In fact, it is generally the right thing to do. If I need a plumber to fix my toilet or a dentist to repair my tooth, I try to find the best person for the job. Well, maybe not the best; I do not conduct a global search. But I certainly want someone well qualified.

In filling jobs, merit matters, for at least two reasons. One is efficiency. I will be better off if my plumber or dentist is capable rather than incompetent. The other is fairness. It would be wrong to discriminate against the most qualified applicant out of racial or religious or sexist prejudice and hire a less-qualified person instead. Even if, for the sake of indulging my prejudice, I were willing to accept a shoddy plumbing repair or root canal, the discrimination would still be unfair. The more qualified candidates could rightly complain that they were victims of injustice.

If hiring based on merit is a good and sensible practice, what possibly could be wrong with a meritocracy? How can so benign a principle as merit fuel a torrent of resentment so potent as to transform the politics of democratic societies around the world? When exactly did merit turn toxic, and how?

WHY MERIT MATTERS

The idea that society should allocate economic rewards and positions of responsibility according to merit is appealing for several reasons. Two of these reasons are generalized versions of the case for merit in hiring—efficiency and fairness. An economic system that rewards effort, initiative, and talent is likely to be more productive than one that pays everyone the same, regardless of contribution, or that hands out desirable social positions based on favoritism. Rewarding people strictly on their merits also has the virtue of fairness; it does not discriminate on any basis other than achievement.

A society that rewards merit is also attractive on aspirational grounds. Not only does it promote efficiency and renounce discrimination; it also affirms a certain idea of freedom. This is the idea that our destiny is in our hands, that our success does not depend on forces beyond our control, that it's up to us. We are not victims of circumstance but masters of our fate, free to rise as far as our effort and talents and dreams will take us.

This is an exhilarating vision of human agency, and it goes hand in hand with a morally comforting conclusion: We get what we deserve. If my success is my own doing, something I've earned through talent and hard work, I can take pride in it, confident that I deserve the rewards my achievements bring. A meritocratic society, then, is doubly inspiring: it affirms a powerful notion of freedom, and it gives people what they have earned for themselves and therefore deserve.

Inspiring though it is, the principle of merit can take a tyrannical turn, not only when societies fail to live up to it, but also—indeed especially—when they do. The dark side of the meritocratic ideal is embedded in its most alluring promise, the promise of mastery and self-making. This promise comes with a burden that is difficult to bear. The meritocratic ideal places great weight on the notion of personal responsibility. Holding people responsible for what they do is a good thing, up to a point. It respects their capacity to think and act for themselves, as moral agents and as citizens. But it is one thing to hold people responsible for acting morally;

34

it is something else to assume that we are, each of us, wholly responsible for our lot in life.

Even the phrase "our lot in life" draws on a moral vocabulary that suggests certain limits to unbridled responsibility. To speak of one's "lot" suggests the drawing of lots, a result determined by fate, fortune, or divine providence, not our own effort.[1] It points beyond merit and choice to the realm of luck and chance, or on some accounts, grace. This reminds us that the most consequential early debates about merit were not about income and jobs but about God's favor: Is it something we earn or receive as a gift?

A COSMIC MERITOCRACY

The notion that our fate reflects our merit runs deep in the moral intuitions of Western culture. Biblical theology teaches that natural events happen for a reason. Favorable weather and a bountiful harvest are divine rewards for good behavior; drought and pestilence are punishments for sin. When a ship encounters stormy seas, people ask who on the crew has angered God.[2]

From the distance of our scientific age, this way of thinking may seem innocent, even childlike. But it is not as distant as it first appears. In fact, this outlook is the origin of meritocratic thinking. It reflects the belief that the moral universe is arranged in a way that aligns prosperity with merit and suffering with wrongdoing. This is not far from the familiar contemporary view that wealth signifies talent and hard work and that poverty signifies indolence.

Two features of the biblical outlook offer an intimation of contemporary meritocracy. One is its emphasis on human agency; the other is its harshness toward those who suffer misfortune. It might seem that contemporary meritocracy emphasizes human agency and will, while the biblical version attributes all power to God. It is he, after all, who doles out the punishments and rewards—the floods, the droughts, the crop-saving rains.

But in fact, this is a highly anthropocentric picture, in which God spends most of his time responding to the promptings of human beings—rewarding their goodness, punishing their sins. God becomes, paradoxically, beholden to us, compelled, insofar as he is just, to give us the treatment we have earned. Although God is the one who bestows the rewards and punishments, he does so according to people's merits, not arbitrarily. So even in the presence of God, humans are seen to earn and therefore to deserve their fate.

Second, this meritocratic way of thinking gives rise to harsh attitudes toward those who suffer misfortune. The more acute the suffering, the greater the suspicion that the victim has brought it on himself. Recall the book of Job. A just and righteous man, Job is subjected to unspeakable pain and suffering, including the death of his sons and daughters in a storm. Ever faithful to God, Job cannot fathom why such suffering has been visited upon him. (He does not realize that he is the victim of a cosmic wager, in which God seeks to prove to Satan that Job's faith will not waver, whatever hardship he encounters.)

As Job mourns the loss of his family, his friends (if one can call them friends) insist that he must have committed some egregious sin, and they press Job to imagine what that sin might be.[3] This is an early example of the tyranny of merit. Armed with the assumption that suffering signifies sin, Job's friends cruelly compound his pain by claiming that, in virtue of some transgression or other, Job must be to blame for the death of his sons and daughters. Although he knows he is innocent, Job shares his companions' theology of merit, and so cries out to God asking why he, a righteous man, is being made to suffer.

When God finally speaks to Job, he rejects the cruel logic of blaming the victim. He does so by renouncing the meritocratic assumption that Job and his companions share. Not everything that happens is a reward or a punishment for human behavior, God proclaims from the whirlwind. All rain is not for the sake of watering the crops of the righteous, nor is every drought for the sake of punishing the wicked. It rains, after all, in places where no one lives—in the wilderness, which is empty of human life. Creation is not only for the sake of human beings. The cosmos is bigger and God's ways more mysterious than the anthropomorphic picture suggests.[4]

God confirms Job's righteousness but chastises him for presuming to grasp the moral logic of God's rule. This represents a radical departure from the theology of merit that informs Genesis and Exodus.[5] In renouncing the idea that he presides over a cosmic meritocracy, God asserts his unbounded power and teaches Job a lesson in humility. Faith in God means accepting the grandeur and mystery of creation, not expecting God to dispense rewards and punishments based on what each person merits or deserves.

SALVATION AND SELF-HELP

The question of merit reappears in Christian debates about salvation: Can the faithful earn salvation through religious observance and good works, or is God entirely free to decide whom to save, regardless of how people live their lives?[6] The first option seems more just, as it rewards goodness and punishes sin. But theologically, it poses a problem, for it calls into question God's omnipotence. If salvation is something we can earn and therefore deserve, then God is bound, so to speak, to recognize our merit. Salvation becomes at least partly a matter of self-help, and this implies a limit to God's infinite power.

The second option, viewing salvation as an unearned gift, affirms God's omnipotence but in doing so raises a different problem: If God is responsible for everything in the world, then he must be responsible for the existence of evil. But if God is just, how can he allow suffering and evil he has the power to prevent? If God is all-powerful, the existence of evil seems to imply that he is unjust. Theologically, it is difficult if not impossible to hold the following three views simultaneously—that God is just, that God is omnipotent, and that evil exists.[7]

One way of resolving this difficulty is to attribute free will to human beings. This shifts the responsibility for evil from God to us. If, in addition to laying down the law, God gave each of us the freedom to decide whether to obey or disobey it, then we are responsible if we choose to do wrong rather than right. Those who act badly will deserve whatever punishment God metes out, in this world or the next. Their suffering will not constitute an evil, but rather just punishment for their transgression.[8]

An early proponent of this solution was a fifth-century British monk named Pelagius. Although he is not well-known, some recent commentators have argued that, as a champion of free will and individual responsibility in early Christian theology, Pelagius was a forerunner of liberalism.[9]

In his day, however, Pelagius's solution generated fierce opposition, not least from Augustine, the most formidable Christian philosopher of the age. For Augustine, attributing free will to humans denies the omnipotence of God and undermines the significance of his ultimate gift, the sacrifice of Christ on the cross. If human beings are so self-sufficient that they can earn salvation on their own, through good works and performing sacraments, then the Incarnation becomes unnecessary. Humility in the face of God's grace gives way to pride in one's own efforts.[10]

Despite Augustine's insistence on salvation by grace alone, the practices of the Church brought merit back in. Rites and rituals—baptism, prayer, attending Mass, performing the sacraments—cannot persist for long without prompting a sense of efficacy among the participants. It is not easy to sustain the belief that faithful religious observance and good works do not win God's favor or generate merit in his eyes. When faith is embodied in outward observance, mediated and reinforced by a complex array of Church practices, a theology of gratitude and grace slides, almost inevitably, toward a theology of pride and self-help. This at least is how Martin Luther viewed the Roman Church of his time, eleven centuries after Augustine had inveighed against salvation by merit.

The Protestant Reformation was born as an argument against merit. Martin Luther's case against the Catholic Church of his day was only partly about the sale of indulgences, the corrupt practice by which rich people tried to buy their way to salvation. (Strictly speaking, the payment was thought to expedite penance and shorten one's stay in purgatory.) His broader point, following Augustine, was that salvation is wholly a matter of God's grace and cannot be influenced by any effort to win God's favor, whether through good works or the performance of rites. We can no more pray our way to heaven than buy our way in. For Luther, election is a gift that is entirely unearned. Seeking to improve our chances by taking communion or attending Mass or otherwise trying to persuade God of our merit is presumptuous to the point of blasphemy.[11]

Luther's stringent doctrine of grace was resolutely anti-meritocratic. It rejected salvation by good works and left no room for human freedom or self-making. And yet, paradoxically, the Protestant Reformation he launched led to the fiercely meritocratic work ethic the Puritans and their successors would bring to America. In *The Protestant Ethic and the Spirit of Capitalism*, Max Weber explains how this happened.[12]

Like Luther, John Calvin, whose theology inspired the Puritans, held that salvation was a matter of God's grace, not determined by human merit or deservingness. Who will be saved and who damned is predestined, not subject to change based on how people live their lives. Even the sacraments cannot help. Although they must be observed to increase the glory of God, "they are not a means to the attainment of grace."[13]

The Calvinist doctrine of predestination created unbearable suspense. It is not hard to see why. If you believe that your place in the afterlife is more important than anything you care about in this world, you desperately want to know whether you are among the elect or the damned. But God does not announce this in advance. We cannot tell by observing people's conduct who is chosen and who is damned. The elect are "God's invisible Church."[14]

As Weber writes, "The question, Am I one of the elect? must sooner or later have arisen for every believer and have forced all other interests into the background. And how can I be sure of this state of grace?" The persistence and urgency of this question led Calvinists to a certain version of the work ethic. Since every person is called by God to work in a vocation, working intensely in that calling is a sign of salvation.[15]

The point of such work is not to enjoy the wealth it produces but to glorify God. Working for the sake of lavish consumption would be a distraction from this end, a kind of corruption. Calvinism combined strenuous work with asceticism. Weber points out that this disciplined approach to work—working hard but consuming little—yields the accumulation of wealth that fuels capitalism. Even when the original religious motivations fall away, the Protestant ethic of work and asceticism provides the cultural basis for capitalist accumulation.

But for our purposes, the significance of this drama consists in the tension that develops between merit and grace. A lifetime of disciplined work in one's calling is not, to be sure, a route to salvation, but rather a way of knowing whether one is (already) among the elect. It is a *sign* of salvation, not its source.

But it proved difficult if not impossible to resist the slide from viewing such worldly activity as a sign of election to viewing it as a source. Psychologically, it is hard to bear the notion that God will take no notice of faithful work that increases his glory. Once I am encouraged to infer from my good works that I am among the elect, it is hard to resist the thought that my good works have somehow contributed to my election. Theologically, the notion of salvation by works, a meritocratic idea, was already present in the background—both in the Catholic emphasis on rites and sacraments and in the Jewish notion of winning God's favor by observing the law and upholding the ethical precepts of the Sinai covenant.

As the Calvinist notion of work in a calling evolved into the Puritan work ethic, it was hard to resist its meritocratic implication—that salvation is earned, and that work is a source, not merely a sign, of salvation. "In practice this means that God helps those who help themselves," Weber observes. "Thus the Calvinist, as it is sometimes put, himself creates his own salvation, or, as would be more correct, the conviction of it." Some Lutherans protested that such a view amounts to a "reversion to the doctrine of salvation by works," precisely the doctrine Luther considered an affront to God's grace.[16]

The Calvinist doctrine of predestination, combined with the idea that the elect must prove their election through work in a calling, leads to the notion that worldly success is a good indication of who is destined for salvation. "For everyone without exception God's Providence has prepared a calling, which he should profess and in which he should labour," Weber explains. This confers divine sanction on the division of labor and supports a "providential interpretation of the economic order."[17]

Proving one's state of grace through worldly activity brings meritocracy back in. The monks of the Middle Ages constituted a kind of "spiritual aristocracy," pursuing their ascetic calling far removed from worldly pursuits. But with Calvinism, Christian asceticism "strode into the market-place of life" and "slammed the door of the monastery behind it." All Christians were called to work and to prove their faith in worldly activity. "By founding its ethic in the doctrine of predestination," Calvinism substituted for "the spiritual aristocracy of monks outside of and above the world the spiritual aristocracy of the predestined saints of God within the world."[18]

Confident of their election, this spiritual aristocracy of the elect looked down with disdain on those apparently destined for damnation. Here Weber glimpses what I would call an early version of meritocratic hubris. "The consciousness of divine grace of the elect and holy was accompanied by an attitude toward the sin of one's neighbor, not of sympathetic understanding based on consciousness of one's own weakness, but of hatred and contempt for him as an enemy of God bearing the signs of eternal damnation."[19]

The Protestant work ethic, then, not only gives rise to the spirit of capitalism. It also promotes an ethic of self-help and of responsibility for one's fate congenial to meritocratic ways of thinking. This ethic unleashes a torrent of anxious, energetic striving that generates great wealth but at the same time reveals the dark side of responsibility and self-making. The humility prompted by helplessness in the face of grace gives way to the hubris prompted by belief in one's own merit.

PROVIDENTIAL THINKING: THEN AND NOW

For Luther, Calvin, and the Puritans, debates about merit were about salvation—do the chosen earn and therefore deserve their election, or is salvation a gift of grace beyond our control? For us, debates about merit are about worldly success—do the successful earn and therefore deserve their success, or is prosperity due to factors beyond our control?

At first glance, these two debates seem to have little in common. One is religious, the other secular. But on closer inspection, the meritocracy of our day bears the mark of the theological contest from which it emerged. The Protestant work ethic began as a tense dialectic of grace and merit, helplessness and self-help. In the end, merit drove out grace. The ethic of mastery and self-making overwhelmed the ethic of gratitude and humility. Working and striving became imperatives of their own, detached from Calvinist notions of predestination and the anxious search for a sign of salvation.

It is tempting to attribute the triumph of mastery and merit to the secular bent of our time. As faith in God recedes, confidence in human agency gathers force; the more we conceive ourselves as self-made and self-sufficient, the less reason we have to feel indebted or grateful for our success.

But even today, our attitudes toward success are not as independent of providential faith as we sometimes think. The notion that we are free human agents, capable of rising and succeeding by our own effort, is only one aspect of meritocracy. Equally important is the conviction that those who succeed deserve their success. This triumphalist aspect of meritocracy generates hubris among the winners and humiliation among the losers. It reflects a residual providential faith that persists in the moral vocabulary of otherwise secular societies.

"The fortunate [person] is seldom satisfied with the fact of being fortunate," Max Weber observed. "Beyond this, he needs to know that he has a *right* to his good fortune. He wants to be convinced that he 'deserves' it, and above all, that he deserves it in comparison with others. He wishes to be allowed the belief that the less fortunate also merely experience [their] due."[20]

The tyranny of merit arises, at least in part, from this impulse. Today's secular meritocratic order moralizes success in ways that echo an earlier providential faith: Although the successful do not owe their power and wealth to divine intervention—they rise thanks to their own effort and hard work—their success reflects their superior virtue. The rich are rich because they are more deserving than the poor.

This triumphalist aspect of meritocracy is a kind of providentialism without God, at least without a God who intervenes in human affairs. The successful make it on their own, but their success attests to their virtue. This way of thinking heightens the moral stakes of economic competition. It sanctifies the winners and denigrates the losers.

The cultural historian Jackson Lears explains how providentialist thinking persisted even as Calvinist notions of predestination and innate human sinfulness fell away. For Calvin and the Puritans, "everyone was equally base in the sight of God." Since no one was deserving, salvation had to depend on God's grace.[21]

> But when liberalizing theologians began to emphasize human be-
> ings' ability to save themselves, success began to signify a conver-
> gence of personal merit and providential plan. Gradually and
> haltingly but unmistakably, the Protestant belief in Providence . . .
> became a way of providing spiritual sanctions for the economic sta-
> tus quo . . . Providence implicitly underwrote inequalities of
> wealth.[22]

Lears sees in American public culture an uneven contest between an ethic of fortune and a more muscular ethic of mastery. The ethic of fortune appreciates the dimensions of life that exceed human understanding and control. It sees that the cosmos does not necessarily match merit with reward. It leaves room for mystery, tragedy, and humility. It is the sensibility of Ecclesiastes: "I returned, and saw under the sun, that the race is not to the swift, nor the battle to the strong, neither yet bread to the wise, nor yet riches to men of understanding, nor yet favour to men of skill; but time and chance happeneth to them all."[23]

The ethic of mastery, by contrast, puts "human choice at the center of the spiritual order."[24] This does not imply a renunciation of God but a recasting of his providential role. Lears shows that the ethic of mastery and control emerges from within evangelical Protestantism, and eventually predominates. It brings a shift from "a covenant of grace to what Luther had reviled, a covenant of works." By the mid-eighteenth century, "the works in question were not sacred rituals (as in traditional Catholicism), but secular moral strivings."[25] But those secular strivings still derived their virtue from a providential plan.

> Providence still governed all, according to Protestant belief . . . But
> human beings could freely choose to participate in the unfolding of

God's plan, could somehow align themselves with God's purpose. Evangelical rationality balanced belief in an overarching providence with an unprecedented celebration of human effort.[26]

Combining human striving with providential sanction creates rocket fuel for meritocracy. It banishes the ethic of fortune and promises to align worldly success with moral deservingness. Lears sees this as a moral loss. "A culture less intent on the individual's responsibility to master destiny might be more capacious, more generous, more gracious." A keener awareness of the unpredictable character of fortune and fate "might encourage fortunate people to imagine their own misfortune and transcend the arrogance of the meritocratic myth—to acknowledge how fitfully and unpredictably people get what they deserve."[27]

Lears assesses the moral and civic damage in stark terms:

The culture of control continues to sustain the smug, secular version of Christian providentialism that has framed American morality for two centuries, though the favored idiom is now technocratic rather than religious. The hubris of the providential view lies in its tendency to sanctify the secular; in its glib assurance not merely that we are all part of a divine—or "evolutionary"—plan, but also that we can actually see that plan at work in prevailing social and economic arrangements, even in the outcome of global power struggles.[28]

The providentialist notion that people get what they deserve reverberates in contemporary public discourse. It comes in two versions—one hubristic, the other punitive. Both versions assert a demanding notion of responsibility for our fate, be it prosperous or calamitous. The financial crisis of 2008 produced a notable example of providential hubris. Risky and greedy behavior by Wall Street banks had brought the global economy to the brink of meltdown, requiring a massive taxpayer bailout. Even as homeowners and Main Street businesses struggled to recover, leading Wall Street bankers were soon paying themselves tens of billions of dollars in bonuses. Asked how he could defend such lavish pay in the face of public outrage, Lloyd Blankfein, CEO of Goldman Sachs, replied that he and his fellow bankers were "doing God's work."[29]

The punitive version of providentialism has recently been voiced by some Christian conservatives in the aftermath of deadly hurricanes and other disasters. When Hurricane Katrina devasted the city of New Orleans in 2005, Reverend Franklin Graham declared that the storm was divine retribution for a "wicked city" known for Mardi Gras, "sex perversion," orgies, and other sinful activities.[30] When an earthquake claimed more than 200,000 lives in Haiti in 2009, the televangelist Pat Robertson attributed the disaster to a pact with the devil that Haitian slaves allegedly made when they rebelled against France in 1804.[31]

Days after the 9/11 terrorist attack on the World Trade Center in New York City, Reverend Jerry Falwell, appearing on Robertson's Christian television program, interpreted the attack as divine retribution for America's sins:

> The abortionists have got to bear some burden for this because God will not be mocked. And when we destroy 40 million little innocent babies, we make God mad. I really believe that the pagans, and the abortionists, and the feminists, and the gays and the lesbians who are actively trying to make that an alternative lifestyle, the ACLU [American Civil Liberties Union] . . . all of them who have tried to secularize America, I point the finger in their face and say, "You helped this happen."[32]

Explaining epic disasters as divine punishment is not exclusive to Christian providentialism. When a devastating earthquake and tsunami struck Japan in 2011, triggering a meltdown at nuclear power plants, Tokyo governor Shintaro Ishihara, an outspoken nationalist, described the event as divine retribution (*tenbatsu*) for Japan's materialism. "We need a tsunami to wipe out egoism, which has rusted onto the mentality of Japanese over a long period of time," he said.[33]

HEALTH AND WEALTH

In recent decades, American Christianity has produced a buoyant new vari-
ant of providentialist faith called the prosperity gospel. Led by televange-
lists and preachers in some of the country's biggest megachurches, it teaches
that God rewards faith with wealth and health. Far from conceiving grace
as a mysterious, unearned gift of God, the prosperity gospel emphasizes
human agency and will. E. W. Kenyon, an early-twentieth-century evangelist who laid the groundwork for the movement, urged Christians to proclaim: "God's ability is mine. God's strength is mine. His success is mine. I
am a winner. I am a conqueror."[34]

Kate Bowler, a historian of the prosperity gospel, writes that its teaching
is summarized in the phrase "I am blessed," where the evidence of being
blessed is being healthy and wealthy.[35] Joel Osteen, a celebrity prosperity
evangelist whose Houston church is the largest in America, told Oprah
Winfrey that "Jesus died that we might live an abundant life."[36] His bestsell-
ing book offers examples of the blessings that flow from faith, including the
mansion in which he lives and the time he was upgraded to business class
on a flight.[37]

It might seem that a gospel of blessedness would prompt humility in the
face of good fortune, rather than the meritocratic conviction that health
and wealth are signs of virtue. But as Bowler observes, "blessed" is a term
that blurs the distinction between gift and reward.

> It can be a term of pure gratitude. "Thank you, God. I could not
> have secured this for myself." But it can also imply that it was de-
> served. "Thank you, me. For being the kind of person who gets it
> right." It is a perfect word for an American society that says it be-
> lieves the American dream is based on hard work, not luck.[38]

Although about one million Americans attend megachurches that preach
the prosperity gospel, its resonance with the American faith in striving and
self-help give it a broader influence. A *Time* magazine poll found that nearly

a third of American Christians agree that "if you give your money to God, God will bless you with more money," and 61 percent believe that "God wants people to be prosperous."[39]

By the early twenty-first century, the prosperity gospel, with its appeal to hard work, upward mobility, and positive thinking, was hard to distinguish from the American dream itself. "The prosperity movement did not simply give Americans a gospel worthy of a nation of self-made men," Bowler writes. "It affirmed the basic economic structures on which individual enterprise stood." And it reinforced the belief that prosperity is a sign of virtue. Like earlier success gospels, it trusted the market "to mete out rewards and punishment in fortune or failure. The virtuous would be richly compensated while the wicked would eventually stumble."[40]

Part of the appeal of the prosperity gospel is its emphasis "on the individual's responsibility for his or her own fate."[41] This is a heady, empowering notion. Theologically, it asserts that salvation is an achievement, something we earn. In worldly terms, it gives people confidence that, with sufficient effort and faith, they can achieve health and wealth. It is relentlessly meritocratic. As with all meritocratic ethics, its exalted conception of individual responsibility is gratifying when things go well but demoralizing, even punitive, when things go badly.

Consider health. What could be more empowering than the belief that our health is in our hands, that the sick can be healed through prayer, that illness can be averted by living well and loving God? But this hyper-agency has a dark side. Illness, when it comes, is not merely a misfortune but a verdict on our virtue. Even death adds insult to injury. "If a believer gets sick and dies," Bowler writes, "shame compounds the grief. Those who are loved and lost are just that—those who have lost the test of faith."[42]

The harsh face of prosperity gospel thinking can be seen in the debate about health care.[43] When Donald Trump and Republicans in Congress attempted to repeal and replace Obamacare, most argued that their market-friendly alternative would increase competition and reduce costs, while protecting people with pre-existing conditions. But Mo Brooks, a conservative Republican congressman from Alabama, made a different argument. He acknowledged that the Republican plan would require those with greater health needs to pay more. But this was a virtue, not a vice, because it would reward those who led good lives. Allowing insurance companies to charge higher premiums to those with higher health care costs was not only cost-effective but morally justified. Higher premiums for the sick would reduce the cost "to those people who lead good lives, they're healthy, they've done the things to keep their bodies healthy. And right now, those are the people—who've done things the right way—that are seeing their costs skyrocketing."[44]

The congressman's case against Obamacare reiterates the harsh meritocratic logic that runs from the Puritans to the prosperity gospel: If prosperity is a sign of salvation, suffering is a sign of sin. This logic is not necessarily tied to religious assumptions. It is a feature of any ethic that conceives human freedom as the unfettered exercise of will and attributes to human beings a thoroughgoing responsibility for their fate.

In 2009, as Obamacare was first being debated, John Mackey, the founder of Whole Foods, wrote an op-ed in *The Wall Street Journal* arguing against a right to health care. His argument relied on libertarian not religious assumptions. And yet, like preachers of the prosperity gospel, he asserted a strenuous notion of individual responsibility, arguing that good health is mainly our own doing.

Many of our health-care problems are self-inflicted: two-thirds of Americans are now overweight and one-third are obese. Most of the diseases that kill us and account for about 70% of all health-care spending—heart disease, cancer, stroke, diabetes and obesity—are mostly preventable through proper diet, exercise, not smoking, minimal alcohol consumption and other healthy lifestyle choices.[45]

Many of those who fall prey to ill health, he argued, have no one to blame but themselves. This is due not to their lack of faith in God but to their lack of attention to scientific and medical evidence showing that a plant-based, low-fat diet "will help prevent and often reverse most degenerative diseases that kill us and are expensive to treat. We should be able to live largely disease-free lives until we are well into our 90s and even past 100 years of age." Although he did not explicitly claim that those who fall ill deserve their disease, he insisted that such people should expect no help from their fellow citizens. "We are all responsible for our own lives and our own health."[46]

For Mackey, as for the prosperity gospel evangelists, good health is a sign of virtue—whether pursued in the pews of a megachurch or in the organic-produce aisles of Whole Foods.

LIBERAL PROVIDENTIALISM

Viewing health and wealth as matters of praise and blame is a meritocratic way of looking at life. It concedes nothing to luck or grace and holds us wholly responsible for our fate; everything that happens is a reward or punishment for the choices we make and for the way we live. This way of thinking celebrates a thoroughgoing ethic of mastery and control and gives rise to meritocratic hubris. It prompts the successful to believe they are "doing God's work" and to look down on victims of misfortune—hurricanes, tsunamis, ill health—as blameworthy for their condition.

Such hubris is not only found among prosperity gospel conservatives and libertarian critics of the welfare state. It is also a prominent feature of liberal and progressive politics. One example is the rhetorical trope of explaining America's power and prosperity in providential terms, as a consequence of its divinely ordained or righteous status. In her speech accepting the Democratic nomination for president in 2016, Hillary Clinton proclaimed, "In the end, it comes down to what Donald Trump doesn't get: America is great because America is good."[47] She used this language often during her campaign, as she sought to persuade voters that Trump's promise to "make America great again" was inconsistent with his malevolence and venality.

But there is no necessary connection between being good and being great. For nations as for persons, justice is one thing, power and wealth another. A glance at history shows that great powers are not necessarily righteous, and morally admirable countries are not necessarily powerful.

The phrase "America is great because America is good" is by now so familiar that we forget its providential presuppositions. It echoes the long-standing conviction that America has a divinely inspired mission in the world, a manifest destiny to conquer a continent or to make the world safe for democracy. But even as the sense of divine mandate recedes, politicians reiterate the claim that our greatness derives from our goodness.

The slogan itself is relatively recent. The first president to use it was Dwight D. Eisenhower, who attributed it, mistakenly, to Alexis de Tocqueville, author of the classic work *Democracy in America*. Speaking in 1953, Eisenhower cited "a wise French visitor who came to America" seeking the source of America's success. Eisenhower quoted the visitor as follows: "Not until I went into the churches of America and heard her pulpits flame with righteousness did I understand the secret of her genius and power. America is great because America is good—and if America ever ceases to be good, America will cease to be great."[48]

Although these sentences do not appear in Tocqueville's work,[49] they proved popular with subsequent presidents, especially Republicans. Presidents Gerald Ford, Ronald Reagan, and George H. W. Bush all used them on inspirational occasions, often when speaking to religious audiences.[50] In a 1984 address to a convention of Christian evangelicals, Ronald Reagan drew explicitly on the providential basis of the slogan:

> All our material wealth and all our influence have been built on our
> faith in God and the bedrock values that follow from that faith. The
> great French philosopher Alexis de Tocqueville, 150 years ago, is
> said to have observed that America is great because America is good.
> And if she ever ceases to be good, she will cease to be great.[51]

In the 1990s, Democrats, seeking to infuse their rhetoric with spiritual resonance, began citing the slogan. As president, Bill Clinton used it nine times; John Kerry and Hillary Clinton both invoked it during their presidential campaigns.[52]

THE RIGHT SIDE OF HISTORY

The claim that America is great because it is good is the bright, uplifting side of the idea that hurricanes are punishment for sin. It is the meritocratic faith applied to a nation. According to a long providential tradition, worldly success is a sign of salvation, or in secular terms, of goodness. But this way of interpreting America's role in history poses a challenge for liberals: If wealthy and powerful countries owe their might to their virtue, can't the same be said of wealthy and powerful citizens?

Many liberals and progressives, especially those with egalitarian commitments, resist the claim that the rich are rich because they are more deserving than the poor. They see this as an ungenerous, moralizing argument used by those who oppose taxing the rich to help the disadvantaged. Against the claim that affluence signifies superior virtue, egalitarian liberals emphasize the contingency of fortune. They point out that success or failure in market societies has as much to do with luck and circumstance as with character and virtue. Many of the factors that separate winners from losers are arbitrary from a moral point of view.

But it is not easy to embrace the moralizing, providential notion that powerful nations owe their greatness to their goodness and at the same time reject the moralizing, meritocratic notion that wealthy individuals owe their fortunes to their virtue. If might signifies right for countries, the same could be said of the "1 percent." Morally and theologically, providentialism abroad and meritocracy at home stand or fall together.

Although politicians of recent decades did not acknowledge this tension explicitly, they gradually resolved it by accepting meritocratic ways of thinking, abroad and at home. The meritocratic outlook implicit in "great-because-good" providentialism found parallel expression in domestic debates about solidarity, responsibility, and the welfare state. Beginning in the 1980s and 1990s, liberals increasingly accepted elements of conservative critiques of the welfare state, including their demanding notion of personal responsibility. Although they did not go so far as to attribute all health and wealth to virtuous behavior, politicians such as Bill Clinton in the U.S. and

Tony Blair in Britain sought to tie welfare eligibility more closely to the personal responsibility and deservingness of the recipients.[53]

The providential aspect of contemporary liberalism can also be glimpsed in another rhetorical turn that touches both foreign and domestic policy. This is the habit of defending one's policies or political allies as being on "the right side of history" and criticizing opponents for being on "the wrong side of history." One might think that debates about "the right side" and "the wrong side" of history would have been at their high point during the Cold War, when Communist and anti-Communist superpowers faced off against each other and claimed that their systems would win the future. Surprisingly, however, no American president used these terms in the context of Cold War debates.[54]

It was not until the 1990s and 2000s that "the right side" and "the wrong side" of history became a staple of political rhetoric, and then mostly by Democrats. President George W. Bush used the phrase only once, telling an audience of U.S. Army soldiers in 2005 that Middle East terrorists were "losing the struggle because they are on the wrong side of history." He added that, thanks to the U.S. invasion of Iraq, "the tide of freedom" was surging across the Middle East. A year later, his vice president, Richard Cheney, speaking on an aircraft carrier, defended the Iraq War, assuring U.S. troops that "our cause is necessary; our cause is just; and we are on the right side of history."[55]

But for the most part, this triumphalist rhetoric was the language of Democratic presidents. Bill Clinton used it twenty-five times during his presidency, Barack Obama thirty-two times.[56] Sometimes Obama used it as Bush and Cheney had done, in describing the struggle against radical Islamic terrorism: "Al Qaida and its affiliates are small men on the wrong side of history," Obama declared in a speech at the U.S. Military Academy in West Point. Addressing the U.S. Air Force Academy, he said that ISIL terrorists would never be "strong enough to destroy Americans or our way of life," in part "because we're on the right side of history."[57]

But Clinton and Obama also used this triumphalist rhetoric in other contexts. This reflected their confidence, following the fall of the Berlin

Wall and the breakup of the Soviet Union, that history was moving ineluctably toward the spread of liberal democracy and free markets. In 1994, Clinton expressed optimism for the prospects of Boris Yeltsin, Russia's first democratically elected president, saying, "He believes in democracy. He's on the right side of history." Responding to democratic stirrings in the Muslim world, Obama, in his first inaugural address, issued a stern warning to tyrants and despots: "To those who cling to power through corruption and deceit and the silencing of dissent, know that you are on the wrong side of history."[58]

When, in 2009, Iranians engaged in street protests against their repressive regime, Obama praised them, saying, "Those who stand up for justice are always on the right side of history." When the Arab Spring of 2011 prompted hope that democracy would displace autocracy in North Africa and the Middle East, Obama also invoked history's verdict. He stated that the Libyan dictator Muammar Qadhafi was "on the wrong side of history" and supported his removal from power. Questioned about his administration's muted support for pro-democracy protestors in Egypt's Tahrir Square, Obama replied: "I think history will end up recording that at every juncture in the situation in Egypt, that we were on the right side of history."[59]

There are two problems with arguing from history before it happens. First, predicting how things will turn out is notoriously tricky. Ousting Saddam Hussein did not bring freedom and democracy to the Middle East. Even the hopes of the Arab Spring soon gave way to a winter of renewed autocracy and repression. From the vantage point of Vladimir Putin's Russia, Yeltsin's democratic moment now looks ephemeral.

Second, even if history's course could be predicted, it offers no basis for moral judgment. As things turned out, Putin not Yeltsin was on the right side of history, at least in the sense that his autocratic way of governing Russia has prevailed. In Syria, the tyrant Bashar al-Assad survived a brutal civil war, and in this sense was on the right side of history. But this does not mean that his regime is morally defensible.

THE ARC OF THE MORAL UNIVERSE

Those who defend their cause as being on the right side of history might reply that they are thinking of the longer sweep of history. But this reply depends on a further assumption: given enough time, and notwithstanding the fitful pace of progress, history bends toward justice. This assumption brings out the providentialism implicit in arguments that appeal to the right side of history. Such arguments rest on the belief that history unfolds in a way that is directed by God, or by a secular bent toward moral progress and improvement.

Barack Obama held this view and spoke of it often. He frequently cited the saying of Martin Luther King, Jr., that "the arc of the moral universe is long, but it bends toward justice." So fond was Obama of this quotation that, as president, he cited it thirty-three times in speeches and proclamations and had it woven into a rug in the Oval Office.[60]

This providential faith provides the moral warrant for talk about "the right side" and "the wrong side" of history. It also supports the claim that America (or any country) is great because it is good. For only if a nation is doing God's work, or advancing history's march toward freedom and justice, can its greatness be a sign of its goodness.

Believing that one's projects and purposes are aligned with God's plan, or with a vision of freedom and justice unfolding in history, is a potent source of hope, especially for people struggling against injustice. King's teaching that the arc of the moral universe "bends toward justice" inspired civil rights marchers of the 1950s and 1960s to carry on, even in the face of violent opposition by segregationists. King drew this memorable phrase from a sermon by Theodore Parker, a nineteenth-century abolitionist minister from Massachusetts. Parker's version, less succinct than King's, showed how providential theology can serve as a wellspring of hope for the oppressed:

Look at the facts of the world. You see a continual and progressive triumph of the right. I do not pretend to understand the moral universe; the arc is a long one, my eye reaches but little ways. I cannot calculate the curve and complete the figure by the experience of sight; I can divine it by conscience. And from what I see I am sure it bends toward justice. Things refuse to be mismanaged long. Jefferson trembled when he thought of slavery and remembered that God is just. Ere long all America will tremble.[61]

In King's hands, as in Parker's, the faith that the arc of the moral universe bends toward justice is a stirring, prophetic call to act against injustice. But the same providential faith that inspires hope among the powerless can prompt hubris among the powerful. This can be seen in the changing sensibility of liberalism in recent decades, as the moral urgency of the civil rights era gave way to a complacent triumphalism in the aftermath of the Cold War.

The collapse of the Soviet Union and the fall of the Berlin Wall led many in the West to assume that history had vindicated their model of liberal democracy and free-market capitalism. Empowered by this assumption, they promoted a neoliberal version of globalization that included free-trade agreements, the deregulation of finance, and other measures to ease the flow of goods, capital, and people across national boundaries. They confidently expected that the expansion of global markets would increase global interdependence, lessen the likelihood of war among nations, temper nationalist identities, and promote respect for human rights. The salubrious effects of global commerce and new information technologies might even loosen the grip of authoritarian regimes and coax them in the direction of liberal democracy.

Things did not turn out this way. The globalization project would bring on a financial crisis in 2008 and, eight years later, a fierce political backlash. Nationalism and authoritarianism would not fade away but gain momentum around the world and come to threaten liberal institutions and norms within democratic societies.

But in the 1980s and 1990s, as market-friendly globalization gathered force, the elites who promoted it had little doubt about where history was heading. From the early 1980s to 2008, the use of "the right side of history" increased more than eightfold in books tracked by Google.[62]

Proponents of globalization were confident that history was on their side. Urging Congress to pass NAFTA (the North American Free Trade Agreement) in 1993, Bill Clinton tried to assuage fears that the deal threatened the job prospects of American workers. But his greatest concern was that a defeat for NAFTA would be a blow to globalization: "The thing that I'm most worried about is that it will put America on the wrong side of history . . . as we move toward the 21st century. That overwhelms every other concern." Speaking in Berlin in 1998, Clinton praised Germany for "making a difficult transition to a global economy." Though many German citizens "may not yet feel the benefits," he said, Germany's embrace of globalization placed it "clearly on the right side of history."[63]

For liberals, being on the right side of history did not mean embracing unbridled free-market economics. It meant promoting global capitalism abroad while combatting discrimination and expanding equal opportunity at home. Health insurance reform, family and medical leave legislation, tax credits for college tuition, and an executive order preventing federal contractors from discriminating against LGBT employees were among the policies that Clinton and Obama, at various times, identified with "the right side of history." In a speech endorsing Obama at the 2008 Democratic National Convention, Clinton recalled winning the presidency despite Republican charges that he was too young and inexperienced to be commander in chief. "It didn't work in 1992, because we were on the right side of history. And it won't work in 2008, because Barack Obama is on the right side of history."[64]

Opposing discrimination and expanding opportunity are worthy causes. Hillary Clinton made them the central themes of her 2016 presidential campaign. But by then, when neoliberal globalization had produced vast inequalities of income and wealth, an economy dominated by finance, a political system in which money spoke louder than citizens, and a rising tide of angry nationalism, the project of improving equality of opportunity seemed inadequate to the moment, a pale expression of providential hope.

When Obama spoke of the arc of the moral universe bending toward justice, he added an assurance that King had not: "Eventually, America gets it right."[65] But this changed the spirit of King's message.

Over time, Obama's providentialism became less a prophetic call for change than a kind of righteous repose, a comforting reassertion of American exceptionalism. Progress "doesn't always go in a straight line," he explained at a 2012 fundraising event in Beverly Hills, California, "it goes in zigs and zags. And there are times where the body politic takes a wrong turn, and there are times where there are folks who are left out. But what makes America exceptional is that, eventually, we get it right. What Dr. King called the arc of the moral universe, it bends towards justice. That's what makes America different. That's what makes America special."[66]

In 1895, Katharine Lee Bates, a Wellesley College professor and social reformer, published a patriotic poem called "America the Beautiful." Fifteen years later, a church organist set it to music. The song, an ode to American goodness, became one of America's most popular patriotic songs; many wanted it to become the national anthem.[67]

Unlike "The Star-Spangled Banner," America's official anthem, "America the Beautiful" was a pacific hymn. It celebrated the country's "purple mountained majesty," not "the rockets' red glare, the bombs bursting in air." The song's refrain was a prayer asking for God's grace:

America! America!
God shed His grace on thee.
And crown thy good with brotherhood
From sea to shining sea![68]

But the line about God's grace was open to two interpretations. It could be read as expressing a wish: "[May] God shed His grace on thee." Or it could be read in the past tense, as a statement of fact: "God [has] shed His grace on thee."[69]

It is clear from the rest of the lyrics that the poet intends the first meaning, a prayer for God's grace. The next line makes this clear. It does not say that God "crowned" thy good with brotherhood; it expresses the hope that he will do so.

Inevitably, many Americans interpret the line "God shed His grace on thee" in the second way, as a statement of fact. This reflects the assertive rather than the aspirational strand of American providentialism. God's grace is not an unearned gift but something we deserve and have in fact achieved. "America is great because America is good."

The balance between merit and grace is not easy to sustain. From the Puritans to the preachers of the prosperity gospel, the ethic of earning and achieving has exerted an almost irresistible allure, threatening always to override the humbler ethic of hoping and praying, of gratitude and gift. Merit drives out grace, or else recasts it in its own image, as something we deserve.

On October 28, 2001, just weeks after the 9/11 attacks, Ray Charles, the legendary African American soul singer and musician, blind since childhood, performed an electrifying rendition of "America the Beautiful" prior to game two of the World Series. Charles was renowned for performing the song as no one else could, evoking aching sorrow and redemptive joy. That night, as he always did, Charles added a riff that allowed his listeners to conclude that America's grace was not a hope and a prayer but a fait accompli:

America! America!
God done shed His grace on thee. Oh yes he did.
And crowned thy good—I doubt you remember—saving brotherhood,
From sea to shining sea.[70]

As the last chords echoed in the stadium, four F-16 fighter jets streaked overhead. The plaintive poignance of Charles's song gave way to something harder, less forgiving. Here was the assertive face of providential faith. The arc of the moral universe may bend toward justice, but God helps those who help themselves.

3

THE RHETORIC OF RISING

These days, we view success the way the Puritans viewed salvation—not as a matter of luck or grace, but as something we earn through our own effort and striving. This is the heart of the meritocratic ethic. It celebrates freedom—the ability to control my destiny by dint of hard work—and deservingness. If I am responsible for having accrued a handsome share of worldly goods—income and wealth, power and prestige—I must deserve them. Success is a sign of virtue. My affluence is my due.

This way of thinking is empowering. It encourages people to think of themselves as responsible for their fate, not as victims of forces beyond their control. But it also has a dark side. The more we view ourselves as self-made and self-sufficient, the less likely we are to care for the fate of those less fortunate than ourselves. If my success is my own doing, their failure must be their fault. This logic makes meritocracy corrosive of commonality. Too strenuous a notion of personal responsibility for our fate makes it hard to imagine ourselves in other people's shoes.

Over the past four decades, meritocratic assumptions have deepened their hold on the public life of democratic societies. Even as inequality has widened to vast proportions, the public culture has reinforced the notion that we are responsible for our fate and deserve what we get. It is almost as if globalization's winners needed to persuade themselves, and everyone else, that those perched on top and those at the bottom have landed where they belong. Or if not, that they would land where they belong if only we could remove unfair barriers to opportunity. Political argument between mainstream center-right and center-left parties in recent decades has consisted mainly of a debate about how to interpret and implement equality of opportunity, so that people will be able to rise as far as their efforts and talents will take them.

STRIVING AND DESERVING

I first noticed the rising tide of meritocratic sentiment by listening to my students. Having taught political philosophy at Harvard since 1980, I am sometimes asked how student opinions have changed over the years. I generally find this question difficult to answer. In classroom debates about the subjects I teach—justice, markets and morals, the ethics of new technologies—students have always voiced a wide range of moral and political views. I have not noticed any decisive trend, with one exception: Beginning in the 1990s and continuing to the present, more and more of my students seem drawn to the conviction that their success is their own doing, a product of their effort, something they have earned. Among the students I teach, this meritocratic faith has intensified.

At first, I assumed this was because they came of age during the era of Ronald Reagan and had absorbed the individualistic philosophy of the time. But these were not, for the most part, politically conservative students. Meritocratic intuitions reach across the political spectrum. They emerge with special intensity in discussions of affirmative action in college admissions. Whether students are for or against affirmative action policies, most voice the conviction that they worked hard to qualify for admission to Harvard and therefore merited their place. The suggestion that they were admitted due to luck or other factors beyond their control provokes strong resistance.

It is not hard to understand the growing meritocratic sentiment among students in selective colleges. Over the past half century, admission to elite colleges has become increasingly daunting. As recently as the mid-1970s, Stanford accepted nearly a third of those who applied. In the early 1980s, Harvard and Stanford admitted about one applicant in five; in 2019, they accepted fewer than one in twenty. As competition for admission has intensified, the adolescent years of children who aspire to top colleges (or whose parents aspire for them) have become a battleground of fevered striving—a highly scheduled, pressure-packed, stress-inducing regime of Advanced Placement courses, private college counselors, SAT tutors, athletic and other extracurricular activities, internships and good deeds in distant lands designed to impress college admissions committees—all supervised by anxious hyper-parents seeking the best for their kids.

It is difficult to emerge from this gauntlet of stress and striving without believing that you have earned, through effort and hard work, whatever success may come your way. This does not make students selfish or ungenerous. Many devote copious amounts of time to public service and other good works. But the experience does make them staunch meritocrats; like their Puritan forebears, they believe they deserve the success their hard work has won.

The meritocratic sensibility I've noticed among college students is not only an American phenomenon. In 2012, I gave a talk at Xiamen University, on the southeast coast of China. My subject was the moral limits of markets. Recent headlines had told of a Chinese teenager who sold one of his kidneys to buy an iPhone and iPad.[1] I asked the students what they thought about this case. In the debate that ensued, many students took the libertarian view: If the teenager freely agreed, without pressure or coercion, to sell his kidney, he should have the right to do so. Others disagreed, arguing that it is unfair for the rich to be able to extend their lives by buying kidneys from the poor. A student toward the back of the hall offered a reply: Having earned their wealth, rich people are meritorious and so deserve to live longer.

I was taken aback by this brazen application of meritocratic thinking. In retrospect, I realize that it is morally akin to the prosperity gospel belief that health and wealth are signs of God's favor. Of course, the Chinese student who voiced it was probably not steeped in Puritan or providential traditions. But he and his classmates had come of age during China's turn to a market society.

The notion that those who prosper deserve the money they make runs deep in the moral intuitions of the students I have encountered during visits, over the past decade, to a number of Chinese universities. Notwithstanding the cultural differences, these Chinese students, like my Harvard students, are the winners of a hyper-competitive admissions process that unfolds against the background of a hyper-competitive market society. It is no wonder that they resist the thought that we are indebted for our success and attracted to the idea that we earn, and therefore deserve, whatever rewards the system bestows on our efforts and talents.

MARKETS AND MERIT

As Deng Xiaoping was launching China's market reforms in the late 1970s and early 1980s, Margaret Thatcher in the United Kingdom and Ronald Reagan in the United States were seeking to move their societies toward a greater reliance on markets. This period of market faith set the stage for the rise of meritocratic values and practices in the decades that followed.

To be sure, markets do not necessarily rest on meritocratic assumptions. The most familiar arguments for markets are about utility and freedom. The first argues that markets create incentives that boost GDP and maximize the general welfare; the second argues that markets leave people free to choose what value to place on the goods they exchange.

But the market triumphalism of the 1980s prompted the articulation of a third, meritocratic rationale: Provided they operate within a fair system of equal opportunity, markets give people what they deserve. As long as everyone has an equal chance to compete, market outcomes reward merit.

The meritocratic ethic was implicit, at times, in the free-market conservativism of Thatcher and Reagan. But it came to its fullest articulation in the politics of the center-left figures who succeeded them. This is due to a distinctive feature of center-left political argument in the 1990s and since:

Rather than challenge the premise of Thatcher and Reagan's market faith, political figures such as Tony Blair and Bill Clinton accepted it and sought to soften its harshest features.

They accepted the Reagan-Thatcher notion that market mechanisms are the primary instruments for achieving the public good. But they wanted to ensure that markets operated under fair conditions. All citizens, whatever their race or class, religion or ethnicity, gender or sexual orientation, should be able to compete on equal terms for the rewards that markets bestow. For the center-left liberals, equality of opportunity required more than the absence of discrimination; it also required access to education, health care, child care, and other services that enable people to compete effectively in the labor market.

Here then was the argument of center-left, market-friendly liberalism from the 1990s to 2016: Enabling everyone to compete on equal terms was not only compatible with a market society but a way to fulfill its underlying principles. Two such principles were fairness and productivity. Eliminating discrimination and expanding opportunity would make markets more fair, and enlisting a wider pool of talent would make markets more productive. (Bill Clinton often advanced the fairness argument under cover of the productivity argument, as when he said, "We don't have a person to waste.")[2]

But beyond fairness and productivity, the liberal argument also gestured toward a third, more potent ideal implicit in the case for markets: Enabling people to compete solely on the basis of effort and talent would bring market outcomes into alignment with merit. In a society where opportunities were truly equal, markets would give people their just deserts.

Over the past four decades, the language of merit and deservingness has become central to public discourse. One aspect of the meritocratic turn displays the hard side of meritocracy. This aspect finds expression in the demanding notions of personal responsibility that have accompanied attempts to rein in the welfare state and to shift risks from governments and companies to individuals.[3] A second aspect of the meritocratic turn is more aspirational. It finds expression in what might be called the rhetoric of rising, the promise that those who work hard and play by the rules deserve to rise as far as their talents and dreams will take them. The rhetoric of personal responsibility and the rhetoric of rising, having animated political argument in recent decades, eventually contributed to the populist backlash against meritocracy.

THE RHETORIC OF RESPONSIBILITY

In the 1980s and 1990s, the rhetoric of responsibility figured prominently in debates about the welfare state. Through much of the twentieth century, arguments over the welfare state were arguments about solidarity, about what we owe one another as citizens. Some held more demanding notions of solidarity, others more limited ones. Since the 1980s, debates about the welfare state have been less about solidarity than about the extent to which the disadvantaged are responsible for their misfortune. Some assert more demanding notions of personal responsibility, others more restrictive ones.

Expansive conceptions of personal responsibility are a clue that meritocratic assumptions are in play. The more thoroughgoing our responsibility for our fate, the more we merit praise or blame for the way our lives turn out.

The Reagan-Thatcher critique of the welfare state argued that people should be held responsible for their own well-being, and that the community owed help only to those whose misfortune was not their own fault. "We will never abandon those who, through no fault of their own, must have our help," Reagan declared in a State of the Union address. "But let us work to see how many can be freed from the dependency of welfare and made self-supporting."[4] "Through no fault of their own" is a revealing phrase. It begins as a trope of generosity; those who are needy "through no fault of their own" have a claim on the community's help. But, like all attributions of responsibility, it also has a harsh side. If those who are victims of circumstance deserve our help, those who had a hand in their own misfortune arguably do not.

In presidential rhetoric, the phrase "through no fault of their own" was first used by Calvin Coolidge and Herbert Hoover. It implies a stringent notion of personal responsibility; those whose poverty or ill health is due to bad choices they have made do not deserve government help and should be left to fend for themselves. Franklin D. Roosevelt employed the phrase from time to time, in the course of arguing that people thrown out of work by the Great Depression could hardly be blamed for being unemployed.[5]

Ronald Reagan, seeking to reduce the role of government, used the phrase more frequently than any prior president. But each of his Democratic successors, Bill Clinton and Barack Obama, employed it more than twice as often as Reagan did.[6] In doing so, they, like Reagan, implicitly distinguished between the deserving and the undeserving poor. Those who struggled due to forces beyond their control were deserving of government assistance; those who were responsible for their misfortune, possibly not.

In 1992, Clinton campaigned for the presidency promising to "end welfare as we know it." As president, he connected the rhetoric of responsibility with the rhetoric of rising, evoking both the hard side and the aspirational face of meritocracy. "We must do what America does best," he proclaimed in this first Inaugural Address. "Offer more opportunity to all and demand more responsibility from all. It is time to break the bad habit of expecting something for nothing from our Government or from each other."[7]

The rhetoric of responsibility and the rhetoric of rising had this in common: both gestured toward the ideal of self-reliance and self-making. In the 1980s and 1990s, responsibility meant getting off welfare and finding a job. Opportunity meant acquiring the education and skills to compete effectively in the labor market. If opportunities were equal, people would rise based on their efforts and talents, and their success would be the measure of their merit. "All Americans have not just a right but a solemn responsibility to rise as far as their God-given talents and determination can take them," Clinton declared. "Opportunity and responsibility: They go hand in hand. We can't have one without the other."[8]

Clinton echoed Reagan's argument that welfare should be restricted to those who were needy "through no fault of their own." "Government's role," Clinton stated, is to "create economic opportunity and to help people who, through no fault of their own, have sustained economic burdens."[9] In 1996, he signed into law a welfare reform measure, opposed by many of his fellow Democrats, that demanded "personal responsibility," required welfare recipients to work, and limited the time they could stay on welfare.[10]

The new emphasis on responsibility, and its meritocratic implications, reached across the Atlantic. As Clinton was enacting welfare reform in the name of "personal responsibility," Tony Blair, soon to become prime minister of Britain, was sounding a similar message: "We need a new settlement on welfare for a new age, where opportunity and responsibility go together." Blair was explicit about the meritocratic inspiration of his politics. "New Labour is committed to meritocracy," he wrote. "We believe that people should be able to rise by their talents, not by their birth or the advantages of privilege."[11]

A few years later, in Germany, Chancellor Gerhard Schröder justified welfare reform in similar terms:

> With these measures, we are weatherizing our welfare state against the storms of globalization. In doing this we will, in every respect, need to increase responsibility: More personal responsibility for ourselves and more common responsibility for the opportunities of our children . . . In terms of social policy this means: Everybody has the same opportunities. But it also means that everybody has the duty to seize their opportunities.[12]

The rhetoric of responsibility is by now so familiar that it is easy to miss its distinctive meaning in recent decades, and its connection to meritocratic understandings of success. Political leaders have long spoken of responsibility, typically referring to citizens' duties to their country and fellow citizens. But as Yascha Mounk points out, responsibility now refers to "our responsibility to take care of ourselves—and to suffer the consequences if we fail to do so." The welfare state has become less "responsibility buffering" and more "responsibility tracking." Limiting welfare eligibility to those who fall on hard times through bad luck rather than bad behavior is an example, an attempt to treat people according to their merits.[13]

AS FAR AS YOUR TALENTS WILL TAKE YOU

The rhetoric of rising is also novel in a way that can easily escape notice. Ideals of equal opportunity and upward mobility have long been a part of the American dream. They also inspire many other societies. The notion that people should be able to rise "as far as their talents and hard work will take them" is familiar to the point of cliché. It is hardly controversial. Mainstream politicians constantly invoke it. No one argues against it.

So it is surprising to discover that this slogan is relatively new. It only became prominent in American political discourse in the last four decades. Ronald Reagan was the first U.S. president to make it a mainstay of his political rhetoric. Speaking at a White House briefing for Black members of his administration, he made explicit the connection between merit and the right to rise. "All Americans have the right to be judged on the sole basis of individual merit," he said, "and to go just as far as their dreams and hard work will take them." For Reagan, the rhetoric of rising was not only about overcoming discrimination. It had many uses, including arguing for tax cuts. Lower taxes would "knock down the barriers on the road to success so that all Americans can go as far as their hard work, skill, imagination, and creativity will take them."[14]

Bill Clinton adopted Reagan's slogan and used it frequently. "The American dream that we were all raised on is a simple but powerful one: If you work hard and play by the rules, you should be given a chance to go as far as your God-given ability will take you." By the 2000s, the rhetoric of rising had become a bipartisan rhetorical reflex. Republicans George W. Bush, John McCain, and Marco Rubio all invoked it. But no American president was as attached to the slogan as Barack Obama, who used it more than all previous presidents combined. In fact, it was arguably the central theme of his presidency.[15]

"When it comes to higher education," Obama told a gathering of educators at the White House, what ultimately matters "is making sure that bright, motivated young people . . . have the chance to go as far as their talents and their work ethic and their dreams can take them." He viewed a college education as the primary vehicle of upward mobility. "Now, as a nation, we don't promise equal outcomes, but we were founded on the idea [that] everybody should have an equal opportunity to succeed. No matter who you are, what you look like, where you come from, you can make it. That's an essential promise of America. Where you start should not determine where you end up. And so I'm glad that everybody wants to go to college."[16]

On another occasion, Obama cited the example of his wife, Michelle, who had grown up in a working-class family but attended Princeton and Harvard Law School and was able to rise. "Michelle and her brother were able to get an unbelievable education and go as far as their dreams would take them." This supported Obama's belief that "what makes America so exceptional, what makes us so special, is this basic bargain, this basic idea that in this country, no matter what you look like, no matter where you come from, no matter what your last name is, no matter what setbacks you may experience, in this country, if you work hard, if you are willing to take responsibility, then you can make it. You can get ahead."[17]

Echoing Reagan and Clinton, Obama's rhetoric of rising pointed toward meritocracy. It emphasized non-discrimination ("no matter what you look like, no matter where you come from"), insisted on hard work, and admonished citizens to "take responsibility" for themselves. Here then was the link between the rhetoric of rising and the meritocratic ethic: If opportunities are truly equal, then not only will people rise as far as their talents and hard work will take them; their success will be their own doing, and they will deserve the rewards that come their way.

GETTING WHAT YOU DESERVE

As the rhetoric of rising became prominent, the language of merit and deservingness found growing expression throughout the public culture. Recall the ubiquitous McDonald's advertising slogan (and jingle) of the 1970s and 1980s: "You deserve a break today." Or consider books and newspapers.

According to Google Ngram, which tracks the frequency of words and phrases in books, the use of the phrase "you deserve" more than tripled from 1970 to 2008. In *The New York Times*, "you deserve" appeared more than four times as often in 2018 as it did in the year Ronald Reagan took office.[18]

Some invocations of deservingness were explicitly related to meritocratic thinking. For example, a 1988 *New York Times* article described a growing market for motivational tapes with hypnotic, subliminal messages murmured under the sound of ocean waves. One such message: "I deserve to do better than Dad. I deserve to succeed. I deserve to reach my goals. I deserve to be rich." But as the language of deservingness infused popular culture, it became a soothing, all-purpose promise of success, as in the headline that accompanied a recent *New York Times* recipe: "You Deserve More Succulent Chicken." (The secret to achieving the tender chicken you deserve? "Don't overcook it.")[19]

As the language of merit and desert became prominent in everyday life, something similar was happening in academic philosophy. In the 1960s and 1970s, the leading Anglo-American philosophers rejected meritocracy on the grounds that what people earn in the market depends on contingencies beyond their control, such as demand for one's talents and whether one's talents are common or rare. But by the 1980s and 1990s, an influential group of philosophers, perhaps reflecting the "rhetoric of responsibility" prevalent in the politics of the day, revived the case for merit. Known as "luck egalitarians," they argued that society's obligation to help the disadvantaged depends on figuring out who among the needy are responsible for their misfortune and who are victims of bad luck. Only those who bear no responsibility for their plight, they maintained, deserve help from the government.[20]

Among politicians, the language of merit and deservingness accompanied the rhetoric of rising. In the 1960s and 1970s, U.S. presidents rarely sought to sway their audiences by telling them what they deserved. John F. Kennedy never used the term "you deserve." That changed with Reagan, who used "you deserve" more often than his five predecessors combined.[21] Speaking to a group of business leaders in 1983, for example, he said that those who succeed by their own efforts deserve to be rewarded.

> This nation was not built on a foundation of envy and resentment. The dream I've always believed in is, no matter who you are, no matter where you come from, if you work hard, pull yourself up and succeed, then, by golly, you deserve life's prize. And trying for that prize made America the greatest nation on Earth.[22]

After Reagan, "you deserve" became a non-partisan fixture of presidential discourse. Clinton used it twice as often as Reagan; Obama, three times as often, in contexts ranging from the quotidian to the consequential. Speaking in a city that had received a job-producing Defense Department administrative center, Clinton said, "You got it because you deserve it." Addressing a group of warehouse workers, Obama declared, "If you put in a hard day's work, you deserve decent pay for it." Speaking at a community college in Ohio, he defended tax cuts for the middle class, saying, "You deserve a break; you deserve some help."[23]

In the United Kingdom, the faith in meritocracy voiced by Tony Blair in the 1990s continued to inform British politics, even after the Brexit vote. In 2016, shortly after becoming prime minister, Theresa May set out her "vision for a truly meritocratic Britain." Speaking of "ordinary, working-class people," May declared, "They deserve a better deal." The better deal she offered consisted in living up to meritocratic principles.[24]

> I want Britain to be the world's great meritocracy—a country where everyone has a fair chance to go as far as their talent and their hard work will allow . . . I want Britain to be a place where advantage is based on merit not privilege; where it's your talent and hard work that matter, not where you were born, who your parents are or what your accent sounds like.[25]

Notwithstanding their talk of rising and deserving, most American politicians do not speak explicitly about meritocracy. Obama was an exception.

For example, in an interview with an ESPN sports commentator, he mused that what attracts people to sports is that "it's one of the few places where it's a true meritocracy. There's not a lot of BS. Ultimately, who's winning, who's losing, who's performing, who's not—it's all laid out there."[26]

During her 2016 presidential campaign, Hillary Clinton drew frequently on the rhetoric of rising and deserving: "Our campaign is about the fundamental belief that, in America, every person, no matter what you look like, who you are, who you love, you should have the chance to go as far as your hard work and dreams will take you." She vowed, if elected, to "make it possible for you to get the chances and the opportunities you deserve to have." At one campaign rally, she declared, "I want this to be a true meritocracy. I'm tired of inequality. I want people to feel like they can get ahead if they work for it."[27]

POPULIST BACKLASH

To Hillary Clinton's misfortune, the rhetoric of rising had, by 2016, lost its capacity to inspire. Donald Trump, the candidate who defeated her, did not speak about upward mobility or the belief that Americans can rise as far as their talent and hard work will take them. As best I can determine, Trump never used this slogan during his campaign, nor has he used it during his presidency. Instead, he offered blunt talk of winners and losers, and promised to make America great again. But his vision of greatness had nothing to do with fulfilling the meritocratic project that had animated American public discourse for the previous four decades.

In fact, there is reason to think that populist antipathy toward meritocratic elites played a part in Trump's election, and in the surprising vote in Britain, earlier that year, to leave the European Union. Elections are complicated events, and it is difficult to say conclusively what prompts voters to vote as they do. But many working-class supporters of Trump, Brexit, and populist parties in other countries seemed less interested in promises of upward mobility than in reassertions of national sovereignty, identity, and pride. They resented meritocratic elites, experts, and professional classes, who had celebrated market-driven globalization, reaped the benefits, consigned working people to the discipline of foreign competition, and who seemed to identify more with global elites than with their fellow citizens.

Not all populist grievances against the established order were reactions against meritocratic hubris. Some were entangled with xenophobia, racism, and hostility to multiculturalism. But the populist backlash was provoked, at least in part, by the galling sense that those who stood astride the hierarchy of merit looked down with disdain on those they considered less accomplished than themselves. This populist complaint is not without warrant. For decades, meritocratic elites intoned the mantra that those who work hard and play by the rules can rise as far as their talents will take them. They did not notice that for those stuck at the bottom or struggling to stay afloat, the rhetoric of rising was less a promise than a taunt.

This is how Trump voters may have heard Hillary Clinton's meritocratic mantra. For them, the rhetoric of rising was more insulting than inspiring. This is not because they rejected meritocratic beliefs. To the contrary: They embraced meritocracy, but believed it described the way things already worked. They did not see it as an unfinished project requiring further government action to dismantle barriers to achievement. This is partly because they feared such intervention would favor ethnic and racial minorities, thus violating rather than vindicating meritocracy as they saw it. But it is also because, having worked hard to achieve a modicum of success, they had accepted the harsh verdict of the market in their own case, and were invested in it, morally and psychologically.

A survey conducted after the 2016 election asked Trump supporters and opponents to agree or disagree with several statements about how well the United States conformed to meritocratic principles, including the following: "Overall, U.S. society is equitable and fair." "Individuals are personally responsible for their position in society." "Opportunities for economic advancement are available to anyone who cares to look for them." "Society has reached a point where white Americans and racial/ethnic minority Americans have equal opportunities for achievement."[28] Unsurprisingly, well-off respondents agreed with these statements more readily than those from lesser economic backgrounds. But independent of class status, Trump supporters agreed more strongly with each of these statements than did non-supporters.[29] Trump supporters resented liberals' rhetoric of rising, not because they rejected meritocracy, but because they believed it described the prevailing social order. They had submitted to its discipline, had accepted the hard judgment it pronounced on their own merits, and believed others should do the same.

The tyranny of merit arises from more than the rhetoric of rising. It consists in a cluster of attitudes and circumstances that, taken together, have made meritocracy toxic. First, under conditions of rampant inequality and stalled mobility, reiterating the message that we are responsible for our fate and deserve what we get erodes solidarity and demoralizes those left behind by globalization. Second, insisting that a college degree is the primary route to a respectable job and a decent life creates a credentialist prejudice that undermines the dignity of work and demeans those who have not been to college; and third, insisting that social and political problems are best solved by highly educated, value-neutral experts is a technocratic conceit that corrupts democracy and disempowers ordinary citizens.

CAN YOU MAKE IT IF YOU TRY?

When politicians reiterate a hallowed verity with mind-numbing frequency, there is reason to suspect that it is no longer true. This is the case with the rhetoric of rising. It is no accident that the rhetoric of rising was at its most fulsome at a time when inequality was approaching daunting proportions. When the richest 1 percent take in more than the combined earnings of the entire bottom half of the population,[30] when the median income stagnates for forty years,[31] the idea that effort and hard work will carry you far begins to ring hollow.

This hollowness produces two kinds of discontent. One is the frustration that arises when the system falls short of its meritocratic promise, when those who work hard and play by the rules are unable to advance. The other is the despair that arises when people believe the meritocratic promise has already been fulfilled, and they have lost out. This is a more demoralizing discontent, because it implies that, for those left behind, their failure is their fault.

Americans, more than most, adhere to the belief that hard work brings success, that our destiny is in our hands. According to global public opinion surveys, most Americans (77 percent) believe that people can succeed if they work hard; only half of Germans think so. In France and Japan, majorities say hard work is no guarantee of success.[32]

Asked what factors are "very important to getting ahead in life," Americans overwhelmingly (73 percent) put hard work first, reflecting the enduring hold of the Protestant work ethic. In Germany, barely half consider hard work very important to getting ahead; in France, only one in four does.[33]

As with all such surveys, the attitudes people express depend on how the question is framed. When it comes to explaining why some people are rich and others poor, Americans are less certain about the role of effort than when asked generally about work and success. Asked whether the rich are rich because they work harder than others or because they had advantages in life, Americans are evenly divided. Asked why people are poor, a majority say it is due to circumstances beyond their control; only three in ten say poverty is due to a lack of effort.[34]

Belief in the efficacy of work as a route to success reflects the broader conviction that we are masters of our destiny, that our fate is in our hands. Americans profess greater faith in human mastery than do citizens of most other countries. The majority of Americans (57 percent) disagree with the statement "success in life is pretty much determined by forces outside our control." By contrast, majorities in most other countries, including most European countries, view success as determined mainly by forces outside our control.[35]

These views about work and self-help have implications for solidarity and the mutual obligations of citizens. If everyone who works hard can be expected to succeed, then those who fall short have no one to blame but themselves, and it is hard to make the case for helping them. This is the harsh side of meritocracy.

If those who land on top, and those who land on the bottom, are wholly responsible for their fate, then social positions reflect what people deserve. The rich are rich thanks to their own doing. If, however, the most fortunate members of society are indebted for their success—to good luck or God's grace or the community's support—then the moral case for sharing one another's fate is stronger. It is easier to make the case that we are all in this together.

This may explain why the United States, with its robust faith that we are masters of our fate, has a less-generous welfare state than the social democracies of Europe, whose citizens are more inclined to attribute their life circumstance to forces outside their control. If everyone can succeed through effort and hard work, then government need simply ensure that jobs and opportunities are truly open to all. American politicians of the center-left and center-right may disagree about what policies equality of opportunity actually requires. But they share the assumption that the aim is to provide everyone, whatever his or her starting point in life, a chance to rise. They agree, in other words, that mobility is the answer to inequality—and that those who rise will have earned their success.

But the American faith in the ability to rise through effort and grit no longer fits the facts on the ground. In the decades following World War II, Americans could expect that their children would do better, economically, than they had. Today, this is no longer the case. Of children born in the 1940s, almost all (90 percent) earned more than their parents. Of children born in the 1980s, only half surpassed their parents' earnings.[36]

It is also harder to climb from poverty to affluence than the popular belief in upward mobility would suggest. Of those born poor in America, few make it to the top. In fact, most do not even make it to the middle class. Studies of upward mobility typically divide the income ladder into five rungs. Of those born on the bottom rung, only around 4 to 7 percent rise to the top, and only about a third reach the middle rung or higher. Although the exact numbers vary from one study to the next, very few Americans live out the "rags to riches" story celebrated in the American dream.[37]

In fact, there is less economic mobility in the United States than in many other countries. Economic advantages and disadvantages carry over from one generation to the next more frequently than in Germany, Spain,

Japan, Australia, Sweden, Canada, Finland, Norway, and Denmark. In the
U.S. and the U.K., nearly half of the economic advantage of high-earning
parents is passed on to their children. That is more than twice the earnings
advantage that children inherit in Canada, Finland, Norway, and Denmark
(where mobility is highest).[38]

Danish and Canadian children, it turns out, are far more likely to rise
from poverty to affluence than U.S. children.[39] By these measures, the
American dream is alive and well and living in Copenhagen.

The American dream is also flourishing in Beijing. An article in *The
New York Times* recently posed the following scenario:

> Imagine you have to make a bet. There are two 18-year-olds, one in
> China, the other in the United States, both poor and short on pros-
> pects. You have to pick the one with the better chance at upward
> mobility.
>
> Which would you choose?
>
> Not long ago, the answer might have seemed simple. The "Amer-
> ican Dream," after all, had long promised a pathway to a better life
> for anyone who worked hard.
>
> But the answer today is startling: China has risen so quickly that
> your chances of improving your station in life there vastly exceed
> those in the United States.[40]

Given China's unprecedented economic growth since 1980, this conclusion is less surprising than it seems. Rich and poor alike realized income
gains in China, while in the U.S., the gains of growth have gone mainly to
those at the top. Although the U.S. remains a much wealthier country per
capita than China, today's generation of Chinese young people is richer
than their parents' generation.[41]

More surprising is the fact that, according to the World Bank, levels
of income inequality in China are about the same as in the U.S. Moreover, China now has greater intergenerational mobility than the U.S. This
means that in the U.S., the land of opportunity, how much you make is
more closely tied to where you started out than it is in China.[42]

When my students encounter these findings, they are disquieted. Most have an instinctive faith in American exceptionalism, in the idea that America is a place where those who work hard can get ahead. This belief in upward mobility is America's traditional answer to inequality. Yes, America may have greater income inequality than other democracies, they reason. But here, unlike the more rigid, class-bound societies of Europe, inequality matters less, because no one is consigned to the class of his or her birth.

But once they learn that the U.S. has more inequality and less mobility than many other countries, they are troubled and perplexed. Some resist what the mobility data shows, pointing to their own experience of striving and succeeding. A conservative student of mine from Texas responded that, in his experience, all that really matters is how hard one works. "Everyone in my high school understood the rules," he said. "If you work hard in school and do well, you get into a good college and get a good job. If not, you work in the oil fields. And that's how things turned out." Others, while recalling their strenuous effort during high school years, acknowledge the sources of support that helped them succeed.

Some of my students argue that, even if the American dream is at odds with the facts, it is important not to spread the news; better to preserve the myth so that people will continue to believe it is possible to rise as far as their talents and hard work will take them. This would turn the American dream into what Plato described as a "noble lie," a belief that, though untrue, sustains civic harmony by inducing citizens to accept certain inequalities as legitimate. In Plato's case, it was the myth that God created people with different metals in their souls, giving divine sanction to an arrangement in which a guardian class led by a philosopher-king governs the city.[43] In our case, it would be the myth that, in America, despite the sizable gap between rich and poor, even those on the bottom can make it if they try.

My students are not the only ones who are mistaken about the prospects of rising. When researchers asked members of the public in the U.S. and Europe how likely it is to rise from poverty to affluence in their countries, the American and European respondents generally got it wrong. Interestingly, however, they got it wrong in opposite ways: Americans overestimated the chance of rising, and Europeans underestimated it.[44]

SEEING AND BELIEVING

These results reveal something important about the way we understand social and political arrangements. We perceive the world in the light of our hopes and fears. At first glance, it might seem that people are simply ill-informed about the mobility that prevails in their societies. But what is interesting, what calls out for interpretation, is that the misperceptions have a certain shape. Europeans, whose societies are more equal and more mobile than the United States, are overly pessimistic about the possibility of rising, while Americans are overly optimistic. Why is this so?

In both cases, beliefs and convictions shape perceptions. Americans' strong attachment to individual initiative, together with their willingness to accept inequality, leads them to exaggerate the possibility of rising through hard work. Europeans' skepticism that individual effort conquers all, together with their lesser tolerance of inequality, leads them to underestimate the possibility of rising.

This tendency to view the world through the lens of our ideals and expectations sheds light on how the meritocratic promise can be demoralizing, even humiliating, for working-class and middle-class voters. On the face of it, this is puzzling: Who could object to proposals to break down barriers, level the playing field, and improve educational opportunities so that everyone, not only those born to privilege, can have a chance at the American dream? Wouldn't the rhetoric of rising appeal to working-class and middle-class voters, who could benefit from the educational opportunities, job training, child care, family leave, and other policies that liberals and progressives were offering?

No, not necessarily. By 2016, as the baleful effects of globalization on ordinary workers became clear, the rhetoric of rising offered by liberal elites conveyed a harsh suggestion. Even in the face of rising inequality, it insisted that we are responsible for our fate, and that we therefore deserve the success or misfortune that comes our way.

This way of viewing inequality fueled meritocratic hubris. It reinforced the belief that those who had reaped the benefits of globalization deserved their bounty, and that those left behind deserved their meager lot. Larry Summers, an economic advisor to President Obama, put it bluntly: "One of the challenges in our society is that the truth is kind of a disequalizer. One of the reasons that inequality has probably gone up in our society is that people are being treated closer to the way that they're supposed to be treated."[45]

It might be argued, in defense of the rhetoric of rising, that it describes the opportunity to compete on equal terms as an ideal worth aiming at, not as a fact of the world in which we live. But merit has a way of overreaching. It begins as an ideal but slides into a claim about the way things are.

Although the rhetoric of rising is aspirational, pointing to a promise that has yet to be redeemed, its articulation invariably turns congratulatory: "Here in America, everyone who works hard can rise." Like most powerful rhetoric, it commingles the aspirational with the congratulatory; it asserts the hope as if it were a fact.

Obama's rhetoric is a case in point. In a 2012 radio address he said, "This is a country where no matter what you look like or where you come from, if you're willing to study and work hard, you can go as far as your talents will take you. You can make it if you try."[46]

Obama's listeners would not be mistaken to think their president was describing the way things actually worked in America, not offering an ideal of a more equal, more mobile society that he hoped to bring about. He spoke in a congratulatory vein, praising America for having achieved a society in which hard work, not inherited privilege, was the key to success.

And yet, as he continued, he shifted from congratulation to aspiration: "I am only the President of the United States today because of the chance my education gave me, and I want every child in America to have that chance. That's what I'm fighting for. And as long as I have the privilege of being your President, that's what I'm going to keep fighting for."[47]

This tendency to move from fact to hope and back again is not a slip of the tongue or philosophical confusion but a characteristic feature of political rhetoric. It plays out with special poignance in the rhetoric of rising. Its commingling of hope and fact muddies the meaning of winning and losing. If meritocracy is an aspiration, those who fall short can always blame the system; but if meritocracy is a fact, those who fall short are invited to blame themselves.

In recent years, they have been invited, above all, to blame themselves for failing to acquire a college degree. One of the most galling features of meritocratic hubris is its credentialism.

CREDENTIALISM:

THE LAST ACCEPTABLE

PREJUDICE

For years, Michael Cohen had served as Donald Trump's personal attorney and fixer. In February 2019, he testified before Congress. By then he had turned on his former boss and was revealing some of the unsavory activities he undertook on Trump's behalf, including paying hush money to a porn star to prevent her from disclosing an affair with Trump. During his testimony, Cohen also revealed another task he had performed at Trump's behest: threatening to sue the colleges Trump had attended, and the College Board, if they ever made public his college grades or SAT scores.[1]

Trump was presumably embarrassed by his academic record and apparently feared that making it public would damage his presidential candidacy, or at least his reputation. Cohen highlighted the hypocrisy in Trump's attempt to hide his academic records. Some years earlier, Trump had insisted that President Obama make his academic records public. "I heard he was a terrible student, terrible," Trump declared in 2011. "How does a bad student go to Columbia and then to Harvard? . . . Let him show his records."[2]

Cohen's disclosure of his attempt to keep Trump's grades and SAT scores from public view attracted less attention than his more salacious testimony about paying off the porn star. But as a sign of the times, it was more consequential. What it revealed was the public significance of credential-ism. By the 2000s, how well one did in college, or even on college entrance exams, loomed large enough to cast glory or disrepute on a president. Don-ald Trump certainly thought so. He first attempted to discredit Obama by demanding his birth certificate, casting doubt on his citizenship. When that failed, he leveled against Obama the next most potent insult he could imagine, casting doubt on his meritocratic credentials.

WEAPONIZING COLLEGE CREDENTIALS

Trump's line of attack reflected his own insecurity. Throughout his candi-dacy and his presidency, Trump boasted often about his intellectual cre-dentials. A study of presidential word choice found that he spoke at a fourth-grade vocabulary level, the lowest of any president in the past cen-tury; his own secretary of state reportedly described him as a "moron," and his secretary of defense said his understanding of world affairs was that of a fifth or sixth grader. Stung by these and other disparaging remarks about his intellect, Trump was at pains to insist that he was a "smart person," in fact a "very stable genius." Asked during his 2016 presidential campaign to name the foreign-policy experts he was consulting, he replied, "I'm speak-ing with myself, number one, because I have a very good brain and I've said a lot of things . . . My primary consultant is myself." He repeatedly asserted that he had a high IQ and that his critics had low ones, an insult he directed especially against African Americans.[3]

Enamored with the genetics of IQ, Trump often pointed out that his uncle had been a professor at MIT ("an academic genius"), evidence that he, Trump, had "good genes, very good genes." Shortly after appointing his first cabinet, he proclaimed, "We have by far the highest IQ of any Cabinet ever assembled!" In a bizarre speech to employees of the Central Intel-ligence Agency on the day after his inauguration, Trump sought to allay what he imagined to be doubts about his intellect: "Trust me, I'm, like, a smart person."[4]

He frequently felt the need to remind audiences of his college credentials, having spent two years at Fordham before transferring to the University of Pennsylvania, where he took undergraduate classes at the Wharton School of Finance. He boasted that he went to "the hardest school to get into, the best school in the world . . . super genius stuff."[5] Campaigning in 2016, he complained that his need constantly to recite and defend his intellectual credentials arose from media bias against conservatives.

> If I ran as a liberal Democrat, they would say I'm one of the smartest people anywhere in the world. It's true! But when you're a conservative Republican they try—oh, do they do a number. That's why I always start off: "Went to Wharton, was a good student, went there, went there, did this, built a fortune." You know I have to give my, like, credentials all the time, because we're a little disadvantaged.[6]

Though animated by his own grievances and insecurities, Trump's repeated insistence that he was "a smart person," however plaintive and comic it seemed to his critics, proved to be a political asset. It resonated with the aggrieved working-class supporters who attended his rallies and who, like him, resented the meritocratic hubris of elites. Trump's protestations displayed the humiliation a meritocratic society can inflict. He both reviled elites and craved their respect. At a campaign-style rally in 2017, he lashed out against elites, then claimed to be one himself:

> Now, you know, I was a good student. I always hear about the elite. You know, the elite—they're elite? I went to better schools than they did. I was a better student than they were. I live in a bigger, more beautiful apartment. And I live in the White House too, which is really great. I think—you know what? I think we're the elites. They're not the elites.[7]

Trump was not the only political figure to display defensiveness in the face of questions about his meritocratic credentials. In 1987, during his first presidential campaign, Joe Biden took umbrage when a voter pressed him to say what law school he attended and where he placed in the class:

I think I probably have a much higher IQ than you do, I suspect. I went to law school on a full academic scholarship—the only one in my class to have a full academic scholarship . . . and in fact ended up in the top half of my class. I was the outstanding student in the political science department at the end of my year. I graduated with three degrees from undergraduate school and 165 credits—only needed 123 credits—and I'd be delighted to sit down and compare my IQ to yours.[8]

Fact-checking found that Biden's reply was replete with exaggeration. He had received a partial scholarship based on financial need, finished toward the bottom of his class, received one undergraduate degree not three (though he did have a double major), and so on.[9] What is striking, however, is not that politicians inflate their college credentials, but that they feel the need to do so.

Even those whose meritocratic credentials are not in doubt sometimes invoke them with defensive self-righteousness. Consider the 2018 Senate confirmation hearings of Brett Kavanaugh, nominated by Trump (and eventually confirmed) for a seat on the U.S. Supreme Court. Late in the proceedings, Kavanaugh's confirmation was placed in doubt when a woman accused him of having sexually assaulted her at a party during their high school years.

When senators questioned him about the alleged drunken sexual assault, Kavanaugh not only denied the charge, but offered an oddly incongruous meritocratic defense, describing how hard he worked during high school, and how he won admission to Yale College and later, Yale Law School.

Asked about apparent references in his high school yearbook to drinking and sexual exploits, he replied, "I was at the top of my class academically, busted my butt in school. Captain of the varsity basketball team. Got in Yale College. When I got into Yale College, got into Yale Law School . . . That's the number one law school in the country. I had no connections there. I got there by busting my tail in college."[10]

Kavanaugh's meritocratic credentials had not been challenged. It is hard to fathom their relevance to the question of whether, when he was eighteen years old, he had become drunk and sexually assaulted a young woman at a party. But by 2018, credentialism had become so pervasive a basis of judgment that it served as a kind of all-purpose rhetoric of credibility, deployed in moral and political combat far beyond the campus gates.

The weaponization of college credentials shows how merit can become a kind of tyranny. It is worth reconstructing how it came about. The age of globalization brought vast inequalities and stagnant wages for the working class. In the U.S., the richest 10 percent captured most of the gains, and the bottom half received virtually none. Liberal and progressive parties of the 1990s and 2000s did not address this inequality directly, by seeking structural reform of the economy. Instead, they embraced market-driven globalization and addressed the uneven benefits it bestowed by seeking a fuller equality of opportunity.

This was the point of the rhetoric of rising. If barriers to achievement could be dismantled, then everyone would have an equal chance to succeed; regardless of race or class or gender, people could rise as far as their talent and effort would take them. And if opportunities were truly equal, those who rose highest could be said to deserve their success and the rewards it brings. This was the meritocratic promise. It was not a promise of greater equality, but a promise of greater and fairer mobility. It accepted that the rungs on the income ladder were growing farther apart and offered simply to help people compete more fairly to clamber up the rungs.

It is easy to see why some would find this political project less than inspiring, especially for political parties once dedicated to more demanding visions of justice and the common good. But put aside, for the moment, the question of whether the meritocratic ideal is an adequate basis for a just society and consider the attitudes toward success and failure it promotes.

EDUCATION AS THE ANSWER TO INEQUALITY

Those who embraced the meritocratic project knew that true equality of opportunity required more than rooting out discrimination. It required leveling the playing field, so that people from all social and economic backgrounds could equip themselves to compete effectively in a knowledge-based, global economy. This led the mainstream parties of the 1990s and 2000s to make education the centerpiece of their response to inequality, stagnant wages, and the loss of manufacturing jobs. "Think about every problem, every challenge we face," said George H. W. Bush in 1991. "The solution to each starts with education." In Britain, Tony Blair, setting out his centrist, reform-minded agenda for the Labour Party in 1996, put it emphatically: "Ask me for my three main priorities for government and I tell you: education, education and education."[11]

Bill Clinton expressed the importance of education, and its connection to jobs, with a rhyming couplet: "What you can earn depends on what you can learn." In the new era of global competition, he argued, workers without a college degree would struggle to find good jobs at decent wages. "We think everybody ought to be able to go to college, because what you can earn depends on what you can learn." Clinton invoked this couplet in speeches and remarks more than thirty times during his presidency. It reflected the common sense of the time and had bipartisan appeal. Senator John McCain, a Republican, often used it during his 2008 presidential campaign.[12]

Barack Obama also saw higher education as the solution to the economic woes of American workers. "In the old days," he told an audience at a technology college in Brooklyn, "if you were willing to work hard, you didn't necessarily need a great education."[13]

If you'd just gone to high school, you might get a job at a factory or in the garment district. Or you might be able to just get a job that allowed you to earn your wages, keep pace with people who had a chance to go to college. But those days are over, and those days are not coming back.

We live in a 21st-century global economy. And in a global economy, jobs can go anywhere. Companies, they're looking for the best-educated people, wherever they live . . . Now you've got billions of

people from Beijing to Bangalore to Moscow, all of whom are competing with you directly . . . If you don't have a good education, then
it is going to be hard for you to find a job that pays a living wage.[14]

After delivering this hard news about global competition, Obama assured
his audience that more education was the solution and concluded with an
upbeat rendition of the rhetoric of rising: He would keep fighting "to make
sure that no matter who you are, where you come from, what you look like,
this country will always be a place where you can make it if you try."[15]

Here then was the basic argument of liberal and progressive politics
in the decades leading up to Brexit, Trump, and the populist revolt: The
global economy, as if a fact of nature, had somehow come upon us and
was here to stay. The central political question was not how to reconfigure
it but how to adapt to it, and how to alleviate its devastating effect on the
wages and job prospects of workers outside the charmed circle of the elite
professions.

The answer: Improve the educational credentials of workers so that
they, too, could "compete and win in the global economy." If equality of
opportunity was the primary moral and political project, expanding access
to higher education was the overriding policy imperative.

Toward the end of the Clinton-Obama era, some commentators generally
sympathetic to the Democratic Party questioned the meritocratic liberalism that had come to define it—embracing globalization, valorizing a college degree, and believing that the talented and well-credentialed deserved
to land on top. Christopher Hayes, an author and host of an MSNBC television program, observed that in recent years the left had had its greatest
successes on issues that involved "making the meritocracy more meritocratic," such as combating racial discrimination, including women in
higher education, and advancing gay rights. But it had failed in areas "that
fall outside the meritocracy's purview," such as "mitigating rising income
inequality."[16]

Within the framework of a system that seeks equal opportunity rather than any semblance of equality in outcomes, it is inevitable that the education system will be asked to do the heavy lifting . . . And as inequality steadily increases, we ask more and more of the educational system, looking for it to expiate the society's other sins.[17]

Thomas Frank, an author with populist sensibilities, criticized liberals' focus on education as the remedy for inequality: "To the liberal class, every big economic problem is really an education problem, a failure by the losers to learn the right skills and get the credentials everyone knows you'll need in the society of the future." Frank found this response to inequality implausible and self-serving:

[It] isn't really an answer at all; it's a moral judgment, handed down by the successful from the vantage of their own success. The professional class is defined by its educational attainment, and every time they tell the country that what it needs is more schooling, they are saying: Inequality is not a failure of the system; it is a failure of you.[18]

Frank argued that all the education talk distracted Democrats from thinking clearly about the policies that had led to inequality. Noting that productivity rose during the 1980s and 1990s but that wages did not, he doubted that inequality was due mainly to a failure of education. "The real problem was one of inadequate worker power, not inadequate worker smarts. The people who produced were losing their ability to demand a share in what they made. The people who owned were taking more and more." Failing to see this led Democrats "to ignore what was happening in the real economy— from monopoly power to financialization to labor-management relations— in favor of a moral fantasy that required them to confront no one."[19]

Frank's mention of a "moral judgment handed down by the successful" touched on something important. Encouraging more people to go to college is a good thing. Making college more accessible to those of modest means is even better. But as a solution to inequality and the plight of workers who lost out in the decades of globalization, the single-minded focus on education had a damaging side effect: eroding the social esteem accorded those who had not gone to college.

It did so in two ways, both having to do with attitudes corrosive of the dignity of work and of the working class. First, most Americans do not have a college degree. For those who go about their day in the company of the managerial-professional classes, this can come as a surprise. Although graduation rates have climbed in recent decades, only about one in three American adults has graduated from a four-year college.[20] When meritocratic elites tie success and failure so closely to one's ability to earn a college degree, they implicitly blame those without one for the harsh conditions they encounter in the global economy. They also absolve themselves of responsibility for promoting economic policies that heighten the wage premium a college degree commands.

Second, by telling workers that their inadequate education is to blame for their troubles, meritocrats moralize success and failure and unwittingly promote credentialism—an insidious prejudice against those who have not been to college.

The credentialist prejudice is a symptom of meritocratic hubris. As meritocratic assumptions tightened their hold in recent decades, elites fell into the habit of looking down on those who do not rise. The constant call for working people to improve their condition by getting a college degree, however well intentioned, eventually valorizes credentialism and undermines social recognition and esteem for those who lack the credentials the system rewards.

THE BEST AND THE BRIGHTEST

Obama was emblematic of the meritocratic thinking that by the early 2000s had become the common sense of the professional classes. As Jonathan Alter writes, "At some level Obama bought into the idea that top-drawer professionals had gone through a fair sorting process, the same process that had propelled him and Michelle to the Ivy League, and were therefore in some way deserving of their elevated status."[21]

In a book chronicling the first year of Obama's presidency, Alter observed that a quarter of his appointees had some connection (as alumni or faculty) to Harvard, and more than 90 percent of early appointees had advanced degrees. "Obama's faith lay in cream rising to the top. Because he himself was a product of the great American postwar meritocracy, he could never fully escape seeing the world from the status ladder he had ascended."[22]

Obama's fondness for the highly credentialed persisted throughout his presidency. By the middle of his second term, two-thirds of his cabinet-rank appointees had attended an Ivy League college, and thirteen of twenty-one had attended Harvard or Yale. All but three held advanced degrees.[23]

Having well-educated people run the government is generally desirable, provided they possess sound judgment and a sympathetic understanding of working people's lives—what Aristotle called practical wisdom and civic virtue. But history shows little connection between prestigious academic credentials and either practical wisdom or an instinct for the common good in the here and now. One of the most ruinous examples of credentialism gone awry is described in David Halberstam's classic book *The Best and the Brightest*. It shows how John F. Kennedy assembled a team with glittering credentials who, for all their technocratic brilliance, led the United States into the folly of the Vietnam War.[24]

Alter saw a similarity between Kennedy's team and Obama's, who "shared the Ivy League as well as a certain arrogance and a detachment from the everyday lives of most Americans."[25] As things turned out, Obama's economic advisors contributed to a folly of their own, less lethal than Vietnam but consequential nonetheless for the shape of American politics. Insisting on a Wall Street–friendly response to the financial crisis, they bailed out the banks without holding them to account, discredited the Democratic Party in the eyes of many working people, and helped pave the way to Trump.

This failure of political judgment was not unrelated to meritocratic hubris. Frank describes a "widely shared view among Democrats that Wall Street is a place of enormous meritocratic prestige, on a level equivalent to a high-end graduate school."[26]

Obama deferred to Wall Street in so many ways because investment banking signifies professional status like almost nothing else. For the kind of achievement-conscious people who filled the administration, investment bankers were more than friends—they were fellow professionals; people of subtle minds, sophisticated jargon, and extraordinary innovativeness.[27]

Frank argues that this reflexive respect for investment bankers "blinded the Democrats to the problems of megabanks, to the need for structural change, and to the epidemic of fraud that overswept the business." He cites Neil Barofsky, a former federal prosecutor who served as the government watchdog for the bank bailout, and who wrote a scathing book about what he saw. The book's title and subtitle convey his conclusion—*Bailout: An Inside Account of How Washington Abandoned Main Street While Rescuing Wall Street*.[28]

While it is true that Wall Street executives had been generous donors to Obama's campaign, his administration's gentle treatment of the financial industry was not only political payback. Barofsky suggests a further, meritocratic explanation—the belief among policy makers that well-credentialed, sophisticated investment bankers deserved the massive amounts they were paid.

The Wall Street fiction that certain financial executives were preternaturally gifted supermen who deserved every penny of their staggering paychecks and bonuses was firmly ingrained in Treasury's psyche. No matter that the financial crisis had demonstrated just how unremarkable the work of those executives had turned out to be, that belief system endured at Treasury across administrations. If a Wall Street executive was contracted to receive a $6.4 million "retention" bonus, the assumption was that he must be worth it.[29]

Beyond the role it may have played in policy-making, credentialism seeped into Democrats' mode of expression in the 1990s and 2000s, and subtly reshaped the terms of public discourse. In every age, politicians and opinion makers, publicists and advertisers, reach for a language of judgment and evaluation they hope will persuade. Such rhetoric typically draws upon evaluative contrasts: just versus unjust, free versus unfree, progressive versus reactionary, strong versus weak, open versus closed. In recent decades, as meritocratic modes of thinking have gained ascendance, the reigning evaluative contrast has become smart versus dumb.

Until recently, the adjective "smart" mainly described persons. In American English, to call someone "smart" is to praise his or her intelligence. (In British English, "clever" conveys this meaning.) As the digital age dawned, "smart" came to describe things—high-tech devices and machines such as "smart cars," "smart phones," "smart bombs," "smart thermostats," "smart toasters," and so on. But the digital age arrived in tandem with the age of meritocracy; it is therefore not surprising that "smart" also came to describe ways of governing.

THE SMART THING TO DO

Prior to the 1980s, U.S. presidents rarely used the word "smart," and when they did, it was typically in the traditional sense. ("The American people are smart.") George H. W. Bush began using the word in its new, digital-age sense. He spoke of "smart cars," "smart freeways," "smart weapons," "smart schools." The use of "smart" in presidential rhetoric exploded with Bill Clinton and George W. Bush, each of whom used it more than 450 times. Obama used it more than 900 times.[30]

The same trend can be seen in general parlance. In books, the use of "smart" climbed steadily from 1975 to 2008, increasing nearly threefold; the use of "stupid" doubled. In The New York Times, the appearance of "smart" increased fourfold from 1980 to 2000, and by 2018 had nearly doubled again.[31]

As a measure of meritocracy's hold on the public mind, the growing frequency of "smart" is less revealing than its changing meaning. Not only did "smart" refer to digital systems and devices; it increasingly became a general term of praise, and a way of arguing for one policy rather than another. As an evaluative contrast, "smart versus dumb" began to displace ethical or ideological contrasts, such as "just versus unjust" or "right versus wrong." Both Clinton and Obama frequently argued that their favored policy was "not just the right thing to do; it's the smart thing to do." This rhetorical tick suggested that, in a meritocratic age, being smart carried more persuasive heft than being right.

"Fighting AIDS worldwide is not just the right thing to do; it's the smart thing," Clinton assured the American public. "In our tightly connected world, infectious disease anywhere is a threat to public health everywhere." Adding a prescription drug benefit to Medicare was "not just the right thing to do; medically speaking, it's the smart thing to do." Raising the minimum wage was "not only the right thing to do for working families; it's the smart thing to do for our economy."[32]

Employing the same idiom, Obama declared that "empowering women isn't just the right thing to do; it's the smart thing to do. When women succeed, nations are more safe, more secure, and more prosperous." Speaking before the U.N. General Assembly, he said the same of development aid: "It's not just the right thing to do, it's the smart thing to do." Obama invoked this double-barreled appeal to ethics and smarts on issues ranging from immigration reform to extending unemployment insurance.[33]

The "smart thing to do" always pointed to a prudential or self-interested reason that did not depend on moral considerations. Clinton and Obama were of course not the first political leaders to buttress moral arguments with prudential ones; what is striking is that the prudential considerations were now a matter of being "smart."

Defending one's policies as smart rather than dumb is closely akin to credentialist ways of talking about people. When Hillary Clinton, newly appointed as secretary of state, announced several of her State Department deputies, she made this connection explicit: "In my testimony before the Senate Foreign Relations Committee, I spoke about the use of smart power. At the heart of smart power are smart people, and these talented individuals are among the smartest I know."[34]

At a time of intense partisanship, the language of smart and dumb has an understandable appeal; it seems to offer a refuge from ideological combat, a mode of political argument that steps back from moral controversy and seeks consensus on the basis of what's smart, sensible, prudent. Obama was drawn to this seemingly non-partisan, meritocratic way of thinking and speaking. On issues related to racial, ethnic, and gender equality, Obama made eloquent, full-throated moral arguments. But when it came to foreign affairs or economic policy, he instinctively reached for the non-ideological language of smart versus dumb.

The most important speech of his early political career came in 2002, when, as a state senator in Illinois, he declared his opposition to the Iraq War. It was this stance that, six years later, would distinguish him from Hillary Clinton and help propel him to his party's nomination for president. Even before ascending to the national political stage, Obama saw political choices in terms of smart versus dumb. "I don't oppose all wars," the young state senator told the anti-war rally in Chicago. "What I am opposed to is a dumb war."[35]

When, during his second term as president, Obama was asked to articulate his foreign policy doctrine, he summed it up in a single, blunt sentence: "Don't do stupid shit."[36]

When Obama found himself at loggerheads with Republicans in 2013 over how to reduce the budget deficit while avoiding automatic, across-the-board spending cuts, he again resorted to the language of smart versus dumb. "There is a sensible way of doing things, and there is a dumb way of doing things," he told shipbuilders in Virginia. At a press conference a few days later, he said, "We shouldn't be making a series of dumb, arbitrary cuts." Instead, he favored "smart spending cuts" and "smart entitlement reform."[37]

Obama maintained that the smart spending cuts and smart revenue raising measures he favored were sensible, non-partisan measures that should be exempt from ideological wrangling. "I don't think that is partisan. It's the kind of approach that I've proposed for two years. It's what I ran on last year."[38] He did not explain how a policy that, by his own account, he ran on during his presidential campaign could be considered non-partisan.

ELITES LOOKING DOWN

Elites seemed oblivious not only to the partisan character of their "smart" policies, but also to the hubristic attitudes their persistent talk of "smart" and "dumb" expressed. By 2016, many working people chafed under the sense that well-schooled elites looked down on them with condescension. This complaint, which burst forth in the populist backlash against elites, was not without warrant. Survey research bears out what many working-class voters sensed; at a time when racism and sexism are out of favor (discredited though not eliminated), credentialism is the last acceptable prejudice. In the United States and Europe, disdain for the poorly educated is more pronounced, or at least more readily acknowledged, than prejudice against other disfavored groups.

In a series of surveys conducted in the United Kingdom, the Netherlands, and Belgium, a team of social psychologists found that college-educated respondents have more bias against less-educated people than they do against other disfavored groups. The researchers surveyed the attitudes of well-educated Europeans toward a range of people who are typically victims of discrimination—Muslims, people of Turkish descent living in Western Europe, people who are poor, obese, blind, and less educated. They found that the poorly educated were disliked most of all.[39]

In a similar study conducted in the United States, the researchers offered a revised list of disfavored groups, including African Americans, the working class, and people who are poor, obese, and less-educated. The American respondents also ranked the less-educated at the bottom.[40]

Beyond showing the disparaging views that college-educated elites have of less-educated people, the authors of the study offer several intriguing conclusions. First, they challenge the familiar notion that educated elites are morally more enlightened than people with less education, and therefore more tolerant. The authors conclude that well-educated elites are no less biased than less-educated folk; "it is rather that [their] targets of prejudice are different." Moreover, the elites are unembarrassed by their prejudice. They may denounce racism and sexism but are unapologetic about their negative attitudes toward the less-educated.[41]

Second, the reason for this lack of embarrassment relates to the meritocratic emphasis on individual responsibility. Elites dislike those with lesser educations more than they dislike poor people or members of the working class, because they consider poverty and class status to be, at least in part, due to factors beyond one's control. By contrast, they consider low educational achievement to represent a failure of individual effort, and therefore the fault of those who do not make it to college. "Compared to the working class, the less-educated were perceived to be more responsible and more blameworthy, they elicited more anger, and they were liked less."[42]

Third, this adverse judgment of the less-educated is not unique to elites; it is shared by the less-educated respondents themselves. This shows how deeply the meritocratic view of achievement has penetrated social life and how demoralizing it can be for those who do not go to college. "There are no indications that less educated people resist the negative attributions made about them." To the contrary, they "even seem to internalize" these adverse judgments. The "less educated are seen as responsible and blameworthy for their situation, even by the less-educated themselves."[43]

Finally, the authors suggest that the relentless emphasis, in a meritocratic society, on the importance of going to college reinforces the social stigma against those who lack a college degree. "The suggestion that education is a universal social problem solver may increase the risk that groups with low levels of socioeconomic status will be especially negatively evaluated while strengthening the ideology of meritocracy." This makes people more willing to accept inequality and more likely to believe that success reflects merit. "If education is regarded as an individual's own responsibility, then people are likely to be less critical of social inequality that stems from differences in education . . . If educational outcomes are seen as largely deserved, then their consequences are, too."[44]

GOVERNMENT BY DEGREE

By the 2000s, citizens without a college degree were not only looked down upon; in the United States and Western Europe, they were virtually absent from elective office. In the U.S. Congress, 95 percent of House members and 100 percent of senators are college graduates. This means that the credentialed few govern the uncredentialed many. Although about two-thirds of American adults do not have a college degree, only a tiny handful are members of Congress.

It has not always been this way. Although the well-educated have always been disproportionately represented in Congress, as recently as the early 1960s about one-fourth of senators and one-fourth of members of the House were elected despite lacking a college degree. Over the past half decade, Congress has become more diverse with regard to race, ethnicity, and gender, but less diverse with regard to educational credentials and class.[45]

One consequence of the diploma divide is that very few members of the working class ever make it to elective office. In the U.S., about half of the labor force is employed in working-class jobs, defined as manual labor, service industry, and clerical jobs. But fewer than 2 percent of the members of Congress worked in such jobs before their election. In state legislatures, only 3 percent come from working-class backgrounds.[46]

Credentialism is also changing the face of representative government in Britain and Europe. In Britain, as in the U.S., those with diplomas govern those without. In the United Kingdom as a whole, about 70 percent do not have a university degree; in Parliament, only 12 percent do not. Nearly nine of ten MPs have degrees; one-fourth of MPs went to Oxford or Cambridge.[47]

Over the past four decades, Britain's Labour Party has undergone an especially striking shift in the educational and class background of its MPs. In 1979, 41 percent of Labour MPs were elected to Parliament without having received a university degree; by 2017, only 16 percent managed to do so.

This rising tide of credentialism was accompanied by a precipitous decline in working-class MPs, who now constitute only 4 percent of the House of Commons. The class composition of the Labour Party, which tradition-ally represented the working class, underwent the most dramatic change. In 1979, 37 percent of Labour MPs came from a manual occupation back-ground. By 2015, only 7 percent did. As Oliver Heath, a British political scientist, observes, "Such changes in MPs' occupational background have made parliament much less representative of the broader British popula-tion, and the Labour party much less representative of the working class whose interests it was traditionally supposed to represent."[48]

The less-educated members of society are also disappearing from par-liaments throughout Western Europe, where the pattern is similar to the American and British experience. In Germany, France, the Netherlands, and Belgium, representative government has become almost exclusively the preserve of the highly credentialed. Even in rich countries such as these, about 70 percent of the adult population do not have college degrees. But very few of them find their way into parliament.[49]

In Germany's Bundestag, 83 percent of MPs are university graduates; fewer than 2 percent have the high school vocational track (*Hauptschule*) as their highest degree. In France, the Netherlands, and Belgium, 82 to 94 percent of representatives in parliament have university degrees. Among cabinet members in these countries, the educational credentials are even higher. In Angela Merkel's 2013 cabinet, for example, nine of the fifteen ministers had PhDs, and all but one of the others had master's degrees. The cachet of a PhD is so considerable in German politics that scandals rage over plagiarism in doctoral dissertations, forcing cabinet ministers to resign.[50]

The virtual absence from government of non–college graduates is a development of the meritocratic age. But it is not unprecedented. It is more than a little troubling to notice that this is a reversion to the way things were before most working people had the right to vote. The highly creden-tialed profile of today's European parliaments resembles the one that pre-vailed in the late nineteenth century, when property qualifications limited suffrage. In Germany, France, the Netherlands, and Belgium, most mem-bers of mid- to late-nineteenth-century parliaments had college degrees.[51]

This changed in the twentieth century, when universal suffrage and the rise of socialist and social democratic parties democratized the composition of parliaments. From the 1920s to the 1950s, MPs without college degrees served in substantial numbers, accounting for one-third to one-half of legislators. Beginning in the 1960s, the portion of degree holders began to climb, and by the 2000s, non–college graduates were as rare in national legislatures as they were in the days of aristocrats and landed gentry.[52]

Some might argue that government by well-educated university graduates is something to welcome not regret. Surely we want highly qualified engineers to build our bridges and well-trained doctors to perform our appendectomies. So why not seek elected representatives who attended the best universities? Aren't highly educated leaders more likely than those with less-distinguished credentials to give us sound public policies and reasoned political discourse?

No, not necessarily. Even a cursory glance at the parlous state of political discourse in Congress and in the parliaments of Europe should give us pause. Governing well requires practical wisdom and civic virtue—an ability to deliberate about the common good and to pursue it effectively. But neither of these capacities is developed very well in most universities today, even those with the highest reputations. And recent historical experience suggests little correlation between the capacity for political judgment, which involves moral character as well as insight, and the ability to score well on standardized tests and win admission to elite universities. The notion that "the best and the brightest" are better at governing than their less-credentialed fellow citizens is a myth born of meritocratic hubris.

Two of the four iconic American presidents on Mount Rushmore (George Washington and Abraham Lincoln) lacked a college degree. The last U.S. president without a diploma, Harry S. Truman, is generally ranked among America's best presidents.[53]

Franklin D. Roosevelt, a Harvard alumnus himself, conceived and enacted the New Deal with an eclectic team of advisors more capable but far less credentialed than those who served recent Democratic presidents. This is due, at least in part, to the fact that in the 1930s, the economics profession did not exert the hold on Washington policy-making it acquired in recent decades.[54] Thomas Frank describes the varied backgrounds of those who launched the New Deal:

> Harry Hopkins, Roosevelt's closest confidant, was a social worker from Iowa. Robert Jackson, the U.S. Attorney General whom Roosevelt appointed to the Supreme Court, was a lawyer who had no law degree. Jesse Jones, who ran Roosevelt's bailout program, was a businessman from Texas with no qualms about putting the nation's most prominent financial institutions into receivership. Marriner Eccles, the visionary whom Roosevelt appointed to run the Federal Reserve, was a small-town banker from Utah with no advanced degrees. Henry Wallace, who was probably the nation's greatest agriculture secretary, studied at Iowa State.[55]

The rising credentialism of recent decades has also failed to improve governance in the United Kingdom. Today, only 7 percent of the British population attends private schools, and fewer than 1 percent attend Oxford or Cambridge universities. But the governing elites are drawn disproportionately from these places. Nearly two-thirds of Boris Johnson's 2019 cabinet attended private schools, and almost half are Oxbridge graduates. Since World War II, most Conservative cabinet ministers, and about a third of ministers in Labour governments, have come from private school backgrounds.[56] But one of the most successful British governments since the war was its least credentialed and most broadly representative in class terms.

In 1945, Clement Attlee's Labour Party defeated Winston Churchill's Conservatives. Attlee was an Oxford graduate, but only one in four of his cabinet ministers came from private schools, a lower proportion than in any British cabinet since. Seven of his ministers had worked as coal miners.[57]

Attlee's highly regarded foreign secretary, Ernest Bevin, who became one of the architects of the postwar world, had left school at the age of eleven and risen through the ranks as a union leader. Herbert Morrison, leader of the House of Commons and deputy prime minister, had left school at fourteen and risen to prominence through local government, helping create London's public transport system. The health minister, Aneurin Bevan, who had left school at thirteen and worked as a miner in Wales, led the creation of Britain's National Health Service. Attlee's government, considered "the most significant reforming administration of twentieth century Britain," empowered the working classes and, according to his biographer, "set the ethical terms on which Britain's new social contract was founded."[58]

Turning Congress and parliaments into the exclusive preserve of the credentialed classes has not made government more effective, but it has made it less representative. It has also alienated working people from mainstream parties, especially those of the center-left, and polarized politics along educational lines. One of the deepest divides in politics today is between those with and those without a college degree.

THE DIPLOMA DIVIDE

In 2016, two-thirds of whites without a college degree voted for Donald Trump. Hillary Clinton won more than 70 percent of voters with advanced degrees. Electoral studies found that education, not income, best predicted support for Trump. Among voters with similar incomes, those with more education voted for Clinton, while those with less voted for Trump.[59]

The diploma divide accounted for the most significant vote swings from the previous presidential election. In 48 of the 50 counties with the highest proportion of college graduates, Hillary Clinton actually did better than Barack Obama four years earlier. In 47 of the 50 counties with the lowest proportion of college graduates, she did considerably worse. No wonder Trump proclaimed, celebrating one of his early primary victories, "I love the poorly educated!"[60]

Throughout much of the twentieth century, parties of the left attracted those with less education, while parties of the right attracted those with more. In the age of meritocracy, this pattern has been reversed. Today, people with more education vote for left-of-center parties, and those with less support parties of the right. The French economist Thomas Piketty has shown that this reversal has unfolded, in striking parallel, in the U.S., the U.K., and France.[61]

From the 1940s to the 1970s, those without a university degree voted reliably for the Democratic Party in the United States, the Labour Party in Britain, and the various left-of-center parties in France. During the 1980s and 1990s, the diploma gap narrowed considerably, and by the 2000s and 2010s, parties of the left had lost the support of voters without a college education.[62]

The reversal is complicated by the fact that wealthy voters still generally support parties of the right, even as the majority of highly educated voters favor the center-left. And in the United States, African American, Latino, and Asian American voters of all educational backgrounds continue to support the Democratic Party. But by the 2010s, education had become the most decisive political divide, and parties that once represented workers increasingly represented meritocratic elites.[63]

In the United States, as the Democratic Party came to be identified with the professional classes, white voters without a college education turned away from it. This trend continued after the election of Trump. In the 2018 congressional elections, 61 percent of non-college-educated white voters supported Republicans, and only 37 percent voted for Democrats. The deepening diploma divide can also be seen by looking at the thirty congressional districts with the highest proportion of college graduates. In 1992, when Bill Clinton was elected president, these districts divided evenly; half elected Democrats to Congress, and half elected Republicans. In 2018, Democrats won all but three of them.[64]

In the United Kingdom, the Labour Party's base of support has seen a similar shift. As recently as the early 1980s, about one-third of Labour Party MPs came from working-class backgrounds. By 2010, fewer than one in ten did. According to Oliver Heath, the decline of working-class MPs in the Labour ranks had a "substantial impact on the relative popularity of the party among working class voters," who increasingly viewed the party as "ruled by an out of touch metropolitan elite."[65]

The disaffection was first reflected in declining turnout among less-educated voters. Then, in 2016, it found expression in the vote to leave the European Union. Low-income voters were more likely than high-income voters to favor Brexit. But educational differences were more pronounced.

Over 70 percent of voters with no college education voted for Brexit, while over 70 percent of those with a postgraduate degree voted to remain.[66]

The pattern can also be seen in regional voting disparities. Of the twenty local authorities with the lowest percentage of college graduates, fifteen voted to leave. Of the twenty most highly educated areas, all voted to remain.[67]

In France, despite its different party system, the same educational divide has developed over the past few decades. Since the 1980s, non–university graduates have moved away from the Socialists and other left parties, which have become the parties of educational elites. In the 1950s and 1960s, left parties were working-class parties; the share of non-graduates voting for the left was about 20 percentage points higher than among university graduates. By the 1980s, the gap had closed, and by the 2010s, it had reversed; now the share of university graduates voting for the left is 10 percentage points higher than the share of non-graduates doing so—a shift of 30 points.[68]

Piketty speculates that the transformation of left parties from worker parties into parties of intellectual and professional elites may explain why they have not responded to the rising inequality of recent decades. Meanwhile, those who lack high-powered educational credentials resent the globalization that elites promote, and turn to populist, nativist candidates, such as Trump in the United States, and Marine Le Pen, who leads a nationalist, anti-immigrant party in France.[69]

In 2017, Emmanuel Macron, a liberal centrist, defeated Le Pen for the presidency of France. Macron's election was hailed by some commentators as a sign that the populist revolt could be quelled by a young, attractive candidate offering a market-friendly globalization program reminiscent of Clinton, Blair, and Obama. Like his meritocratic counterparts in the U.S. and the U.K., he drew his strongest support from voters with university educations and advanced degrees.[70]

But Macron's popularity soon faded, and his government was confronted with a series of street protests by citizens who donned the yellow safety vests (*gilets jaunes*) worn by stranded motorists. The protesters, mainly middle- and working-class residents of areas outside Paris, were angered by an increase in gas taxes, Macron's aloof manner, and economic policies that did little for those left behind by globalization. When, in the midst of the crisis, a senior politician from Macron's party was asked what mistakes by the government had provoked the protests, he replied, "We were probably too intelligent, too subtle."[71]

The relentless credentialism of our day has driven working-class voters toward populist and nationalist parties and deepened the divide between those with and those without a university degree. It has also led to increasingly partisan views of higher education, the institution most emblematic of the meritocratic project. As recently as 2015, Republicans and Democrats alike said that colleges and universities have a positive effect on the country. This is no longer the case. Today, 59 percent of Republicans believe that colleges and universities have a negative effect on the way things are going in the country, and only 33 percent view higher education favorably. By contrast, Democrats overwhelming believe (67 percent to 18 percent) that colleges and universities have a positive effect.[72]

One of the casualties of meritocracy's triumph may be the loss of broad public support for higher education. Once widely seen as an engine of opportunity, the university has become, at least for some, a symbol of credentialist privilege and meritocratic hubris.

The rhetoric of rising, with its single-minded focus on education as the answer to inequality, is partly to blame. Building a politics around the idea that a college degree is a condition of dignified work and social esteem has a corrosive effect on democratic life. It devalues the contributions of those without a diploma, fuels prejudice against less-educated members of society, effectively excludes most working people from representative government, and provokes political backlash.

TECHNOCRATIC TALK

Closely connected to these credentialist ills is the technocratic turn of public discourse. The more policy-making is described as a matter of "smart versus dumb," the greater the case for having "smart" people (experts and elites) decide things, rather than allowing citizens to debate and decide what policies to enact. For meritocratic elites, the rhetoric of "smart" and "dumb" seems to offer a non-partisan alternative to moral and ideological disagreement. But such disagreement lies at the heart of democratic politics. Too determined an effort to rise above the messy terrain of partisan disagreement can lead to a technocratic public discourse that diverts politics from questions of justice and the common good.

Barack Obama is a case in point. When speaking about redeeming the promise of equal rights for all Americans, his rhetoric could soar to heights of eloquence unmatched by any political figure of his day. His "Amazing Grace" eulogy in Charleston, South Carolina, honoring the memory of parishioners murdered in church by a hate-filled gunman, was one of the most stirring speeches by an American president in modern times.

And yet, when it came to his view of democratic governance, Obama was at heart a technocrat. As this may seem a harsh claim about a popular president, let me explain. To govern a democratic society requires contending with disagreement. Governing in the face of disagreement presupposes a view about how disagreements arise, and how they might be overcome in this or that moment, for this or that public purpose. Obama believed that the primary source of democratic disagreement is that ordinary citizens lack sufficient information.

If lack of information is the problem, the solution is for those with a fuller grasp of the facts to make decisions on behalf of their fellow citizens, or at least to enlighten them, to tell them what they need to know to make sensible decisions of their own. Presidential leadership is less about moral persuasion than about gathering and promulgating facts.

Obama articulated this vision of governing with remarkable clarity in a 2007 speech to Google employees, early in his campaign for the presidency. One of the things he had learned while traveling the country, he told them, is that "the American people at their core are a decent people. There's a generosity of spirit there, and there's common sense there, but it's not tapped." The reason:

Mainly people—they're just misinformed, or they are too busy, they're trying to get their kids to school, they're working, they just don't have enough information, or they're not professionals at sorting out all the information that's out there, and so our political process gets skewed. But if you give them good information, their instincts are good and they will make good decisions. And the president has the bully pulpit to give them good information.[73]

Ever since Theodore Roosevelt coined the term a century earlier, the "bully pulpit" has referred to the presidency as a place of moral inspiration and exhortation. Now the bully pulpit would be a venue for facts and data, for good information. This is the essence of a technocratic conception of politics, and it carries more than a whiff of meritocratic hubris. If the ordinary people who populate the land, however "decent," are "not professionals" at sorting out information, then the true professionals must do the sorting for them and provide them the facts they need.

Obama saw this as the way to heal America's "skewed" political process. The challenge was not to break up the large concentrations of economic power that bore down on the political process, or to awaken in the public a keener sense of the common good. It was to provide better, more accurate information. "I'm really looking forward to doing that, because I am a big believer in reason and facts and evidence and science and feedback," he told his Google audience. "I want to restore that sense of decisions being based on facts to the White House."[74]

It might be thought that this statement of technocratic faith was intended mainly to win supporters in the tech industry. But throughout his presidency and since, Obama has been true to this vision of politics. Further examples of this way of thinking highlight the affinity between technocratic politics and neoliberalism. To a far greater extent than previous presidents, Obama drew upon jargon familiar among academic economists and corporate executives. In making his case for health care reform, for example, he spoke less about the moral argument for universal coverage than about the need "to bend the cost curve," by which he meant reducing the rising cost of health expenditures. Although "bending the cost curve" did not stir much passion on the hustings, he used some version of this phrase more than sixty times in arguing the merits of his health care plan.[75]

In recent years, economists have argued for the use of market incentives to elicit desirable behavior. This emphasis on incentives has become so widespread that it has given rise to a new verb, "incentivize." Like many social scientists, management consultants, and business executives of the early twenty-first century, Obama embraced "incentivize" as a way of describing how market mechanisms could achieve desired outcomes. He offered policies to "incentivize" technological development, small business hiring, clean energy development, improved water management, good cybersecurity practices, weatherization programs, healthier nutrition, efficient health care delivery, positive school climates, responsible business conduct, and a host of other goals.

Incentivizing was a technocratic concept that fit well with Obama's instinct for avoiding partisan or ideological wrangling. It deployed a financial inducement to bring about a public purpose, and so seemed to strike a comfortable middle ground between a government mandate and an unfettered market choice. Where previous presidents had scarcely used the word, Obama spoke of "incentivizing" this or that behavior on more than one hundred occasions.[76]

More than any other aspect of his political rhetoric, Obama's constant talk of "smart" policies highlighted the connection between technocracy and meritocracy. For Obama, "smart" was the ultimate term of praise: "smart diplomacy," "smart foreign policy," "smart regulations," "smart growth," "smart spending cuts," "smart investments in education," "smart immigration policy," "smart infrastructure projects," "smart law enforcement," "smart government," "smart trade policy," "smart energy policy," "smart climate policy," "smart entitlement reform," "smart market reforms," "smart environmental regulations," "smart counterterrorism policy," "climate-smart agriculture," "smart development," "smart market-oriented innovation," and above all, "smart grids." During his presidency, Obama spoke in praise of "smart grids" or "smart grid technologies" on more than one hundred occasions. Overall, he used the adjective "smart" in connection with policies and programs more than nine hundred times.[77]

One of the defects of the technocratic approach to politics is that it places decision-making in the hands of elites, and so disempowers ordinary citizens. Another is that it abandons the project of political persuasion. Incentivizing people to act responsibly—to conserve energy or to watch their weight or to observe ethical business practices—is not only an alternative to coercing them; it is also an alternative to persuading them.

TECHNOCRACY VERSUS DEMOCRACY

The ideologically evasive, economistic talk emanating from meritocratic elites has coincided with a time when public discourse is increasingly rude and shrill, with partisans shouting and tweeting past one another. What the technocratic discourse and the shouting matches have in common is a failure to engage in a substantive way with the moral convictions that animate democratic citizens; neither cultivates the habit of reasoning together about competing conceptions of justice and the common good.

The populist upheavals of 2016—the Brexit vote in Britain and the election of Trump in the United States—repudiated meritocratic elites and the neoliberal, technocratic approach to politics. Replying to economists' predictions that leaving the European Union would bring economic hardship to the United Kingdom, a leading Brexit proponent replied, "The people in this country have had enough of experts."[78]

For his part, Obama struggled to make sense of the political earthquake that occurred at the end of his presidency. In 2018, two years after Trump was elected to succeed him, Obama conceded that proponents of globalization "did not adapt quickly enough to the fact that there were people being left behind." The Washington consensus "got a little too comfortable. Particularly after the Cold War, you had this period of great smugness on the part of America and American elites thinking we got this all figured out."[79]

But Obama's primary diagnosis of polarized politics in the age of Trump had to do with the public's inability to agree on basic facts. The reason we are "seeing so much gridlock and venom and polarization in our politics," he said, is partly because "we don't have a common baseline of facts and information." Those who watched Fox News and those who read *The New York Times* inhabited "entirely different realities," with "not just different opinions but different facts . . . It's like, epistemological."[80]

He offered a vivid illustration of what he saw as clashing realities:

> The biggest challenge we're going to have over the next 10, 15, 20 years is to return to a civic conversation in which if I say this is a chair, we agree this is a chair. Now we can disagree on whether it's a nice chair, whether we should replace the chair, whether you want to move it over there. But you can't say it's an elephant.[81]

Of course, the factual disputes that figure in political debate are not as simple as describing a piece of furniture. But the "elephant" in the room was climate change. What Obama meant is that it is hard to have a reasoned debate about climate change with people who deny its existence, or the human role in bringing it about.

Obama surely had in mind that his successor, abetted by climate change deniers, had withdrawn the United States from the Paris climate accord that he, Obama, had signed. He attributed this not only to ideological disagreement but to a rejection of science by Trump and his Republican supporters.

In fact, the slogan "I believe in science" has become a rallying cry for Democrats. Hillary Clinton proclaimed it in her speech accepting the nomination in 2016, Obama used it as president, and a number of candidates seeking the 2020 presidential nomination made it a refrain on the campaign trail. That the slogan implicitly relegates science to the realm of faith seems not to have diminished its popularity.[82]

In support of his long-held belief in the primacy of facts, Obama was fond of quoting Senator Daniel Patrick Moynihan, who once told an obdurate opponent, "You are entitled to your own opinion, but you are not entitled to your own facts." In telling the story, Obama sometimes added that Moynihan "was very smart" and his opponent "wasn't as smart."[83]

But attributing political disagreement to a simple refusal to face facts or accept science misunderstands the interplay of facts and opinion in political persuasion. The idea that we should all agree on the facts, as a pre-political baseline, and then proceed to debate our opinions and convictions, is a technocratic conceit. Political debate is often about how to identify and characterize the facts relevant to the controversy in question. Whoever succeeds in framing the facts is already a long way to winning the argument. Moynihan to the contrary, our opinions direct our perceptions; they do not arrive on the scene only after the facts are cut and dried.

DEBATING CLIMATE CHANGE

If the primary source of opposition to action on climate change were a lack of information or a refusal to accept science, one would expect opposition to be stronger among those with less education and scientific knowledge. But this is not the case. Studies of public opinion show that the more people know about science, the more polarized are their views on climate change.

Republicans are more skeptical than Democrats about global warming, and the partisan divide increases with education. Among Republicans with a high school education or less, 57 percent believe global warming is generally exaggerated. Among Republicans who are college graduates, 74 percent think so. Among Democrats, more education leads to greater concern with climate change. Of Democrats with a high school education or less, 27 percent consider global warming exaggerated; of Democrats with college degrees, only 15 percent think so.[84]

The partisan gap in climate change concern is thus almost twice as large (59 percent) among those with college degrees as among those with a high school education (30 percent). The same pattern holds true of beliefs about the human role in bringing about climate change. Asked whether "global warming is caused by natural changes in the environment," most Republicans say "yes," and most Democrats say "no." But the partisan gap among college graduates (53 percent) is much greater than among those with less education (19 percent).[85]

More detailed studies have found that political polarization on climate change tracks not only general levels of education but also scientific knowledge. People with greater scientific knowledge, as measured by science courses taken and tests of scientific literacy, are more likely than those who know less about science to adhere to their party's views on climate change.[86]

These findings challenge the idea that those unwilling to support measures to alleviate climate change are simply ill-informed about science. The partisan divide on climate change is not mainly about facts and information but about politics. It is a mistake to assume that the more people know about science, the more likely they are to converge on measures to combat climate change. The technocrat's belief that, if only we could agree on the facts, we could then have a reasoned debate about policy, misconceives the project of political persuasion.

Speaking in 2018 at MIT, Obama imagined the rational debate the country could have about climate change, if only everyone agreed on the basic facts:

> You and I can have an argument about climate change in which you conclude, "we're not going to stop the Chinese and the Indians from burning a bunch of coal, it's gone on for a pretty long time, we're just going to have to adapt, and maybe we'll invent some new energy source in the nick of time, and that's why I'm opposed to the Paris Accords."
>
> I'll come back and say, "well no, it turns out if we just invest in some smart technology and we create a smart regulatory framework that incentivizes investment in clean energy, we can actually solve this problem now, and if we don't it's going to be catastrophic."[87]

Obama wished we could have a wholesome debate such as this, and he lamented that the climate change deniers had made it impossible.[88]

But such a debate, even if possible, would be an impoverished mode of political argument. It assumes that our only choice is between resignation and imprudence on the one hand, and a value-neutral technocratic fix on the other. But this misses the deeper moral and political considerations that underlie the climate change controversy.

The appeal of the technocratic position, but also its weakness, is its seemingly frictionless value neutrality. Talk of "smart technology" and "smart regulatory frameworks" glides over the moral and political questions that make climate change a daunting and difficult issue: What would it take to counter the outsize influence of the fossil fuel industry on democratic politics? Should we reconsider the consumerist attitudes that lead us to treat nature instrumentally, as a dumping ground for what Pope Francis has called our "throwaway culture"?[89] And what about those who oppose government action to reduce carbon emissions, not because they reject science, but because they do not trust government to act in their interest, especially in a large-scale reconfiguration of the economy, and do not trust the technocratic elites who would design and implement this reconfiguration?

These are not scientific questions to be answered by experts. They are questions about power, morality, authority, and trust, which is to say they are questions for democratic citizens.

One of the failures of the well-credentialed, meritocratic elites who have governed for the past four decades is that they have not done very well at putting questions such as these at the heart of political debate. Now, as we find ourselves wondering whether democratic norms will survive, complaints about the hubris of meritocratic elites and the narrowness of their technocratic vision may seem trifling. But theirs was the politics that led to this moment, that produced the discontent that populist authoritarians exploit. Facing up to the failures of meritocracy and technocracy is an indispensable step toward addressing that discontent and reimagining a politics of the common good.

SUCCESS ETHICS

Consider two societies, both unequal, and to the same degree. Of every hundred dollars in national income, the richest 20 percent receive $62, while the poorest 20 percent get only $1.70. If you pooled the entire income of the bottom half of the society, you would have only $12.50, far less than the amount taken in by the richest 1 percent alone ($20.20). Disparities of wealth are even greater.[1]

If you are troubled by stark inequalities of income and wealth, you might well consider these two societies unjust. But before deciding, you might ask for some further information. You might want to know, for example, how these unequal distributions arose.

MERITOCRACY VERSUS ARISTOCRACY

Imagine, then, that the first society is an aristocracy, in which income and wealth are determined by the accident of birth and passed down from one generation to the next. Those born to noble families are wealthy, and those born to peasant families are poor. The same will be true of their children and their children's children. And imagine that the second society is a meritocracy. Its inequalities in income and wealth are not the result of hereditary privilege but the result of what people have earned through effort and talent.

Learning this would likely lead you to prefer the second society to the first. An aristocracy is unjust, because it consigns people to the class of their birth. It does not let them rise. A meritocracy, by contrast, enables people to improve their condition by exercising their talent and ingenuity. This is a powerful argument in its favor. To be sure, a meritocracy does not do away with inequality. Precisely because people differ in their talents and ambitions, some rise higher than others. But at least it can be said that these inequalities reflect people's merits rather than the circumstances of their birth.

Those who worry about inequality might still press for further information. They will suspect that, even in the meritocratic society, at least some of those at the top have benefited from a favorable starting point in life—loving, supportive, and possibly affluent families, good schools with dedicated teachers, and so on. Before declaring the meritocratic society just, these skeptics will want to know that policies are in place to ensure that all children, regardless of family background, have the educational and cultural opportunities to reach their full potential.

One way of thinking about what makes for a just society is to ask what kind of society you would choose if you did not know whether you would grow up in a rich family or a poor one. By this standard, most people would agree that a meritocracy with truly equal opportunity is more just than an aristocracy. But for the moment, put the question of justice aside and consider another feature of the two unequal societies we have imagined. Suppose you knew in advance whether you would land on top or on the bottom. Which of these two societies would you rather live in if you were rich, and which would you prefer if you were poor?

Remember, both societies are highly unequal. If you land in the top 1 percent, your average income will be (let's imagine) $1.3 million per year; if you land in the bottom 20 percent, it will be only $5,400 per year.[2] That is quite a difference. You might conclude that, since the gap between rich and poor is equally stark in both societies, knowing which position you will occupy does not help you decide which society to prefer.

But income and wealth would not be your only consideration. If you were rich, you might prefer the society that enabled you to bequeath your wealth and privilege to your children. This would argue for the aristocratic society. If you were poor, you might prefer the society that enabled you, or your children, a chance to rise. This would argue for the meritocratic society.

Further reflection, however, suggests a countervailing consideration in each case. People care not only about how much money they have but also about what their wealth or poverty signifies for their social standing and self-esteem. If you were born into the upper reaches of an aristocracy, you would be aware that your privilege was your good fortune, not your own doing. Whereas if you ascended, through effort and talent, to the apex of a meritocracy, you could take pride in the fact that your success was earned rather than inherited. Unlike aristocratic privilege, meritocratic success brings a sense of achievement for having earned one's place. From this point of view, it is better to be rich in a meritocracy than in an aristocracy.

For similar reasons, being poor in a meritocracy is demoralizing. If, in a feudal society, you were born into serfdom, your life would be hard, but you would not be burdened by the thought that you were responsible for your subordinate position. Nor would you labor under the belief that the landlord for whom you toiled had achieved his position by being more capable and resourceful than you. You would know he was not more deserving than you, only luckier.

If, by contrast, you found yourself on the bottom rung of a meritocratic society, it would be difficult to resist the thought that your disadvantage was at least partly your own doing, a reflection of your failure to display sufficient talent and ambition to get ahead. A society that enables people to rise, and that celebrates rising, pronounces a harsh verdict on those who fail to do so.

MERITOCRACY'S DARK SIDE

The term "meritocracy" was invented under the shadow of this worry. Michael Young was a British sociologist affiliated with the Labour Party. In 1958, he wrote a book called *The Rise of the Meritocracy*.[3] For Young, meritocracy described a dystopia, not an ideal. He wrote at a time when the British class system was breaking down, giving way to a system of educational and professional advancement based on merit. This was a good thing, because it enabled gifted children of the working class to develop their talents and escape a life consigned to manual labor.

But Young also glimpsed the dark side of meritocracy. Writing as if he were a historian looking back from the year 2033, he described with uncanny clarity the moral logic of the meritocratic society that was beginning to unfold in the postwar Britain of his day. Without defending the class-bound order that was passing, Young suggested that its moral arbitrariness and manifest unfairness at least had this desirable effect: It tempered the self-regard of the upper class and prevented the working class from viewing its subordinate status as personal failure.

Those who were "catapulted" to the top by their parents' riches and influence "could not say to themselves with complete conviction 'I am the best man for the job' because they knew that they had not won their place in open competition and, if they were honest, had to recognize that a dozen of their subordinates would have been as good, or perhaps better."[4]

> The upper-class man had to be insensitive indeed not to have noticed, at some time in his life, that a private in his regiment, a butler or "charlady" in his home, a driver of taxi or bus, or the humble workman with lined face and sharp eyes in the railway carriage or country pub—not to have noticed that amongst such people was intelligence, wit, and wisdom at least equal to his own.[5]

Even if some "upper-class men" deceived themselves into believing they deserved their place at the top, their subordinates were under no such illusion.

They knew "that many bosses were there not so much because of what they knew, as who they knew, and who their parents were." Knowing the system was rigged empowered the working class to challenge it politically. (This was the point of having a Labour Party.) Equally important, the arbitrariness of the class system spared workers from judging themselves by the inferior status society had assigned them.[6]

> The worker said to himself: "Here I am, a workman. Why am I a workman? Am I fit for nothing else? Of course not. Had I had a proper chance I would have shown the world. A doctor? A brewer? A minister? I could have done anything. I never had the chance. And so I am a worker. But don't think that at bottom I am any worse than anyone else."[7]

Young suggests that being clear-eyed about the moral arbitrariness of one's rank has a certain advantage; it prevents both the winners and the losers from believing they deserve their lot in life. This does not vindicate the class system. But it does shed light on a paradoxical feature of a meritocratic order. Allocating jobs and opportunities according to merit does not reduce inequality; it reconfigures inequality to align with ability. But this reconfiguration creates a presumption that people get what they deserve. And this presumption deepens the gap between rich and poor.

> Now that people are classified by ability, the gap between the classes has inevitably become wider. The upper classes are . . . no longer weakened by self-doubt and self-criticism. Today the eminent know that success is just reward for their own capacity, for their own efforts, and for their own undeniable achievement. They deserve to belong to a superior class. They know too, that not only are they of higher caliber to start with, but that a first-class education has been built upon their native gifts.[8]

Not only did Young anticipate the meritocratic hubris of elites; he glimpsed their affinity for technocratic expertise, their tendency to look down on those who lacked their lustrous credentials, and the corrosive effect of these attitudes on public discourse. The rising elites "come as close as anyone to understanding the full and ever-growing complexity of our technical civilization. They are trained in science, and it is scientists who have inherited the earth." Their superior intellect and education give them little reason or occasion to engage in serious discussion with those who lack a college degree.

How can they carry on a two-sided conversation with the lower classes when they [the elites] speak another, richer, and more exact language? Today, the elite know that . . . their social inferiors are inferiors in other ways as well—that is, in the two vital qualities, of intelligence and education, which are given pride of place in the more consistent value system of the twenty-first century.[9]

"One of our characteristic modern problems," Young observed (and remember, he was "observing" as if living in 2033), is that "some members of the meritocracy . . . have become so impressed with their own importance as to lose sympathy with the people whom they govern." He added sardonically that some meritocrats were "so tactless that even people of low caliber have been quite unnecessarily offended."[10] (Hillary Clinton's statement during the 2016 campaign that half of Donald Trump's supporters were "a basket of deplorables" comes to mind.)[11]

Resentment against elites was compounded by the self-doubt that a meritocracy inflicts on those who fail to rise.

Today all persons, however humble, know they have had every chance . . . Are they not bound to recognize that they have an inferior status—not as in the past because they were denied opportunity; but because they *are* inferior? For the first time in human history the inferior man has no ready buttress for his self-regard.[12]

Young anticipated that this toxic brew of hubris and resentment would fuel a political backlash. He concluded his dystopian tale by predicting that, in

2034, the less-educated classes would rise up in a populist revolt against the meritocratic elites. In 2016, as Britain voted for Brexit and America for Trump, that revolt arrived eighteen years ahead of schedule.

MERITOCRACY RECONSIDERED

The two societies I described above are not purely hypothetical. The income inequalities that beset them are the ones that prevail in the United States today.[13] For the most part, these inequalities are defended, when they are defended at all, on something like meritocratic grounds. No one argues that the rich should be rich because they were born to wealthy parents. Critics of inequality may complain that those who would abolish inheritance taxes, say, are implicitly endorsing hereditary privilege. But no one defends hereditary privilege outright or disputes the principle that careers should be open to talents.

Most of our debates about access to jobs, education, and public office proceed from the premise of equal opportunity. Our disagreements are less about the principle itself than about what it requires. For example, critics of affirmative action in hiring and college admissions argue that such policies are inconsistent with equality of opportunity, because they judge applicants on factors other than merit. Defenders of affirmative action reply that such policies are necessary to make equality of opportunity a reality for members of groups that have suffered discrimination or disadvantage.

At the level of principle at least, and political rhetoric, meritocracy has won the day. In democracies throughout the world, politicians of the center-left and center-right claim that their policies are the ones that will enable all citizens, whatever their race or ethnicity, gender or class, to compete on equal terms and to rise as far as their efforts and talents will take them. When people complain about meritocracy, the complaint is usually not about the ideal but about our failure to live up to it: The wealthy and powerful have rigged the system to perpetuate their privilege; the professional classes have figured out how to pass their advantages on to their children, converting the meritocracy into a hereditary aristocracy; colleges that claim to select students on merit give an edge to the sons and daughters of the wealthy and the well-connected. According to this complaint, meritocracy is a myth, a distant promise yet to be redeemed.[14]

This complaint is certainly valid. But what if the problem runs deeper? What if the real problem with meritocracy is not that we have failed to achieve it but that the ideal is flawed? What if the rhetoric of rising no longer inspires, not simply because social mobility has stalled but, more fundamentally, because helping people scramble up the ladder of success in a competitive meritocracy is a hollow political project that reflects an impoverished conception of citizenship and freedom?

To explore this larger question, we need to examine two objections to meritocracy as a moral and political project. One is about justice; the other is about attitudes toward success and failure. The first objection doubts that even a fully realized meritocracy, in which jobs and pay perfectly reflected people's efforts and talents, would be a just society. The second objection worries that even if a meritocracy were fair, it would not be a good society. It would generate hubris and anxiety among the winners and humiliation and resentment among the losers—attitudes at odds with human flourishing and corrosive of the common good.

Philosophical critiques of meritocracy focus mainly on the first objection. For reasons we will explore, most contemporary philosophers reject the notion that society should allocate jobs and pay based on what people deserve. This puts philosophers at odds with the moral intuitions that inform common opinion, and it is worth trying to figure out who is right—the philosophers or the public.

Although the first objection, about justice, is the more familiar one in philosophical circles, the second objection, about hubris and humiliation, may be more consequential for understanding our current political condition. The populist protest against meritocratic elites is not only about fairness but also about social esteem. To understand this protest is to identify and assess the grievances and resentments that animate it. Are they legitimate or misdirected? Insofar as they are legitimate, what might be done to address them?

WOULD A PERFECT MERITOCRACY BE JUST?

Imagine that, one day, we managed to remove all unfair obstacles to success, so that everyone, including those from humble backgrounds, could compete with the children of the privileged on a level playing field. Imagine that we achieved in fact what we proclaim in principle, that all citizens should have an equal chance to rise as far as their talents and hard work can take them.

Of course, such a society would be difficult to achieve. Overcoming discrimination would not be enough. The institution of the family complicates the project of giving everyone an equal chance. It is not easy to offset the advantages that affluent parents confer on their children. I am not thinking mainly of inherited wealth. A robust estate tax could deal with that. I am thinking of the everyday ways that conscientious, well-to-do parents help their kids. Even the best, most inclusive educational system would be hard pressed to equip students from poor backgrounds to compete on equal terms with children from families that bestow copious amounts of attention, resources, and connections.

But suppose this could be done. Suppose we could fulfill the promise of giving every child an equal chance to compete for success in school, in the workplace, and in life. Would this make for a just society?

It is tempting to say, "Yes, of course. Isn't this what the American dream is all about—creating an open, mobile society in which the child of a farm worker or a penniless immigrant can rise to become a CEO?" And while this dream holds a special allure for Americans, it also resonates in democratic societies throughout the world.

A perfectly mobile society is an inspiring ideal for two reasons. First, it expresses a certain idea of freedom. Our fate should not be fixed by the circumstances of our birth but should be ours to decide. Second, it gestures to the hope that what we achieve reflects what we deserve. If we are free to rise based on our own choices and talents, it seems fair to say that those who succeed deserve their success.

Despite its powerful appeal, however, there is reason to doubt that even a perfectly realized meritocracy would be a just society. To begin, it is important to notice that the meritocratic ideal is about mobility, not equality. It does not say there is anything wrong with yawning gaps between rich and poor; it only insists that the children of the rich and the children of the poor should be able, over time, to swap places based on their merits—to rise or fall as a result of their effort and talent. No one should be stuck at the bottom, or ensconced at the top, due to prejudice or privilege.

What matters for a meritocracy is that everyone has an equal chance to climb the ladder of success; it has nothing to say about how far apart the rungs on the ladder should be. The meritocratic ideal is not a remedy for inequality; it is a justification of inequality.

This is not, in itself, an argument against it. But it raises a question: Is the inequality that results from meritocratic competition justified? Defenders of meritocracy say yes; provided everyone competes on a level playing field, the outcome is just. Even a fair competition has winners and losers. What matters is that everyone starts the race at the same starting point, having had equal access to training, coaching, nutrition, and so on. If so, the winner of the race deserves the prize. There is no injustice in the fact that some run faster than others.

DO WE DESERVE OUR TALENTS?

Whether this argument is convincing depends on the moral status of talents. Recall the rhetoric of rising that figures so prominently in public discourse these days. However humble our origins, the politicians proclaim, we should all be able to rise as far as our talent and hard work will take us. But why exactly that far? Why assume that our talents should determine our destiny, and that we merit or deserve the rewards that flow from them?

There are two reasons to question this assumption. First, my having this or that talent is not my doing but a matter of good luck, and I do not merit or deserve the benefits (or burdens) that derive from luck. Meritocrats acknowledge that I do not deserve the benefits that arise from being born into a wealthy family. So why should other forms of luck—such as having a particular talent—be any different? If I won a million dollars in the state lottery, I would be delighted at my good fortune. But it would be folly to claim I had earned the windfall, or that my winning had anything to do with my merit. Similarly, if I bought a lottery ticket and failed to win, I might be disappointed, but I could not complain that I had been denied something I deserved.

Second, that I live in a society that prizes the talents I happen to have is also not something for which I can claim credit. This too is a matter of good fortune. LeBron James makes tens of millions of dollars playing basketball, a hugely popular game. Beyond being blessed with prodigious athletic gifts, LeBron is lucky to live in a society that values and rewards them. It is not his doing that he lives today, when people love the game at which he excels, rather than in Renaissance Florence, when fresco painters, not basketball players, were in high demand.

The same can be said of those who excel in pursuits our society values less highly. The world champion arm wrestler may be as good at arm wrestling as LeBron is at basketball. It is not his fault that, except for a few pub patrons, no one is willing to pay to watch him pin an opponent's arm to the table.[15]

Much of the appeal of the meritocratic faith consists in the idea that our success is our own doing, at least under the right conditions. Insofar as the economy is a field of fair competition, untainted by privilege or prejudice, we are responsible for our fate. We succeed or fail based on our merits. We get what we deserve.

This is a liberating picture, for it suggests we can be self-made human agents, the authors of our fate, the masters of our destiny. It is also morally satisfying, because it suggests the economy can answer to the ancient notion of justice as giving people their due.

But the recognition that our talents are not our own doing complicates this picture of self-making. It puts in doubt the meritocratic faith that overcoming prejudice and privilege is sufficient to bring about a just society. If our talents are gifts for which we are indebted—whether to the genetic lottery or to God—then it is a mistake and a conceit to assume we deserve the benefits that flow from them.

DOES EFFORT MAKE US WORTHY?

Defenders of meritocracy reply by invoking effort and hard work. They argue that those who rise by dint of hard work are responsible for the success their efforts bring, and worthy of praise for their industriousness. This is true, up to a point. Effort matters, and no one, however gifted, succeeds without working to cultivate his or her talents. Even the most gifted musician must devote long hours of practice to become good enough to play at Carnegie Hall. Even the most gifted athlete must spend strenuous years of training to make the Olympic team.

Notwithstanding the importance of effort, however, success rarely comes from hard work alone. What sets Olympic medal winners and NBA stars apart from lesser athletes is not only their strenuous training regimes. Many basketball players practice as hard as LeBron, but few can match his exploits on the court. I could train night and day but I will never swim faster than Michael Phelps. Usain Bolt, the gold medal sprinter considered the fastest runner in the world, acknowledged that his training partner Yohan Blake, also a gifted sprinter, works harder than he does. Effort isn't everything.[16]

The defenders of meritocracy know this, of course. They do not claim that the hardest-working athlete deserves the gold medal, or that the most industrious scientist deserves the Nobel Prize, or that the worker who expends the most effort deserves the highest pay, regardless of results.

They know that success is an amalgam of talent and effort that is not easy to disentangle. Success breeds success, and those who lack the talents society rewards may find it hard to summon the motivation to strive. But the meritocratic argument is not mainly a sociological claim about the efficacy of effort. It is above all a moral claim about human agency and freedom.

The meritocratic emphasis on effort and hard work seeks to vindicate the idea that, under the right conditions, we are responsible for our success and thus capable of freedom. It also seeks to vindicate the faith that, if the competition is truly fair, success will align with virtue; those who work hard and play by the rules will earn the rewards they deserve.

We want to believe that success, in sports and in life, is something we earn, not something we inherit. Natural gifts and the advantages they bring embarrass the meritocratic faith. They cast doubt on the conviction that praise and rewards flow from effort alone. In the face of this embarrassment, we inflate the moral significance of effort and striving. This distortion can be seen, for example, in television coverage of the Olympics, which focuses less on the feats the athletes perform than on heart-rending stories of the hardships they have overcome, the obstacles they have surmounted, and the struggles they have waged to triumph over injury, or a difficult child-hood, or political turmoil in their native land.[17]

It can be seen in the overwhelming majority (77 percent) of Americans who, despite the difficulty of rising, believe that "most people can succeed if they are willing to work hard."[18] I see a similarly exaggerated emphasis on striving in my Harvard students who, despite their impressive talents and often favorable life circumstances, invariably attribute their admission to effort and hard work.

If the meritocratic ideal is flawed because it ignores the moral arbitrariness of talent and inflates the moral significance of effort, it remains to ask what alternative conceptions of justice are available—and what notions of freedom and desert they offer instead.

TWO ALTERNATIVES TO MERITOCRACY

Over the past half century, two competing accounts of a just society have shaped political argument in most democratic societies. One might be called free-market liberalism, the other welfare state liberalism (or "egalitarian liberalism"). These two public philosophies stand in a complex relation to meritocracy. Both offer compelling arguments against the meritocratic idea that a just society distributes income and wealth based on what people deserve.

In practice, however, each generates attitudes toward success that are difficult to distinguish from meritocratic ones. Neither offers an account of the common good sufficiently robust to counter the hubris and humiliation to which meritocracies are prone. Despite rejecting the notion that the winners in a competitive market society morally deserve their winnings, these public philosophies offer no antidote to the tyranny of merit. It is instructive nonetheless to see why, despite their disagreements, they both reject merit as the basis of justice.

Free-Market Liberalism

Perhaps the most influential case for free-market liberalism in the twentieth century was advanced by Friedrich A. Hayek, an Austrian-born economist-philosopher. A source of inspiration for Margaret Thatcher and other proponents of laissez-faire capitalism, Hayek opposed government efforts to reduce economic inequality, argued against progressive taxation, and viewed the welfare state as antithetical to freedom.

In his book *The Constitution of Liberty* (1960), Hayek argues that the only equality compatible with freedom is the purely formal equality of all citizens before the law. Careers should be open to everyone, but the state should not try to create a level playing field by providing equal or compensatory educational opportunities, a project he viewed as unrealistic and ultimately coercive. Unless the family were abolished, children would inevitably grow up in families that varied in the advantages they afforded, and any attempt to give all children an equal prospect for success would involve intolerable state coercion. Hayek rejects the notion "that all must be assured an equal start and the same prospects" for success. Such a principle would require the state to control "all conditions relevant to a particular individual's prospects," a far-reaching project that Hayek considers "the opposite of freedom."[19]

Given his opposition to the redistribution of income, one might expect Hayek to insist that the free market gives people the economic rewards they deserve. But he does not. In fact, he argues that market outcomes have nothing to do with rewarding merit. They simply reflect the value consumers place on the goods and services sellers have to offer. Hayek draws a distinction between merit and value. Merit involves a moral judgment about what people deserve, whereas value is simply a measure of what consumers are willing to pay for this or that good.[20]

It is a mistake, Hayek argues, to over-moralize economic rewards by assuming they reflect the merit of those who receive them. One of the reasons Hayek wants to deflate this moralizing notion is to disarm a familiar objection to the inequalities of income and wealth produced by unfettered markets. The most compelling objection to inequality, he suggests, arises from the concern that "the differences in reward do not correspond to any recognizable differences in the merits of those who receive them."[21]

Hayek's reply to this objection is revealing. Rather than try to show that those who earn handsome rewards in the market morally deserve them, he rejects the idea that economic rewards reflect people's merits, or moral desert. This is the force of his distinction between merit and value. In a free society, my income and wealth will reflect the value of the goods and services I have to offer, but this value is determined by contingencies of supply and demand. It has nothing to do with my merit or virtue, or the moral importance of the contribution I make.

To illustrate Hayek's point, consider an example. Some people argue that hedge fund managers do not deserve to make vastly more money than schoolteachers; managing money is far less admirable and important than teaching and inspiring young people. A defender of free markets might reply that hedge fund managers are responsible for investing the hard-earned pensions of teachers, firefighters, and college endowments, and so the moral importance of their work makes them worthy of the vast sums they earn. But Hayek does not offer this kind of reply. His argument is more radical. It rejects the very idea that the money people make should reflect what they deserve.

Hayek supports this argument by observing that my having the talents society happens to prize is not my doing, but morally contingent, a matter of good luck:

> The inborn as well as the acquired gifts of a person clearly have a value to his fellows which does not depend on any credit due to him

for possessing them. There is little a man can do to alter the fact that his special talents are very common or exceedingly rare. A good mind or a fine voice, a beautiful face or a skillful hand, and a ready wit or an attractive personality are in large measure as independent of a person's efforts as the opportunities or the experiences he has had. In all these instances the value which a person's capacities or services have for us and for which he is recompensed has little relation to anything that we can call moral merit or deserts.[22]

For Hayek, denying that economic rewards are a matter of merit is a way of fending off demands for redistribution by those who believe that hedge fund managers do not deserve to make more than teachers. Hayek is able to reply that, even if we consider the vocation of teaching to be more admirable than managing money, wages and salaries are not awards for good character or worthy achievement but simply payments that reflect the economic value of the goods and services market participants have to offer.

Unlike Hayek, defenders of welfare state liberalism favor taxing the rich to help the poor. Surprisingly, however, they share Hayek's view that the distribution of income and wealth should not be based on what people merit or deserve.

Welfare State Liberalism

Welfare state liberalism (or "egalitarian liberalism") finds its fullest philosophical expression in the work of John Rawls, the noted twentieth-century American political philosopher. In his classic work *A Theory of Justice* (1971), Rawls argues that even a system of fair equality of opportunity, one that fully compensated for the effects of class differences, would not make for a just society. The reason: If people competed on a truly level playing field, the winners would be those endowed with the greatest talent. But differences of talent are as morally arbitrary as differences of class.[23]

"Even if it works to perfection in eliminating the influence of social contingencies," Rawls argues, a fair meritocracy "still permits the distribution of wealth and income to be determined by the natural distribution of abilities and talents."[24] Income inequalities due to natural talents are no more just than inequalities that arise from class differences. "From a moral standpoint the two seem equally arbitrary."[25] So even a society that achieved true equality of opportunity would not necessarily be a just society. It would have also to contend with the inequalities that arise due to differences in people's native abilities.

How to contend with them? Some defenders of meritocracy worry that the only alternative to equality of opportunity is equality of result, a kind of leveling equality that would handicap the gifted to prevent them from gaining a competitive edge. In a short story called "Harrison Bergeron," the author Kurt Vonnegut, Jr., imagines a dystopian future in which those with superior intelligence, physical strength, and good looks are required to wear elaborate encumbrances and disguises to offset their natural advantages.[26]

But Rawls shows that this is not the only way to compensate for unequal talents. "No one deserves his greater natural capacity nor merits a more favorable starting place in society. But it does not follow that one should eliminate these distinctions. There is another way to deal with them."[27] Rather than handicap the talented, Rawls would have the winners share their winnings with those less fortunate than themselves. Don't make the best runners wear lead shoes; let them run at full speed. But acknowledge in advance that the winnings do not belong to them alone. Encourage the gifted to cultivate and exercise their talents, but with the understanding that the rewards those talents reap in the market should be shared with the community as a whole.

Rawls calls this way of dealing with unequal talents "the difference principle." It departs from meritocracy, not by preventing the gifted from exercising their talents but by denying that they merit or deserve the rewards those talents command in a market society.

"The difference principle represents," Rawls writes, "an agreement to regard the distribution of natural talents as a common asset and to share in the benefits of this distribution whatever it turns out to be. Those who have been favored by nature, whoever they are, may gain from their good fortune only on terms that improve the situation of those who have lost out." Society should be arranged "so that these contingencies work for the good of the least fortunate."[28]

The meritocrat might reply that, even if our natural talents are a matter of good luck, our effort is up to us. We therefore deserve what we earn by dint of effort and hard work. Rawls disagrees. "Even the willingness to make an effort, to try, and so to be deserving in the ordinary sense is itself dependent upon happy family and social circumstances." Even effort cannot save the idea that market rewards should reflect moral desert.

> The assertion that a man deserves the superior character that enables him to make the effort to cultivate his abilities is equally problematic; for his character depends in large part upon fortunate family and social circumstances for which he can claim no credit. The notion of desert seems not to apply to these cases.[29]

Like Hayek, Rawls emphasizes the moral arbitrariness of talent and rejects the idea that market outcomes reflect merit or desert. But for Rawls, this argues for redistributive taxation, not against it. To those who would deny the state the right to tax a portion of their hard-earned income, claiming they deserve it, Rawls replies that the amount of money we make depends on factors that are arbitrary from a moral point of view. It is not my doing that the market prizes the talents I have, or that I possess those talents in the first place. So I cannot rightly complain if the tax laws require me to turn over a portion of my income to pay for schools or roads or help for the poor.

It might be argued that, even if I do not morally deserve the benefits the market bestows on my talents, it is a further question how these benefits should be distributed. Should society distribute them to the community as a whole, or to the least fortunate members of society, or (as Hayek thinks) simply let them lie where they fall? Rawls's argument that market earnings reflect factors arbitrary from a moral point of view is a powerful negative argument; it undermines the meritocratic claim that the rich deserve the money they make. But it does not establish that the community has a legitimate moral claim to this money, or some portion of it.

This would depend on showing that we are indebted in various ways to the community that makes our success possible and therefore obligated to contribute to its common good.[30]

Politically as well as philosophically, welfare state liberals are better at articulating the negative argument—against the individual's sole claim to her success—than the affirmative argument—for the individual's debt to the community. Recall Barack Obama's attempt to evoke the mutual dependence and obligation of citizens during his 2012 re-election campaign:

> [I]f you've been successful, you didn't get there on your own. You didn't get there on your own. I'm always struck by people who think, well, it must be because I was just so smart. There are a lot of smart people out there. It must be because I worked harder than everybody else. Let me tell you something—there are a whole bunch of hardworking people out there.
>
> If you were successful, somebody along the line gave you some help. There was a great teacher somewhere in your life. Somebody helped to create this unbelievable American system that we have that allowed you to thrive. Somebody invested in roads and bridges. If you've got a business—you didn't build that. Somebody else made that happen.[31]

Republicans seized on the last two sentences to portray Obama as an apostle of big government who was hostile to entrepreneurs. Of course, he did not mean that my business or yours was actually built by "somebody else." He was trying to say that the successful are not solely responsible for their success, but indebted to the community that makes it possible, not only by building roads and bridges but also by cultivating our talents and valuing our contributions. "You're not on your own, we're in this together," he added a few sentences later.[32]

More than a slip of the tongue, Obama's awkward attempt to describe the moral debt the successful owe their fellow citizens reflects a weakness in the philosophy of welfare state liberalism, which fails to provide a sense of community adequate to the solidarity it requires. This may account for the faltering legitimacy of the welfare state in recent decades, not only in the United States but also in Europe, where public services and safety nets have traditionally been more generous. It may also account for the inability of liberal democracies to resist the rampant inequality of recent decades and the rising tide of meritocratic sentiment, in political rhetoric and public attitudes, that has rationalized it.

REJECTING MERIT

Both Hayek and Rawls reject merit or desert as the basis of justice. For Hayek, denying that economic rewards are a matter of merit is a way of resisting demands for redistribution.

For Rawls, the renunciation of merit and desert serves the opposite political position. It is a way of countering objections to redistribution by wealthy people who claim, for example, that they deserve the money they have earned, and that it is therefore wrong to tax a portion of those earnings for redistributive purposes. Rawls can reply that making a lot of money is not a measure of a person's merit or virtue; it simply reflects the happy coincidence of the skills a person has to offer with the abilities the market demands. Once just tax laws are in place, people are entitled to keep whatever portion of their earnings the tax code specifies. But they cannot rightly claim that the tax laws should be written in the first place to honor or reward their merits and achievements.[33]

Although Rawls and Hayek differ politically, their rejection of merit as the basis of justice highlights two philosophical commitments they share. One is about the difficulty of coming to agreement, in pluralist societies, about which virtues and qualities of character are worthy of reward. The other is about freedom. "Reward according to merit must in practice mean reward according to assessable merit," Hayek writes, "merit that other people can recognize and agree upon and not merit merely in the sight of some higher power." The difficulty of identifying merit gives rise to a deeper problem. Given the inevitable disagreement about which activities are meritorious or worthy of praise, any attempt to base distributive justice on moral merit rather than economic value would lead to coercion. "A society in which the position of the individual was made to correspond to human ideas of moral merit would therefore be the exact opposition of a free society."[34]

Rawls also points to widespread disagreement about merit and desert, and worries that basing justice on desert is at odds with freedom. Unlike Hayek, Rawls does not conceive freedom in market terms. For Rawls, freedom consists in pursuing our own conception of the good life while respecting the right of others to do the same. This means abiding by principles of justice that we and our fellow citizens would all agree to if each of us set aside our particular interests and advantages. Thinking about justice from this point of view—without knowing whether we would be rich or poor, strong or weak, healthy or unhealthy—would not lead us to affirm whatever distribution of income resulted from the market. To the contrary, Rawls argues, it would lead us to accept only those inequalities that help the least-advantaged members of society.

Although Rawls rejects the distribution of income that results from a free market, he does have this in common with Hayek: Rawls's principles of justice do not seek to reward merit or virtue. In pluralist societies, people disagree about what counts as meritorious or virtuous, as these judgments depend on controversial conceptions of the best way to live. From Rawls's point of view, to base principles of justice on one such conception would be to undermine freedom; it would impose on some the values of others, and so fail to respect each person's right to choose and pursue his or her own conception of the good life.

And so, despite their differences, both Hayek and Rawls reject the idea that economic rewards should reflect what people deserve. In doing so, they acknowledge that they are challenging conventional wisdom. The notion that justice means giving people what they deserve seems deeply embedded in untutored common opinion. Rawls notes the "tendency for common sense to suppose" that income and wealth should be distributed according to moral desert, and Hayek admits that his renunciation of merit "may appear at first so strange and even shocking" that he must "ask the reader to suspend judgment" until he can explain.[35]

But even as free-market liberalism and welfare state liberalism set the terms of public discourse over the past half century, they did not dislodge the widely held conviction that what people earn should reflect what they deserve.[36] To the contrary, during those decades, meritocratic attitudes toward success tightened their hold, even as mobility stalled and inequality deepened.

MARKETS AND MERIT

Here then is a puzzling feature of contemporary politics: Why, despite the rejection of meritocratic assumptions by the leading public philosophies of the day, do political rhetoric and public attitudes cleave to the notion that economic rewards either do align or should align with merit and desert? Is it simply that philosophy is too distant from the world to have any bearing on the way ordinary citizens think and act? Or do certain features of free-market liberalism and welfare state liberalism open the way to meritocratic understandings of success that they officially reject?

I believe the second is the case. A closer look at these two versions of liberalism reveals that their renunciation of merit and desert is not as thoroughgoing as may first appear. Both reject the meritocratic notion that, in a fair competition, the rich are more deserving than the poor. But the alternatives they offer can nonetheless give rise to attitudes characteristic of meritocratic societies—hubris among the successful and resentment among the disadvantaged.

This can be seen most clearly in Hayek's distinction between merit and value. Hayek rightly observes that conceiving income inequalities as reflections of unequal merit adds insult to injury. "A society in which it was generally presumed that a high income was proof of merit and a low income of the lack of it, in which it was universally believed that position and remuneration corresponded to merit . . . would probably be much more unbearable to the unsuccessful ones than one in which it was frankly recognized that there was no necessary connection between merit and success."[37] Hayek cites the British Labour Party figure Anthony Crosland, whose influential book *The Future of Socialism* (1956) also emphasized the demoralizing effect that a meritocracy can have on those who do not rise:

> When opportunities are known to be unequal, and the selection clearly biased towards wealth or lineage, people can comfort themselves for failure by saying that they never had a proper chance— the system was unfair, the scales too heavily weighted against them. But if the selection is obviously by merit, this source of comfort disappears, and failure induces a total sense of inferiority, with no excuse or consolation; and this, by a natural quirk of human nature, actually increases the envy and resentment at the success of others.[38]

Hayek argues that keeping in mind the difference between merit and value renders income inequalities less invidious. If everyone knew such inequalities had nothing to do with people's merit, the rich would be less proud and the poor less resentful than they would otherwise be. But if, as Hayek claims, economic value is a legitimate basis for inequality, it is not so clear that invidious attitudes toward success are undercut.

For consider: How different, really, is the story the successful tell themselves if they believe their success measures the value of their contribution rather than their virtue or merit? And how different is the story the disadvantaged tell themselves if they believe their struggles do not reflect poorly on their character, only on the meager value of what they have to offer?

Morally and psychologically, the distinction between merit and value becomes vanishingly thin. This is especially true in market societies, where money is the measure of most things. In such societies, reminding the wealthy that their wealth reflects (only) the superior value of their contributions to society is an unlikely antidote to hubris and self-congratulation. And reminding the poor that their poverty reflects (only) the inferior value of their contributions is hardly a bracing tonic to their self-esteem.

The ease with which judgments of value can slide into judgments of merit reflects the familiar but questionable assumption that a person's market value is a good measure of his or her contribution to society. Hayek accepts this assumption uncritically. He simply points out that our market value is determined by factors beyond our control and so is not a measure of our merit. But he does not consider the possibility that the value of a person's contribution to society could be something other than his or her market value.

Once market value is taken as a proxy for social contribution, however, it is hard to resist the thought that people deserve, as a matter of justice, whatever income corresponds to their market value, or "marginal product" in the economist's jargon. According to standard economic analysis, perfectly competitive markets pay each worker the value of his or her "marginal product," the value of output attributable to that worker.

If, notwithstanding the complexity of the economy, it is possible to identify and individuate each person's market value in this way, and if market value is the true measure of social contribution, then it is a short step to concluding that people morally deserve to be paid according to their "marginal product," or market value.

A recent version of this argument has been advanced by Harvard economist N. Gregory Mankiw, who served as an economic advisor to President George W. Bush. Mankiw begins by stating a widely held and intuitively appealing moral principle: "People should get what they deserve. A person who contributes more to society deserves a higher income that reflects those greater contributions." He offers, as examples, Steve Jobs, the founder of Apple, and J. K. Rowling, author of the wildly popular Harry Potter books. Most people agree that they deserve the millions they have made, Mankiw suggests, because their high earnings reflect the great value to society of iPhones and riveting adventure tales.[39]

Mankiw would extend this reasoning to all incomes in a competitive market economy: Morality should endorse the results that competitive markets generate, for care workers and hedge fund managers alike. Since "each person's income reflects the value of what he contributed to society's production of goods and services," Mankiw argues, "one might easily conclude that, under these idealized conditions, each person receives his just deserts."[40]

The assertion that people morally deserve whatever income a competitive free market assigns them goes back to the early days of neoclassical economics. Critics of this notion, including some economists generally friendly to free markets, have long pointed out its defects. As we have seen, Hayek rejects this notion on the grounds that what people earn depends on native abilities that are no doing of the person endowed with them. It also depends on the vagaries of supply and demand. Whether the talents I have to offer are rare or plentiful is no doing of mine, and yet decisive for the income they command in the market. Mankiw's "just deserts" theory ignores these contingencies.

MARKET VALUE VERSUS MORAL VALUE

Perhaps the most devastating critique of the idea that market outcomes reflect moral desert was advanced in the 1920s by Frank Knight, one of the founders of neoclassical economics. Knight, a critic of the New Deal, taught at the University of Chicago, where his students included Milton Friedman and others who would become leading libertarian economists. And yet Knight took trenchant aim at the notion that markets reward merit. "It is a common assumption . . . that productive contribution is an ethical measure of desert," he wrote. But "an examination of the question will readily show that productive contribution can have little or no ethical significance."[41]

Knight offers two arguments against attributing moral desert to market outcomes. One is the argument about talents taken up by Hayek and Rawls, both of whom cite him.[42] Having talents that enable me to cater to market demand is no more my own doing than inheriting valuable property. "It is hard to see that . . . possession of the capacity to furnish services which are in demand . . . constitutes an ethical claim to a superior share of the social dividend, except to the extent that the capacity is itself the product of conscientious effort." Moreover, the income my talents command depends on how many other people also possess them. Having talents that happen to be scarce and yet highly prized certainly boosts my income, but it is nothing for which I can claim credit. "It is hard to see how it is more meritorious merely to be different from other people than it is to be like them."[43]

Knight's second argument is more far reaching. It questions an assumption that Hayek takes for granted. This is the assumption that equates market value with social contribution. As Knight points out, meeting market demand is not necessarily the same thing as making a truly valuable contribution to society.

Serving market demand is simply a matter of satisfying whatever wants and desires people happen to have. But the ethical significance of satisfying such wants depends on their moral worth. Evaluating their worth involves moral judgments, admittedly contestable, that economic analysis cannot provide. So even setting aside the question of talents, it is a mistake to assume that the money people make by catering to consumer preferences reflects merit or moral desert. Its ethical significance depends on moral considerations that no economic model can supply.

> We cannot accept want-satisfaction as a final criterion of value because we do not in fact regard our wants as final; instead of resting in the view that there is no disputing about tastes, we dispute about them more than anything else; our most difficult problem in valuation is the evaluation of our wants themselves and our most troublesome want is the desire for wants of the "right" kind.[44]

Knight's insight drives a wedge between two concepts that Hayek conflates — the value of an economic contribution as measured by the market and its actual value. Consider the high school chemistry teacher in the television series *Breaking Bad*, who employs his expertise as a chemist to make the highly sought-after (though illegal) drug methamphetamine. The meth he cooks is so pure that it commands millions on the drug market, and the income he reaps far exceeds his modest pay as a teacher. Most would agree, however, that his contribution as a teacher has far greater value than his contribution as a drug dealer.

The reason has nothing to do with market imperfections or the fact that laws banning drugs limit the supply and so boost the profits of those who peddle them illegally. Even if meth were legal, a talented chemist might still make more money producing meth than teaching students. But this does not mean that a meth dealer's contribution is more valuable than a teacher's.

Or consider the billionaire casino mogul Sheldon Adelson. One of the richest men in the world, he makes thousands of times more than a nurse or a doctor. But even assuming the markets for casino moguls and health care providers are perfectly competitive, there is no reason to believe that their market value reflects the true value of their contributions to society. This is because the value of their contributions depends on the moral importance of the ends they serve, not on how effectively they satisfy consumer demand. Caring for people's health is morally more important than catering to their desire to play slot machines.

Knight further argues that "the wants which an economic system operates to gratify are largely produced by the workings of the system itself." The economic order does not simply satisfy pre-existing demand; "its activity extends to the formation and radical transformation, if not to the outright creation, of the wants themselves." Any ethical assessment of an economic system must therefore consider "the kind of wants which it tends to generate or nourish," not only its efficiency in satisfying "wants as they exist at any given time."[45]

These considerations lead Knight to reject the notion Mankiw defends, that in a perfectly competitive market, people morally deserve the marginal product of their labor. Knight derides such claims as "the familiar ethical conclusions of apologetic economics."[46]

Although Knight, a skeptic of ambitious projects of social reform, is remembered as a leading proponent of laissez-faire economics, he inveighed against the idea that market prices are the measure of moral desert or ethical value.

> The product or contribution is always measured in terms of price, which does not correspond closely with ethical value or human significance. The money value of a product is a matter of the "demand," which in turn reflects the tastes and purchasing power of the buying public and the availability of substitute commodities. All these factors are largely created and controlled by the workings of the economic system itself . . . Hence their results can have in themselves no ethical significance as standards for judging the system.[47]

Although Knight does not claim to offer an ethical theory that could assess the moral importance of various wants and desires, he rejects the view, familiar among economists, that there is no judging tastes, that it is impossible to rank some wants as higher or worthier than others. An economic system should be judged less by its efficiency in satisfying consumer demand than "by the wants which it generates [and] the type of character which it forms in its people . . . Ethically, the creation of the right wants is more important than want-satisfaction."[48]

By challenging the assumption that the market value of productive contributions has ethical significance, Knight offers a critique of meritocracy more thoroughgoing than Hayek's, and one less susceptible to self-congratulation. Hayek tells the wealthy that although their wealth is no measure of their merit, it does reflect the superior value of their contribution to society. For Knight, this is overly flattering. Being good at making money measures neither our merit nor the value of our contribution. All the successful can honestly say is that they have managed—through some unfathomable mix of genius or guile, timing or talent, luck or pluck or grim determination—to cater effectively to the jumble of wants and desires, however weighty or frivolous, that constitute consumer demand at any given moment. Satisfying consumer demand is not valuable in itself; its value depends, case by case, on the moral status of the ends it serves.

DESERVING OR ENTITLED?

It remains to ask how egalitarian liberalism also fuels meritocratic hubris, despite rejecting the idea that people morally deserve the economic rewards that markets confer. To begin, it is important to clarify what Rawls means by rejecting desert as the basis of justice. He does not mean that no one has a legitimate claim to the income or position he or she acquires. In a just society, those who work hard and play by the rules are entitled to what they earn.

Here Rawls makes a subtle but important distinction—between moral desert and what he calls "entitlements to legitimate expectations." The difference is this: Unlike a desert claim, an entitlement can arise only once certain rules of the game are in place. It can't tell us how to set up the rules in the first place. Rawls's point is that we cannot know who is entitled to what until we first identify the principles of justice that should govern those rules and, more broadly, the basic structure of society.[49]

Here is how this distinction bears on the debate over meritocracy: To base justice on moral desert would be to set up the rules for the sake of rewarding the virtuous and the meritorious. Rawls rejects this. He thinks it is a mistake to regard an economic system—or, for that matter, a constitution—as a scheme for honoring virtue or cultivating good character. Considerations of justice are prior to considerations of merit and virtue.

This is the heart of Rawls's case against meritocracy. In a just society, those who become wealthy or attain prestigious positions are entitled to their success, not because it testifies to their superior merit but only insofar as these benefits are part of a system that is fair to everyone, including the worst-off members of society.

"A just scheme, then, answers to what men are entitled to; it satisfies their legitimate expectations as founded upon social institutions. But what they are entitled to is not proportional to nor dependent upon their intrinsic worth." The principles of justice that define people's duties and rights "do not mention moral desert, and there is no tendency for distributive shares to correspond to it."[50]

At stake in Rawls's renunciation of merit are two issues—one political, the other philosophical. Politically, Rawls wants to show that the affluent cannot legitimately object to redistributive taxation by claiming that their wealth is their due, something they morally deserve. This is the argument about the moral arbitrariness of talent and other contingencies that contribute to success. If success in a market economy depends heavily on luck, then it is hard to claim that the money we make is a reward for superior merit or desert.

> None of the precepts of justice aims at rewarding virtue. The premiums earned by scarce natural talents, for example, are to cover the costs of training and to encourage the efforts of learning, as well as to direct ability to where it best furthers the common interest. The distributive shares that result do not correlate with moral worth, since the initial endowment of natural assets and the contingencies of their growth and nurture in early life are arbitrary from a moral point of view.[51]

Philosophically, the assertion that principles of justice must be defined independent of considerations of merit, virtue, or moral desert is an instance of a more general feature of Rawls's liberalism. This is the claim that the "right" (the framework of duties and rights that governs society as a whole) is prior to the "good" (the various conceptions of virtue and the good life that people pursue within the framework). Principles of justice that affirmed a particular conception of merit, virtue, or moral desert would not be neutral toward the competing conceptions of the good life that citizens in pluralist societies espouse. Such principles would impose on some the values of others and so fail to respect everyone's right to choose and pursue their own way of life.

Rawls explains the priority of justice over merit by way of an analogy: We don't set up the institution of property because we believe thieves have bad character and we want an institution that will enable us to punish them for it. That would be, so to speak, a "meritocratic" theory of punishment. It would put the good before the right. But this gets the moral logic backward. Instead, we set up the institution of property for reasons of efficiency and justice; then, if people steal, we enforce the law by punishing them. Having violated the rights of others, they become worthy of punishment. The point of the punishment is to penalize thieves for committing an injustice, not to stigmatize them for bad character (though this may be a side effect).[52]

Rawls argues that a meritocratic approach to economic rewards would also reverse the proper relation between the right and the good. "For a society to organize itself with the aim of rewarding moral desert as a first principle would be like having the institution of property in order to punish thieves."[53]

ATTITUDES TOWARD SUCCESS

On the face of it, Rawls's non-meritocratic way of thinking about economic success should be humbling for the successful and consoling for the disadvantaged. It should restrain the tendency toward meritocratic hubris among elites and prevent the loss of self-esteem for those who lack power or wealth. If I truly believe my success is due to my good fortune rather than my own doing, I am more likely to feel an obligation to share this good fortune with others.

These sentiments are in short supply these days. Humility among the successful is not a prominent feature of contemporary social and economic life. One impetus to populist backlash is a widespread sense among working people that elites look down on them. To the extent this is the case, it could simply show that the contemporary welfare state falls short of Rawls's idea of a just society. Or it could suggest that egalitarian liberalism does not challenge the self-satisfaction of elites after all.

It is certainly true that the contemporary welfare state, especially in the United States, does not live up to Rawls's vision of a just society. Many of the inequalities of income and power we witness today do not arise from a system of fair equality of opportunity or work to the advantage of the least well-off. This leads liberals to interpret working-class resentment against elites as a complaint about injustice. If this is the only basis of anger against elites, the solution is to double down on the project of expanding opportunity and improving the economic prospects of the least well-off.

But this is not the only way of interpreting the populist backlash against elites. The hubristic attitudes toward success that invite this backlash could well be fueled by the sense of entitlement that Rawls's philosophy affirms, even as it rejects moral desert. For consider: Even a society that is perfectly just, as Rawls defines justice, admits certain inequalities—those that result from fair equality of opportunity and that work to the advantage of the least well-off. Imagine how, consistent with Rawlsian principles, a wealthy CEO could justify his or her advantages to a lower-paid worker on the factory floor:

> I am not worthier than you nor morally deserving of the privileged position I hold. My generous compensation package is simply an incentive necessary to induce me, and others like me, to develop our talents for the benefit of all. It is not your fault that you lack the talents society needs, nor is it my doing that I have such talents in abundance. This is why some of my income is taxed away to help people like you. I do not morally deserve my superior pay and position, but I am entitled to them under fair rules of social cooperation. And remember, you and I would have agreed to these rules had we thought about the matter before we knew who would land on top and who at the bottom. So please do not resent me. My privileges make you better off than you would otherwise be. The inequality you find galling is for your own good.[54]

To be sure, this rationale would not justify all inequalities of income, wealth, power, and opportunity that exist today. What it reveals, however, is that meritocratic attitudes toward success are not necessarily softened or displaced by liberal theories of distributive justice. Entitlements to legitimate expectations may be as potent a source of meritocratic hubris and working-class resentment as claims based on merit, virtue, or desert.

Recall the analogy with punishment. Even if the reason for punishing theft is to uphold the institution of property, a characteristic side effect of such punishment is to stigmatize thieves. Similarly, even if the reason for paying surgeons more than janitors is that such pay differentials are part of a just basic structure that works to the advantage of the least well-off, a predictable side effect of such pay differentials is to honor the special talents and contributions of surgeons. Over time, these normative "side effects" shape attitudes toward success (and failure) that are hard to distinguish from meritocratic ones.

Social esteem flows, almost ineluctably, to those who enjoy economic and educational advantages, especially if they earn those advantages under fair terms of social cooperation. Liberals might reply that, provided all members of society are accorded equal respect as citizens, the allocation of social esteem is not a political matter. Deciding what abilities and achievements are worthy of admiration is a matter of social norms and personal values—a matter of the good, not the right.[55]

But this reply overlooks the fact that the allocation of honor and recognition is a political question of central importance and has long been regarded as such. Aristotle considered justice to be mainly about the distribution of offices and honors, not the distribution of income and wealth. Today's populist revolt against elites is animated in large part by anger among working-class voters at what they take to be the disdain of the professional classes for those without a college degree. Insisting on the priority of the right over the good makes social esteem a matter of personal morality, and so blinds liberals to the politics of hubris and humiliation.

But it is folly to insist that the condescending attitudes of the credentialed, professional classes toward blue-collar workers is a matter of social norms that politics cannot or should not address. Questions of honor and recognition cannot be neatly separated from questions of distributive justice. This is especially true when it turns out that patronizing attitudes toward the disadvantaged are implicit in the case for compensating them. Sometimes these attitudes find explicit expression. As Thomas Nagel, a liberal egalitarian philosopher, has written, "when racial and sexual injustice have been reduced, we shall still be left with the great injustice of the smart and the dumb, who are so differently rewarded for comparable effort."[56]

"The smart and the dumb" is a telling phrase. It confirms populists' worst suspicions about liberal elites. Far from the democratic sensibility of Rawls, who seeks a society in which we "share one another's fate,"[57] Nagel's phrase lays bare the meritocratic hubris to which some versions of welfare state liberalism are prone.

CHANCE AND CHOICE

The tendency of welfare state liberalism to fuel the politics of hubris and humiliation became more explicit in the work of liberal egalitarian philosophers of the 1980s and 1990s. Building on Rawls's argument that the distribution of talents is arbitrary from a moral point of view, these philosophers argued that a just society should compensate people for bad luck of all kinds—being born poor, disabled, or with meager talents, or suffering accidents and misfortunes in the course of life. As one such philosopher wrote, "Distributive justice stipulates that the lucky should transfer some or all of their gains due to luck to the unlucky."[58]

At first glance, this "luck egalitarian" philosophy, as it came to be known, seems a generous response to the accidents of fortune. In seeking to redress the undeserved benefits and burdens that the lottery of life bestows, it seems to offer a humane alternative to a competitive meritocratic society.

On closer inspection, however, the luck egalitarian philosophy requires exacting judgments of merit and desert. Because it argues that people should be compensated only insofar as their misfortune is due to factors beyond their control, it conditions public assistance (for welfare, say, or health care) on whether a needy person is needy due to bad luck or bad choices. This requires policy makers to figure out who among the poor are victims of circumstance and hence deserving of help and who are responsible for their poverty and therefore undeserving.[59]

Elizabeth Anderson, a trenchant critic of luck egalitarianism, calls this distinction between the deserving and undeserving poor a revival of "Poor

Law thinking."[60] It puts the state in the position of interrogating needy citizens to determine whether they might have averted their poverty by making better choices. This parsing of responsibility is a morally unattractive way of conceiving the obligations that democratic citizens owe one another, for at least two reasons.

First, it bases our obligation to help those in need not on compassion or solidarity but on how they came to be needy in the first place. In certain cases, this makes moral sense. Most people would agree that a capable person who refuses to work simply out of indolence, even when decent jobs are available, has a weak case for public support. Having chosen not to work, the person is responsible for the consequences. But some luck egalitarians assert a far more expansive notion of responsibility. They argue that even the failure to buy insurance for various possible adversities constitutes the kind of choice that makes people responsible for most any misfortune that befalls them. If, for example, an uninsured person suffers grievous injury in a car crash, the luck egalitarian wants to know whether she could have purchased an insurance policy. Only if no such policies were available or affordable would the community be obligated to help with the hospital bills.[61]

Second, beyond its severity toward the imprudent, luck egalitarianism demeans those who do qualify for public assistance by casting them as helpless victims. Here there is a paradox. Luck egalitarians place great moral weight on people's ability to choose. They seek to compensate for chance so people's income and life prospects can reflect their own choices. But this demanding ethic of responsibility and choice carries a harsh implication: those who need help must be able to show that their neediness is not their own doing. To qualify for public assistance, they must present themselves—and conceive of themselves—as victims of forces beyond their control.[62]

This perverse incentive spills beyond the self-image of the claimants into the terms of public discourse. Liberals who defend the welfare state on the basis of luck egalitarianism are led, almost unavoidably, to a rhetoric of victimhood that views welfare recipients as lacking agency, as incapable of acting responsibly.[63]

But helping the disadvantaged on the grounds that they are victims of circumstances beyond their control carries a high moral and civic price.

It supports the disparaging view that welfare recipients have little to contribute and are incapable of acting responsibly. And as Anderson rightly observes, denying that those in need of public support can exercise meaningful choice is hard to reconcile with respecting them as equal citizens, capable of sharing in self-government.[64]

In short, luck egalitarianism "offers no aid to those it labels irresponsible, and humiliating aid to those it labels innately inferior," Anderson writes. "Like the Poor Law regime, it abandons those disadvantaged through their own choices to their miserable fates and defines the deserving disadvantaged in terms of their innate inferiority of talent, intelligence, ability, or social appeal."[65]

As with other versions of liberalism, the luck egalitarian philosophy begins by rejecting merit and desert as the basis of justice but ends by reasserting meritocratic attitudes and norms with a vengeance. For Rawls, these norms re-enter in the guise of entitlements to legitimate expectations. For the luck egalitarians, they enter through an emphasis on individual choice and personal responsibility.

The notion that we do not deserve the benefits and burdens that flow from luck—including the luck of having or lacking the talents society rewards—seems to undercut the meritocratic notion that, under conditions of fair competition, we deserve what we earn. Advantages due to chance, not choice, are undeserved. But the line between chance and choice is complicated by the fact that sometimes people choose to take chances. Skydivers risk life and limb for the thrill. Young people who feel invincible choose not to buy health insurance. Gamblers flock to casinos.

Luck egalitarians say that those who choose to take risks are responsible for their fates when their bets go badly. The community owes help only to victims of bad luck they have not courted—being struck by a meteor, for example. Those who lose a bet they have willingly made can claim no help from the winners. Ronald Dworkin makes this point with his distinction between "brute luck" (the meteor victim) and "option luck" (the losing gambler).[66]

The contrast between chance and choice makes judgments of merit and desert unavoidable. Although no one deserves to lose at gambling, the losing gambler, having chosen to bear the risk, deserves no help from the community in paying his gambling debts. He is responsible for his misfortune.

Of course, it can sometimes be unclear what counts as genuine choice. Some gamblers suffer from addiction, and slot machines are programmed to manipulate gamblers to keep them playing. In these cases, gambling is less a choice than a coercive practice that preys on the vulnerable. But insofar as people freely choose to bear certain risks, the luck egalitarian considers them responsible for the consequences. They deserve their fate, at least in the sense that no one owes them help in meeting it.

Beyond familiar disputes about what counts as a truly voluntary choice, the distinction between chance and choice is blurred by another consideration—the possibility of insurance. If my house burns down, this is surely bad luck. But what if affordable fire insurance were available and I had failed to buy it, hoping that no fire would ever occur and that I could save money by avoiding the yearly premium with impunity? Although the fire itself is "brute luck," my failure to insure against it is a choice that converts the unfortunate incident into "option luck." Having chosen not to buy an insurance policy, I am responsible for the consequences and cannot expect taxpayers to compensate me for the loss of my house.

Of course, insurance is not available for all accidents and contingencies. Some people have the good luck to be born with the talents society prizes while others are born disabled in ways that make it hard to earn a living. Dworkin thinks the concept of insurance can be extended to deal with these contingencies as well. Since it is impossible to buy insurance before one is born, Dworkin suggests that we estimate the average amount people would pay to insure against being born with meager talents and use that figure to redistribute income from the talented to the untalented. The idea is to compensate for the unequal distribution of native ability by taxing those who have won out in the genetic lottery.[67]

There is reason to doubt that it is possible to calculate the premiums and payouts of a hypothetical insurance policy for the lack of native talent.

But if it could be done, and if the talented were taxed and the untalented were compensated accordingly, and if, furthermore, everyone had fair access to jobs and educational opportunities, then the luck egalitarian's ideal of a just society would be realized. All income differences due to undeserved gifts and handicaps would be compensated for, and all remaining inequalities would reflect factors for which we are responsible, such as effort and choice. And so the luck egalitarian's attempt to banish the effects of accident and misfortune points to a meritocratic ideal after all: a distribution of income based not on morally arbitrary contingencies but on what people deserve.[68]

Luck egalitarianism defends inequalities that arise from effort and choice. This highlights a point of convergence with free-market liberalism. Both emphasize personal responsibility and make the community's obligation to help the needy conditional on showing that their neediness is no fault of their own. Luck egalitarians seek, by their own account, to defend the welfare state from free-market critics by accepting "the most powerful idea in the arsenal of the anti-egalitarian right: the idea of choice and responsibility."[69] This reduces the disagreement between free-market and egalitarian liberals to a debate about the conditions under which a person's choices can be considered truly free rather than burdened by circumstance or necessity.

VALORIZING TALENT

Although free-market and egalitarian liberalism both reject merit as a first principle of justice, they ultimately share a meritocratic bent. Neither effectively counters the morally unattractive attitudes toward success and failure to which meritocracies are prone—hubris among the winners and humiliation among the losers. This has partly to do with their insistence on parsing personal responsibility. It also reflects their valorization of talent. Even as they insist that one's native abilities are a matter of luck and hence arbitrary from a moral point of view, they take talent, and in particular, natural or innate talent, incredibly seriously.

This is especially true of egalitarian liberals, who attribute income inequality in large part to the results of the genetic lottery. They devise elaborate measures, such as Dworkin's hypothetical insurance scheme, to calculate and compensate for differences of "natural" or "innate" or "inborn" talent that, unlike social and cultural advantages, cannot be offset by equal educational opportunities. They base the case for redistribution on this biologistic conception of talent, as a genetic fact given prior to social arrangements. But this way of conceiving talent, as a kind of inborn excellence, is a hubristic conceit. Even as egalitarian liberals seek to remedy "the great injustice of the smart and the dumb,"[70] they valorize "the smart" and denigrate "the dumb."

One need not enter the fraught debate about the genetic basis of intelligence in order to see that the staggering inequalities of income and wealth we witness today have little to do with innate differences in intelligence. The notion that the outsize earnings of people who work in finance, business, and elite professions is due to their genetic superiority is far-fetched. While it may be true that the achievements of geniuses such as Einstein or virtuosos such as Mozart are the result of innate gifts, it is absurd to think that such surpassing natural genius is what separates hedge fund managers from high school teachers.

As Elizabeth Anderson observes, it is doubtful "that inferior native endowments have much to do with observed income inequalities in capitalist economies." Most differences in income "are due to the fact that society has invested far more in developing some people's talents than others and that it puts very unequal amounts of capital at the disposal of each worker. Productivity attaches mainly to work roles, not to individuals."[71]

Natural talents, undeserved though they be, attract praise in meritocratic societies. This is partly because they are admired for their own sake. But it is also because they are thought to account for the vast winnings of the successful.

If a meritocracy enables people to rise "as far as their God-given talents will take them," it is tempting to assume that the most successful are the most gifted. But this is a mistake. Success at making money has little to do with native intelligence, if such a thing exists.[72] By fixating on natural talent as a primary source of income inequality, egalitarian liberals exaggerate its role and, inadvertently, enlarge its prestige.

MERITOCRACY'S RISE

"Meritocracy" was born as a term of abuse but became a term of praise and aspiration. "New Labour is committed to meritocracy," proclaimed Tony Blair in 1996, the year before he became prime minister of Britain. "We believe that people should be able to rise by their talents, not by their birth or the advantages of privilege."[73] In 2001, campaigning for a second term, he said his mission was "to break down the barriers that hold people back, to create real upward mobility, a society that is open and genuinely based on merit and the equal worth of all." He promised "a strictly meritocratic programme," aimed at "opening up economy and society to merit and talent."[74]

Michael Young, by then eighty-five years old, was dismayed. In an essay in *The Guardian*, he complained that Blair was celebrating an ideal that he (Young) had debunked in his satirical work four decades earlier. Young now feared his dark prediction had come true. "I expected that the poor and the disadvantaged would be done down, and in fact they have been . . . It is hard indeed in a society that makes so much of merit to be judged as having none. No underclass has ever been left as morally naked as that."[75]

Meanwhile, the rich and the powerful, "insufferably smug," were riding high. "If meritocrats believe, as more and more of them are encouraged to do, that their advancement comes from their own merits, they can feel they deserve whatever they can get." As a result, "inequality has been becoming more grievous with every year that passes, and without a bleat from the leaders of the party who once spoke up so trenchantly and characteristically for greater equality."[76]

He did not know what could be done "about this more polarized meritocratic society." But he wished that "Mr. Blair would drop the word from his public vocabulary, or at least admit to the downside."[77]

For the last several decades, the language of merit has dominated public discourse, with little recognition of the downside. Even in the face of deepening inequality, the rhetoric of rising has provided, for mainstream parties of the center-left and center-right, the primary language of moral progress and political improvement. "Those who work hard and play by the rules should be able to rise as far as their talents will take them." Meritocratic elites had become so accustomed to intoning this mantra that they failed to notice it was losing its capacity to inspire. Tone-deaf to the mounting resentments of those who had not shared in the bounty of globalization, they missed the mood of discontent. The populist backlash caught them by surprise. They did not see the insult implicit in the meritocratic society they were offering.

6

THE SORTING MACHINE

If meritocracy is the problem, what is the solution? Should we hire people based on nepotism or prejudice of various kinds, rather than their ability to do the job? Should we go back to the days when Ivy League colleges admitted the privileged sons of white, Protestant, upper-class families with little regard for their academic promise? No. Overcoming the tyranny of merit does not mean that merit should play no role in the allocation of jobs and social roles.

Instead, it means rethinking the way we conceive success, questioning the meritocratic conceit that those on top have made it on their own. And it means challenging inequalities of wealth and esteem that are defended in the name of merit but that foster resentment, poison our politics, and drive us apart. Such rethinking should focus on the two domains of life most central to the meritocratic conception of success: education and work.

In the next chapter, I will show how the tyranny of merit undermines the dignity of work, and how we might renew it. In this chapter, I show how higher education has become a sorting machine that promises mobility on the basis of merit but entrenches privilege and promotes attitudes toward success corrosive of the commonality democracy requires.

Colleges and universities preside over the system by which modern societies allocate opportunity. They confer the credentials that determine access to high-paying jobs and prestigious positions. For higher education, this role is a mixed blessing.

Making colleges and universities the animating heart of meritocratic aspiration confers on them enormous cultural authority and prestige. It has made admission to elite colleges the object of fevered ambition and enabled a number of American universities to amass multibillion-dollar endowments. But converting these institutions into the bulwark of a meritocratic order may not be good for democracy, for the students who compete to attend them, or even for the colleges and universities themselves.

JAMES CONANT'S MERITOCRATIC COUP D'ÉTAT

The notion of competitive college admissions as the gateway to opportunity is by now so familiar that it is easy to forget its novelty. The meritocratic mission of American higher education is of relatively recent origin, a product of the 1950s and 1960s. During the early decades of the twentieth century, admission to Harvard, Yale, and Princeton, the influential "big three" of the Ivy League, depended largely on having attended one of the private boarding schools that catered to upper-class families of the Protestant elite. Academic ability mattered less than coming from the right social background and being able to afford the tuition. Each college had its own entrance exams, but even these were flexibly administered; many who failed to get a passing grade were nonetheless admitted. Women were excluded, Black students were barred from Princeton and scarce at Harvard and Yale, and Jewish enrollment was restricted by formal or informal quotas.[1]

The notion of elite colleges as meritocratic institutions, whose purpose was to recruit and train the most talented students, whatever their backgrounds, to become leaders of society, found its most influential articulation in the 1940s, by James Bryant Conant, the president of Harvard University. Conant, a chemist who served as a scientific advisor to the

Manhattan Project during World War II, was troubled by the emergence, at Harvard and throughout American society, of a hereditary upper class. Such an elite was contrary to America's democratic ideals, he believed, and ill-suited to governing at a time when the country needed intelligence and scientific prowess as never before.

Nicholas Lemann, author of an illuminating history of aptitude testing in American higher education, describes the problem as Conant saw it. At Harvard and other leading universities, "rich heedless young men with servants, whose lives revolved around parties and sports, not studying, set the tone for college life." These men went on to dominate the leading law firms, Wall Street banks, the Foreign Service, research hospitals, and university faculties.[2]

> All the good places were reserved for members of a certain group . . .
> all-male, Eastern, high-Protestant, privately educated . . . No Catholics or Jews were allowed, except in rare cases that required of them a careful extirpation of any accent or other noticeable expression of their alien culture. Nonwhites weren't in close enough range of membership in the elite to be excluded. And even the fiercest social reformers of the day didn't think to suggest that women ought routinely to participate in running the country.[3]

Conant's ambition was to upend this hereditary elite and replace it with a meritocratic one. His goal, Lemann writes, was

> to depose the existing, undemocratic American elite and replace it with a new one made up of brainy, elaborately trained, public-spirited people drawn from every section and every background. These people (men, actually) would lead the country. They would manage the large technical organizations that would be the backbone of the late-twentieth-century United States and create, for the first time ever, an organized system that would provide opportunity to all Americans.[4]

It was, in Lemann's words, "an audacious plan for engineering a change in the leadership group and social structure of the country—a kind of quiet, planned coup d'état."[5]

To pull off this meritocratic coup d'état, Conant needed a way to identify the most promising high school students, however modest their family backgrounds, and recruit them for elite college educations. He began by creating a Harvard scholarship for talented students from public schools in the Midwest, who would be chosen based on a test of intellectual aptitude. In commissioning this test, Conant insisted that it measure native intelligence, not mastery of academic subjects, to avoid giving an advantage to those who had attended privileged secondary schools. The test he chose for this purpose, a version of an IQ test used by the army during World War I, was called the Scholastic Aptitude Test (SAT).

In time, Conant's scholarship program was extended to students nationwide. The test he used to select them, the SAT, eventually came to be used to determine admission to colleges and universities across the country. As Lemann observes, the SAT "would become not just a way of handing out a few scholarships at Harvard, but the basic mechanism for sorting the American population."[6]

Conant's attempt to transform Harvard into a meritocratic institution was part of a broader ambition to remake American society on meritocratic principles. He set out his vision in "Education for a Classless Society," an address he delivered at the University of California and published in *The Atlantic* in 1940. Conant wanted to reclaim for American society the principle of equality of opportunity, now threatened by "the development of a hereditary aristocracy of wealth." He cited Frederick Jackson Turner, the Harvard historian who had argued that the closing of the frontier cut off the traditional avenue of American opportunity—the ability to move west, to cultivate land, and to rise through effort and ingenuity unshackled by class-bound hierarchy. "The most distinctive fact" of the early period of American democracy, Turner had written, "was the freedom of the individual to rise under conditions of social mobility."[7]

Turner, writing at the end of the nineteenth century, was perhaps the first to use the term "social mobility."[8] Conant called this concept "the heart of my argument" and used it to define his ideal of a classless society.

> A high degree of social mobility is the essence of the American ideal of a classless society. If large numbers of young people can develop their own capacities irrespective of the economic status of their parents, then social mobility is high. If, on the other hand, the future of a young man or woman is determined almost entirely by inherited privilege or the lack of it, social mobility is nonexistent.[9]

If social mobility is high, Conant explained, "sons and daughters must and can seek their own level, obtain their own economic rewards, engage in any occupation irrespective of what their parents might have done."[10]

But what, in the absence of an open frontier, could serve as the instrument of the mobility a fluid, classless society required? Conant's answer was education. As more and more Americans were attending high school, the secondary school system was becoming "a vast engine" which, if operated properly, could "aid us in recapturing . . . opportunity, a gift that once was the promise of the frontier."

According to Conant's vision, however, the opportunity that widespread high school enrollment made possible consisted less in the education it provided than in the chance it presented to sort and rank students as candidates for higher education. In a highly industrialized society, "abilities must be assessed, talents must be developed, ambitions guided. This is the task for our public schools."[11]

Although Conant believed it was important to educate all future citizens as members of a political democracy, this civic purpose of the public schools was secondary to their sorting function. More important than educating young people for citizenship was equipping them "to step on to the first rung of whatever ladder of opportunity seems most appropriate." Conant acknowledged that this sorting role "may seem an overwhelming burden to put upon our education system," but he hoped the public schools could be "reconstructed for this specific purpose."[12] The public schools offered a broad recruiting ground for a new, meritocratic elite.

In support of his notion of culling from each generation those best suited for higher education and public leadership, Conant enlisted a formidable ally—Thomas Jefferson. Like Conant, Jefferson opposed an aristocracy of wealth and birth and wanted to replace it with an aristocracy of virtue and talents. Jefferson also believed that a well-designed educational system could be the mechanism for "the selection of the youths of genius from among the classes of the poor." Nature had not vested talent exclusively in the wealthy but had "scattered [it] with equal hand" among all ranks of society. The challenge was to find it and cultivate it so that the most talented and virtuous could be educated and equipped to govern.[13]

Jefferson had proposed a system of public education for Virginia with this aim in mind. Those who did best in free primary schools would be chosen to "receive at public expense a higher degree of education at a district school." Those who excelled there would receive scholarships to attend the College of William and Mary and become leaders of society. "Worth and genius would thus have been sought out from every condition of life, and completely prepared by education for defeating the competition of wealth and birth for public trusts."[14]

Jefferson's plan was not adopted, but for Conant, it offered an inspiring precedent for the selective system of higher education he favored, one based on equality of opportunity and social mobility. Jefferson had not used either of those terms. He wrote instead of a "natural aristocracy" of talent and virtue that he hoped would prevail over "an artificial aristocracy founded on wealth and birth."[15] And he described his competitive scholarship plan in language that would have been impolitic in Conant's more democratic age: "Twenty of the best geniuses will be raked from the rubbish annually and be instructed, at the public expense."[16]

INTIMATIONS OF THE TYRANNY OF MERIT

Seen in retrospect, Jefferson's indelicate language highlights two potentially objectionable features of a meritocratic system of education that our language of social mobility and equal opportunity obscures: First, a fluid, mobile society based on merit, though antithetical to hereditary hierarchy, is not antithetical to inequality; to the contrary, it legitimates inequalities that arise from merit rather than birth. Second, a system that celebrates and rewards "the best geniuses" is prone to denigrate the rest, implicitly or explicitly, as "rubbish." Even as he proposed a generous scholarship scheme, Jefferson offered an early instance of our own meritocratic tendency to valorize the "smart" and stigmatize the "dumb."

Conant addressed these two potential objections to a meritocratic order, the first more directly than the second. Regarding inequality, he frankly acknowledged that his ideal of a classless society did not aim at a more equal distribution of income and wealth. He sought a more mobile society, not a more equal one. What mattered was not easing the gap between rich and poor but ensuring that people traded places in the economic hierarchy from one generation to the next, some moving up and others moving down from the status of their parents. "For one generation at least and perhaps two, considerable differences in economic status as well as extreme differentiation of employment may exist without the formation of classes." Power and privilege may be unequal provided they are "automatically redistributed at the end of each generation."[17]

As for the distasteful image of raking "geniuses" from "the rubbish," Conant did not think the sorting he proposed would valorize those sorted in or denigrate those sorted out. "We must proceed from the premise that there are no educational privileges, even at the most advanced levels of instruction," he wrote. "No one channel should have a social standing above the other."[18]

As things turned out, Conant was too sanguine on both counts. Making higher education meritocratic did not bring about a classless society, nor did it avoid disparaging those excluded for the lack of talent. Some would say these developments simply reflect a failure to realize meritocratic ideals. But as Conant acknowledged, sorting for talent and seeking equality are two different projects.

Conant's meritocratic vision was egalitarian in the sense that he wanted to open Harvard and other elite universities to the most talented students in the country, however modest their social and economic backgrounds.

At a time when Ivy League colleges were dominated by families of estab-lished privilege, this was a noble ambition. But Conant was not concerned with expanding access to higher education. He did not want to increase the number of students attending college; he wanted simply to ensure that those who did attend were truly the most capable. The country "would benefit by an elimination of at least a quarter, or perhaps one-half, of those now enrolled in advanced university work," he wrote in 1938, "and the sub-stitution of others of more talent in their place." In line with this view, he opposed the GI Bill, enacted by FDR in 1944, which provided free college education for returning veterans. The nation did not need more students going to college, Conant thought; it needed better ones.[19]

During Conant's two decades as president, Harvard's admissions policy fell short of the meritocratic ideals he advocated. By the end of his tenure, in the early 1950s, Harvard still rarely rejected the sons of alumni, admit-ting more than 87 percent of them.[20] It continued to favor applicants from elite New England boarding schools, accepting most who applied, while holding public school applicants to higher academic standards. This was partly because the prep school students were "paying guests" who did not need financial aid but also because their "upper crust" pedigree brought the cultural cachet that Ivy League schools still prized.[21] Restrictions on the admission of Jewish students were quietly eased but not eliminated, reflecting a persisting fear that having too many Jews "would drive away the upper-class Protestant boys whom Harvard most wished to enroll."[22] The admission of women and attempts to recruit students from racial and ethnic minorities lay in the future.

CONANT'S MERITOCRATIC LEGACY

Although the Harvard of his day did not fully implement them, the merito-cratic ideals Conant proclaimed have since come to define the self-understanding of American higher education. The arguments he advanced in the 1940s about the role of colleges and universities in a democratic society have become the conventional wisdom of our day. No longer in dispute, they have devolved into the routine rhetorical fare of commencement addresses and public pronouncements by college presidents: Higher education should be open to talented students of all social and economic backgrounds, ideally without regard for their ability to pay. Although only the wealthiest colleges can afford need-blind admissions and financial aid, it is widely agreed that merit not wealth should be the basis of admission. While most colleges evaluate applicants on an array of factors, including academic promise, character, athletic prowess, and extracurricular activities, academic merit is measured mainly by high school grades and scores on the SAT, the standardized test of intellectual aptitude that Conant championed.

To be sure, the meaning of merit is fiercely contested. In debates over affirmative action, for example, some argue that counting race and ethnicity as factors in admission violates merit; others reply that the ability to bring distinctive life experiences and perspectives to the classroom and the wider society is a merit relevant to a university's mission. But the fact that our debates about college admissions are typically arguments about merit testifies to the hold of meritocratic ideals.

Perhaps most deeply embedded is Conant's notion of higher education as the primary gateway to opportunity, a source of upward mobility that keeps society fluid by offering all students, whatever their social or economic background, the chance to rise as far as their talents will take them. Drawing on this idea, college presidents ritualistically remind us that excellence and opportunity go hand in hand. The fewer the social and economic barriers to college attendance, the greater the ability of colleges to recruit the most outstanding students and equip them to succeed. As each entering class arrives on campus for first-year orientation, they are lavished with praise for their excellence and diversity, and for the talent and effort that have led to their admission.[23]

Rhetorically and philosophically, Conant's meritocratic ideology has won the day. But it has not played out the way he expected.

SAT SCORES TRACK WEALTH

First, the SAT, it turns out, does not measure scholarly aptitude or native intelligence independent of social and educational background. To the contrary, SAT scores are highly correlated with wealth. The higher your family income, the higher your SAT score. At each successive rung on the income ladder, average SAT scores increase.[24] For scores that put students in contention for the most selective colleges, the gap is especially stark. If you come from a family with an annual income greater than $200,000, your chance of scoring above 1400 (out of 1600) is one in five. If you come from a poor family (less than $20,000 per year), your chance is one in fifty.[25] Those in high-scoring categories are also, overwhelmingly, children of parents with college degrees.[26]

Beyond the general educational advantages well-off families can provide, the SAT scores of the privileged are boosted by the use of private test-prep courses and tutors. Some, in places like Manhattan, charge as much as $1,000 per hour for one-on-one tutoring. As meritocratic competition for college admission has intensified in recent decades, tutoring and test prep has become a billion-dollar industry.[27]

For years, the College Board, which administers the SAT, insisted that its test measured aptitude and that scores were unaffected by tutoring. It recently dropped that pretense and entered a partnership with the Khan Academy to provide free online SAT practice to all test takers. Although this was a worthy undertaking, it did little to level the test-prep playing field, as College Board officials hoped and claimed it would. Unsurprisingly perhaps, students from families with higher incomes and education levels made greater use of the online help than did students from disadvantaged backgrounds, resulting in an even greater scoring gap between the privileged and the rest.[28]

For Conant, a test of aptitude or IQ held promise as a democratic measure of academic ability, untainted by educational disadvantage and the vagaries of high school grades. This is why he opted for the SAT to choose his scholarship students. He would be surprised to learn that high school grades are better than SAT scores at identifying low-income students who are likely to succeed in college.

Comparing the predictive power of test scores and grades is a tangled matter. For two-thirds of students, they are more or less aligned. But for those whose SAT scores and grades are discrepant, the SAT helps the privileged and hurts the disadvantaged.[29]

While high school grades are to some extent correlated with family income, SAT scores are more so. This is partly because, contrary to long-standing claims by the testing industry, the SAT is coachable. Private tutoring helps, and a profitable industry has arisen to teach high school students the gimmicks and tricks to boost their scores.[30]

MERITOCRACY ENTRENCHES INEQUALITY

Second, the system of meritocratic admission that Conant promoted did not lead to the classless society he hoped it would produce. Inequalities of income and wealth have deepened since the 1940s and 1950s, and the social mobility that Conant saw as the remedy for a stratified society has not come about. The haves and have-nots have not been trading places from one generation to the next. As we have seen, relatively few children of the poor rise to affluence, and relatively few children of affluence fall below the ranks of the upper middle class. Notwithstanding the American dream of rising from rags to riches, upward mobility is less common in the United States than in many European countries, and there is no evidence of improvement in recent decades.

More to the point, higher education in the age of meritocracy has not been an engine of social mobility; to the contrary, it has reinforced the advantages that privileged parents confer on their children. Of course, the demographic and academic profile of students on elite college campuses has changed for the better since the 1940s. The hereditary aristocracy of white, Anglo-Saxon, Protestant wealth that Conant sought to displace no longer predominates. Women are admitted on equal terms with men, colleges actively recruit for racial and ethnic diversity, and about half of today's

Ivy League students identify themselves as students of color.[31] The quotas and informal practices limiting Jewish enrollment that prevailed during the first half of the twentieth century have disappeared.

The favoritism that Harvard, Yale, and Princeton long accorded young men from upper-class boarding schools receded in the 1960s and 1970s. So did the routine admission to Ivy League colleges of any minimally qualified son of an alumnus. Academic standards improved and median SAT scores increased. The best-endowed colleges and universities adopted need-blind admissions and generous financial-aid policies, removing a major financial barrier for promising students of modest means.

These are the undeniable achievements. And yet, the meritocratic revolution in higher education did not bring about the social mobility and broad opportunity that its early proponents expected and that educational leaders and politicians continue to promise. America's selective colleges and universities ousted the complacent, entitled, hereditary elite that worried Conant. But this aristocracy of inherited privilege has given way to a meritocratic elite that is now as privileged and entrenched as the one it replaced.

Though far more inclusive in terms of gender, race, and ethnicity, this meritocratic elite has not produced a fluid, mobile society. Instead, today's credentialed, professional classes have figured out how to pass their privileges on to their children, not by bequeathing them large estates but by equipping them with the advantages that determine success in a meritocratic society.

Notwithstanding its newfound role as the arbiter of opportunity and the engine of upward mobility, higher education has not provided a significant counterweight to the rising inequality of recent times. Consider the class composition of higher education today, especially in its most selective domains:

- Most students at selective colleges and universities are from affluent families; very few are from low-income backgrounds. More than 70 percent of those who attend the hundred or so most competitive colleges in the United States come from the top quarter of the income scale; only 3 percent come from the bottom quarter.[32]

- The wealth gap in college enrollment is most acute at the top. At Ivy League colleges, Stanford, Duke, and other prestigious places, there are more students from the wealthiest 1 percent of families than from the entire bottom half of the country. At Yale and Princeton, only about one student in fifty comes from a poor family (bottom 20 percent).[33]

- If you come from a rich family (top 1 percent), your chances of attending an Ivy League school are 77 times greater than if you come from a poor family (bottom 20 percent). Most young people from the bottom half of the income scale attend a two-year college or none at all.[34]

Over the last two decades, elite private colleges have offered more generous financial aid, and the federal government has increased college funding for students of modest means. Harvard and Stanford, for example, now provide free tuition, room, and board to any student whose family makes less than $65,000 per year. Despite these measures, however, the share of students from low-income families at selective colleges has changed little since 2000 and in some cases has drifted downward. The percentage of "first generation" students (the first in their families to attend college) at Harvard today is no higher than it was in 1960. Jerome Karabel, the author of a history of admissions policies at Harvard, Yale, and Princeton, concludes that "the children of the working class and the poor are about as unlikely to attend the Big Three [Harvard, Yale, and Princeton] today as they were in 1954."[35]

WHY ELITE COLLEGES ARE NOT ENGINES OF MOBILITY

The academic reputations, scientific contributions, and rich educational offerings of America's leading colleges and universities are admired throughout the world. But these institutions are not effective engines of upward mobility. Recently, the economist Raj Chetty and a team of colleagues undertook a comprehensive study of the role of colleges in promoting inter-generational mobility, examining the economic trajectory of 30 million college students from 1999 to 2013. For each college in the United States, they calculated the proportion of its students who rose from the bottom rung on the income ladder to the top (i.e., from the bottom quintile to the top quintile). They asked, in other words, what proportion of students at each college came from a poor family but wound up earning enough to reach the top 20 percent. Their finding: higher education today does surprisingly little to promote upward mobility.[36]

This is especially true at elite private colleges. Although attending a place like Harvard or Princeton does give a poor kid a good chance of rising, such places enroll so few poor kids to begin with that their mobility rate is low. Only 1.8 percent of Harvard students (and only 1.3 percent at Princeton) rise from the bottom to the top of the income scale.[37]

One might expect things to be different at the major public universities. But they, too, enroll so many already-affluent students that they contribute little to upward mobility. The mobility rate at the University of Michigan at Ann Arbor is only 1.5 percent. Its class-skewed profile is similar to Harvard's: two-thirds of its students come from well-off families (top quintile). Poor kids are even scarcer in Ann Arbor (fewer than 4 percent) than at Harvard. A similar pattern holds true at the University of Virginia, with a mobility rate of only 1.5 percent, due largely to the fact that fewer than 3 percent of its students come from poor families.[38]

Chetty and his team did identify some less-famous public universities and state colleges with higher mobility rates. These schools are both accessible to low-income students and successful at helping them rise. Cal State University at Los Angeles, for example, and the State University of New York at Stony Brook enable nearly 10 percent of their students to rise from the bottom rung to the top, about five times the mobility rate of Ivy League colleges and the most selective public universities.[39]

But these institutions are the exception. Taken together, the 1,800 colleges and universities Chetty studied—private and public, selective and non-selective—enabled fewer than 2 percent of their students to rise from the bottom fifth of the income scale to the top fifth.[40] Some might ask whether propelling students, in one generation, from the bottom quintile ($20,000 family income or less) to the top ($110,000 income or more) is too demanding a test of mobility. But even more modest ascents are relatively rare. At elite private colleges and universities, only about one student in ten manages to rise even two rungs (two quintiles) on the income ladder.[41]

American colleges and universities enable surprisingly few students to rise, despite the fact that attending such places does enhance one's economic prospects. College graduates, especially from prestigious places, do have a major edge in landing lucrative jobs. But these schools have little impact on upward mobility, because most of their students are well-off in the first place. American higher education is like an elevator in a building that most people enter on the top floor.

In practice, most colleges and universities do less to expand opportunity than to consolidate privilege. For those who look to higher education as the primary vehicle of opportunity, this is sobering news. It calls into question an article of faith in contemporary politics—that the answer to rising inequality is greater mobility, and that the way to increase mobility is to send more people to college.

Although this vision of opportunity is invoked by politicians across the ideological spectrum, it fits less and less well with the lived experience of a great many people, especially those who lack a college degree but aspire nonetheless to dignified work and a decent life. This is a reasonable aspiration that a meritocratic society ignores at its peril. For the credentialed classes, it is easy to forget that most of our fellow citizens do not have a college degree. Constantly admonishing them to better their condition by getting one ("what you earn depends on what you learn") can be more insulting than inspiring.

What then to do about higher education? Should it retain its current role as the arbiter of opportunity? And should we continue to assume that opportunity consists in equal access to the meritocratic tournament that college admissions has become? Some say yes, provided we can improve the fairness of the tournament. They argue that the dearth of low-income students in higher education points not to a flaw in meritocratic admissions but to a failure to implement them consistently. According to this view, the cure for meritocracy's ills is a more thoroughgoing meritocracy, one that gives talented students equal access to college whatever their social and economic background.

MAKING MERITOCRACY MORE FAIR

On its face, this is a sensible position. Improving educational opportunities for poor but gifted students is an unqualified good. In recent decades, colleges and universities have made important strides in recruiting African American and Latinx students but have done little to increase the proportion of lower-income students. In fact, as public debate has raged about affirmative action for racial and ethnic minorities, colleges have quietly practiced what amounts to affirmative action for the wealthy.

For example, many selective colleges and universities give preference to the children of alumni ("legacies," as they are called), on the grounds that admitting them builds community spirit and generates gifts to the endowment. At elite colleges, alumni children are as much as six times more likely than other applicants to win admission. Overall, Harvard admits only one applicant in twenty; of legacy applicants, it accepts one out of three.[42]

Some schools also ease academic standards to admit children of wealthy donors who are not alumni, reasoning that it is worth accepting some less-than-stellar students in exchange for a new library or scholarship fund. During a fundraising campaign in the late 1990s and early 2000s, Duke University devoted about one hundred places per year in the entering class to children of wealthy donors who might not otherwise have been admitted. Although some faculty worried about compromising academic standards, the policy helped boost Duke's endowment and improve its competitive standing.[43] Documents filed in a recent court case about Harvard's admissions policy revealed that nearly 10 percent of its students are admitted with the help of donor connections.[44]

Preferences for recruited athletes is another boon to affluent applicants. It is sometimes assumed that lowering academic standards for athletes, especially in high-profile sports such as football and basketball, helps enroll students from underrepresented minorities and low-income backgrounds. But on the whole, applicants who benefit from athletic preferences are disproportionately wealthy and white. This is because most of the sports for which elite colleges recruit are pursued mainly by well-off kids—squash, lacrosse, sailing, crew, golf, water polo, fencing, even horseback riding.[45]

Preferential admission for athletes is not limited to powerhouse football schools such as Michigan and Ohio State, whose bowl-bound teams fill massive stadiums. At Williams College, a small, prestigious liberal arts college in New England, 30 percent of the class consists of athletic recruits.[46] Few of these student athletes come from disadvantaged backgrounds. A study of nineteen selective colleges and universities co-authored by the former president of Princeton found that recruited athletes enjoy greater admissions advantages than either underrepresented minorities or alumni children, and that only 5 percent of them come from the bottom quarter of the income scale.[47]

Colleges could try to address this unfairness in various ways. They could undertake class-based affirmative action by according students from poor families the same preferences they currently give legacies, donor children, and recruited athletes. Or they could reduce the advantages they give wealthy applicants by ending these preferences altogether. In addition, colleges could offset the advantages affluent applicants enjoy due to SAT scores inflated by private tutoring and test prep by no longer requiring these standardized tests, as the University of Chicago and other schools have recently done. Studies have shown that SAT scores are more likely than high school grades to be distorted as predictors of academic performance by socioeconomic background; relying on them less would enable colleges to enroll more students of modest means with little if any loss in rates of academic success.[48]

These are steps that colleges could take on their own. Government could also intervene to make college admission less biased in favor of the privileged. Senator Edward Kennedy, himself a legacy student at Harvard, once proposed requiring private colleges to make public the acceptance rates for alumni children and report their socioeconomic profile. Daniel Markovits, a Yale law professor and critic of meritocratic inequality, would go further. He has proposed denying private universities their tax-exempt status unless they admit at least half of their students from the bottom two-thirds of the income scale, ideally by expanding enrollments.[49]

These measures, whether undertaken by the colleges themselves or by government mandate, would ease the inequality that makes higher education a weak force for social mobility. They would reduce the unfairness of the system by improving access for the less-privileged. These are compelling reasons to consider them.

But focusing only on the unfairness of the current system begs a bigger question at the heart of Conant's meritocratic revolution: Should colleges and universities take on the role of sorting people based on talent to determine who gets ahead in life?

There are at least two reasons to doubt that they should. The first concerns the invidious judgments such sorting implies for those who get sorted out, and the damaging consequences for a shared civic life. The second concerns the injury the meritocratic struggle inflicts on those who get sorted in and the risk that the sorting mission becomes so all-consuming that it diverts colleges and universities from their educational mission. In short, turning higher education into a hyper-competitive sorting contest is unhealthy for democracy and education alike. Consider each of these dangers in turn.

SORTING AND THE ALLOCATION OF SOCIAL ESTEEM

Conant was aware of the risk that converting universities into sorting mechanisms could sow social discord, but he thought this risk could be avoided. His goal was to use testing and tracking to direct each person to the social role that made best use of his talents (he still assumed that only men's talents needed to be tested and tracked), without implying that the most talented people were worthier than others. He did not believe that educational sorting would generate judgments of social superiority or prestige, as the old system of inherited privilege had done.[50]

Conant's faith that it is possible to sort people without judging them ignores the moral logic and psychological appeal of the meritocratic regime he helped launch. One of the primary arguments for a meritocracy over a hereditary aristocracy is that those who rise due to their own merits have earned their success and therefore deserve the rewards their merits bring. Meritocratic sorting is bound up with judgments about earning and deserving. These are inescapably public judgments, about whose talents and achievements are worthy of honor and recognition.

Conant's conviction that higher education should shift power away from the hereditary upper class and seek out talented scientists and intellectuals was not only a way of filling socially necessary roles; it was also an argument about what qualities of intellect and character a modern, technologically advanced society should value and reward. So it was implausible to deny that the new system of sorting was also a new basis for allocating social status and esteem. This was the point of Michael Young's *Rise of the Meritocracy* (1958), published just a few years after Conant stepped down as president of Harvard. Young saw what Conant either failed or refused to see, that the new meritocracy carried with it a new, exacting basis for judging who was deserving and who was not.

Those following Conant who helped carry out the meritocratic makeover of higher education were explicit about the connection between sorting and judging. In a book entitled *Excellence* (1961), John W. Gardner, a foundation president who would later serve as secretary of Health, Education, and Welfare in Lyndon Johnson's administration, expressed the spirit of the new meritocratic age. "We are witnessing a revolution in society's attitude toward men and women of high ability and advanced training. For the first time in history, such men and women are very much in demand on a very wide scale." Unlike previous societies, which were run by the few and could therefore afford to squander talent, a modern technological society governed by complex organizations needed to mount a relentless search for talent, to seek it out wherever it was to be found. The imperatives of this "great talent hunt" now set the task for education—to become a "rigorous sorting-out process."[51]

Unlike Conant, Gardner acknowledged the harsh aspect of merito-cratic sorting. "As education becomes increasingly effective in pulling the bright youngster to the top, it becomes an increasingly rugged sorting-out process for everyone concerned . . . The schools are the golden avenue of opportunity for able youngsters; but by the same token they are the arena in which less able youngsters discover their limitations." This was the down-side of equality of opportunity. It enabled "every young person [to] go as far as his ability and ambition would take him, without obstacles of money, social standing, religion or race." But there was "pain involved for those who lacked the necessary ability."[52]

Such pain was inevitable, Gardner thought, and a price worth paying, given the urgent need to cull and cultivate talent. He acknowledged that the pain became especially acute as some students qualified for college and others fell short. "If a society sorts people out efficiently and fairly according to their gifts, the loser knows that the true reason for his lowly status is that he is not capable of better. That is a bitter pill for any man."[53]

For Young, this insight was the heart of the case against meritocracy. For Gardner, it was an unfortunate side effect. "Because college has gained extraordinary prestige," he conceded, it had come to define success. "Today attendance at college has become virtually a prerequisite of high attain-ment in the world's eyes, so that it becomes, in the false value framework we have created, the only passport to a meaningful life." Gardner gamely argued that "achievement should not be confused with human worth" and that individuals were worthy of respect regardless of their achievements. But he seemed to understand that the meritocratic society he was helping bring about left little room for the distinction between educational achieve-ment and social esteem.[54]

> The plain fact is that college education is firmly associated in the public mind with personal advancement, upward social mobility, market value and self-esteem. And if enough of the American peo-ple believe that one must attend college in order to be accorded re-spect and confidence, then the very unanimity of opinion makes the generalization true.[55]

A few years later, Kingman Brewster, the president of Yale, also acknowledged the close connection between sorting students based on merit and turning college admission into a badge of social recognition and esteem. Brewster, who brought Yale into the meritocratic era, encountered resistance from influential members of his governing board to his attempts to base admission less on family legacy and more on academic talent. In 1966, Yale adopted need-blind admissions, which meant admitting students without regard for their financial need and providing them sufficient financial support to enroll. Brewster argued, shrewdly but insightfully, that the new policy would not only enable Yale to attract strong students from modest backgrounds; it would also increase Yale's appeal to wealthy students, who would be drawn to a college known to accept students based on their merits not their money. Now that "the pocketbook was no longer relevant to admission," he wrote, "the privileged took pride in the feeling that they had made it on the merits rather than on the basis of something ambiguously called 'background.'"[56]

Once, people took pride in sending their children to places where they could rub elbows with upper-class blue bloods. Now people took pride in sending their children to places that signified their superior merit.

The shift to meritocratic admissions heightened the prestige of colleges that could attract the most outstanding students. Prestige was typically measured by the average SAT scores of the students they admitted and also, perversely, by the number of applicants they were able to reject. Increasingly, colleges were ranked by their selectivity, and selectivity loomed larger in students' choices.

Until the 1960s, college-bound students typically enrolled in places close to home. As a result, academic ability was spread broadly across a range of colleges and universities. But as the meritocratic recasting of higher education took form, college choice became more strategic. Students, especially those from high-income families, began to seek out the most selective college that would accept them.[57]

Caroline M. Hoxby, an economist who studies higher education, calls this trend the "re-sorting of higher education." The gap between highly selective and less-selective colleges widened. Students with high SAT scores clamored for admission to the handful of colleges with other high-scoring students, and college admission became a winner-take-all competition. Although many assume that getting into college is harder today than in the past, this is not generally the case. The majority of colleges and universities in the United States accept most students who apply.[58]

Only at a narrow slice of elite colleges have admissions rates plunged in recent decades. These are the places that capture the headlines and animate the admissions frenzy that blights the teenage years of college-bound kids from affluent families. In 1972, as the "re-sorting" was already well under way, Stanford accepted one-third of those who applied. Today, it accepts less than 5 percent. Johns Hopkins, which accepted the majority of its applicants (54 percent) in 1988, now accepts only 9 percent. The University of Chicago experienced one of the most precipitous drops, from a 77 percent acceptance rate in 1993 to 6 percent in 2019.[59]

All told, forty-six colleges and universities now accept fewer than 20 percent of applicants. Several of these schools were the desired destination of students whose parents perpetrated the 2019 college admissions scandal. But only 4 percent of U.S. undergraduates attend these hyper-selective colleges. More than 80 percent attend schools that accept more than half of their applicants.[60]

What accounts for the re-sorting that, over the past fifty years, has concentrated high-scoring students in a relatively small group of highly selective colleges? Hoxby offers an economist's explanation: lower transportation costs made it easier to travel to colleges far from home, and lower information costs made it easier to find out how your SAT score compared with those of other students. In addition, the most prestigious colleges spend more on the education of each student, so for those who can get in, enrolling at such places is a sound investment in one's "human capital"—even allowing for the expected donation to the college fund later in life.[61]

But the fact that this "re-sorting" coincided with the meritocratic transformation of higher education suggests a further explanation: Selective colleges and universities became irresistibly attractive because they stood at the apex of the emerging hierarchy of merit. Prompted by their parents, ambitious, well-off students flooded the gates of prestigious campuses not only because they wanted to study in the company of academically gifted students, but because these colleges conferred the greatest meritocratic prestige. More than a matter of bragging rights, the kudos associated with attending a highly selective college carry over into employment opportunities after graduation. This is not mainly because employers believe students learn more at elite colleges than at less-selective places, but because employers have faith in the sorting function these colleges perform and value the meritocratic honor they bestow.[62]

WOUNDED WINNERS

The winner-take-all re-sorting of higher education was undesirable for two reasons. First, it reinforced inequality, as the colleges that fared best in the selectivity sweepstakes were generally the ones with the highest proportion of wealthy students. Second, it exacted a damaging toll on the winners. Unlike the old hereditary elite, which assumed its place at the top without much fuss or bother, the new meritocratic elite wins its place through strenuous striving.

Although the new elite has now taken on a hereditary aspect, the transmission of meritocratic privilege is not guaranteed. It depends on "getting in." This gives meritocratic success a paradoxical moral psychology. Collectively and retrospectively, its results are almost pre-ordained, given the overwhelming predominance on elite campuses of affluent kids. But to those in the midst of the hyper-competitive struggle for admission, it is impossible to view success as anything other than the result of individual effort and achievement. This is the standpoint that generates the conviction among the winners that they have earned their success, that they have made it on their own. This belief can be criticized as a form of meritocratic hubris; it attributes more than it should to individual striving and forgets the advantages that convert effort into success. But there is also poignance in this belief, for it is forged in pain—in the soul-destroying demands that meritocratic striving inflicts upon the young.

Prosperous parents are able to give their kids a powerful boost in the bid for admission to elite colleges, but often at the cost of transforming their high school years into a high-stress, anxiety-ridden, sleep-deprived gauntlet of Advanced Placement courses, test-prep tutoring, sports training, dance and music lessons, and a myriad of extracurricular and public service activities, often under the advice and tutelage of private admissions consultants whose fees can cost more than four years at Yale. Some of these consultants advise parents to seek disability diagnoses for their children, to get them extra time on standardized tests. (In one wealthy Connecticut suburb, 18 percent of students receive such diagnoses, more than six times the national average.) Other consultants specialize in creating customized summer foreign travel programs designed to produce compelling fodder for college application essays.[63]

This meritocratic arms race tilts the competition in favor of the wealthy and enables affluent parents to pass their privilege on to their kids. This way of transmitting privilege is doubly objectionable. For those who lack the apparatus of advantage, it is unfair; for children entangled in the apparatus, it is oppressive. The meritocratic struggle gives rise to a culture of invasive, achievement-driven, pushy parenting that does not serve teenagers well. The rise of helicopter parenting coincides with the decades when meritocratic competition intensified. In fact, the use of "parent" as a verb only became common in the 1970s, when the need to prepare children for academic success came to be seen as a pressing parental responsibility.[64]

From 1976 to 2012, the amount of time American parents devoted to helping their children with their homework increased more than fivefold.[65] As the college admission stakes grew, anxious, intrusive parenting became a common affliction. A 2009 *Time* magazine cover story sounded the alarm: "The Case Against Over-Parenting: Why It Is Time for Mom and Dad to Cut the Strings." We had become "so obsessed with our kids' success," *Time* observed, "that parenting turned into a form of product development." The drive to manage childhood now began early. "Among 6-to-8-year-olds, free playtime dropped 25% from 1981 to '97, and homework more than doubled."[66]

In an intriguing study, the economists Matthias Doepke and Fabrizio

Zilibotti offer an economic explanation for the rise of helicopter parenting, which they define as "the heavily involved, time-intensive, controlling child-rearing approach that has become widespread over the last three decades." They argue that such parenting is a rational response to rising inequality and increasing returns to education. Although intensive parenting has increased in many societies in recent decades, it is most pronounced in places where inequality is greatest, such as the United States and South Korea, and less prevalent in countries such as Sweden and Japan, where inequality is less acute.[67]

Understandable though it may be, parents' drive to direct and manage their children's lives for meritocratic success has taken a harsh psychological toll, especially on pre-college teenagers. In the early 2000s, Madeline Levine, a psychologist who treats young people in Marin County, California, an affluent suburb of San Francisco, began noticing that many outwardly successful teens from well-off families were extremely unhappy, disconnected, and lacking in independence. "Scratch the surface, and many of them are . . . depressed, anxious, and angry . . . They are overly dependent on the opinions of parents, teachers, coaches, and peers and frequently rely on others not only to pave the way on difficult tasks but to grease the wheels of everyday life as well." She began to realize that, rather than insulating these young people from life's difficulties, affluence and a high degree of parental involvement were contributing to their unhappiness and fragility.[68]

In a book entitled *The Price of Privilege*, Levine described what she called a "mental health epidemic among privileged youth." Traditionally, psychologists had assumed that "at-risk" youth were disadvantaged kids in the inner city, "growing up in harsh and unforgiving circumstances."[69] Without denying their plight, Levine observed that America's new at-risk group consisted of teens from affluent, well-educated families.

> In spite of their economic and social advantages, they experience among the highest rates of depression, substance abuse, anxiety disorders, somatic complaints, and unhappiness of any group of children

in this country. When researchers look at kids across the socioeconomic spectrum, they find that the most troubled adolescents often
come from affluent homes.[70]

Levine cited research by Suniya S. Luthar, who has documented the "coun-
terintuitive notion that upper-middle-class youth, who are en route to the
most prestigious universities and well-paying careers in America," suffer
higher rates of emotional distress than other teens, a pattern that continues
once they reach college. Compared with the general population, full-time
college students are "2.5 times more likely to meet diagnostic criteria of
substance abuse or dependence (23% vs. 9%)," and half of all full-time college students report binge drinking and abuse of illegal or prescription
drugs.[71]

What accounts for the inordinate levels of emotional distress among
young people from affluent families? The answer has largely to do with the
meritocratic imperative—the unrelenting pressure to perform, to achieve,
to succeed. "For children and parents alike," Luthar writes, "it is nearly
impossible to ignore the ubiquitous, pervasive message emblazoned from
their early years onward: there is one path to ultimate happiness—having
money—that in turn comes from attending prestigious colleges."[72]

Those who prevail on the battlefield of merit emerge triumphant but
wounded. I see this in my students. The habit of hoop-jumping is hard
to break. Many still feel so driven to strive that they find it difficult to use
their college years as a time to think, explore, and critically reflect on who
they are and what is worth caring about. An alarming number struggle
with mental health issues. The psychic toll of navigating the meritocratic
gauntlet is not restricted to the Ivy League. A recent study of 67,000 undergraduates at more than a hundred colleges in the United States found
that "college students face unprecedented levels of distress," including rising rates of depression and anxiety. One in five college students reported
thoughts of suicide in the previous year, and one in four was diagnosed or
treated for a mental health disorder.[73] The suicide rate among young people
(ages 20–24) increased 36 percent from 2000 to 2017; more now die from
suicide than homicide.[74]

Beyond these clinical conditions, psychologists have found a subtler affliction bearing down on this generation of college students: a "hidden epidemic of perfectionism." Years of anxious striving leave young people with a fragile sense of self-worth, contingent on achievement and vulnerable to the exacting judgments of parents, teachers, admissions committees, and ultimately, themselves. "Irrational ideals of the perfect self have become desirable—even necessary—in a world where performance, status and image define a person's usefulness and value," write Thomas Curran and Andrew P. Hill, the authors of the study. Surveying more than 40,000 American, Canadian, and British college students, the authors report a sharp increase in perfectionism from 1989 to 2016, including a 32 percent increase in perfectionist attitudes tied to social and parental expectations.[75]

Perfectionism is the emblematic meritocratic malady. At a time when young people are relentlessly "sorted, sifted, and ranked by schools, universities, and the workplace, neoliberal meritocracy places a strong need to strive, perform, and achieve at the center of modern life."[76] Success or failure at meeting the demand to achieve comes to define one's merit and self-worth.

Those who tend the levers and pulleys of the meritocracy machine are not unaware of its human costs. In an honest, insightful essay about the risk of burnout, Harvard College admissions officers worried that those who spend their high school and college years jumping through hoops of high achievement wind up as "dazed survivors of some bewildering life-long boot-camp." The essay, first published in 2000, is still posted, as a kind of cautionary tale, on the Harvard admissions website.[77]

STILL HOOP-JUMPING

Having fomented and rewarded achievement mania by their admissions policies, elite colleges do little to dial it back once students arrive on campus. The instinct for sorting and competing invades college life, where students re-enact the ritual of accepting and rejecting. Here is an example:

Harvard College has more than four hundred extracurricular clubs and organizations. Some, such as the orchestra and varsity football team, require certain abilities and so legitimately hold tryouts. But today, "comping," or competing for admission to student organizations, whether or not they demand special skills, has become commonplace. The culture of comping is so extreme that some students experience freshman year as "Rejection 101," a lesson in dealing with the disappointment of failing to make the cut.[78]

Like the colleges themselves, the student organizations boast about their low acceptance rates. The Harvard College Consulting Group declares itself "the most selective pre-professional student group on Harvard's campus," with an acceptance rate below 12 percent. The Crimson Key Society, which organizes Freshman Orientation Week and runs campus tours, also advertises its selectivity; only 11.5 percent of applicants are accepted. "We don't want to just put anyone in front of tourists," the Society's comp director explains. But the need for talent seems less compelling than the impulse to re-enact the trauma—and the rush—of meritocratic competition. "You jump through this huge hoop of getting into Harvard," a first-year student told *The Harvard Crimson*, "and you just want to jump through more to get this adrenaline going again."[79]

The rise of the comping culture illustrates the conversion of college into basic training for a competitive meritocracy, an education in packaging oneself and applying for stuff. This in turn reflects a broader shift in the role of colleges and universities: their credentialing function now looms so large that it overwhelms their educational function. The sorting and striving crowd out teaching and learning. College deans and presidents abet this tendency by saying, as if self-effacingly, that students learn more outside their classes than in them. This could mean (and perhaps once meant) that students learn from their classmates through informal, ongoing discussion of questions that arise in their courses and readings. But increasingly it refers to networking.

Closely akin to the comping and networking is obsessing about grades. Although I cannot prove that students' preoccupation with grades has intensified in recent decades, it certainly feels that way. In 2012, in one of the largest Ivy League cheating scandals in memory, some seventy students had to withdraw from Harvard College for cheating on a take-home exam.[80] In 2017, the College's Honors Council was deluged with cases of academic dishonesty, as more than sixty students in an introductory computer science course were referred for possible cheating.[81] But cheating is not the only manifestation of grade obsession. At one well-known law school, faculty members are instructed not to tell students when grades for the previous semester will be released, as experience has shown that advance notice of this momentous event generates too much anxiety. The release of grades is now carefully timed to enable distressed students to seek the help of counseling services.

HUBRIS AND HUMILIATION

When Conant set Harvard, and higher education, the task of testing and sorting the American population, I doubt he imagined the relentless meritocratic competition this project would unleash. Today, the role of colleges and universities as arbiters of opportunity is so entrenched that it is difficult to imagine alternatives. But the time has come to do so. Rethinking the role of higher education is important, not only to repair the damaged psyches of the privileged but also to repair the polarized civic life that meritocratic sorting has produced.

In seeking to dismantle the sorting machine that Conant set in motion, it is worth noticing that the regime of merit exerts its tyranny in two directions at once. Among those who land on top, it induces anxiety, a debilitating perfectionism, and a meritocratic hubris that struggles to conceal a fragile self-esteem. Among those it leaves behind, it imposes a demoralizing, even humiliating sense of failure.

These two tyrannies share a common moral source—the abiding meritocratic faith that we are, as individuals, wholly responsible for our fate: If we succeed, it is thanks to our own doing, and if we fail, we have no one to blame but ourselves. Inspiring though it seems, this strenuous notion of individual responsibility makes it hard to summon the sense of solidarity and mutual obligation that could equip us to contend with the rising inequality of our time.

It would be a mistake to think that higher education is solely responsible for the inequalities of income and social esteem we witness today. The project of market-driven globalization, the technocratic turn of contemporary politics, and the oligarchic capture of democratic institutions are all complicit in this condition. But before turning, in chapter 7, to the vexed question of work in a globalized economy, it is worth considering what might be done to alleviate the harsh effects of meritocratic sorting, and to do so from both directions—attending to the wounds it inflicts on those it picks out as winners and to the indignities it inflicts on those it marks as losers.

Consider first a modest proposal for reforming college admission, if only to illustrate how we might begin to ease the debilitating cycle of sorting and striving.

A LOTTERY OF THE QUALIFIED

One approach to reform would seek to improve access to elite colleges by reducing reliance on the SAT and by eliminating preferences for legacies, athletes, and donor children.[82] Although such reforms would make the system less unfair, they do not challenge the notion of higher education as a sorting project, whose role is to seek out talent and allocate opportunity and rewards to those who possess it. But the sorting project is the problem. Making it more truly meritocratic entrenches it more deeply.

So consider this instead: Each year, more than 40,000 students apply for the roughly 2,000 places that Harvard and Stanford have to offer. Admissions officers tell us that a great many of those who apply are qualified to do the work at Harvard or Stanford and do it well. The same is presumably true at the dozens of selective colleges and universities that attract many more qualified applicants than they are able to accept. (In 2017, eighty-seven colleges and universities accepted fewer than 30 percent of applicants.)[83] As early as 1960, when the number of applicants was less daunting, a longtime member of Yale's admissions committee was quoted as saying, "You sometimes have the nasty feeling that you could take all the thousands of [applications] . . . and you could throw them down the stairs, pick up any thousand, and produce as good a class as the one that will come out of the committee meeting."[84]

My proposal takes that suggestion seriously. Of the 40,000-plus applicants, winnow out those who are unlikely to flourish at Harvard or Stanford, those who are not qualified to perform well and to contribute to the education of their fellow students. This would leave the admissions committee with, say, 30,000 qualified contenders, or 25,000, or 20,000. Rather than engage in the exceedingly difficult and uncertain task of trying to predict who among them are the most surpassingly meritorious, choose the entering class by lottery. In other words, toss the folders of the qualified applicants down the stairs, pick up 2,000 of them, and leave it at that.[85]

This proposal does not ignore merit altogether; only those qualified are admitted. But it treats merit as a threshold qualification, not an ideal to be maximized.[86] This is sensible, first of all, on practical grounds. Even the wisest admissions officers cannot assess, with exquisite precision, which eighteen-year-olds will wind up making the most truly outstanding contributions, academic or otherwise. Although we valorize talent, it is, in the context of college admissions, a vague and watery concept. Perhaps it is possible to identify a math prodigy at an early age, but talent in general is a more complicated, less predictable thing.

Consider how difficult it is to assess even more narrowly defined talents and skills. Nolan Ryan, one of the greatest pitchers in the history of baseball, holds the all-time record for most strikeouts and was elected on the first ballot to baseball's Hall of Fame. When he was eighteen years old, he was not signed until the twelfth round of the baseball draft; teams chose 294 other, seemingly more promising players before he was chosen.[87] Tom

Brady, one of the greatest quarterbacks in the history of football, was the 199th draft pick.[88] If even so circumscribed a talent as the ability to throw a baseball or a football is hard to predict with much certainty, it is folly to think that the ability to have a broad and significant impact on society, or on some future field of endeavor, can be predicted well enough to justify fine-grained rankings of promising high school seniors.

But the most compelling reasons for a lottery of the qualified is to combat the tyranny of merit. Setting a threshold of qualification and letting chance decide the rest would restore some sanity to the high school years, and relieve, at least to some extent, the soul-killing, résumé-stuffing, perfection-seeking experience they have become. It would also deflate meritocratic hubris, by making clear what is true in any case, that those who land on top do not make it on their own but owe their good fortune to family circumstance and native gifts that are morally akin to the luck of the draw.

I can imagine at least four objections:

1. What about academic quality?

That depends on setting the right threshold. I have a hunch that, at least for the top sixty or eighty colleges and universities, the quality of classroom discussion and academic performance would not be noticeably different. My hunch could be wrong, but there is an easy way to find out. Begin with an experiment: Admit half the class using the existing system and half by a lottery of the qualified, and then compare academic performance at the time of graduation (and career success some years later). Stanford actually came close to trying this experiment in the late 1960s, but the plan was scuttled due to opposition by the dean of admissions.[89]

2. What about diversity?

In principle, the lottery could be adjusted to ensure diversity along any particular dimension a college deemed compelling by assigning each student in a favored category two lottery tickets, or three. This could produce the desired diversity without giving up on the aspect of chance. One variation worth considering: To counteract the hereditary tendency of meritocratic admissions as currently practiced, colleges could first admit a certain number of qualified applicants whose parents did not attend college, and then run the lottery.

3. What about legacies and donor children?

Ideally, colleges should stop giving preference to children of alumni. But for colleges that want to continue to do so, they could assign each alumni child two lottery tickets rather than one (as with diversity categories above), or more, if the college deemed it necessary. It is worth noting that, to replicate the current rate of legacy admissions, some schools would have to assign each alumni child five or six lottery tickets. This would at least make vivid the advantage they are conferring on privileged kids and perhaps prompt debate about whether such preferences should continue.

Favoritism for children of big donors who are not alumni should also be eliminated. But if colleges cannot resist the financial benefit of selling some places in the entering class, they could simply set aside a handful of seats to be auctioned off or sold outright. This would be a more honest way of acknowledging the compromises some colleges currently make under cover of merit. As in the current system, the recipients of the bought places would not be publicly identified, but at least they would no longer be buying a bogus presumption of superior merit.

4. Wouldn't admission by lottery render selectivity less meaningful and so erode the prestige of the top colleges and universities?

Yes, perhaps. But is this really an objection? Only if you believe that the prestige-driven "re-sorting" of higher education in recent decades has improved the quality of teaching and learning. But this is highly doubtful. Drawing high-scoring students from a broader range of colleges across the country into a smaller circle of hyper-selective places has deepened inequality but done little if anything to improve education. The anxious striving and hoop-jumping that meritocratic sorting has induced has rendered students less open to the exploratory character of a liberal arts education. Scaling back the sorting and the prestige-mongering would be a virtue not a drawback of the lottery system.

If a sizable number of elite colleges and universities began admitting qualified students by lottery, they would alleviate, at least to some degree, the stress of high school years. College-bound teenagers and their parents would realize that, beyond demonstrating the ability to perform well in college-level courses, students would no longer need to devote their adolescence to an arms race of activities and achievements designed to impress admissions committees. Helicopter parenting might recede, to the benefit of the emotional well-being of parents and children alike. Spared the scars of the battlefield of merit, young people might arrive in college less prone to hoop-jumping and more open to personal and intellectual exploration.

These changes would ease the damage the tyranny of merit inflicts on the winners. But what about everyone else? Only about 20 percent of graduating high school seniors are swept up in the frenzy to get into prestigious colleges. What about the 80 percent who attend less-competitive universities, or two-year community colleges, or none at all? For them, the tyranny of merit is not about a soul-killing competition for admission but about a demoralizing world of work that offers meager economic rewards and scant social esteem to those who lack meritocratic credentials.

DISMANTLING THE SORTING MACHINE

An adequate response requires an ambitious project: We should power down the meritocratic sorting machine by lowering the stakes of winning admission to highly selective colleges and universities. More broadly, we should figure out how to make success in life less dependent on having a four-year college degree.

Any attempt to honor work must begin by taking seriously the various forms of learning and training that prepare people to undertake it. This means reversing the retreat from public higher education, overcoming the neglect of technical and vocational education, and breaking down the sharp distinction, in funding and prestige, between four-year colleges and other post-secondary educational settings.

One impediment to reducing meritocratic sorting in higher education is that, in the United States at least, much of it is carried out by private colleges and universities. Nevertheless, these institutions, private though they are, rely on substantial federal funding, especially for student financial aid and federally sponsored research. In some cases, they hold vast endowments, which generate income that is traditionally tax-exempt. (The Republican tax bill of 2017 imposed a tax on the endowment income of a small number of wealthy colleges.)[90] In principle, the federal government could use this leverage to require private colleges and universities to expand enrollment, admit more students from disadvantaged backgrounds, or even to adopt some version of the admissions lottery proposal.[91]

It is unlikely, however, that such measures would by themselves lower the stakes of getting in to at least one selective college. Of greater significance would be measures to broaden access to four-year public colleges and universities, and to devote greater support to community colleges, technical and vocational education, and job training. These are, after all, the educational settings in which the majority of Americans learn the skills they need to make a decent living.

Government funding for state colleges and universities has fallen in recent decades, and tuition has increased, to the point where the public character of these institutions is in doubt.[92] In 1987, public colleges received three times more revenue per student from state and local governments than from tuition. But as government funding fell, tuition rose. By 2013, public higher education derived as much of its revenue from tuition as from state and local support.[93]

Many leading public universities are now public in name only.[94] At the University of Wisconsin–Madison, for example, only 14 percent of the budget comes from state appropriations.[95] At the University of Virginia, state funding accounts for just 10 percent of the budget.[96] At the University of Texas at Austin, state appropriations provided 47 percent of the budget in the mid-1980s; today, only 11 percent. Meanwhile, the share from tuition increased more than fourfold.[97]

As public support recedes and tuition rises, student debt has skyrocketed. Today's generation of students set out on their careers burdened by a mountain of debt. Over the past fifteen years, the total amount of student loan debt increased more than fivefold. By 2020, it exceeded $1.5 *trillion*.[98]

The most glaring indication of the meritocratic tilt in college finance is the gap between federal support for higher education and support for technical and vocational training. Isabel Sawhill, an economist at the Brookings Institution, offers a striking account of the disparity:

> Contrast the small amount being spent on employment and training with the amount spent on higher education in the form of grants, loans, and tax credits. For the academic year 2014–2015, a total of $162 billion was spent to help people go to college. In contrast, the Department of Education spends about $1.1 billion annually on career and technical education.[99]

Sawhill adds that, even combining career and technical education funding with expenditures to help displaced workers find new jobs, "we are only spending about $20 billion per year on these work-related programs at the federal level."[100]

The amount the U.S. spends on training or retraining workers is not only small compared with the amount we spend on higher education. It is also minuscule compared with the amounts other countries spend. Economists speak of "active labor market policies" to describe government programs that help equip workers with the skills the job market needs. Such policies respond to the fact that the labor market does not work smoothly on its own; training and placement programs are often needed to help workers find jobs suited to their skills. Sawhill points out that economically advanced countries spend an average of 0.5 percent of GDP on active labor market programs. France, Finland, Sweden, and Denmark spend more than 1 percent of GDP on such programs. The U.S. spends only about 0.1 percent—less than we spend on prisons.[101]

The American indifference to active labor market policies may reflect the market faith that supply and demand (in this case, for labor) automatically align, without outside help. But it also reflects the meritocratic conviction that higher education is the primary avenue to opportunity. "One reason the United States may have neglected employment and training," Sawhill writes, "is because the emphasis has been on financing higher education. The assumption seems to be that everyone needs to go to college."[102]

But as we have seen, only about one-third of Americans earn a bachelor's degree. For everyone else, access to a well-paying job depends on forms of education and training that we woefully neglect. Despite its aspirational appeal, the meritocratic insistence that a four-year college degree is the gateway to success distracts us from taking seriously the educational needs of most people. This neglect not only hurts the economy; it expresses a lack of respect for the kind of work the working class does.

THE HIERARCHY OF ESTEEM

Repairing the damage the sorting machine inflicts requires more than increased funding for job training. It requires us to rethink the way we value different kinds of work. One way to begin is by dismantling the hierarchy of esteem that accords greater honor and prestige to students enrolled in name-brand colleges and universities than to those in community colleges or in technical and vocational training programs. Learning to become a plumber or electrician or dental hygienist should be respected as a valuable contribution to the common good, not regarded as a consolation prize for those who lack the SAT scores or financial means to make it to the Ivy League.

Higher education derives much of its prestige from its avowedly higher purpose: not only to equip students for the world of work but also to prepare them to be morally reflective human beings and effective democratic citizens, capable of deliberating about the common good. Having spent a career teaching moral and political philosophy, I certainly believe in the importance of moral and civic education. But why assume that four-year colleges and universities have, or should have, a monopoly on this mission? A more capacious notion of educating citizens for democracy would resist the sequestration of civic education in universities.

It should be acknowledged, first of all, that elite colleges and universities are not doing very well at this task.[103] For the most part, they place relatively little curricular emphasis on moral and civic education, or on the kind of historical studies that prepare students to exercise informed practical judgment about public affairs. The growing prominence of supposedly value-neutral social science, together with the proliferation of narrow, highly specialized courses, has left little room for courses that expose students to big questions of moral and political philosophy and invite them to reflect critically on their moral and political convictions.

There are exceptions, of course. And many colleges and universities require students to take some course or other that deals with ethical or civic themes. But for the most part, our leading colleges and universities today are better at inculcating technocratic skills and orientations than the ability to reason and deliberate about fundamental moral and civic questions. This technocratic emphasis may have contributed to the failure of governing elites over the past two generations, and to the morally impoverished terms of public discourse.

But even if my assessment of the state of moral and civic education at elite colleges is too harsh, there is no reason why four-year colleges should be the sole setting for courses in moral reasoning and civic argument. Civic education out of doors, so to speak, has a long tradition.

An inspiring example is the demand made by the Knights of Labor, one of America's first major labor unions, for reading rooms in factories, so that workers could inform themselves about public affairs. This demand grew out of a republican tradition that viewed civic learning as embedded in the world of work.[104]

As the cultural historian Christopher Lasch observed, foreign visitors to America in the nineteenth century were struck by its broad equality of condition. By this they meant neither an equal distribution of wealth nor even the opportunity to rise, but rather an independence of mind and judgment that put all citizens on a roughly equal footing:

Citizenship appeared to have given even the humbler members of society access to the knowledge and cultivation elsewhere reserved for the privileged classes . . . Labor's contribution to the general well-being took the form of mind as well as muscle. American mechanics, it was said, "are not untaught operatives, but an enlightened, reflective people, who not only know how to use their hands, but are familiar with principles." Mechanics' magazines returned to this theme again and again.[105]

Lasch makes the broader point that the egalitarian character of American society in the nineteenth century was less about social mobility than about the general diffusion of intelligence and learning across all classes and vocations.[106] This is the kind of equality that meritocratic sorting destroys. It seeks to concentrate intelligence and learning in the citadel of higher education and promises access to the citadel through a fair competition. But this way of allocating access to learning undermines the dignity of labor and corrupts the common good. Civic education can flourish in community colleges, job training sites, and union halls as well as on ivy-strewn campuses. There is no reason to suppose that aspiring nurses and plumbers are less suited to the art of democratic argument than aspiring management consultants.

CHASTENING MERIT'S HUBRIS

The most potent rival to merit, to the notion that we are responsible for our lot and deserve what we get, is the notion that our fate exceeds our control, that we are indebted for our success, and also for our troubles—to the grace of God, or the vagaries of fortune, or the luck of the draw. The Puritans found, as we saw in chapter 2, that a thoroughgoing ethic of grace is almost impossible to sustain. Living by the belief that we have no hand in whether we will be saved in the next world or successful in this one is hard to reconcile with the idea of freedom and with the conviction that we get what we deserve. This is why merit tends to drive out grace; sooner or later, the successful assert, and come to believe, that their success is their own doing, and that those who lose out are less worthy than they.

But even in its triumph, the meritocratic faith does not deliver the self-mastery it promises. Nor does it provide a basis for solidarity. Ungenerous to the losers and oppressive to the winners, merit becomes a tyrant. And when it does, we can enlist its ancient rival to rein it in. This is what, in one small domain of life, the admissions lottery tries to do. It summons chance to chasten merit's hubris.

Reflecting on the tyranny that merit inflicts on affluent, competitive kids brings to mind two experiences from my own teenage years.

The mania for sorting and tracking filtered down into the public junior high school and high school I attended in Pacific Palisades, California, in the late 1960s. So heavily tracked were these schools that, despite the fact that some 2,300 students attended my high school, I found myself constantly in the company of the same 30 or 40 kids in the top track. My eighth-grade math teacher took tracking to an extreme. The class may have been Algebra or Geometry; I don't remember which. But I do remember the seating arrangement. Three of the six rows were so-called honors rows, in which students were seated in precise order of their grade point average. This meant that seating assignments changed with each test or quiz. To heighten the drama, the teacher announced the new seating arrangement before handing back each graded exercise. I was good in math but not the best. I typically shuttled between the second desk and the fourth or fifth. A girl named Kay, a math whiz, almost always occupied the first desk.

As a fourteen-year-old kid, I thought this was how school worked. The better you did, the higher you were ranked. Everyone knew who the best math students were, and who had triumphed or bombed on this or that quiz. Although I didn't realize it at the time, this was my first encounter with meritocracy.

By the time we reached tenth grade, the tracking and ranking was taking its toll. Most of the top-track students had become obsessed with grades, not only our own, but everyone else's too. We were intensely competitive, so much so that our preoccupation with grades threatened to swamp our intellectual curiosity.

My tenth-grade biology teacher, Mr. Farnham, a wry, bow-tied man whose classroom teemed with snakes, salamanders, fish, mice, and other fascinating wildlife, found this troubling. One day, he gave us a pop quiz. He told us to take out a piece of paper, number from one to fifteen, and answer true or false. When students complained that he had not given us any questions, he told us to think of a statement for each question and write down whether it was true or false. Students asked anxiously whether this arbitrary quiz would be graded, and whether it would count. "Yes, of course," he said.

At the time, I found this an amusing if eccentric classroom joke. But in retrospect, I see that Mr. Farnham was trying, in his way, to push back against the tyranny of merit. He was trying to get us to step back from the sorting and the striving long enough to marvel at the salamanders.

RECOGNIZING WORK

From the end of World War II to the 1970s, it was possible for those without a college degree to find good work, support a family, and lead a comfortable middle-class life. This is far more difficult today. Over the past four decades, the earnings difference between college and high school graduates—what economists call the "college premium"—has doubled. In 1979, college graduates made about 40 percent more than high school graduates; by the 2000s they made 80 percent more.[1]

Although the age of globalization brought rich rewards to the well-credentialed, it did nothing for most ordinary workers. From 1979 to 2016, the number of manufacturing jobs in the United States fell from 19.5 million to 12 million.[2] Productivity increased, but workers reaped a smaller and smaller share of what they produced, while executives and shareholders captured a larger share.[3] In the late 1970s, CEOs of major American companies made 30 times more than the average worker; by 2014, they made 300 times more.[4]

The median income of American males has been stagnant, in real terms, for half a century. Although per capita income has increased 85 percent since 1979, white men without a four-year college degree make less now, in real terms, than they did then.[5]

ERODING THE DIGNITY OF WORK

It is not surprising that they are unhappy. But economic hardship is not the only source of their distress. The meritocratic age has also inflicted a more insidious injury on working people: eroding the dignity of work. By valorizing the "brains" it takes to score well on college admission tests, the sorting machine disparages those without meritocratic credentials. It tells them that the work they do, less valued by the market than the work of well-paid professionals, is a lesser contribution to the common good, and so less worthy of social recognition and esteem. It legitimates the lavish rewards the market bestows on the winners and the meager pay it offers workers without a college degree.

This way of thinking about who deserves what is not morally defensible. For reasons we explored earlier (chapter 5), it is a mistake to assume that the market value of this or that job is the measure of its contribution to the common good. (Recall the richly compensated meth dealer and the modestly paid high school teacher.) But over the last several decades, the idea that the money we make reflects the value of our social contribution has become deeply embedded. It echoes throughout the public culture.

Meritocratic sorting helped entrench this idea. So did the neoliberal, or market-oriented, version of globalization embraced by mainstream parties of the center-right and center-left since the 1980s. Even as globalization produced massive inequality, these two outlooks—the meritocratic and the neoliberal—narrowed the grounds for resisting it. They also undermined the dignity of work, fueling resentment of elites and political backlash.

Since 2016, pundits and scholars have debated the source of populist discontent. Is it about job loss and stagnant wages or cultural displacement? But this distinction is too sharply drawn. Work is both economic and cultural. It is a way of making a living and also a source of social recognition and esteem.

This is why the inequality brought about by globalization produced such anger and resentment. Those left behind by globalization not only struggled while others prospered; they also sensed that the work they did was no longer a source of social esteem. In society's eyes, and perhaps also their own, their work no longer signified a valued contribution to the common good.

Working-class men without a college degree voted overwhelmingly for Donald Trump. Their attraction to his politics of grievance and resentment suggests they were distressed by more than economic hardship alone. So does an expression of futility that was mounting in the years leading up to Trump's election: As the circumstances of work for those without meritocratic credentials became bleak, growing numbers of working-age men dropped out of the labor force altogether.

In 1971, 93 percent of white working-class men were employed. By 2016, only 80 percent were. Of the 20 percent who did not have jobs, only a small fraction of them were looking for work. As if defeated by the indignities of a labor market indifferent to their skills, most had simply given up. The abandonment of work was especially acute among those who had not been to college. Of Americans whose highest academic qualification was a high school diploma, only 68 percent were employed in 2017.[6]

DEATHS OF DESPAIR

But giving up on work was not the most grievous expression of the damaged morale of working-class Americans. Many were giving up on life itself. The most tragic indication is the increase in "deaths of despair." The term was coined by Anne Case and Angus Deaton, two Princeton economists who recently made a disquieting discovery. Throughout the twentieth century, as modern medicine pushed back disease, life expectancy steadily increased. But from 2014 to 2017, it stalled and even declined. For the first time in a century, life expectancy in the United States decreased for three straight years.[7]

This was not because medical science stopped finding new cures and treatments for disease. Mortality rates were going up, Case and Deaton found, due to an epidemic of deaths caused by suicides, drug overdoses, and alcoholic liver disease. They called them "deaths of despair" because they were, in various ways, self-inflicted.[8]

Such deaths, which had been mounting for more than a decade, were especially frequent among white adults in middle age. For white men and women aged 45–54, deaths of despair increased threefold from 1990 to 2017.[9] By 2014, for the first time, more people in this group were dying of drugs, alcohol, and suicide than from heart disease.[10]

Among those who live at some distance from working-class communities, the crisis was barely noticed at first, the scale of loss obscured by the lack of public attention. But by 2016, more Americans were dying each year from drug overdose than died during the entire Vietnam War.[11] The New York Times columnist Nicholas Kristof offers another stark comparison: More Americans now die deaths of despair *every two weeks* than died during eighteen years of war in Afghanistan and Iraq.[12]

What might account for this grim epidemic? A telling clue can be found in the educational background of those most vulnerable to it. Case and Deaton discovered that "the increase in deaths of despair was almost all among those without a bachelor's degree. Those with a four-year degree are mostly exempt; it is those without a degree who are most at risk."[13]

The overall death rate for white men and women in middle age (ages 45–54) has not changed much over the past two decades. But mortality varies greatly by education. Since the 1990s, death rates for college graduates declined by 40 percent. For those without a college degree, they rose by 25 percent. Here then is another advantage of the well-credentialed. If you have a bachelor's degree, your risk of dying in middle age is only one quarter of the risk facing those without a college diploma.[14]

Deaths of despair account for much of this difference. People with less education have long been at greater risk than those with college degrees of dying from alcohol, drugs, or suicide. But the diploma divide in death has become increasingly stark. By 2017, men without a bachelor's degree were three times more likely than college graduates to die deaths of despair.[15]

It might be thought that the underlying cause is unhappiness borne of poverty, and that educational differences figure only because those with lesser educations are likely to be poor. Case and Deaton consider this possibility but find it unpersuasive. The dramatic increase in deaths of despair from 1999 to 2017 does not correspond to a general increase in poverty. They also looked state by state and found no convincing correlation between deaths by suicide, drug overdose, and alcohol, and rising poverty levels.

Something more than material deprivation was inciting the despair, something distinctive to the plight of people struggling to make their way in a meritocratic society without the credentials it honors and rewards. The deaths of despair, Case and Deaton conclude, "reflect a long-term and slowly unfolding loss of a way of life for the white, less educated working class."[16]

> The widening gap between those with and those without a degree is not only in death but also in quality of life; those without a degree are seeing increases in their levels of pain, ill health, and serious mental distress, and declines in their ability to work and to socialize. The gap is also widening in earnings, in family stability, and in community. A four-year degree has become *the* key marker of social status, as if there were a requirement for nongraduates to wear a circular scarlet badge bearing the letters BA crossed through by a diagonal red line.[17]

This condition sadly vindicates Michael Young's observation that "in a society that makes so much of merit" it is hard "to be judged as having none. No underclass has ever been left as morally naked as that."[18]

It is also eerily reminiscent of John Gardner's argument for "excellence" and educational sorting in the early 1960s. In acknowledging meritocracy's downside, he was more prescient than he knew. Those who "saw the beauty of a system in which every young person could go as far as his ability and ambition would take him" easily overlooked "the pain involved for those who lacked the necessary ability," Gardner wrote. "Yet pain there is and must be."[19]

Two generations later, when Oxycontin was the drug that dulled the pain, the rising tide of death revealed a dark consequence of meritocratic sorting—a world of work that accords little dignity to those who have been sorted out.

SOURCES OF RESENTMENT

During the Republican primaries of 2016, Donald Trump, then an insurgent candidate running against the establishment, did best in places that had the highest rates of deaths of despair. A county-by-county electoral analysis found that, even controlling for income, the death rate among middle-aged whites was strongly correlated with support for Trump. So was the lack of a bachelor's degree.[20]

One of the reasons mainstream pundits and politicians were shocked and perplexed by Trump's election is that they were oblivious to (and in some cases complicit in) the culture of elite condescension that had been building for some time. This culture arose, in large part, from the meritocratic sorting project and the inequality brought about by market-driven globalization. But it finds expression throughout American life. The working-class fathers on television sitcoms, such as Archie Bunker in *All in the Family* and Homer Simpson in *The Simpsons*, are mostly buffoons. Media scholars have found that television's blue-collar dads are depicted as ineffectual and dumb, the butt of jokes, often dominated by their more competent and sensible wives. Fathers from upper-middle-class and professional backgrounds are more favorably portrayed.[21]

Elite disparagement of the working class can be heard in common parlance. Joan Williams, a professor at Hastings College of Law in San Francisco, has criticized progressives for their "class cluelessness."[22]

Too often in otherwise polite society, elites (progressives emphatically included) unselfconsciously belittle working-class whites. We hear talk of "trailer trash" in "flyover states" afflicted by "plumber's butt"—open class insults that pass for wit. This condescension affects political campaigns, as in Hillary Clinton's comment about "deplorables" and Barack Obama's about people who "cling to guns or religion."[23]

Williams acknowledges that "economic resentment has fueled racial anxiety that, in some Trump supporters (and Trump himself), bleeds into open racism. But to write off white working-class anger as nothing more than racism is intellectual comfort food, and it is dangerous."[24]

Barbara Ehrenreich, a journalist who writes about work and class, makes a similar observation. She quotes W. E. B. Du Bois, writing in 1935: "It must be remembered that the white group of laborers, while they received a low wage, were compensated in part by a sort of public and psychological wage." Unlike African Americans, white working-class citizens were "admitted freely with all classes of white people to public functions, public parks, and the best public schools."[25] This "public and psychological wage" is what today goes by the name of "white privilege."

After the civil rights movement, the racial segregation that upheld this perverse psychological wage subsidy fell away, Ehrenreich suggests, leaving poor whites without "the comfort of knowing that someone was worse off and more despised than they were." Liberal elites who "feel righteous in their disgust for lower-class white racism" are right to condemn the racism.[26] But they fail to see how attributing "white privilege" to disempowered white working-class men and women is galling; it ignores their struggle to win honor and recognition in a meritocratic order that has scant regard for the skills they have to offer.

Katherine J. Cramer, a political scientist at the University of Wisconsin–Madison, spent five years interviewing people in rural communities across Wisconsin, and emerged with a nuanced account of the politics of resentment.[27] Residents of rural communities believed that too much tax money and government attention went to undeserving people. "The undeserving included racial minorities on welfare," Cramer wrote, "but it also included lazy urban professionals like me working desk jobs and producing nothing more than ideas." Racism is part of their resentment, she explained, but it is intertwined with a more basic concern "that people like them, in places like theirs, were overlooked and disrespected."[28]

In one of the most compelling chronicles of working-class discontent, Arlie Russell Hochschild, a sociologist at the University of California, Berkeley, embedded herself in Louisiana bayou country. In kitchen table conversations with conservative Southern working people, she sought to understand why those who stood in desperate need of government help—not least to contend with the oil and chemical companies that brought environmental disaster to their communities—nonetheless despised and distrusted the federal government. She composed a story, an interpretive reconstruction of what she learned, describing "the hopes, fears, pride, shame, resentment, and anxiety in the lives of those [she] talked with."[29]

Her story was an interwoven tale of economic deprivation and cultural dislocation. Economic progress had become harder, "restricted to a small elite." For the bottom 90 percent, the American dream machine "had stopped due to automation, off-shoring, and the growing power of multinationals vis-à-vis their workforces. At the same time, for that 90 percent, competition between white men and everyone else had increased—for jobs, for recognition, and for government funds."[30] To make matters worse, those who believed they had been waiting patiently in line for their chance at the American dream found that other people were cutting in line ahead of them—Blacks, women, immigrants, refugees. They resented the people they viewed as line cutters (the beneficiaries of affirmation action, for example) and were angry at the political leaders who allowed them to get away with it.[31]

When those waiting their turn complained about the line cutters, elites called them racists, "rednecks," "white trash," and other insulting names. Hochschild offered this sympathetic account of the predicament confronting her beleaguered working-class hosts:

> You are a stranger in your own land. You do not recognize yourself in how others see you. It is a struggle to feel seen and honored. And to feel honored you have to feel—and feel seen as—moving forward. But through no fault of your own, and in ways that are hidden, you are slipping backward.[32]

Any serious response to working-class frustrations must combat the elite condescension and credentialist prejudice that have become rife in the public culture. It must also put the dignity of work at the center of the political agenda. This is not as easy as it may seem. People of various ideological persuasions will hold competing notions about what it means for a society to respect the dignity of work, especially at a time when globalization and technology, with their seemingly inevitable bent, threaten to undermine it. But the way a society honors and rewards work is central to the way it defines the common good. Thinking through the meaning of work would force us to confront moral and political questions we otherwise evade, but that lurk, unaddressed, beneath the surface of our present discontents: What counts as a valuable contribution to the common good, and what do we owe one another as citizens?

RENEWING THE DIGNITY OF WORK

As inequality increased in recent years, and as working-class resentment gathered force, some politicians responded by speaking of the dignity of work. Bill Clinton used the term more than any previous president, and Donald Trump refers to it frequently.[33] It has become a popular rhetorical gesture for politicians across the political spectrum, though mainly in the service of familiar political positions.[34]

Some conservatives argue that cutting welfare honors the dignity of work by making life harder for the idle and weaning them from dependence on government. Trump's secretary of agriculture claimed that reducing access to food stamps "restores the dignity of work to a sizable segment of our population." Defending a 2017 bill that cut taxes for corporations and mainly benefited the wealthy, Trump stated that his goal was "for every American to know the dignity of work, the pride of a paycheck."[35]

For their part, liberals sometimes appeal to the dignity of work in seeking to strengthen the safety net and boost the purchasing power of working people—raising the minimum wage, offering policies for health care, family leave, and child care, and providing a tax credit for low-income families.

But this rhetoric, backed by these substantial policy proposals, failed to address the working-class anger and resentment that led to Trump's 2016 victory. Many liberals found this puzzling. How could so many people who stood to benefit economically from these measures vote for a candidate who opposed them?

One familiar answer is that white working-class voters, swayed by fear of cultural displacement, overlooked or overrode their economic interests to "vote with their middle finger," as some commentators put it. But this explanation is too quick. It draws too sharp a distinction between economic interests and cultural status. Economic concerns are not only about money in one's pocket; they are also about how one's role in the economy affects one's standing in society. Those left behind by four decades of globalization and rising inequality were suffering from more than wage stagnation; they were experiencing what they feared was growing obsolescence. The society in which they lived no longer seemed to need the skills they had to offer.

Robert F. Kennedy, seeking his party's nomination for president in 1968, understood this. The pain of unemployment was not simply that the jobless lacked an income but that they were deprived of the opportunity to contribute to the common good. "Unemployment means having nothing to do—which means having nothing to do with the rest of us," he explained. "To be without work, to be without use to one's fellow citizens, is to be in truth the Invisible Man of whom Ralph Ellison wrote."[36]

What Kennedy glimpsed about the discontent of his time is what contemporary liberals miss about ours. They have been offering working-class and middle-class voters a greater measure of distributive justice—fairer, fuller access to the fruits of economic growth. But what these voters want even more is a greater measure of contributive justice—an opportunity to win the social recognition and esteem that go with producing what others need and value.

The liberal emphasis on distributive justice rightly offers a counterweight to a single-minded focus on maximizing GDP. It arises from the conviction that a just society aims not only to maximize the overall level of prosperity; it also seeks a fair distribution of income and wealth. According to this view, policies expected to increase GDP—such as free-trade agreements, or policies that encourage companies to outsource labor to low-wage countries—can be defended only if the winners compensate the losers. For example, the increased profits of companies and individuals who gain from globalization could be taxed to strengthen the social safety net and to provide income support or job retraining for displaced workers.

This approach has informed the thinking of mainstream center-left (and some center-right) parties in the United States and Europe since the 1980s: Embrace globalization and the increased prosperity it brings but use the gains to offset the loss that domestic workers suffer as a result. The populist protest amounts to a renunciation of this project. Looking back across the wreckage, we can see why this project failed.

First of all, it was never really implemented. Economic growth occurred but the winners did not compensate the losers. Instead, neoliberal globalization brought an unabated increase in inequality. Almost all of the gains of economic growth went to those at the top, and most working people saw little or no improvement, even after taxes. The redistributive aspect of the project fell by the wayside, due in part to the growing power of money in politics, what some call the "oligarchic capture" of democratic institutions.

But there was a further problem. The focus on maximizing GDP, even if accompanied by help for those left behind, puts the emphasis on consumption rather than production. It invites us to think of ourselves more as consumers than as producers. In practice, of course, we are both. As consumers, we want to get the most for our money, to buy goods and services as cheaply as possible, whether they are made by low-wage workers overseas or well-paid American workers. As producers, we want satisfying and remunerative work.

It falls to politics to reconcile our identities as consumers and as producers. But the globalization project sought to maximize economic growth, and hence the welfare of consumers, with little regard for the effect of outsourcing, immigration, and financialization on the well-being of producers. The elites who presided over globalization not only failed to address the inequality it generated; they also failed to appreciate its corrosive effect on the dignity of work.

WORK AS RECOGNITION

Policy proposals to compensate for inequality by increasing the purchasing power of working- and middle-class families, or to shore up the safety net, will do little to address the anger and resentment that now run deep. This is because the anger is about the loss of recognition and esteem. While diminished purchasing power certainly matters, the injury that most animates the resentment of working people is to their status as producers. This injury is the combined effect of meritocratic sorting and market-driven globalization.

Only a political agenda that acknowledges this injury and seeks to renew the dignity of work can speak effectively to the discontent that roils our politics. Such an agenda must attend to contributive as well as distributive justice.[37] This is because the anger abroad in the land is, at least in part, a crisis of recognition. And it is in our role as producers, not consumers, that we contribute to the common good and win recognition for doing so.

The contrast between consumer and producer identities points to two different ways of understanding the common good. One approach, familiar among economic policy makers, defines the common good as the sum of everyone's preferences and interests. According to this account, we achieve the common good by maximizing consumer welfare, typically by maximizing economic growth. If the common good is simply a matter of satisfying consumer preferences, then market wages are a good measure of who has contributed what. Those who make the most money have presumably made the most valuable contribution to the common good, by producing the goods and services that consumers want.

A second approach rejects this consumerist notion of the common good in favor of what might be called a civic conception. According to the civic ideal, the common good is not simply about adding up preferences or maximizing consumer welfare. It is about reflecting critically on our preferences—ideally, elevating and improving them—so that we can live worthwhile and flourishing lives. This cannot be achieved through economic activity alone. It requires deliberating with our fellow citizens about how to bring about a just and good society, one that cultivates civic virtue and enables us to reason together about the purposes worthy of our political community.[38]

The civic conception of the common good requires, then, a certain kind of politics, one that provides venues and occasions for public deliberation. But it also suggests a certain way of thinking about work. From the standpoint of the civic conception, the most important role we play in the economy is not as consumers but as producers. For it is as producers that we develop and exercise our abilities to provide goods and services that fulfill the needs of our fellow citizens and win social esteem. The true value of our contribution cannot be measured by the wage we receive, for wages depend, as the economist-philosopher Frank Knight pointed out (see chapter 5), on contingencies of supply and demand. The value of our contribution depends instead on the moral and civic importance of the ends our efforts serve. This involves an independent moral judgment that the labor market, however efficient, cannot provide.

The notion that economic policy is ultimately for the sake of consumption is today so familiar that it is hard to think our way beyond it. "Consumption is the sole end and purpose of all production," Adam Smith declared in The Wealth of Nations, "and the interest of the producer ought to be attended to, only so far as it may be necessary for promoting that of the consumer."[39] John Maynard Keynes echoed Smith, proclaiming that consumption "is the sole end and object of all economic activity,"[40] and most contemporary economists agree. But an older tradition of moral and political thought held otherwise. Aristotle argued that human flourishing depends on realizing our nature through the cultivation and exercise of our abilities. The American republican tradition taught that certain occupations—first agriculture, then artisan labor, then free labor broadly understood—cultivate the virtues that equip citizens for self-rule.[41]

In the twentieth century, the producer ethic of the republican tradition gradually gave way to consumerist notions of freedom, and to a political economy of economic growth.[42] But the idea that, even in a complex society, work draws citizens together in a scheme of contribution and mutual recognition did not disappear altogether. At times, it has found inspiring expression. Speaking to striking sanitation workers in Memphis, Tennessee, shortly before he was assassinated, Rev. Martin Luther King, Jr., tied the dignity of sanitation workers to their contribution to the common good.

> One day our society will come to respect the sanitation workers if it is to survive, for the person who picks up our garbage is in the final analysis as significant as the physician, for if he doesn't do his job, diseases are rampant. All labor has dignity.[43]

In a 1981 Encyclical Letter, "On Human Work," Pope John Paul II stated that through work man "achieves fulfillment as a human being and indeed in a sense becomes 'more a human being.'" He also saw work as bound up with community. "[T]his brings it about that man combines his deepest human identity with membership of a nation, and intends his work also to increase the common good developed together with his compatriots."[44]

A few years later, the National Conference of Catholic Bishops issued a Pastoral Letter elaborating Catholic social teaching on the economy, giving explicit definition to "contributive" justice. All persons "have an obligation to be active and productive participants in the life of society," and government has "a duty to organize economic and social institutions so that people can contribute to society in ways that respect their freedom and the dignity of their labor."[45]

Some secular philosophers voice similar views. The German social theorist Axel Honneth has argued that contemporary conflicts over the distribution of income and wealth can best be understood as conflicts over recognition and esteem.[46] Although he traces this idea to the philosophy of Hegel, a notoriously difficult thinker, it is intuitively plausible to any sports fan who has followed salary disputes involving highly paid athletes. When fans complain about a player who already makes millions but is holding out for more, the athlete invariably replies, "It's not about the money. It's about respect."

This is what Hegel means by the struggle for recognition. More than a system for satisfying needs efficiently, the labor market, according to Hegel, is a system of recognition. It not only remunerates work with an income but publicly recognizes each person's work as a contribution to the common good. Markets by themselves do not provide workers with skills or confer recognition, so Hegel proposed an institution akin to trade associations or guilds to ensure that workers' skills were adequate to make contributions seen as worthy of public esteem. In short, Hegel argued that the capitalist organization of work emerging in his time could be ethically justified only on two conditions, described succinctly by Honneth: "first, it must provide a minimum wage; second, it must give all work activities a shape that reveals them to be a contribution to the common good."[47]

Eighty years later, the French social theorist Émile Durkheim built on Hegel's account of work, arguing that the division of labor can be a source of social solidarity, provided everyone's contribution is remunerated according to its real value for the community.[48] Unlike Smith, Keynes, and many present-day economists, Hegel and Durkheim did not see work mainly as a means to the end of consumption. Instead, they argued that work, at its best, is a socially integrating activity, an arena of recognition, a way of honoring our obligation to contribute to the common good.

CONTRIBUTIVE JUSTICE

In our deeply polarized time, when large numbers of working people feel ignored and unappreciated, when we desperately need sources of social cohesion and solidarity, it might seem that these more robust notions of the dignity of work would find their way into mainstream political argument. But this has not been the case. Why not? Why is the reigning political agenda resistant to the contributive aspect of justice, and to the producer-centered ethic that underlies it?

The answer might seem simply to lie in our love of consumption, along with the belief that economic growth delivers the goods. But something deeper is at stake. Beyond the material benefits it promises, making economic growth an overriding aim of public policy has a special appeal for pluralist societies like ours that are teeming with disagreement. It seems to spare us the need for contentious debates about morally controversial questions.

People hold various views about what is important in life. We disagree about the meaning of human flourishing. As consumers, we differ in our preferences and desires. In the face of these differences, maximizing consumer welfare seems a value-neutral goal for economic policy. If consumer welfare is the goal, then notwithstanding our disparate preferences, more is better than less. Disagreements inevitably arise about how to distribute the fruits of economic growth—hence the need for debates about distributive justice. But all can agree, or so it would seem, that expanding the economic pie is better than shrinking it.

Contributive justice, by contrast, is not neutral about human flourishing or the best way to live. From Aristotle to the American republican tradition, from Hegel to Catholic social teaching, theories of contributive justice teach us that we are most fully human when we contribute to the common good and earn the esteem of our fellow citizens for the contributions we make. According to this tradition, the fundamental human need is to be needed by those with whom we share a common life. The dignity of work consists in exercising our abilities to answer such needs. If this is what it means to live a good life, then it is a mistake to conceive consumption as "the sole end and object of economic activity."

A political economy concerned only with the size and distribution of GDP undermines the dignity of work and makes for an impoverished civic life. Robert F. Kennedy understood this: "Fellowship, community, shared patriotism—these essential values of our civilization do not come from just buying and consuming goods together." They come instead from "dignified employment at decent pay, the kind of employment that lets a man say to his community, to his family, to his country, and most important, to himself, 'I helped to build this country. I am a participant in its great public ventures.'"[49]

Few politicians speak that way today. In the decades after RFK, progressives largely abandoned the politics of community, patriotism, and the dignity of work, and offered instead the rhetoric of rising. To those who worried about stagnant wages, outsourcing, inequality, and the fear that immigrants and robots were coming for their jobs, governing elites offered bracing advice:

Go to college. Equip yourself to compete and win in the global economy. What you earn will depend on what you can learn. You can make it if you try.

This was an idealism suited to a global, meritocratic, market-driven age. It flattered the winners and insulted the losers. By 2016, its time was up. The arrival of Brexit and Trump, and the rise of hyper-nationalist, anti-immigrant parties in Europe, announced the failure of the project. The question now is what an alternative political project might look like.

DEBATING THE DIGNITY OF WORK

The dignity of work is a good place to start. On the surface, it is hardly a controversial ideal. No politician speaks against it. But a political agenda that takes work seriously—that treats it as an arena of recognition—would raise uncomfortable questions for mainstream liberals and conservatives alike. This is because it would challenge a premise that proponents of market-based globalization widely share—that market outcomes reflect the true social value of people's contributions to the common good.

Thinking about pay, most would agree that what people make for this or that job often overstates or understates the true social value of the work they do. Only an ardent libertarian would insist that the wealthy casino magnate's contribution to society is a thousand times more valuable than that of a pediatrician. The pandemic of 2020 prompted many to reflect, at least fleetingly, on the importance of the work performed by grocery store clerks, delivery workers, home care providers, and other essential but modestly paid workers. In a market society, however, it is hard to resist the tendency to confuse the money we make with the value of our contribution to the common good.

This confusion is not merely the result of sloppy thinking. It is not put to rest by philosophical arguments revealing its flaws. It reflects the allure of the meritocratic hope that the world is arranged in a way that aligns what we receive with what we are due. This is the hope that has fueled providentialist thinking from the Old Testament to present-day talk of being "on the right side of history."

In market-driven societies, interpreting material success as a sign of

213

moral desert is a persisting temptation. It is a temptation we need repeatedly to resist. One way of doing so is to debate and enact measures that prompt us to reflect, deliberately and democratically, on what counts as truly valuable contributions to the common good and where market verdicts miss the mark.

It would be unrealistic to expect that such a debate would produce agreement; the common good is inescapably contestable. But a renewed debate about the dignity of work would disrupt our partisan complacencies, morally invigorate our public discourse, and move us beyond the polarized politics that four decades of market faith and meritocratic hubris have bequeathed.

Consider, as illustrations, two versions of a political agenda focused on the dignity of work and the need to challenge market outcomes to affirm it. One comes from a conservative direction, the other from a progressive one.

The Hubris of the "Open Agenda"

The first comes from a young conservative thinker who once worked as a policy advisor to Republican presidential candidate Mitt Romney. In an insightful book, *The Once and Future Worker*, Oren Cass offers a series of proposals that address the grievances Trump tapped but failed to resolve. Cass argues that the renewal of work in the United States requires Republicans to give up their orthodox embrace of free markets. Rather than push corporate tax cuts and unfettered free trade in hopes of boosting GDP, Republicans should focus on policies that enable workers to find jobs that pay well enough to support strong families and communities. This matters more for a good society, Cass maintains, than economic growth.[50]

One of the policies he proposes to achieve this goal is a wage subsidy for low-income workers—hardly standard Republican fare. The idea is that the government would provide a supplementary payment for each hour worked by a low-wage employee, based on a target hourly-wage rate. The wage subsidy is, in a way, the opposite of a payroll tax. Rather than deduct a certain amount of each worker's earnings, the government would contribute a certain amount, in hopes of enabling low-income workers to make a decent living even if they lack the skills to command a substantial market wage.[51]

A dramatic version of the wage subsidy proposal was enacted by a number of European countries when the coronavirus pandemic of 2020 locked down their economies. Rather than offer unemployment insurance to workers who lost their jobs during the pandemic, as the U.S. government did, Britain, Denmark, and the Netherlands covered 75 to 90 percent of wages for companies that did not lay off workers. The advantage of the wage subsidy is that it enables employers to retain workers on their payroll during the emergency, rather than fire them and force them to rely on unemployment insurance. The U.S. approach, by contrast, cushions workers' lost wages but does not affirm the dignity of work by ensuring that workers keep their jobs.[52]

Other proposals Cass offers are more likely to appeal to conservatives, such as scaling back environmental regulations that cost jobs in manufacturing and mining industries.[53] On the fraught subjects of immigration and free trade, Cass urges that we view these from the standpoint of workers, not consumers. If our goal is the lowest possible consumer prices, he observes, then free trade, outsourcing, and relatively open immigration policies are desirable. But if our main concern is creating a labor market that enables low- and middle-skilled American workers to earn a decent living, raise families, and build communities, then some restrictions on trade, outsourcing, and immigration are justified.[54]

Whatever the merit of Cass's particular proposals, what is interesting about his project is that it works out the implications of shifting our focus from maximizing GDP to creating a labor market conducive to the dignity of work and social cohesion. In doing so, he offers a scathing critique of globalization proponents, who have insisted since the 1990s that the key political divide is no longer between left and right but between "open and closed." Cass rightly points out that this way of framing the globalization debate casts the "highly skilled, college-educated 'winners' of the modern economy" as open-minded and their critics as closed-minded, as if questioning the free flow of goods, capital, and people across national borders were a kind of bigotry. It is hard to imagine a more condescending way of defending neoliberal globalization to those it leaves behind.[55]

The proponents of the "open agenda" insist that the solution for those who do not prosper is better education. "The vision is supposed to be an inspiring one, in which people are lifted upward to greater opportunity," Cass writes. "Its real implications are less exalted; if the economy no longer works for the average worker, it is he who needs to transform into something it likes better." He concludes that "the open agenda is not sustainable in a democracy where the majority finds itself left behind; its arguments are losing force." Citing the danger of "irresponsible populism," Cass states that "the question is not whether the open agenda will lose but rather to what."[56]

Finance, Speculation, and the Common Good

A second approach to renewing the dignity of work, more likely to resonate with political progressives, would highlight an aspect of the globalization agenda that is often overlooked by mainstream politicians—the rising role of finance. The financial industry came dramatically to public attention with the financial crisis of 2008. The debate it provoked was mainly about the terms of the taxpayer bailout and how to reform Wall Street to reduce the risk of future crises.

Far less public attention has been given to the way finance remade the economy in recent decades and subtly transformed the meaning of merit and success. This transformation bears deeply on the dignity of work. Trade and immigration have figured more conspicuously than finance in the populist backlash against globalization; their impact on working-class jobs and status is palpable and visceral. But the financialization of the economy may be more corrosive of the dignity of work, and more demoralizing. This is because it offers perhaps the clearest example in a modern economy of the gap between what the market rewards and what actually contributes to the common good.

The financial industry today looms large in advanced economies, having grown dramatically during the past several decades. In the United States, its share of GDP has nearly tripled since the 1950s, and by 2008, it claimed more than 30 percent of corporate profits. Its employees make 70 percent more than comparably qualified workers in other industries.[57]

This would not be a problem if all this financial activity were productive, if it increased the economy's ability to produce valuable goods and services. But this is not the case. Even at its best, finance is not productive in itself. Its role is to facilitate economic activity by allocating capital to socially useful purposes—new businesses, factories, roads, airports, schools, hospitals, homes. But as finance has exploded as a share of the U.S. economy in recent decades, less and less of it has involved investing in the real economy. More and more has involved complex financial engineering that yields big profits for those engaged in it but does nothing to make the economy more productive.[58]

As Adair Turner, chair of Britain's Financial Services Authority, explained, "There is no clear evidence that the growth in the scale and complexity of the financial system in the rich developed world over the last 20 to 30 years has driven increased growth or stability, and it is possible for financial activity to extract rents [unjustified windfalls] from the real economy rather than to deliver economic value."[59]

This measured judgment is a devastating verdict on the conventional wisdom that led the Clinton administration and its U.K. counterparts to deregulate the financial industry in the 1990s. What it means, in simple terms, is that the complex derivatives and other financial instruments devised by Wall Street in recent decades actually hurt the economy more than they helped it.

Consider a concrete example. In his book *Flashboys*, Michael Lewis tells the story of a company that laid a fiber-optic cable linking Chicago futures traders with New York stock markets. The cable increased the speed of trades on pork belly futures and other speculative bets by a few milliseconds. This minuscule edge was worth hundreds of millions of dollars to high-speed traders.[60] But it is hard to claim that speeding up such transactions from the blink of an eye to something even faster contributes anything of value to the economy.

High-speed trading is not the only financial innovation of dubious economic value; credit default swaps that enable speculators to bet on future prices without investing in any productive activity are hard to distinguish from casino gambling. One party wins and the other loses, money changes hands, but no investment occurs along the way. When companies use profits to buy back shares instead of investing in research and development, or in new equipment, shareholders gain but the productive capacity of the company does not.

In 1984, as financialization was starting to take off, James Tobin, the distinguished Yale economist, offered a prescient warning of the "casino aspect of our financial markets." He worried "that we are throwing more and more of our resources, including the cream of our youth, into financial activities remote from the production of goods and services, into activities that generate high private rewards disproportionate to their social productivity."[61]

It is hard to know exactly what portion of financial activity improves the productive capacity of the real economy and what portion generates unproductive windfalls for the financial industry itself. But Adair Turner, a credible authority, has estimated that in advanced economies such as the U.S. and U.K., only 15 percent of financial flows go into new productive enterprises rather than into speculation on existing assets or fancy derivatives.[62] Even if this underestimates by half the productive aspect of finance, it is a sobering figure. Its implications are not only economic but also moral and political.

Economically, it suggests that much financial activity hinders rather than promotes economic growth. Morally and politically, it reveals a vast discrepancy between the rewards the market bestows on finance and the value of its contribution to the common good. This discrepancy, along with the disproportionate prestige accorded those engaged in speculative pursuits, mocks the dignity of those who earn a living producing useful goods and services in the real economy.

Those who worry about the adverse economic effects of modern finance have proposed various ways to reform it. My concern, however, is with its moral and political implications. A political agenda that recognizes the dignity of work would use the tax system to reconfigure the economy of esteem by discouraging speculation and honoring productive labor.

Generally speaking, this would mean shifting the tax burden from work to consumption and speculation. A radical way of doing so would be to lower or even eliminate payroll taxes and to raise revenue instead by taxing consumption, wealth, and financial transactions. A modest step in this direction would be to reduce the payroll tax (which makes work expensive for employers and employees alike) and make up the lost revenue with a financial transactions tax on high-frequency trading, which contributes little to the real economy.

These and other measures to shift the burden of taxation from labor to consumption and speculation could be done in ways that would make the tax system more efficient and less regressive than it is today. But these considerations, however important, are not the only ones that matter. We should also consider the expressive significance of taxation. By this I mean the attitudes toward success and failure, honor and recognition, embedded in the way we fund our public life. Taxation is not only a way of raising revenue; it is also a way of expressing a society's judgment about what counts as a valuable contribution to the common good.

MAKERS AND TAKERS

On one level, the moral aspect of tax policy is familiar. We commonly argue about the fairness of taxation—whether this or that tax will fall more heavily on the rich or the poor. But the expressive dimension of taxation goes beyond debates about fairness, to the moral judgments societies make about which activities are worthy of honor and recognition, and which ones should be discouraged. Sometimes, these judgments are explicit. Taxes on tobacco, alcohol, and casinos are called "sin taxes" because they seek to discourage activities deemed harmful or undesirable (smoking, drinking, gambling). Such taxes express society's disapproval of these activities by raising the cost of engaging in them. Proposals to tax sugary sodas (to combat obesity) or carbon emissions (to address climate change) likewise seek to change norms and shape behavior.

Not all taxes have this aim. We do not tax income to express disapproval of paid employment or to discourage people from engaging it. Nor is a general sales tax intended as a deterrent to buying things. These are simply ways of raising revenue.

Often, however, moral judgments are implicit in seemingly value-neutral policies. This is especially true when tax touches work, and the various ways people make money. For example, why should income from capital gains be taxed at a lower rate than income from labor? Warren Buffett raised this question when he pointed out that he, a billionaire investor, paid a lower rate of tax than his secretary.[63]

Some argue that taxing investment less heavily than work encourages investment and so promotes economic growth. On one level, this argument is purely practical, or utilitarian; it seeks to increase GDP, not to honor wealthy investors who reap capital gains. But politically, this seemingly practical claim draws some of its persuasive force from a moral assumption—an argument about merit—that lurks just beneath the surface. This is the assumption that investors are "job creators" who should be rewarded with lower taxes.

A stark version of this argument was advanced by Republican congressman Paul Ryan, former Speaker of the U.S. House of Representatives, and a devotee of the libertarian writer Ayn Rand. Ryan, a critic of the welfare state, distinguished between "makers" (those who contribute the most to the economy) and "takers" (those who receive more in government benefits than they pay in taxes). He worried that, as the welfare state grew, the so-called "takers" were coming to outnumber the "makers."[64]

Some objected to Ryan's highly moralized way of speaking about economic contribution. Others accepted his distinction between makers and takers but argued that Ryan had misidentified them. Rana Foroohar, a business columnist at the *Financial Times* and CNN, offers a powerful instance of the second view in an insightful book titled *Makers and Takers: The Rise of Finance and the Fall of American Business.* Citing Adair Turner, Warren Buffett, and other critics of unproductive financialization, Foroohar argues that the primary "takers" in today's economy are those in the financial industry who engage in speculative activity that reaps enormous windfalls without contributing to the real economy:

> All this finance has not made us more prosperous. Instead, it has
> deepened inequality and ushered in more financial crises, which

destroy massive amounts of economic value each time they happen. Far from being a help to our economy, finance has become a hindrance. More finance isn't increasing our economic growth—it is slowing it.[65]

Foroohar concludes that the supposed "makers" are the ones "doing most of the taking in society: paying the least taxes as a percentage of income, grabbing a disproportionate share of the economic pie, and advancing business models that often run counter to growth." The true "makers," she argues, are those who labor in the real economy to provide useful goods and services, and those who invest in this productive activity.[66]

The debate over who is a maker in today's economy, and who a taker, is ultimately an argument about contributive justice, about what economic roles are worthy of honor and recognition. Thinking this through requires public debate about what counts as a valuable contribution to the common good. My proposal to replace some or all of the payroll tax with a financial transactions tax—a "sin tax," in effect, on casino-like speculation that does not help the real economy—is intended as one way of framing such a debate. No doubt there are others. My broader point is that renewing the dignity of work requires that we contend with the moral questions underlying our economic arrangements, questions that the technocratic politics of recent decades have obscured.

One such question is what kinds of work are worthy of recognition and esteem. Another is what we owe one another as citizens. These questions are connected. For we cannot determine what counts as a contribution worth affirming without reasoning together about the purposes and ends of the common life we share. And we cannot deliberate about common purposes and ends without a sense of belonging, without seeing ourselves as members of a community to which we are indebted. Only insofar as we depend on others, and recognize our dependence, do we have reason to appreciate their contributions to our collective well-being. This requires a sense of community sufficiently robust to enable citizens to say, and to believe, that "we are all in this together"—not as a ritual incantation in times of crisis, but as a plausible description of our everyday lives.

Over the past four decades, market-driven globalization and the meritocratic conception of success, taken together, have unraveled these moral ties. Global supply chains, capital flows, and the cosmopolitan identities they fostered made us less reliant on our fellow citizens, less grateful for the work they do, and less open to the claims of solidarity. Meritocratic sorting taught us that our success is our own doing, and so eroded our sense of indebtedness. We are now in the midst of the angry whirlwind this unraveling has produced. To renew the dignity of work, we must repair the social bonds the age of merit has undone.

CONCLUSION:

MERIT AND THE COMMON GOOD

Henry Aaron, one of baseball's greatest players, grew up in the segregated South. His biographer, Howard Bryant, describes how, as a young boy, "Henry would watch as his father was forced to surrender his place in line at the general store to any whites who entered." When Jackie Robinson broke baseball's color line, Henry, then thirteen years old, was inspired to believe that he, too, could play one day in the Major Leagues. Lacking a bat and ball, he practiced with what he had, using a stick to hit bottle caps pitched to him by his brother. He would go on to break Babe Ruth's career record for home runs.[1]

In a poignant observation, Bryant writes, "Hitting, it could be argued, represented the first meritocracy in Henry's life."[2]

It is hard to read this line without loving meritocracy, without seeing it as the ultimate answer to injustice—a vindication of talent over prejudice, racism, and unequal opportunity. And from this thought, it is a small step to the conclusion that a just society is a meritocratic one, in which everyone has an equal chance to rise as far as their talent and hard work will take them.

But this is a mistake. The moral of Henry Aaron's story is not that we should love meritocracy but that we should despise a system of racial injustice that can only be escaped by hitting home runs. Equality of opportunity is a morally necessary corrective to injustice. But it is a remedial principle, not an adequate ideal for a good society.

BEYOND EQUALITY OF OPPORTUNITY

It is not easy to keep hold of this distinction. Inspired by the heroic rise of a few, we ask how others might also be enabled to escape the conditions that weigh them down. Rather than repair the conditions that people want to flee, we construct a politics that makes mobility the answer to inequality.

Breaking down barriers is a good thing. No one should be held back by poverty or prejudice. But a good society cannot be premised only on the promise of escape.

Focusing only, or mainly, on rising does little to cultivate the social bonds and civic attachments that democracy requires. Even a society more successful than ours at providing upward mobility would need to find ways to enable those who do not rise to flourish in place, and to see themselves as members of a common project. Our failure to do so makes life hard for those who lack meritocratic credentials and makes them doubt that they belong.

It is often assumed that the only alternative to equality of opportunity is a sterile, oppressive equality of results. But there is another alternative: a broad equality of condition that enables those who do not achieve great wealth or prestigious positions to live lives of decency and dignity—developing and exercising their abilities in work that wins social esteem, sharing in a widely diffused culture of learning, and deliberating with their fellow citizens about public affairs.

Two of the best accounts of equality of condition appeared in the midst of the Depression. In a book entitled *Equality* (1931), R. H. Tawney, a British economic historian and social critic, argued that equality of opportunity is at best a partial ideal. "Opportunities to 'rise,'" he wrote, "are not a substitute for a large measure of practical equality, nor do they make immaterial the existence of sharp disparities of income and social condition."[3]

Social well-being . . . depends upon cohesion and solidarity. It implies the existence, not merely of opportunities to ascend, but of
a high level of general culture, and a strong sense of common
interests. . . . Individual happiness does not only require that men
should be free to rise to new positions of comfort and distinction;
it also requires that they should be able to lead a life of dignity and
culture, whether they rise or not.[4]

In the same year, across the Atlantic, a writer named James Truslow Adams wrote a paean to his country entitled *The Epic of America*. Few recall
the book, but everyone knows the phrase he coined in its closing pages:
"the American dream." Looking back from our time, it would be easy
to equate his account of the American dream with our rhetoric of rising. America's "distinctive and unique gift to mankind," Adams wrote,
was the dream "of a land in which life should be better and richer and
fuller for every man, with opportunity for each according to his ability or
achievement."[5]

It is not a dream of motor cars and high wages merely, but a dream
of a social order in which each man and each woman shall be able
to attain to the fullest stature of which they are innately capable, and
be recognized by others for what they are, regardless of the fortu-
itous circumstances of birth or position.[6]

But a closer reading reveals that the dream Adams described was not only
about moving up; it was about achieving a broad, democratic equality of
condition. As a concrete example, he pointed to the U.S. Library of Congress, "a symbol of what democracy can accomplish on its own behalf," a
place of public learning that drew Americans from all walks of life:

As one looks down on the general reading room, which alone contains ten thousand volumes which may be read without even the
asking, one sees the seats filled with silent readers, old and young,
rich and poor, black and white, the executive and the laborer, the

general and the private, the noted scholar and the schoolboy, all reading at their own library provided by their own democracy.[7]

Adams considered this scene "to be a perfect working out in a concrete example of the American dream—the means provided by the accumulated resources of the people themselves, [and] a public intelligent enough to use them." If this example could be "carried out in all departments of our national life," Adams wrote, the American dream would become "an abiding reality."[8]

DEMOCRACY AND HUMILITY

We do not have much equality of condition today. Public spaces that gather people together across class, race, ethnicity, and faith are few and far between. Four decades of market-driven globalization has brought inequalities of income and wealth so pronounced that they lead us into separate ways of life. Those who are affluent and those of modest means rarely encounter one another in the course of the day. We live and work and shop and play in different places; our children go to different schools. And when the meritocratic sorting machine has done its work, those on top find it hard to resist the thought that they deserve their success and that those on the bottom deserve their place as well. This feeds a politics so poisonous and a partisanship so intense that many now regard marriage across party lines as more troubling than marrying outside the faith. It is little wonder we have lost the ability to reason together about large public questions, or even to listen to one another.

Merit began its career as the empowering idea that we can, through work and faith, bend God's grace in our favor. The secular version of this idea made for an exhilarating promise of individual freedom: Our fate is in our hands. We can make it if we try.

But this vision of freedom points us away from the obligations of a shared democratic project. Recall the two conceptions of the common good we considered in chapter 7, the consumerist and the civic. If the common good consists simply in maximizing the welfare of consumers, then achieving an equality of condition does not matter in the end. If democracy is simply economics by other means, a matter of adding up our individual interests and preferences, then its fate does not depend on the moral bonds of citizens. A consumerist conception of democracy can do its limited work whether we share a vibrant common life or inhabit privatized enclaves in the company of our own kind.

But if the common good can be arrived at only by deliberating with our fellow citizens about the purposes and ends worthy of our political community, then democracy cannot be indifferent to the character of the common life. It does not require perfect equality. But it does require that citizens from different walks of life encounter one another in common spaces and public places. For this is how we learn to negotiate and abide our differences. And this is how we come to care for the common good.[9]

The meritocratic conviction that people deserve whatever riches the market bestows on their talents makes solidarity an almost impossible project. For why do the successful owe anything to the less-advantaged members of society? The answer to this question depends on recognizing that, for all our striving, we are not self-made and self-sufficient; finding ourselves in a society that prizes our talents is our good fortune, not our due. A lively sense of the contingency of our lot can inspire a certain humility: "There, but for the grace of God, or the accident of birth, or the mystery of fate, go I." Such humility is the beginning of the way back from the harsh ethic of success that drives us apart. It points beyond the tyranny of merit toward a less rancorous, more generous public life.

NOTES

PROLOGUE TO THE PAPERBACK EDITION

1. Margot Sanger-Katz, "On Coronavirus, Americans Still Trust the Experts," *The New York Times*, June 27, 2020, nytimes.com/2020/06/27/upshot/coronavirus-americans-trust-experts .html.
2. The COVID Tracking Project, covidtracking.com/race. Data as of February 21, 2021. Race categories may overlap with Hispanic/Latinx ethnicity.
3. James Clyburn, Interview with FiveThirtyEight, February 26, 2020, abcnews.go.com /fivethirtyeight/video/rep-james-clyburn-settled-endorsing-joe-biden-president-69231417. I am indebted to Elizabeth Anderson for bringing Clyburn's quote to my attention.

INTRODUCTION: GETTING IN

1. Jennifer Medina, Katie Benner, and Kate Taylor, "Actresses, Business Leaders and Other Wealthy Parents Charged in U.S. College Entry Fraud," *The New York Times*, March 12, 2019, nytimes.com/2019/03/12/us/college-admissions-cheating-scandal.html.
2. Ibid. See also "Here's How the F.B.I. Says Parents Cheated to Get Their Kids into Elite Colleges," *The New York Times*, March 12, 2019, nytimes.com/2019/03/12/us/admissions -scandal.html; Affidavit in Support of Criminal Complaint, March 11, 2019, U.S. Department of Justice, justice.gov/file/1142876/download.
3. Lara Trump on *Fox News at Night*, March 12, 2019, facebook.com/FoxNews/videos/lara -trump-weighs-in-on-college-admissions-scandal/2334404040124820.
4. Andrew Lelling, U.S. Attorney, District of Massachusetts, March 12, 2019, CNN transcript of statement, edition.cnn.com/TRANSCRIPTS/1903/12/ath.02.html.
5. Frank Bruni, "Bribes to Get into Yale and Stanford? What Else Is New?," *The New York Times*, March 12, 2019, nytimes.com/2019/03/12/opinion/college-bribery-admissions.html; Eugene Scott, "Why Trump Jr. Mocked the Parents Caught Up in the College Admissions Scandal," *The Washington Post*, March 13, 2019, washingtonpost.com/politics/2019/03/13 /why-trump-jr-mocked-parents-caught-up-college-admissions-scandal. For original reporting on Jared Kushner's case and on the role of money in admissions, see Daniel Golden, *The Price of Admission* (New York: Broadway Books, 2006), pp. 44–46. On Trump's reported donations to the Wharton School, see Luis Ferre Sadurni, "Donald Trump May Have Donated over $1.4 Million to Penn," *Daily Pennsylvanian*, November 3, 2016, thedp .com/article/2016/11/trumps-history-of-donating-to-penn.
6. Singer quoted in Affidavit in Support of Criminal Complaint, March 11, 2019, U.S. Department of Justice, justice.gov/file/1142876/download, p. 13.

7. Andrew Lelling, U.S. Attorney, District of Massachusetts, March 12, 2019, CNN transcript of statement, edition.cnn.com/TRANSCRIPTS/1903/12/ath.02.html.

8. Andre Perry, "Students Need a Boost in Wealth More Than a Boost in SAT Scores," *The Hechinger Report*, May 17, 2019, hechingerreport.org/students-need-a-boost-in-wealth-more-than-a-boost-in-sat-scores.

9. Ron Lieber, "One More College Edge," *The New York Times*, March 16, 2019; Paul Tough, *The Years That Matter Most: How College Makes or Breaks Us* (Boston: Houghton Mifflin Harcourt, 2019), pp. 153–67.

10. "Some Colleges Have More Students from the Top 1 Percent Than the Bottom 60," *The New York Times*, January 18, 2017, nytimes.com/interactive/2017/01/18/upshot/some-colleges-have-more-students-from-the-top-1-percent-than-the-bottom-60.html. The data is from Raj Chetty, John Friedman, Emmanuel Saez, Nicholas Turner, and Danny Yagan, "Mobility Report Cards: The Role of Colleges in Intergenerational Mobility," NBER Working Paper No. 23618, revised version, December 2017, opportunityinsights.org/paper/mobilityreportcards.

11. Caroline M. Hoxby, "The Changing Selectivity of American Colleges," *Journal of Economic Perspectives* 23, no. 4 (Fall 2009), pp. 95–118.

12. Ibid., pp. 95–100; Paul Tough, *The Years That Matter Most*, p. 39.

13. Matthias Doepke and Fabrizio Zilibotti, *Love, Money & Parenting: How Economics Explains the Way We Raise Our Kids* (Princeton: Princeton University Press, 2019), pp. 8–11, 51–84.

1. WINNERS AND LOSERS

1. A cover story in *The Economist* exemplifies this view. See "Drawbridges Up: The New Divide in Rich Countries Is Not Between Left and Right but Between Open and Closed," *The Economist*, July 30, 2016, economist.com/briefing/2016/07/30/drawbridges-up. For a more nuanced view, see Bagehot, "Some Thoughts on the Open v Closed Divide," *The Economist*, March 16, 2018, economist.com/bagehots-notebook/2018/03/16/some-thoughts-on-the-open-v-closed-divide.

2. In this and the following paragraphs of this section, I draw from Michael Sandel, "Right-Wing Populism Is Rising as Progressive Politics Fails—Is It Too Late to Save Democracy?," *New Statesman*, May 21, 2018, newstatesman.com/2018/05/right-wing-populism-rising-progressive-politics-fails-it-too-late-save-democracy; and Michael J. Sandel, "Populism, Trump, and the Future of Democracy," openDemocracy.net, May 9, 2018, opendemocracy.net/en/populism-trump-and-future-of-democracy.

3. In the United States, most of the economic growth since 1980 has gone to the top 10 percent, whose income grew 121 percent; almost none went to the bottom half of the population, whose average income (about $16,000) in 2014 was about the same as it was in real terms in 1980. For working-age men, the median income was "the same in 2014 as in 1964, about $35,000. There has been no growth for the median male worker over half a century." Thomas Piketty, Emmanuel Saez, and Gabriel Zucman, "Distributional National Accounts: Methods and Estimates for the United States," *Quarterly Journal of Economics* 133, issue 2 (May 2018), pp. 557, 578, 592–93, available at eml.berkeley.edu/~saez/PSZ2018QJE.pdf; Facundo Alvaredo, Lucas Chancel, Thomas Piketty, Emmanuel Saez, and Gabriel Zucman, *World Inequality Report 2018* (Cambridge, MA: Harvard University Press, 2018), pp. 3, 83–84. Income distribution data for the U.S. and other countries is also available at the online World Inequality Database, wid.world. See also Thomas Piketty, *Capital in the Twenty-First Century* (Cambridge, MA: Harvard University Press, 2014), p. 297, where Piketty states that from 1977 to 2007, the richest 10 percent absorbed three-quarters of the entire economic growth of the United States.

   In the U.S., the top 1 percent receive 20.2 percent of national income, while the bottom half receive 12.5 percent. In the U.S., the top 10 percent take in nearly half (47 percent) of national income, compared with 37 percent in Western Europe, 41 percent in China, and 55 percent in Brazil and India. See Piketty, Saez, and Zucman, "Distributional National Accounts," p. 575, available at eml.berkeley.edu/~saez/PSZ2018QJE.pdf; Alvaredo, Chancel, Piketty, Saez, and Zucman, *World Inequality Report 2018*, pp. 3, 83–84.

4. Author's search of online archive of speeches and public papers of U.S. presidents at the American Presidency Project, U.C. Santa Barbara, presidency.ucsb.edu.

5. According to a study by the Pew Charitable Trusts, 4 percent of Americans born in the bottom quintile rise to the top quintile as adults, 30 percent rise to the middle quintile or higher, and 43 percent remain stuck in the bottom quintile. "Pursuing the American Dream: Economic Mobility Across Generations," Pew Charitable Trusts, July 2012, p. 6, Figure 3, available at pewtrusts.org/~/media/legacy/uploadedfiles/wwwpewtrustsorg/reports/economic _mobility/pursuingamericandreampdf.pdf. A study by the Harvard economist Raj Chetty and colleagues concludes that 7.5 percent of Americans born in the bottom quintile rise to the top quintile, 38 percent rise to the middle quintile or higher, and 34 percent remain stuck at the bottom. Raj Chetty, Nathaniel Hendren, Patrick Kline, and Emmanuel Saez, "Where Is the Land of Opportunity? The Geography of Intergenerational Mobility in the United States," *Quarterly Journal of Economics* 129, no. 4 (2014), pp. 1553–623; available at rajchetty.com/chettyfiles/mobility_geo.pdf (mobility figures at p. 16 and Table II). According to a study by Scott Winship of the Archbridge Institute, only 3 percent of children born in the bottom quintile make it to the top quintile, and only 26 percent make it to the middle quintile or higher; 46 percent remain stuck at the bottom. Scott Winship, "Economic Mobility in America," Archbridge Institute, March 2017, p. 18, Figure 3, available at archbridgeinst.wpengine.com/wp-content/uploads/2017/04/Contemporary-levels-of -mobility-digital-version_Winship.pdf.

6. Miles Corak, "Income Inequality, Equality of Opportunity, and Intergenerational Mobility," *Journal of Economic Perspectives* 27, no. 3 (Summer 2013), pp. 79–102 (see Figure 1, p. 82), online at pubs.aeaweb.org/doi/pdfplus/10.1257/jep.27.3.79; Miles Corak, "Do Poor Children Become Poor Adults? Lessons from a Cross Country Comparison of Generational Earnings Mobility," IZA Discussion Paper No. 1993, March 2006 (see Table 1, p. 42), at ftp .iza.org/dp1993.pdf; *A Broken Social Elevator? How to Promote Social Mobility* (Paris: OECD Publishing, 2018), online at doi.org/10.1787/9789264301085-en. The OECD study shows similar results to those of Corak, except for Germany, which according to the OECD study is less mobile than the United States. See country comparisons in Figure 4.8, p. 195.

7. Stefanie Stantcheva, "Prisoners of the American Dream," *Project Syndicate*, February 22, 2018, scholar.harvard.edu/files/stantcheva/files/prisoners_of_the_american_dream_by_stefanie _stantcheva_-_project_syndicate_0.pdf.

8. Raj Chetty, John Friedman, Emmanuel Saez, Nicholas Turner, and Danny Yagan, "Mobility Report Cards: The Role of Colleges in Intergenerational Mobility," NBER Working Paper No. 23618, Revised Version, July 2017, equality-of-opportunity.org/papers/coll_mrc_paper.pdf.

9. fivethirtyeight.com/features/even-among-the-wealthy-education-predicts-trump-support/; jrf.org.uk/report/brexit-vote-explained-poverty-low-skills-and-lack-opportunities.

10. Aaron Blake, "Hillary Clinton Takes Her 'Deplorables' Argument for Another Spin," *The Washington Post*, March 13, 2018, washingtonpost.com/news/the-fix/wp/2018/03/12/hillary -clinton-takes-her-deplorables-argument-for-another-spin. Trump won narrowly over Clinton among high-income voters. But he won decisively among voters from rural areas and small cities (62–34 percent), among white voters without a college degree (67–28 percent), and among voters who believe trade with other countries takes away rather than creates more jobs (65–31 percent). See "Election 2016: Exit Polls," *The New York Times*, November 8, 2016, nytimes.com/interactive/2016/11/08/us/politics/election-exit-polls.html.

11. Donald J. Trump, "Remarks Announcing United States Withdrawal from the United Nations Framework Convention on Climate Change Paris Agreement," June 1, 2017, the American Presidency Project, presidency.ucsb.edu/node/328739.

12. For various interpretations of Confucian political meritocracy, see Daniel A. Bell and Chenyang Li, eds., *The East Asian Challenge for Democracy: Political Meritocracy in Comparative Perspective* (New York: Cambridge University Press, 2013); on Plato, see *The Republic of Plato*, translated by Allan Bloom (New York: Basic Books, 1968), Book VI; on Aristotle, see *The Politics of Aristotle*, translated by Ernest Barker (Oxford: Oxford University Press, 1946), Book III, and *The Nicomachean Ethics of Aristotle*, translated by Sir David Ross (Oxford: Oxford University Press, 1925), Books I and VI.

13. Joseph F. Kett, *Merit: The History of a Founding Idea from the American Revolution to the 21st Century* (Ithaca, NY: Cornell University Press, 2013), pp. 1–10, 33–44. Thomas Jefferson to John Adams, October 28, 1813, in Lester J. Cappon, ed., *The Adams-Jefferson Letters: The Complete Correspondence Between Thomas Jefferson and Abigail and John Adams* (Chapel Hill: University of North Carolina, 1959), vol. 2, pp. 387–92.

14. Michael Young, *The Rise of the Meritocracy* (Harmondsworth: Penguin Books, 1958).

15. Ibid., p. 106.

2. "GREAT BECAUSE GOOD": A BRIEF MORAL HISTORY OF MERIT

1. "lot, n." OED Online, Oxford University Press, June 2019, oed.com/view/Entry/110425. Accessed July 16, 2019.

2. For example, Jonah 1:4–16.

3. Job 4:7. I am indebted here and in the following discussion of Job to Moshe Halbertal's fine essay "Job, the Mourner," in Leora Batnitzky and Ilana Pardes, eds., *The Book of Job: Aesthetics, Ethics, and Hermeneutics* (Berlin: de Gruyter, 2015), pp. 37–46.

4. Ibid., pp. 39, 44–45. Halbertal attributes this interpretation of Job to Maimonides. On rain falling where no one lives, see Job 38:25–26.

5. Ibid., pp. 39, 45.

6. I am indebted here and in the paragraphs that follow to the illuminating discussion in Anthony T. Kronman, *Confessions of a Born-Again Pagan* (New Haven, CT: Yale University Press, 2016), esp. pp. 88–98, 240–71, 363–93.

7. Halbertal, "Job, the Mourner," p. 37.

8. Kronman, *Confessions of a Born-Again Pagan*, pp. 240–59; J. B. Schneewind, *The Invention of Autonomy* (Cambridge: Cambridge University Press, 1998), pp. 29–30.

9. Eric Nelson, *The Theology of Liberalism: Political Philosophy and the Justice of God* (Cambridge, MA: Harvard University Press, 2019); Michael Axworthy, "The Revenge of Pelagius," *New Statesman*, December 7, 2018, p. 18; Joshua Hawley, "The Age of Pelagius," *Christianity Today*, June 2019, at christianitytoday.com/ct/2019/june-web-only/age-of-pelagius-joshua-hawley.html.

10. Kronman, *Confessions of a Born-Again Pagan*, pp. 256–71; Schneewind, *The Invention of Autonomy*, p. 272.

11. Kronman, *Confessions of a Born-Again Pagan*, pp. 363–81.

12. Max Weber, *The Protestant Ethic and the Spirit of Capitalism* (originally published 1904–1905), translated by Talcott Parsons (New York: Charles Scribner's Sons, 1958).

13. Ibid., p. 104.

14. Ibid., pp. 109–10.

15. Ibid., pp. 110–15.

16. Ibid., p. 115.

17. Ibid., p. 160.

18. Ibid., pp. 154, 121.

19. Ibid., pp. 121–22.

20. Max Weber, "The Social Psychology of the World Religions," in H. H. Gerth and C. Wright Mills, eds., *From Max Weber: Essays in Sociology* (New York: Oxford University Press, 1946), p. 271. Italics in original.

21. Jackson Lears, *Something for Nothing: Luck in America* (New York: Viking, 2003), p. 34.

22. Ibid.

23. Ibid., pp. 57–62. Ecclesiastes 9:11–12, cited at p. 59.

24. Lears, *Something for Nothing*, p. 60.

25. Ibid., p. 76.

26. Ibid.

27. Ibid., p. 22.

28. Ibid.

29. John Arlidge and Philip Beresford, "Inside the Goldmine," *The Sunday Times* (London), November 8, 2009.

30. Graham quoted in "Hurricane Katrina: Wrath of God?," *Morning Joe* on NBC News, October 5, 2005, at nbcnews.com/id/9600878/ns/msnbc-morning_joe/t/hurricane-katrina -wrath-god/#.XQZz8NNKjuQ.

31. Robertson quoted in Dan Fletcher, "Why Is Pat Robertson Blaming Haiti?" *Time*, Jan. 14, 2010.

32. Falwell quoted in Laurie Goodstein, "After the Attacks: Finding Fault," *The New York Times*, September 15, 2001.

33. Devin Dwyer, "Divine Retribution? Japan Quake, Tsunami Resurface God Debate," ABC News, March 18, 2011, at abcnews.go.com/Politics/japan-earthquake-tsunami-divine-retri bution-natural-disaster-religious/story?id=13167670; Harry Harootunian, "Why the Japa-nese Don't Trust Their Government," *Le Monde Diplomatique*, April 11, at mondediplo .com/2011/04/08japantrust.

34. Kenyon quoted in Kate Bowler, "Death, the Prosperity Gospel and Me," *The New York Times*, February 13, 2016. See also Kate Bowler, *Blessed: A History of the American Prosper-ity Gospel* (New York: Oxford University Press, 2013).

35. Bowler, "Death, the Prosperity Gospel and Me."

36. Osteen quoted in Bowler, ibid.

37. David Van Biema and Jeff Chu, "Does God Want You to Be Rich?" *Time*, September 10, 2006.

38. Bowler, "Death, the Prosperity Gospel and Me."

39. Bowler, *Blessed*, p. 181; polling data in Biema and Chu, "Does God Want You to Be Rich?"

40. Bowler, *Blessed*, p. 226.

41. Ibid.

42. Bowler, "Death, the Prosperity Gospel and Me."

43. See Vann R. Newkirk II, "The American Health Care Act's Prosperity Gospel," *The Atlan-tic*, May 5, 2017.

44. Brooks quoted in Newkirk, ibid., and in Jonathan Chait, "Republican Blurts Out That Sick People Don't Deserve Affordable Care," *New York*, May 1, 2017.

45. John Mackey, "The Whole Foods Alternative to ObamaCare," *The Wall Street Journal*, August 11, 2009. See also Chait, ibid.

46. Mackey, ibid.

47. Hillary Clinton, "Address Accepting the Presidential Nomination at the Democratic Con-vention in Philadelphia, Pennsylvania," July 28, 2016, at presidency.ucsb.edu/documents /address-accepting-the-presidential-nomination-the-democratic-national-convention.

48. President Dwight D. Eisenhower, "Address at the New England 'Forward to '54' Dinner," Boston, Massachusetts, September 21, 1953, at presidency.ucsb.edu/documents/address-the -new-england-forward-54-dinner-boston-massachusetts.

49. See John Pitney, "The Tocqueville Fraud," *The Weekly Standard*, November 12, 1995, at weeklystandard.com/john-j-pitney/the-tocqueville-fraud.

50. Counting variations of the quote, Gerald R. Ford used it six times as president, Ronald Reagan used it ten times, and George H. W. Bush used it six times. Incidence of use was calculated using the searchable document archive of the American Presidency Project, University of California, Santa Barbara, at presidency.ucsb.edu/advanced-search.

51. President Ronald Reagan, "Remarks at the Annual Convention of the National Association of Evangelicals in Columbus, Ohio," March 6, 1984, at presidency.ucsb.edu/documents /remarks-the-annual-convention-the-national-association-evangelicals-columbus-ohio.

52. Incidence of use was calculated using the searchable document archive of the American Presidency Project, University of California, Santa Barbara, at presidency.ucsb.edu /advanced-search. The archive includes all presidential speeches and remarks, and some campaign speeches of presidential candidates who are not incumbent presidents. An archive search shows that John Kerry used the phrase at least once during his 2004 campaign and that Hillary Clinton used the phrase at least seven times during her 2016 campaign.

53. See Yascha Mounk, *The Age of Responsibility: Luck, Choice, and the Welfare State* (Cambridge, MA: Harvard University Press, 2017).

54. The first president to use the phrase was Ronald Reagan, speaking about a free-trade agreement with Canada in 1988, presidency.ucsb.edu/documents/remarks-the-american-coalition -for-trade-expansion-with-canada. But a few months later, in a speech at the American Enterprise Institute, he criticized "the right side of history" as "that unpleasant Marxist phrase" used by those who, in the 1970s, wanted to accept Soviet domination of Eastern Europe, presidency.ucsb.edu/documents/remarks-the-american-enterprise-institute-for-public -policy-research. See generally Jay Nordlinger, "The Right Side of History," *National Review*, March 31, 2011, and David A. Graham, "The Wrong Side of 'the Right Side of History,'" *The Atlantic*, December 21, 2015.

55. President George W. Bush, "Remarks to Military Personnel at Fort Hood, Texas," April 12, 2005, at presidency.ucsb.edu/documents/remarks-military-personnel-fort-hood-texas. Vice President Richard B. Cheney, "Vice President's Remarks at a Rally for Expeditionary Strike Group One," May 23, 2006, at presidency.ucsb.edu/documents/vice-presidents-remarks -rally-for-expeditionary-strike-group-one.

56. Incidence of use was calculated using the searchable document archive of the American Presidency Project, University of California, Santa Barbara, at presidency.ucsb.edu /advanced-search.

57. President Barack Obama, "Commencement Address at the United States Military Academy in West Point, New York," May 22, 2010, at presidency.ucsb.edu/documents/commencement -address-the-united-states-military-academy-west-point-new-york-2; Obama, "Commencement Address at the United States Air Force Academy in Colorado Springs, Colorado," June 2, 2016, at presidency.ucsb.edu/documents/commencement-address-the-united-states-air -force-academy-colorado-springs-colorado-1.

58. President William J. Clinton, "Interview with Larry King," January 20, 1994, at presidency .ucsb.edu/documents/interview-with-larry-king-1; President Barack Obama, "Inaugural Address," January 20, 2009, at presidency.ucsb.edu/documents/inaugural-address-5.

59. President Barack Obama, "The President's News Conference," June 23, 2009, at presidency .ucsb.edu/documents/the-presidents-news-conference-1122; Obama, "The President's News Conference, March 11, 2011, at presidency.ucsb.edu/documents/the-presidents-news-confer ence-1112; Obama, "The President's News Conference," February 15, 2011, at presidency .ucsb.edu/documents/the-presidents-news-conference-1113.

60. Incidence of use was calculated using the searchable document archive of the American Presidency Project, University of California, Santa Barbara, at presidency.ucsb.edu

/advanced-search. On the rug, see Chris Hayes, "The Idea That the Moral Universe Inherently Bends Toward Justice Is Inspiring. It's Also Wrong." At nbcnews.com/think/opinion /idea-moral-universe-inherently-bends-towards-justice-inspiring-it-s-ncna859661, and David A. Graham, "The Wrong Side of 'the Right Side of History.'"

61. Theodore Parker, *Ten Sermons of Religion*, 2nd ed. (Boston: Little, Brown and Company, 1855), pp. 84–85.

62. Google books Ngram at <iframe name="ngram_chart" src="https://books.google.com /ngrams/interactive_chart?content=right+side+of+history&year_start=1980&year_end =2010&corpus=15&smoothing=3&share=&direct_url=t1%3B%2Cright%20side%20of%20 history%3B%2Cc0" width=900 height=500 marginwidth=0 marginheight=0 hspace=0 vspace=0 frameborder=0 scrolling=no></iframe>.

63. President William J. Clinton, "Media Roundtable Interview on NAFTA," November 12, 1993, at presidency.ucsb.edu/documents/media-roundtable-interview-nafta; Clinton, "Remarks to the People of Germany in Berlin," May 13, 1998, at presidency.ucsb.edu/documents /remarks-the-people-germany-berlin.

64. President William J. Clinton, "Remarks at a Campaign Concert for Senator John F. Kerry in Boston," September 28, 1996, at presidency.ucsb.edu/documents/remarks-campaign -concert-for-senator-john-f-kerry-boston; President Barack Obama, "Remarks at a Democratic National Committee Reception in San Jose, California," May 8, 2014, at presidency .ucsb.edu/documents/remarks-democratic-national-committee-reception-san-jose -california; Obama, "Remarks on Signing an Executive Order on Lesbian, Gay, Bisexual, and Transgender Employment Discrimination," July 21, 2014, at presidency.ucsb.edu /documents/remarks-signing-executive-order-lesbian-gay-bisexual-and-transgender -employment; William J. Clinton, "Address at the Democratic National Convention in Denver, Colorado, August 27, 2008, at presidency.ucsb.edu/documents/address-the -democratic-national-convention-denver-colorado.

65. President Barack Obama, "Remarks at a Reception Celebrating Lesbian, Gay, Bisexual, and Transgender Pride Month," June 13, 2013, at presidency.ucsb.edu/documents/remarks -reception-celebrating-lesbian-gay-bisexual-and-transgender-pride-month.

66. President Barack Obama, "Remarks at an Obama Victory Fund 2012 Fundraiser in Beverly Hills, California," June 6, 2012, at presidency.ucsb.edu/documents/remarks-obama-victory -fund-2012-fundraiser-beverly-hills-california.

67. Eric Westervelt, "Greatness Is Not a Given: 'America The Beautiful' Asks How We Can Do Better," National Public Radio, April 4, 2019, at npr.org/2019/04/04/709531017/america-the -beautiful-american-anthem.

68. Katharine Lee Bates, *America the Beautiful and Other Poems* (New York: Thomas Y. Crowell Co., 1911), pp. 3–4.

69. See Mark Krikorian, "God Shed His Grace on Thee," *National Review*, July 6, 2011.

70. A video of Ray Charles's performance of "America the Beautiful" at the 2001 World Series is available at youtube.com/watch?v=HlHMQEegpFs.

3. THE RHETORIC OF RISING

1. Evan Osnos, *Age of Ambition: Chasing Fortune, Truth, and Faith in the New China* (New York: Farrar, Straus and Giroux, 2014), pp. 308–10.

2. As president, Bill Clinton used this phrase 21 times. For example: "[W]e have a heavy responsibility to make sure that no child is denied that opportunity because they happen to be poor or they happen to be born in an area that hasn't had a lot of economic opportunity or they happen to be a member of a racial minority or they happen to be otherwise left behind, because we don't have a person to waste. This is a highly competitive world

and it runs on people power, and we need all the people we can get." William J. Clinton, "Remarks in San Jose, California," August 7, 1996, the American Presidency Project, presidency.ucsb.edu/node/223422.

3. See Yascha Mounk, *The Age of Responsibility: Luck, Choice, and the Welfare State* (Cambridge, MA: Harvard University Press, 2017), and Jacob S. Hacker, *The Great Risk Shift* (New York: Oxford University Press, 2006).

4. Ronald Reagan, "Address Before a Joint Session of Congress on the State of the Union," January 27, 1987, the American Presidency Project, presidency.ucsb.edu/node/252758.

5. Uses of the phrase by Coolidge, Hoover, and FDR can be found at the American Presidency Project, presidency.ucsb.edu/advanced-search.

6. As president, Reagan used the phrase "through no fault of their own" 26 times; Clinton used it 72 times, Obama 56 times. Calculated by the author using the searchable archive at the American Presidency Project, presidency.ucsb.edu/advanced-search.

7. William J. Clinton, "Inaugural Address," January 20, 1993, the American Presidency Project, presidency.ucsb.edu/node/219347.

8. William J. Clinton, "Address Before a Joint Session of the Congress on the State of the Union," January 24, 1995, the American Presidency Project, presidency.ucsb.edu/node/221902.

9. William J. Clinton, "Remarks on Arrival at McClellan Air Force Base, Sacramento, California," April 7, 1995, the American Presidency Project, presidency.ucsb.edu/node/220655.

10. William J. Clinton, "Statement on Signing the Personal Responsibility and Work Opportunity Reconciliation Act of 1996," August 22, 1996, at the American Presidency Project, presidency.ucsb.edu/node/222686.

11. Tony Blair, *New Britain: My Vision of a Young Country* (London: Fourth Estate, 1996), pp. 19, 173. See also pp. 273, 292.

12. Gerhard Schröder, December 31, 2002, quoted in Yascha Mounk, *The Age of Responsibility: Luck, Choice, and the Welfare State* (Cambridge, MA: Harvard University Press, 2017), pp. 220–21. Translated by Mounk. See also pp. 1–6.

13. Mounk, ibid., quote at p. 30; see generally pp. 28–37.

14. Ronald Reagan, "Remarks at a White House Briefing for Black Administration Appointees," June 25, 1984, the American Presidency Project, presidency.ucsb.edu/node/260916; Ronald Reagan, "Radio Address to the Nation on Tax Reform," May 25, 1985, the American Presidency Project, presidency.ucsb.edu/node/259932.

15. William J. Clinton, "Remarks to the Democratic Leadership Council," December 3, 1993, the American Presidency Project, presidency.ucsb.edu/node/218963; Obama used some version of the phrase 50 times during his presidency, Reagan 15 times, Clinton 14 times, George W. Bush 3 times, George H. W. Bush twice, Gerald Ford once, Richard Nixon once. The phrase appeared in three written statements by Nixon and in two by Lyndon Johnson, and did not appear in spoken or written statements by any U.S. president prior to Johnson. Frequencies calculated by author using the searchable archive of presidential speeches at the American Presidency Project, presidency.ucsb.edu/advanced-search.

16. Barack Obama, "Remarks at the White House College Opportunity Summit," December 4, 2014, the American Presidency Project, presidency.ucsb.edu/node/308043.

17. Barack Obama, "Remarks at a Campaign Rally in Austin, Texas," July 17, 2012, the American Presidency Project, presidency.ucsb.edu/node/301979.

18. Google Ngram search at books.google.com/ngrams/graph?content=you+deserve&year_start=1970&year_end=2008&corpus=15&smoothing=3&share=&direct_url=t1%3B%2Cyou%20deserve%3B%2Cc0. According to the searchable online archive of *The New York Times*, "you deserve" appeared 14 times in 1981 and 69 times in 2018. It also showed a steady increase by decade, rising from 111 uses in the 1970s to 175 in the 1980s, 228 in the 1990s, 480 in the 2000s, and 475 in the 2010s (through July 31, 2019).

19. John Lofflin, "What's New in Subliminal Messages: 'I Deserve to Succeed. I Deserve to Reach My Goals. I Deserve to Be Rich,'" *The New York Times*, March 20, 1988, nytimes .com/1988/03/20/business/what-s-new-subliminal-messages-deserve-succeed-deserve -reach-my-goals-deserve-be.html?searchResultPosition=1; David Tanis, "You Deserve More Succulent Chicken," *The New York Times*, March 29, 2019, nytimes.com/2019/03/29 /dining/chicken-paillard-recipe.html?searchResultPosition=1.

20. See the discussion of Friedrich Hayek, John Rawls, and the luck egalitarians in chapter 3.

21. Reagan used "you deserve" 31 times, compared with a total of 27 uses by Presidents Kennedy, Johnson, Nixon, Ford, and Carter, according to the searchable archive of presidential speeches at the American Presidency Project, presidency.ucsb.edu/advanced-search.

22. Ronald Reagan, "Remarks and a Question-and-Answer Session with Members of the Commonwealth Club of California in San Francisco," March 4, 1983, the American Presidency Project, presidency.ucsb.edu/node/262792.

23. Reagan used "you deserve" 31 times, Clinton used it 68 times, and Obama used it 104 times, according to the searchable archive of presidential speeches at the American Presidency Project, presidency.ucsb.edu/advanced-search. William J. Clinton, "Remarks to the Community in San Bernardino, California," May 20, 1994, the American Presidency Project, presidency.ucsb.edu/node/220148; Barack Obama, "Remarks at the Costco Wholesale Corporation Warehouse in Lanham, Maryland," January 29, 2014, the American Presidency Project, presidency.ucsb.edu/node/305268; Barack Obama, "Remarks at Cuyahoga Community College Western Campus in Parma, Ohio," September 8, 2010, the American Presidency Project, presidency.ucsb.edu/node/288117.

24. Theresa May, "Britain, the Great Meritocracy: Prime Minister's Speech," September 9, 2016, at gov.uk/government/speeches/britain-the-great-meritocracy-prime-ministers-speech.

25. Ibid.

26. Barack Obama, Interview with Bill Simmons of ESPN, March 1, 2012, the American Presidency Project, presidency.ucsb.edu/node/327087.

27. Hillary Clinton, "Remarks at the Frontline Outreach Center in Orlando, Florida," September 21, 2016, the American Presidency Project, presidency.ucsb.edu/node/319595; "Remarks at Eastern Market in Detroit, Michigan," November 4, 2016, the American Presidency Project, presidency.ucsb.edu/node/319839; "Remarks at Ohio State University in Columbus, Ohio," October 10, 2016, the American Presidency Project, presidency.ucsb.edu/node/319580.

28. Erin A. Cech, "Rugged Meritocratists: The Role of Overt Bias and the Meritocratic Ideology in Trump Supporters' Opposition to Social Justice Efforts," *Socius: Sociological Research for a Dynamic World* 3 (January 1, 2017), pp. 1–20, journals.sagepub.com/doi/full/10 .1177/2378023117712395.

29. Ibid., pp. 7–12.

30. In the U.S., the top 1 percent receive 20.2 percent of national income, while the bottom half receive 12.5 percent. In the U.S., the top 10 percent take in nearly half (47 percent) of national income, compared with 37 percent in Western Europe, 41 percent in China, and 55 percent in Brazil and India. Thomas Piketty, Emmauel Saez, and Gabriel Zucman, "Distributional National Accounts: Methods and Estimates for the United States, *Quarterly Journal of Economics* 133, issue 2 (May 2018), p. 575, available at eml.berkeley.edu/~saez /PSZ2018QJE.pdf; Alvaredo, Chancel, Piketty, Saez, and Zucman, *World Inequality Report 2018*, pp. 3, 83–84. Income distribution data for the U.S. and other countries is also available at the online World Inequality Database, wid.world.

31. In the United States, most of the economic growth since 1980 has gone to the top 10 percent, whose income grew 121 percent; almost none went to bottom half of the population, whose average income (about $16,000) in 2014 was about the same as it was in real terms in 1980. For working-age men, the median income was "the same in 2014 as in 1964, about

$35,000. There has been no growth for the median male worker over half a century." Piketty, Saez, and Zucman, "Distributional National Accounts," pp. 557, 578, 592–93. See also Thomas Piketty, *Capital in the Twenty-First Century* (Cambridge, MA: Harvard University Press, 2014), p. 297, where Piketty states that from 1977 to 2007, the richest 10 percent absorbed three-quarters of the entire economic growth of the U.S.

32. Americans agree by 77 to 20 percent that "most people can succeed if they are willing to work hard." Germans agree by 51 to 48 percent. In France and Japan, majorities agree more with the statement that "hard work is no guarantee of success for most people," by 54 to 46 percent (France) and 59 to 40 percent (Japan). Pew Global Attitudes Project, July 12, 2012, pewresearch.org/global/2012/07/12/chapter-4-the-casualties-faith-in-hard-work-and -capitalism.

33. Seventy-three percent of Americans say working hard is "very important to getting ahead in life," compared with 49 percent of German and 25 percent of French respondents. Among South Korean and Japanese respondents, the figures were 34 percent and 42 percent respectively. Pew Research Center, Spring 2014 Global Attitudes survey, October 7, 2014, pewre search.org/global/2014/10/09/emerging-and-developing-economies-much-more-optimistic -than-rich-countries-about-the-future/inequality-05.

34. Asked why people are rich, 43 percent say they worked harder, and 42 percent say they had advantages in life. Asked why people are poor, 52 percent cite circumstances beyond their control and 31 percent cite a lack of effort. Democrats and Republicans differ in their responses to these questions. Amina Dunn, "Partisans Are Divided over the Fairness of the U.S. Economy—and Why People Are Rich or Poor," Pew Research Center, October 4, 2018, pewresearch.org/fact-tank/2018/10/04/partisans-are-divided-over-the-fairness-of-the-u-s -economy-and-why-people-are-rich-or-poor.

35. Asked whether "success in life is pretty much determined by forces outside our control," 74 percent of South Koreans, 67 percent of Germans, and 66 percent of Italians agree, compared with only 40 percent of Americans. Pew Research Center, Spring 2014 Global Attitudes survey, October 9, 2014, pewresearch.org/global/2014/10/09/emerging-and-developing -economies-much-more-optimistic-than-rich-countries-about-the-future.

36. Raj Chetty, David Grusky, Maximilian Hell, Nathaniel Hendren, Robert Manduca, and Jimmy Narang, "The Fading American Dream: Trends in Absolute Income Mobility Since 1940," *Science* 356 (6336), 2017, pp. 398–406, available at opportunityinsights.org/paper /the-fading-american-dream. Comparing the earnings of fathers and sons, the shift is even starker: 95 percent of males born in 1940 made more than their fathers; only 41 percent of males born in 1984 exceeded their fathers' earnings.

37. According to a study by the Pew Charitable Trusts, 4 percent of Americans born in the bottom quintile rise to the top quintile as adults, 30 percent rise to the middle quintile or higher, and 43 percent remain stuck in the bottom quintile. "Pursuing the American Dream: Economic Mobility Across Generations," Pew Charitable Trusts, July 2012, p. 6, Figure 3, available at pewtrusts.org/~/media/legacy/uploadedfiles/wwwpewtrustsorg/reports/economic_mobility /pursuingamericandreampdf.pdf. A study by the Harvard economist Raj Chetty and colleagues concludes that 7.5 percent of Americans born in the bottom quintile rise to the top quintile, 38 percent rise to the middle quintile or higher, and 34 percent remain stuck at the bottom. Raj Chetty, Nathaniel Hendren, Patrick Kline, and Emmanuel Saez, "Where Is the Land of Opportunity? The Geography of Intergenerational Mobility in the United States," *Quarterly Journal of Economics* 129, no. 4 (2014), pp. 1553–623; available at rajchetty.com/chettyfiles /mobility_geo.pdf (mobility figures at p. 16 and Table II). According to a study by Scott Winship of the Archbridge Institute, only 3 percent of children born in the bottom quintile make it to the top quintile, and only 26 percent make it to the middle quintile or higher; 46 percent remain stuck at the bottom. Scott Winship, "Economic Mobility in America," Archbridge

Institute, March 2017, p. 18, Figure 3, available at archbridgeinst.wpengine.com/wp-content /uploads/2017/04/Contemporary-levels-of-mobility-digital-version_Winship.pdf.

38. Miles Corak, "Income Inequality, Equality of Opportunity, and Intergenerational Mobility," *Journal of Economic Perspectives* 27, no. 3 (Summer 2013), pp. 79–102 (see Figure 1, p. 82), online at pubs.aeaweb.org/doi/pdfplus/10.1257/jep.27.3.79; Miles Corak, "Do Poor Children Become Poor Adults? Lessons from a Cross Country Comparison of Generational Earnings Mobility," IZA Discussion Paper No. 1993, March 2006 (see Table 1, p. 42), at ftp .iza.org/dp1993.pdf; *A Broken Social Elevator? How to Promote Social Mobility* (Paris: OECD Publishing, 2018), online at doi.org/10.1787/9789264301085-en. The OECD study shows similar results to those of Corak, except for Germany, which according to the OECD study is less mobile than the United States. See country comparisons in Figure 4.8, p. 195.

39. Chetty et al., "Where Is the Land of Opportunity?" p. 16. See also Julia B. Isaacs, Isabel Sawhill, and Ron Haskins, *Getting Ahead or Losing Ground: Economic Mobility in America* (Economic Mobility Project: An Initiative of the Pew Charitable Trusts, 2008), at pewtrusts .org//media/legacy/uploadedfiles/wwwpewtrustsorg/reports/economic_mobility/economic mobilityinamericafullpdf.pdf. Mobility data for the U.S. and Denmark is at Figure 1, p. 40.

40. Javier C. Hernández and Quoctrung Bui, "The American Dream Is Alive. In China," *The New York Times*, November 18, 2018, nytimes.com/interactive/2018/11/18/world/asia/china -social-mobility.html.

41. Ibid.

42. Ibid. World Bank data comparing intergenerational mobility in China and the United States is from Ambar Narayan et al., *Fair Progress?: Economic Mobility Across Generations Around the World* (Washington, DC: World Bank, 2018), pp. 107 (Figure 3.6), 140 (Map 4.1) and 141 (Figure 4.2). The World Bank study is available online at openknowledge.worldbank.org /handle/10986/28428. An OECD study cites data showing mobility in China as being somewhat less than in the U.S. See *A Broken Social Elevator? How to Promote Social Mobility* (Paris: OECD Publishing, 2018), Figure 4.8, p. 195, at doi.org/10.1787/9789264301085-en.

43. *The Republic of Plato*, Book III, 414b–17b. Translated by Allan Bloom (New York: Basic Books, 1968), pp. 93–96.

44. Alberto Alesina, Stefanie Stantcheva, and Edoardo Teso, "Intergenerational Mobility and Preferences for Redistribution," *American Economic Review* 108, no. 2 (February 2018), pp. 521–54. Online at pubs.aeaweb.org/doi/pdfplus/10.1257/aer.20162015.

45. Summers quoted in Ron Suskind, *Confidence Men: Wall Street, Washington, and the Education of a President* (New York: Harper, 2011), p. 197.

46. President Barack Obama, "The President's Weekly Address," August 18, 2012; the American Presidency Project, presidency.ucsb.edu/node/302249.

47. Ibid.

4. CREDENTIALISM: THE LAST ACCEPTABLE PREJUDICE

1. Grace Ashford, "Michael Cohen Says Trump Told Him to Threaten Schools Not to Release Grades," *The New York Times*, February 27, 2019, nytimes.com/2019/02/27/us/politics /trump-school-grades.html; full transcript: Michael Cohen's Opening Statement to Congress, *The New York Times*, February 27, 2019, nytimes.com/2019/02/27/us/politics/cohen -documents-testimony.html?module=inline.

2. Maggie Haberman, "Trump: How'd Obama Get into Ivies?," *Politico*, April 25, 2011, politico.com/story/2011/04/trump-howd-obama-get-into-ivies-053694.

3. Nina Burleigh, "Trump Speaks at Fourth-Grade Level, Lowest of Last 15 Presidents, New Analysis Finds," *Newsweek*, January 8, 2018, newsweek.com/trump-fire-and-fury-smart-genius -obama-774169; data and methodology at blog.factba.se/2018/01/08/; Rebecca Morin, "'Idiot,'

'Dope,' 'Moron': How Trump's Aides Have Insulted the Boss," *Politico*, September 4, 2018, politico.com/story/2018/09/04/trumps-insults-idiot-woodward-806455; Valerie Strauss, "President Trump Is Smarter Than You. Just Ask Him," *The Washington Post*, February 9, 2017, washingtonpost.com/news/answer-sheet/wp/2017/02/09/president-trump-is-smarter-than-you-just-ask-him/; Andrew Restuccia, "Trump Fixates on IQ as a Measure of Worth," *Politico*, May 30, 2019, politico.com/story/2019/05/30/donald-trump-iq-intelligence-1347149; David Smith, "Trump's Tactic to Attack Black People and Women: Insult Their Intelligence," *The Guardian*, August 10, 2018, theguardian.com/us-news/2018/aug/10/trump-attacks-twitter-black-people-women.

4. Strauss, "President Trump Is Smarter Than You. Just Ask Him"; Donald J. Trump, "Remarks at the Central Intelligence Agency in Langley, Virginia," January 21, 2017, the American Presidency Project, presidency.ucsb.edu/node/323537.

5. Trump quoted in Michael Kranish, "Trump Has Referred to His Wharton Degree as 'Super Genius Stuff,'" *The Washington Post*, July 8, 2019, washingtonpost.com/politics/trump-who-often-boasts-of-his-wharton-degree-says-he-was-admitted-to-the-hardest-school-to-get-into-the-college-official-who-reviewed-his-application-recalls-it-differently/2019/07/08/0a4eb414-977a-11e9-830a-21b9b36b64ad_story.html.

6. Strauss, "President Trump Is Smarter Than You. Just Ask Him."

7. Donald J. Trump, "Remarks at a 'Make America Great Again' Rally in Phoenix, Arizona," August 22, 2017, the American Presidency Project, presidency.ucsb.edu/node/331393.

8. Video of Biden comments at youtube.com/watch?v=QWM6EuKxz5A; Trump-Biden comparison discussed in Meghan Kruger, "Who's the Smartest of Them All? Trump and Biden Both Say 'Me,'" *The Washington Post*, July 17, 2019, washingtonpost.com/opinions/whos-the-smartest-of-them-all-trump-and-biden-both-say-me/2019/07/17/30221c46-a8cb-11e9-9214-246e594de5d5_story.html.

9. James R. Dickenson, "Biden Academic Claims 'Inaccurate,'" *The Washington Post*, September 22, 1987, washingtonpost.com/archive/politics/1987/09/22/biden-academic-claims-inaccurate/932eaeed-9071-47a1-aeac-c94a51b668e1.

10. Kavanaugh hearing, transcript, *The Washington Post*, September 27, 2018, washingtonpost.com/news/national/wp/2018/09/27/kavanaugh-hearing-transcript.

11. George H. W. Bush, "Address to the Nation on the National Education Strategy," April 18, 1991, the American Presidency Project, presidency.ucsb.edu/node/266128; Blair quoted in Ewen Macaskill, "Blair's Promise: Everyone Can Be a Winner," *The Guardian*, October 2, 1996, theguardian.com/education/1996/oct/02/schools.uk.

12. William J. Clinton, "Remarks at a Democratic National Committee Dinner," May 8, 1996, the American Presidency Project, presidency.ucsb.edu/node/222520. Clinton used some version of the phrase ("what you learn," or "what you can learn") 32 times, according to a search of the online archive at the American Presidency Project, presidency.ucsb.edu/advanced-search. John McCain's version reversed the lines in Clinton's couplet: "In the global economy, what you learn is what you earn." For example, McCain, "Address at Episcopal High School in Alexandria, Virginia," April 1, 2008, the American Presidency Project, presidency.ucsb.edu/node/277705.

13. Barack Obama, "Remarks at Pathways in Technology Early College High School in New York City," October 25, 2013, the American Presidency Project, presidency.ucsb.edu/node/305195.

14. Ibid.

15. Ibid.

16. Christopher Hayes, *The Twilight of the Elites: America After Meritocracy* (New York: Crown Publishers, 2012), p. 48.

17. Ibid.

18. Thomas Frank, *Listen, Liberal—or What Ever Happened to the Party of the People?* (New York: Metropolitan Books, 2016), pp. 34–35.

19. Ibid., pp. 72–73. For data on the divergence between productivity and pay since 1979, see "Productivity-Pay Gap," Economic Policy Institute, July 2019, epi.org/productivity-pay-gap.

20. In 2018, 35 percent of Americans twenty-five years and over had completed four years of college, up from 25 percent in 1999 and 20 percent in 1988. United States Census Bureau, CPS Historical Time Series Tables, 2018, Table A-2, census.gov/data/tables/time-series /demo/educational-attainment/cps-historical-time-series.html.

21. Jonathan Alter, *The Promise: President Obama, Year One* (New York: Simon and Schuster, 2010), p. 64.

22. Ibid.

23. Patrick J. Egan, "Ashton Carter and the Astoundingly Elite Educational Credentials of Obama's Cabinet Appointees," *The Washington Post*, December 5, 2014, washingtonpost.com /news/monkey-cage/wp/2014/12/05/ashton-carter-and-the-astoundingly-elite-educational -credentials-of-obamas-cabinet-appointees. Cited in Frank, *Listen, Liberal*, p. 164.

24. David Halberstam, *The Best and the Brightest* (New York: Random House, 1969).

25. Alter, *The Promise*, p. 63.

26. Frank, *Listen, Liberal*, p. 40.

27. Ibid., pp. 165–66.

28. Ibid., p. 166; Neil Barofsky, *Bailout: An Inside Account of How Washington Abandoned Main Street While Rescuing Wall Street* (New York: Free Press, 2012).

29. Barofsky, *Bailout*, p. 139.

30. Author search using online archive of presidential speeches at the American Presidency Project, presidency.ucsb.edu/advanced-search.

31. Word frequency in books searched in Google Ngram, books.google.com/ngrams. In *The New York Times*, the word "smart" appeared 620 times in 1980, 2,672 times in 2000. Word searched by year at nytimes.com/search?query=smart.

32. William J. Clinton, "The President's Radio Address," August 19, 2000, the American Presidency Project, presidency.ucsb.edu/node/218332; "Remarks on Proposed Medicare Prescription Drug Benefit Legislation and an Exchange with Reporters," June 14, 2000, the American Presidency Project, presidency.ucsb.edu/node/226899; "The President's Radio Address," September 2, 2000, the American Presidency Project, presidency.ucsb.edu/node/218133.

33. Barack Obama, "Statement on International Women's Day," March 8, 2013, the American Presidency Project, presidency.ucsb.edu/node/303937; "Remarks to the United Nations General Assembly in New York City," September 20, 2016, the American Presidency Project, presidency.ucsb.edu/node/318949; "Remarks on Immigration Reform," October 24, 2013, the American Presidency Project, presidency.ucsb.edu/node/305189; "Remarks at Forsyth Technical Community College in Winston-Salem, North Carolina," December 6, 2010, the American Presidency Project, presidency.ucsb.edu/node/288963.

34. Hillary Clinton quoted in "Press Release—President Obama Announces Key State Department Appointments," March 6, 2009, the American Presidency Project, presidency.ucsb .edu/node/322243.

35. Transcript of Obama's 2002 speech at npr.org/templates/story/story.php?storyId=99591469.

36. Obama quoted in David Rothkopf, *Foreign Policy*, June 4, 2014, foreignpolicy.com/2014/06 /04/obamas-dont-do-stupid-shit-foreign-policy.

37. Barack Obama, "Remarks at Newport News Shipbuilding in Newport News, Virginia," February 26, 2013, the American Presidency Project, presidency.ucsb.edu/node/303848; "The President's News Conference," March 1, 2013, the American Presidency Project, presidency.ucsb.edu/node/303955.

38. Barack Obama, "The President's News Conference," March 1, 2013.

39. Toon Kuppens, Russell Spears, Antony S. R. Manstead, Bram Spruyt, and Matthew J. Easterbrook, "Educationism and the Irony of Meritocracy: Negative Attitudes of Higher

Educated People Towards the Less Educated," *Journal of Experimental Social Psychology* 76 (May 2018), pp. 429–47.

40. Ibid., pp. 441–42.

41. Ibid., pp. 437, 444.

42. Ibid., pp. 438–39, 441–43.

43. Ibid., p. 444.

44. Ibid., pp. 441, 445.

45. Jennifer E. Manning, "Membership of the 116th Congress: A Profile," Congressional Research Service, June 7, 2019, p. 5, crsreports.congress.gov/product/pdf/R/R45583; A. W. Geiger, Kristen Bialik, and John Gramlich, "The Changing Face of Congress in 6 Charts," Pew Research Center, February 15, 2019, pewresearch.org/fact-tank/2019/02/15/the-changing-face-of-congress.

46. Nicholas Carnes, *The Cash Ceiling: Why Only the Rich Run for Office—and What We Can Do About It* (Princeton, NJ: Princeton University Press, 2018), pp. 5–6.

47. Data on MPs is from Rebecca Montacute and Tim Carr, "Parliamentary Privilege—the MPs in 2017," Research Brief, the Sutton Trust, June 2017, pp. 1–3, suttontrust.com/research-paper/parliamentary-privilege-the-mps-2017-education-background. See also Lukas Audickas and Richard Cracknell, "Social Background of MPs 1979–2017," House of Commons Library, November 12, 2018, researchbriefings.parliament.uk/ResearchBriefing/Summary/CBP-7483 #fullreport, which gives a somewhat lower figure (82 percent) for MPs with university degrees. The figure for the general population (70 percent without degrees) is from Bagehot, "People Without Degrees Are the Most Under-represented Group," *The Economist,* May 12, 2018.

48. Ibid., "Social Background of MPs 1979–2017," House of Commons Library, pp. 11–12; Ashley Cowburn, "Long Read: How Political Parties Lost the Working Class," *New Statesman,* June 2, 2017, newstatesman.com/2017/06/long-read-how-political-parties-lost-working-class; Oliver Heath, "Policy Alienation, Social Alienation and Working-Class Abstention in Britain, 1964–2010," *British Journal of Political Science* 48, issue 4 (October 2018), p. 1063, doi.org/10.1017/S0007123416000272.

49. Mark Bovens and Anchrit Wille, *Diploma Democracy: The Rise of Political Meritocracy* (Oxford: Oxford University Press, 2017), pp. 1–2, 5.

50. Ibid., pp. 112–16, 120; Conor Dillon, "Tempting PhDs Lead Politicians into Plagiarism," *DW,* February 13, 2013, p.dw.com/p/17dJu.

51. Bovens and Wille, *Diploma Democracy,* pp. 113–16.

52. Ibid.

53. Jackie Bischof, "The Best US Presidents, as Ranked by Presidential Historians," *Quartz,* February 19, 2017, qz.com/914825/presidents-day-the-best-us-presidents-in-history-as-ranked -by-presidential-historians/; Brandon Rottinghaus and Justin S. Vaughn, "How Does Trump Stack Up Against the Best—and Worst—Presidents?," *The New York Times,* February 19, 2018, nytimes.com/interactive/2018/02/19/opinion/how-does-trump-stack-up-against-the-best -and-worst-presidents.html.

54. See Binyamin Appelbaum, *The Economists' Hour: False Prophets, Free Markets, and the Fracture of Society* (New York: Little, Brown and Company, 2019), pp. 3–18.

55. Frank, *Listen, Liberal,* p. 39.

56. Figures on portion of general population who attend private schools (7 percent) and Oxford or Cambridge (1 percent) are from *Elitist Britain 2019: The Educational Backgrounds of Britain's Leading People* (The Sutton Trust and Social Mobility Commission, 2019), p. 4, suttontrust.com/wp-content/uploads/2019/06/Elitist-Britain-2019.pdf; figures on Boris Johnson cabinet and percentage of cabinet who attended private school over time are from Rebecca Montacute and Ruby Nightingale, Sutton Trust Cabinet Analysis 2019, suttontrust .com/research-paper/sutton-trust-cabinet-analysis-2019.

57. Sutton Trust Cabinet Analysis 2019; Adam Gopnik, "Never Mind Churchill, Clement Attlee Is a Model for These Times," *The New Yorker*, January 2, 2018, newyorker.com/news /daily-comment/never-mind-churchill-clement-attlee-is-a-model-for-these-times.

58. Gopnik, "Never Mind Churchill, Clement Attlee Is a Model for These Times"; the working-class backgrounds of Bevan and Morrison are discussed in Michael Young, "Down with Meritocracy," *The Guardian*, June 28, 2001, theguardian.com/politics/2001/jun/29 /comment. On Bevan's background, see the BBC, "Aneurin Bevan (1897–1960)," bbc.co.uk /history/historic_figures/bevan_aneurin.shtml. The assessments of the Attlee government are from the BBC, "Clement Attlee (1883–1967)," bbc.co.uk/history/historic_figures/attlee _clement.shtml, and John Bew, *Clement Attlee: The Man Who Made Modern Britain* (New York: Oxford University Press, 2017), quoted in Gopnik.

59. On Trump share of non-college white voters, see 2016 exit polls, CNN, cnn.com/election /2016/results/exit-polls; Clinton share of advanced degree holders is from Thomas Piketty, "Brahmin Left vs. Merchant Right: Rising Inequality & the Changing Structure of Political Conflict," WID.world Working Paper Series, March 2018, piketty.pse.ens.fr/files/Piketty2018 .pdf, Figure 3.3b; on education versus income, see Nate Silver, "Education, Not Income, Predicted Who Would Vote for Trump," November 22, 2016, FiveThirtyEight.com, fivethir tyeight.com/features/education-not-income-predicted-who-would-vote-for-trump.

60. Silver, "Education, Not Income, Predicted Who Would Vote for Trump." Trump quoted in Susan Page, "Trump Does the Impossible—Again," *USA Today*, February 25, 2016, usatoday.com/story/news/politics/elections/2016/02/24/analysis-donald-trump-does -impossible-again/80843932.

61. Thomas Piketty, "Brahmin Left vs. Merchant Right: Rising Inequality & the Changing Structure of Political Conflict."

62. Ibid., Figures 1.2c and 1.2d.

63. Ibid., p. 3; 2018 exit polls, CNN, cnn.com/election/2018/exit-polls.

64. 2018 exit polls, CNN, cnn.com/election/2018/exit-polls; Aaron Zitner and Anthony DeBarros, "The New Divide in Politics: Education," *The Wall Street Journal*, November 10, 2018, wsj.com/articles/midterm-results-point-to-a-new-divide-in-politics-education-1541865601.

65. Oliver Heath, "Policy Alienation, Social Alienation and Working-Class Abstention in Britain, 1964–2010," p. 1064, Figure 4; Oliver Heath, "Has the Rise of Middle Class Politicians Led to the Decline of Class Voting in Britain?," February 12, 2015, LSE blogs, blogs.lse.ac.uk /politicsandpolicy/the-rise-of-middle-class-politicians-and-the-decline-of-class-voting-in -britain.

66. "People Without Degrees Are the Most Under-represented Group," *The Economist*, May 12, 2018, economist.com/britain/2018/05/12/people-without-degrees-are-the-most-under -represented-group; Matthew Goodwin and Oliver Heath, "Brexit Vote Explained: Poverty, Low Skills and Lack of Opportunities," Joseph Rowntree Foundation, August 31, 2016, jrf .org.uk/report/brexit-vote-explained-poverty-low-skills-and-lack-opportunities.

67. Goodwin and Heath, "Brexit Vote Explained: Poverty, Low Skills and Lack of Opportunities."

68. Thomas Piketty, "Brahmin Left vs. Merchant Right: Rising Inequality & the Changing Structure of Political Conflict," pp. 13, Figures 2.3a–2.3e.

69. Ibid., pp. 2, 61.

70. Jérôme Fourquet, "Qui sont les Français qui soutiennent Emmanuel Macron?," *Slate*, February 7, 2017, slate.fr/story/136919/francais-marchent-macron.

71. Pascal-Emmanuel Gobry, "The Failure of the French Elite," *The Wall Street Journal*, February 22, 2019. See also Christopher Caldwell, "The People's Emergency," *The New Republic*, April 22, 2019, newrepublic.com/article/153507/france-yellow-vests-uprising-emmanuel -macron-technocratic-insiders.

72. Kim Parker, "The Growing Partisan Divide in Views of Higher Education," Pew Research Center, August 19, 2019, pewsocialtrends.org/essay/the-growing-partisan-divide-in-views-of-higher-education.

73. Obama quoted in Adam J. White, "Google.gov," *The New Atlantis*, Spring 2018, p. 15, the newatlantis.com/publications/googlegov. The video of Obama's talk at Google is at youtube.com/watch?v=m4yVlPqeZwo&feature=youtu.be&t=1h1m42s.

74. Ibid. See also Steven Levy, *In the Plex: How Google Thinks, Works, and Shapes Our Lives* (New York: Simon & Schuster, 2011), p. 317.

75. Author's search of Obama's use of "cost curve," using the online archive of the American Presidency Project, presidency.ucsb.edu/advanced-search.

76. Author's search of Obama's use of "incentivize," using the online archive of the American Presidency Project, presidency.ucsb.edu/advanced-search.

77. Author's search of Obama's use of "smart," using the online archive of the American Presidency Project, presidency.ucsb.edu/advanced-search.

78. Henry Mance, "Britain Has Had Enough of Experts, says Gove," June 3, 2016, *Financial Times*, ft.com/content/3be49734-29cb-11e6-83e4-abc22d5d108c.

79. Peter Baker, "From Obama and Baker, a Lament for a Lost Consensus," *The New York Times*, November 28, 2018, nytimes.com/2018/11/28/us/politics/obama-baker-consensus.html.

80. Quotes from Obama speaking at MIT's Sloan Sports Analytics Conference on February 23, 2018. Although the session was off the record, an audio recording of Obama's remarks is posted on the website of *Reason*, a libertarian magazine, at reason.com/2018/02/26/barack-obama-mit-sloan-sports.

81. Obama quoted in Baker, "From Obama and Baker, a Lament for a Lost Consensus." The exact quote comes from the C-SPAN video of President Obama at Rice University, November 27, 2018, at c-span.org/video/?455056-1/president-obama-secretary-state-james-baker-discuss-bipartisanship.

82. Hillary Clinton, "Address Accepting the Presidential Nomination at the Democratic National Convention in Philadelphia, Pennsylvania," July 28, 2016, the American Presidency Project, presidency.ucsb.edu/node/317862; Barack Obama, "Remarks to the Illinois General Assembly in Springfield, Illinois," February 10, 2016, the American Presidency Project, presidency.ucsb.edu/node/312502; Katie M. Palmer, "Cool Catchphrase, Hillary, but Science Isn't about Belief," *Wired*, July 29, 2016, wired.com/2016/07/cool-catchphrase-hillary-science-isnt-belief.

83. Obama quoted Moynihan on various occasions, including in Barack Obama, *The Audacity of Hope: Thoughts on Reclaiming the American Dream* (New York: Three Rivers Press, 2006), in his campaign appearance at Google in 2007 (quoted in Adam J. White, "Google.gov," *The New Atlantis*, Spring 2018, p. 16), and in his 2018 remarks at MIT, where he added the observation about Moynihan being smart, reason.com/2018/02/26/barack-obama-mit-sloan-sports.

84. Frank Newport and Andrew Dugan, "College-Educated Republicans Most Skeptical of Global Warming," Gallup, March 26, 2015, news.gallup.com/poll/182159/college-educated-republicans-skeptical-global-warming.aspx. In 2018, 69 percent of Republicans and only 4 percent of Democrats considered global warming generally exaggerated; 89 percent of Democrats and only 35 percent of Republicans believed global warming is caused by human activity. See Megan Brenan and Lydia Saad, "Global Warming Concern Steady Despite Some Partisan Shifts," Gallup, March 28, 2018, news.gallup.com/poll/231530/global-warming-concern-steady-despite-partisan-shifts.aspx.

85. Ibid.

86. Caitlin Drummond and Baruch Fischhoff, "Individuals with Greater Science Literacy and Education Have More Polarized Beliefs on Controversial Science Topics," *Proceedings of*

the *National Academy of Sciences* 114, no. 36 (September 5, 2017), pp. 9587–92, doi.org/10 .1073/pnas.1704882114.

87. Obama quoted in Robby Soave, "5 Things Barack Obama Said in His Weirdly Off-the-Record MIT Speech," February 27, 2018, *Reason*, at reason.com/2018/02/26/barack-obama -mit-sloan-sports, which also includes an audio recording of the speech.

88. Ibid.

89. Encyclical Letter Laudato Si' of the Holy Father Francis, "On Care for Our Common Home," May 24, 2015, paragraph 22, w2.vatican.va/content/dam/francesco/pdf/encyclicals /documents/papa-francesco_20150524_enciclica-laudato-si_en.pdf.

5. SUCCESS ETHICS

1. These inequalities are the ones that prevail in the United States today. The income distribution figures are from Thomas Piketty, Emmanuel Saez, and Gabriel Zucman, "Distributional National Accounts: Methods and Estimates for the United States," *Quarterly Journal of Economics* 133, issue 2 (May 2018), p. 575. The distribution of wealth is even more unequal. Most wealth (77 percent) is held by the top 10 percent, and the wealth of the top 1 percent now far exceeds the combined wealth of the bottom 90 percent of the population. See Alvarado et al., eds., *World Inequality Report* 2018, p. 237. A valuable online resource, the World Inequality Database, provides updates, for the U.S. and other countries: wid.world.

2. Piketty, Saez, and Zucman, "Distributional National Accounts," p. 575.

3. Michael Young, *The Rise of the Meritocracy* (Harmondsworth, UK: Penguin Books, 1958).

4. Ibid., p. 104.

5. Ibid., pp. 104–5.

6. Ibid., p. 105.

7. Ibid., p. 106.

8. Ibid.

9. Ibid., pp. 106–7.

10. Ibid., p. 107.

11. Amy Chozick, "Hillary Clinton Calls Many Trump Backers 'Deplorables,' and G.O.P. Pounces," *The New York Times*, September 10, 2016, nytimes.com/2016/09/11/us/politics /hillary-clinton-basket-of-deplorables.html.

12. Young, *The Rise of the Meritocracy*, pp. 108–9.

13. Piketty, Saez, and Zucman, "Distributional National Accounts," p. 575.

14. A vast and growing literature documents the consolidation of meritocratic privilege. Examples include Matthew Stewart, "The Birth of a New American Aristocracy," *The Atlantic*, June 2018, pp. 48–63; "An Hereditary Meritocracy," *The Economist*, January 22, 2015; Richard V. Reeves, *Dream Hoarders* (Washington, DC: Brookings Institution Press, 2017); Robert D. Putnam, *Our Kids: The American Dream in Crisis* (New York: Simon & Schuster, 2015); Samuel Bowles, Herbert Gintis, and Melissa Osborne Groves, eds., *Unequal Chances: Family Background and Economic Success* (Princeton, NJ: Princeton University Press, 2005); Stephen J. McNamee and Robert K. Miller, Jr., *The Meritocracy Myth* (Lanham, MD: Rowman & Littlefield, 3rd ed., 2014).

15. Viewership and financial prospects seem to be improving for arm wrestlers and practitioners of other niche sports. See Paul Newberry, "Arm Wrestling Looks to Climb Beyond Barroom Bragging Rights," Associated Press, September 6, 2018, available at apnews.com /842425dc6ed44c6886f9b3aedaac9141; Kevin Draper, "The Era of Streaming Niche Sports Dawns," *The New York Times*, July 17, 2018.

16. Justin Palmer, "Blake Trains Harder Than Me, but Won't Take 200 Title: Bolt," Reuters, November 12, 2011, available at reuters.com/article/us-athletics-bolt/blake-works-harder -than-me-but-wont-take-200-title-bolt-idUSTRE7AB0DE20111112; Allan Massie, "Can a

Beast Ever Prevail Against a Bolt?," *The Telegraph*, August 6, 2012, available at telegraph.co
.uk/sport/olympics/athletics/9455910/Can-a-Beast-ever-prevail-against-a-Bolt.html.

17. This paragraph draws upon my book *The Case Against Perfection: Ethics in the Age of Genetic Engineering* (Cambridge, MA: Harvard University Press, 2007), pp. 28–29.

18. "Global Attitudes Project," Pew Research Center, July 12, 2012: pewglobal.org/2012/07/12/chapter-4-the-casualties-faith-in-hard-work-and-capitalism.

19. Friedrich A. Hayek, *The Constitution of Liberty* (Chicago: University of Chicago Press, 1960), pp. 92–93.

20. Ibid., pp. 85–102.

21. Ibid., p. 93.

22. Ibid., p. 94.

23. John Rawls, *A Theory of Justice* (Cambridge, MA: Harvard University Press, 1971).

24. Ibid., pp. 73–74.

25. Ibid., p. 75.

26. Kurt Vonnegut, Jr., "Harrison Bergeron" (1961) in Vonnegut, *Welcome to the Monkey House* (New York: Dell Publishing, 1998). See discussion in Michael J. Sandel, *Justice: What's the Right Thing to Do?* (New York: Farrar, Straus and Giroux, 2009), pp. 155–56.

27. Rawls, *A Theory of Justice*, p. 102.

28. Ibid., pp. 101–2.

29. Ibid., p. 104.

30. For elaboration of this claim, see Michael J. Sandel, *Liberalism and the Limits of Justice* (Cambridge: Cambridge University Press, 1982), pp. 96–103, 147–54.

31. "Remarks by the President at a Campaign Event in Roanoke, Virginia," July 13, 2012: obamawhitehouse.archives.gov/the-press-office/2012/07/13/remarks-president-campaign-event-roanoke-virginia.

32. Ibid.

33. For another example of this view, see T. M. Scanlon, *Why Does Inequality Matter?* (Oxford: Oxford University Press, 2018), pp. 117–32.

34. Hayek, *The Constitution of Liberty*, pp. 94, 97.

35. Rawls, *A Theory of Justice*, pp. 310–11; Hayek, *The Constitution of Liberty*, p. 94.

36. For an illuminating discussion of the gap between liberal philosophy and common opinion on the role of desert, see Samuel Scheffler, "Responsibility, Reactive Attitudes, and Liberalism in Philosophy and Politics," *Philosophy & Public Affairs* 21, no. 4 (Autumn 1992), pp. 299–323.

37. Hayek, *The Constitution of Liberty*, p. 98.

38. C. A. R. Crosland, *The Future of Socialism* (London: Jonathan Cape, 1956), p. 235, quoted in Hayek, *The Constitution of Liberty*, p. 440.

39. N. Gregory Mankiw, "Spreading the Wealth Around: Reflections Inspired by Joe the Plumber," *Eastern Economic Journal* 36 (2010), p. 295.

40. Ibid.

41. Frank Hyneman Knight, *The Ethics of Competition* (New Brunswick, NJ: Transaction Publishers, 1997), p. 46. This volume reprints Knight's article "The Ethics of Competition," which originally appeared in *The Quarterly Journal of Economics* xxxvii (1923), pp. 579–624. On Knight generally, see the introduction to the Transaction edition by Richard Boyd.

42. For a valuable account of Rawls's debt to Knight, see Andrew Lister, "Markets, Desert, and Reciprocity," *Politics, Philosophy & Economics* 16 (2017), pp. 47–69.

43. Ibid., pp. 48–49.

44. Ibid., p. 34.

45. Ibid., p. 38.

46. Ibid., p. 41.

47. Ibid., p. 47.

48. Ibid., pp. 43–44.
49. Rawls, *A Theory of Justice*, pp. 310–15.
50. Ibid., p. 311.
51. Ibid., pp. 311–12.
52. Ibid., pp. 312–13.
53. Ibid., p. 313.
54. This explanation of pay differentials is similar in some respects to the letters I imagined a college might send to successful and unsuccessful applicants, explaining the grounds of their acceptance or rejection, in *Liberalism and the Limits of Justice*, pp. 141–42.
55. Scanlon seems to acknowledge the difficulty of disentangling the "right" from the "good" where attitudes toward success and failure are at stake. See Scanlon, *Why Does Inequality Matter?*, pp. 29, 32–35.
56. Thomas Nagel, "The Policy of Preference," *Philosophy & Public Affairs* 2, no. 4 (Summer 1973), reprinted in Nagel, *Mortal Questions* (Cambridge: Cambridge University Press, 1979), p. 104.
57. Rawls, *A Theory of Justice*, p. 102.
58. Richard Arneson, "Rawls, Responsibility, and Distributive Justice," in Marc Fleurbaey, Maurice Salles, and John Weymark, eds., *Justice, Political Liberalism, and Utilitarianism: Themes from Harsanyi and Rawls* (Cambridge: Cambridge University Press, 2008), p. 80.
59. The term "luck egalitarianism" comes from Elizabeth Anderson. My discussion of this doctrine is indebted to her powerful critique of it. See Elizabeth S. Anderson, "What Is the Point of Equality?," *Ethics* 109, no. 2 (January 1999), pp. 287–337.
60. Ibid., p. 311.
61. Ibid., pp. 292, 299–96. On the uninsured driver, Anderson cites Eric Rakowski, *Equal Justice* (New York: Oxford University Press, 1991).
62. Anderson, "What Is the Point of Equality?," pp. 302–11.
63. See Yascha Mounk, *The Age of Responsibility: Luck, Choice, and the Welfare State* (Cambridge, MA: Harvard University Press, 2017), pp. 14–21.
64. Ibid.
65. Ibid., pp. 308, 311.
66. Ronald Dworkin, "What Is Equality? Part 2: Equality of Resources," *Philosophy & Public Affairs* 10, no. 4 (Autumn 1981), p. 293.
67. Ibid., pp. 297–98.
68. As Samuel Scheffler observes, the luck egalitarian's emphasis on the distinction between choice and circumstance tacitly assumes that "people *do* deserve the outcomes of their choices. This would imply that luck egalitarianism is committed to assigning a more fundamental role to desert than its proponents acknowledge." Scheffler, "Justice and Desert in Liberal Theory," *California Law Review* 88, no. 3 (May 2000), p. 967, n. 2.
69. G. A. Cohen, "On the Currency of Egalitarian Justice," *Ethics* 99, no. 4 (July 1989), p. 933.
70. Nagel, "The Policy of Preference," p. 104.
71. Anderson, "What Is the Point of Equality?," p. 325.
72. Joseph Fishkin argues that "there is no such thing as 'natural' talent or effort, unmediated by the opportunities the world has afforded us, which include the circumstances of our birth." He challenges the idea that "genes and environment operate as separate, independent causal forces," an idea he attributes to "the casual popular science of genetics." Human development involves "an interaction among genetic activity, the person, and her environment" that cannot be disaggregated into "natural" and "socially produced" components, as most theories of equal opportunity presuppose. See Joseph Fishkin, *Bottlenecks: A New Theory of Equal Opportunity* (New York: Oxford University Press, 2014), pp. 83–99.
73. Blair quoted in David Kynaston, "The Road to Meritocracy Is Blocked by Private Schools," *The Guardian*, February 22, 2008.

74. Tony Blair, "I Want a Meritocracy, Not Survival of the Fittest," *Independent*, February 9, 2001: independent.co.uk/voices/commentators/i-want-a-meritocracy-not-survival-of-the-fittest-5365602.html.

75. Michael Young, "Down with Meritocracy," *The Guardian*, June 28, 2001.

76. Ibid.

77. Ibid.

6. THE SORTING MACHINE

1. Jerome Karabel, *The Chosen: The Hidden History of Admission and Exclusion at Harvard, Yale, and Princeton* (Boston: Houghton Mifflin, 2005), pp. 21–23, 39–76, 232–36.

2. Nicholas Lemann, *The Big Test: The Secret History of the American Meritocracy* (New York: Farrar, Straus and Giroux, 1999), p. 7.

3. Ibid., p. 8.

4. Ibid., pp. 5–6.

5. Ibid.

6. Ibid., p. 28.

7. James Bryant Conant, "Education for a Classless Society: The Jeffersonian Tradition," *The Atlantic*, May 1940, theatlantic.com/past/docs/issues/95sep/ets/edcla.htm. Conant's quote from Turner on social mobility is from "Contributions of the West to American Democracy," *The Atlantic*, January 1903, reprinted in Frederick Jackson Turner, *The Frontier in American History* (New York: Henry Holt and Co., 1921), p. 266.

8. On Turner being the first to use the term "social mobility," see Christopher Lasch, *The Revolt of the Elites and the Betrayal of Democracy* (New York: W. W. Norton, 1995), p. 73. See also Lemann, *The Big Test*, p. 48. Charles W. Eliot, president of Harvard from 1869 to 1909, used the term "social mobility" in his 1897 essay "The Function of Education in a Democratic Society," as quoted in Karabel, *The Chosen*, p. 41.

9. Conant, "Education for a Classless Society."

10. Ibid.

11. Ibid.

12. Ibid.

13. Ibid. Conant quoting Jefferson, *Notes on the State of Virginia* (1784), edited by William Peden (Chapel Hill: University of North Carolina Press, 1954), Queries 14 and 19.

14. Ibid.

15. Thomas Jefferson to John Adams, October 28, 1813, in Lester J. Cappon, ed., *The Adams-Jefferson Letters: The Complete Correspondence between Thomas Jefferson and Abigail and John Adams* (Chapel Hill: University of North Carolina Press, 1959).

16. Jefferson, *Notes on the State of Virginia* (1784).

17. Ibid.

18. Conant quoted in Lemann, *The Big Test*, p. 47. Lemann drew the quote from an unpublished book Conant wrote in the early 1940s: James Bryant Conant, *What We Are Fighting to Defend*, unpublished manuscript, in the papers of James B. Conant, Box 30, Harvard University Archives.

19. Karabel, *The Chosen*, p. 152; Lemann, *The Big Test*, p. 59.

20. Karabel, *The Chosen*, pp. 174, 189.

21. Ibid., p. 188.

22. Ibid., pp. 172, 193–97.

23. See Andrew H. Delbanco, "What's Happening in Our Colleges: Thoughts on the New Meritocracy," *Proceedings of the American Philosophical Society* 156, no. 3 (September 2012), pp. 306–7.

24. Andre M. Perry, "Students Need More Than an SAT Adversity Score, They Need a Boost in Wealth," *The Hechinger Report*, May 17, 2019, brookings.edu/blog/the-avenue/2019/05/17/students-need-more-than-an-sat-adversity-score-they-need-a-boost-in-wealth/, Figure 1; Zachary A. Goldfarb, "These Four Charts Show How the SAT Favors Rich, Educated Families," *The Washington Post*, March 5, 2014, washingtonpost.com/news/wonk/wp/2014/03/05/these-four-charts-show-how-the-sat-favors-the-rich-educated-families. The College Board last published data on average SAT scores by family income in 2016. See "College-Bound Seniors, Total Group Profile Report, 2016," secure-media.collegeboard.org/digitalServices/pdf/sat/total-group-2016.pdf, Table 10.

25. Paul Tough, *The Years That Matter Most: How College Makes or Breaks Us* (Boston: Houghton Mifflin Harcourt, 2019), p. 171, citing an unpublished analysis of 2017 College Board data by James Murphy, a tutor, testing consultant, and writer.

26. Daniel Markovits, *The Meritocracy Trap* (New York: Penguin Press, 2019), p. 133, citing Charles Murray, *Coming Apart* (New York: Crown Forum, 2012), p. 60, who reports that of college-bound seniors who took the SAT in 2010, 87 percent of students with scores over 700 in the math and verbal tests had a least one parent with a college degree, and 56 percent had a parent with a graduate degree. Murray states (p. 363) that these percentages are unpublished figures provided to him by the College Board. Using data from 1988 to the 1990s, Anthony P. Carnevale and Stephen J. Rose found that, of all students with SAT scores over 1300 (the top 8 percent), 66 percent come from families with high socioeconomic status (top quartile of family income and education), and only 3 percent come from those with low socioeconomic status (bottom quartile). See Carnevale and Rose, "Socioeconomic Status, Race/Ethnicity, and Selective College Admission," in Richard B. Kahlenberg, ed., *America's Untapped Resource: Low-Income Students in Higher Education* (New York: Century Foundation, 2004), p. 130, Table 3.14.

27. Douglas Belkin, "The Legitimate World of High-End College Admissions," *The Wall Street Journal*, March 13, 2019, wsj.com/articles/the-legitimate-world-of-high-end-college-admissions-11552506381; Dana Goldstein and Jack Healy, "Inside the Pricey, Totally Legal World of College Consultants," *The New York Times*, March 13, 2019, nytimes.com/2019/03/13/us/admissions-cheating-scandal-consultants.html; James Wellemeyer, "Wealthy Parents Spend up to $10,000 on SAT Prep for Their Kids," *MarketWatch*, July 7, 2019, marketwatch.com/story/some-wealthy-parents-are-dropping-up-to-10000-on-sat-test-prep-for-their-kids-2019-06-21; Markovits, *The Meritocracy Trap*, pp. 128–29.

28. Tough, *The Years that Matter Most*, pp. 86–92.

29. Ibid., pp. 172–82.

30. Ibid.

31. At Princeton, for example, 56 percent of the Class of 2023 self-identify as students of color. See Princeton University Office of Communications, "Princeton Is Pleased to Offer Admission to 1,895 Students for Class of 2023," March 28, 2019, princeton.edu/news/2019/03/28/princeton-pleased-offer-admission-1895-students-class-2023. At Harvard, the figure for the Class of 2023 is 54 percent. See admissions statistics, Harvard College Admissions and Financial Aid, college.harvard.edu/admissions/admissions-statistics. For percentages at other Ivy League colleges, see Amy Kaplan, "A Breakdown of Admission Rates Across the Ivy League for the Class of 2023," *The Daily Pennsylvanian*, April 1, 2019, thedp.com/article/2019/04/ivy-league-admission-rates-penn-cornell-harvard-yale-columbia-dartmouth-brown-princeton.

32. A study of the top 146 highly selective colleges and universities found that 74 percent of students came from the top quarter of the socioeconomic status scale. Carnevale and Rose, "Socioeconomic Status, Race/Ethnicity, and Selective College Admissions," p. 106, Table 3.1. A similar study of the 91 most competitive colleges and universities found that 72

percent of students came from the top quarter. Jennifer Giancola and Richard D. Kahlenberg, "True Merit: Ensuring Our Brightest Students Have Access to Our Best Colleges and Universities," Jack Kent Cooke Foundation, January 2016, Figure 1, jkcf.org/research/true-merit-ensuring-our-brightest-students-have-access-to-our-best-colleges-and-universities.

33. Raj Chetty, John N. Friedman, Emmanuel Saez, Nicholas Turner, and Danny Yagan, "Mobility Report Cards: The Role of Colleges in Intergenerational Mobility," NBER Working Paper No. 23618, July 2017, p. 1, opportunityinsights.org/wp-content/uploads/2018/03/coll_mrc_paper.pdf. See also "Some Colleges Have More Students from the Top 1 Percent Than the Bottom 60. Find Yours," *The New York Times*, January 18, 2017, nytimes.com/interactive/2017/01/18/upshot/some-colleges-have-more-students-from-the-top-1-percent-than-the-bottom-60.html. The *New York Times* online interactive feature draws on data from the Chetty study to show the economic profile for each of two thousand colleges. For Yale, see nytimes.com/interactive/projects/college-mobility/yale-university; for Princeton, see nytimes.com/interactive/projects/college-mobility/princeton-university.

34. Chetty et al., "Mobility Report Card," p. 1. College enrollment percentages by income status are displayed at nytimes.com/interactive/2017/01/18/upshot/some-colleges-have-more-students-from-the-top-1-percent-than-the-bottom-60.html.

35. Jerome Karabel, *The Chosen*, p. 547.

36. Chetty et al., "Mobility Report Cards," and "Mobility Report Cards," Executive Summary, opportunityinsights.org/wp-content/uploads/2018/03/coll_mrc_summary.pdf.

37. Ibid. For Harvard and Princeton mobility rates, see nytimes.com/interactive/projects/college-mobility/harvard-university, nytimes.com/interactive/projects/college-mobility/princeton-university.

38. Ibid. For University of Michigan and University of Virginia mobility rates, see nytimes.com/interactive/projects/college-mobility/university-of-michigan-ann-arbor, nytimes.com/interactive/projects/college-mobility/university-of-virginia.

39. Chetty et al., "Mobility Report Cards," Table IV; Chetty et al., "Mobility Report Cards," Executive Summary, opportunityinsights.org/wp-content/uploads/2018/03/coll_mrc_summary.pdf.

40. Chetty et al., "Mobility Report Cards," Table II.

41. The percentage of students at each college who move up at least two quintiles is presented in the *New York Times* online interactive feature based on data from Chetty et al. For example, at Harvard, 11 percent of students move up two quintiles; at Yale, 10 percent; and at Princeton, 8.7 percent. See nytimes.com/interactive/projects/college-mobility/harvard-university; the "overall mobility index" for each college shows the likelihood of moving up two or more income quintiles.

42. On legacy admissions generally, see William G. Bowen, Martin A. Kurzweil, and Eugene M. Tobin, *Equity and Excellence in American Higher Education* (Charlottesville: University of Virginia Press, 2005), pp. 103–8, 167–71; Karabel, *The Chosen: The Hidden History of Admission and Exclusion at Harvard, Yale, and Princeton*, pp. 266–72, 283, 359–63, 506, 550–51; Daniel Golden, *The Price of Admission* (New York: Broadway Books, 2006), pp. 117–44. The estimate of "six times as likely" is reported in Daniel Golden, "How Wealthy Families Manipulate Admissions at Elite Universities," *Town & Country*, November 21, 2016, townandcountrymag.com/society/money-and-power/news/a8718/daniel-golden-college-admission. The figure on Harvard legacy admissions is from data made public in a 2018 lawsuit, reported in Peter Arcidiacono, Josh Kinsler, and Tyler Ransom, "Legacy and Athlete Preferences at Harvard," December 6, 2019, pp. 14 and 40 (Table 1), public.econ.duke.edu/~psarcidi/legacyathlete.pdf; and Delano R. Franklin and Samuel W. Zwickel, "Legacy Admit Rate Five Times That of Non-Legacies, Court Docs Show," *The Harvard Crimson*, June 20, 2018, thecrimson.com/article/2018/6/20/admissions-docs-legacy.

43. Daniel Golden, "Many Colleges Bend Rules to Admit Rich Applicants," *The Wall Street Journal*, February 20, 2003, online.wsj.com/public/resources/documents/golden2.htm; see also Golden, *The Price of Admission*, pp. 51–82.

44. Documents produced during the 2018 lawsuit challenging Harvard's use of affirmative action showed that more than 10 percent of Harvard's Class of 2019 was admitted from a list of applicants with donor connections maintained by Harvard administrators. For the six years from the Class of 2014 through the Class of 2019, 9.34 percent of admitted students came from the donor affiliated list. Of these students, 42 percent were accepted, about seven times the overall Harvard acceptant rate during this period. Delano R. Franklin and Samuel W. Zwickel, "In Admissions, Harvard Favors Those Who Fund It, Internal Emails Show," *The Harvard Crimson*, October 18, 2018, thecrimson.com/article/2018/10/18/day-three-harvard-admissions-trial. The overall Harvard acceptance rate during this period was about 6 percent; see Daphne C. Thompson, "Harvard Acceptance Rate Will Continue to Drop, Experts Say," *The Harvard Crimson*, April 16, 2015, thecrimson.com/article/2015/4/16/admissions-downward-trend-experts.

45. Golden, *The Price of Admission*, pp. 147–76.

46. David Leonhardt, "The Admissions Scandal Is Really a Sports Scandal," *The New York Times*, March 13, 2019, nytimes.com/2019/03/13/opinion/college-sports-bribery-admissions.html; Katherine Hatfield, "Let's Lose the Directors' Cup: A Call to End Athletic Recruitment," *The Williams Record*, November 20, 2019, williamsrecord.com/2019/11/lets-lose-the-directors-cup-a-call-to-end-athletic-recruitment.

47. Bowen, Kurzweil, and Tobin, *Equity and Excellence in American Higher Education*, pp. 105–6 (Table 5.1).

48. Tough, *The Years That Matter Most*, pp. 172–82.

49. Daniel Golden, "Bill Would Make Colleges Report Legacies and Early Admissions," *The Wall Street Journal*, October 29, 2003, online.wsj.com/public/resources/documents/golden9.htm; Daniel Markovits, *The Meritocracy Trap* (New York: Penguin Press, 2019), pp. 276–77.

50. See Lemann, *The Big Test*, p. 47, and the passage quoted above (note 18) from an unpublished book Conant wrote in the early 1940s: James Bryant Conant, *What We Are Fighting to Defend*, unpublished manuscript, in the papers of James B. Conant, Box 30, Harvard University Archives.

51. John W. Gardner, *Excellence: Can We Be Equal and Excellent Too?* (New York: Harper & Brothers, 1961), pp. 33, 35–36.

52. Ibid., pp. 65–66.

53. Ibid., pp. 71–72.

54. Ibid., pp. 80–81.

55. Ibid., p. 82.

56. Brewster quoted in Geoffrey Kabaservice, "The Birth of a New Institution," *Yale Alumni Magazine*, December 1999, archives.yalealumnimagazine.com/issues/99_12/admissions.html.

57. Caroline M. Hoxby, "The Changing Selectivity of American Colleges," *Journal of Economic Perspectives* 23, no. 4 (Fall 2009), pp. 95–118.

58. Ibid. On the high acceptance rates at most colleges, see Drew Desilver, "A Majority of U.S. Colleges Admit Most Students Who Apply," Pew Research Center, April 9, 2019, pewresearch.org/fact-tank/2019/04/09/a-majority-of-u-s-colleges-admit-most-students-who-apply/; Alia Wong, "College-Admissions Hysteria Is Not the Norm," *The Atlantic*, April 10, 2019, theatlantic.com/education/archive/2019/04/harvard-uchicago-elite-colleges-are-anomaly/586627.

59. The Stanford admissions rate in 1972 was 32 percent. See Doyle McManus, "Report Shows Admission Preference," *Stanford Daily*, October 23, 1973, archives.stanforddaily.com/1973/10/23?page=1&section=MODSMD_ARTICLE4#article; Camryn Pak, "Stanford Admit

Rate Falls to Record-Low 4.34% for class of 2023," *Stanford Daily*, December 18, 2019, stanforddaily.com/2019/12/17/stanford-admit-rate-falls-to-record-low-4-34-for-class-of-2023/; Johns Hopkins 1988 acceptance rate is from Jeffrey J. Selingo, "The Science Behind Selective Colleges," *The Washington Post*, October 13, 2017, washingtonpost.com/news/grade-point/wp/2017/10/13/the-science-behind-selective-colleges/; Meagan Peoples, "University Admits 2,309 Students for the Class of 2023," *Johns Hopkins News-Letter*, March 16, 2019, jhunewsletter.com/article/2019/03/university-admits-2309-students-for-the-class-of-2023; University of Chicago 1993 acceptance rate is from Dennis Rodkin, "College Comeback: The University of Chicago Finds Its Groove," *Chicago Magazine*, March 16, 2001, chicago mag.com/Chicago-Magazine/March-2011/College-Comeback-The-University-of-Chicago-Finds-Its-Groove/; Justin Smith, "Acceptance Rate Drops to Record Low 5.9 Percent for Class of 2023," *The Chicago Maroon*, April 1, 2019, chicagomaroon.com/article/2019/4/1/uchicago-acceptance-rate-drops-record-low.

60. Drew Desilver, "A Majority of U.S. Colleges Admit Most Students Who Apply," Pew Research Center.

61. Hoxby, "The Changing Selectivity of American Colleges."

62. Tough, *The Years That Matter Most*, pp. 138–42, drawing upon Lauren A. Rivera, *Pedigree: How Elite Students Get Elite Jobs* (Princeton, NJ: Princeton University Press, 2015).

63. Dana Goldstein and Jugal K. Patel, "Extra Time on Tests? It Helps to Have Cash," *The New York Times*, July 30, 2019, nytimes.com/2019/07/30/us/extra-time-504-sat-act.html; Jenny Anderson, "For a Standout College Essay, Applicants Fill Their Summers," *The New York Times*, August 5, 2011, nytimes.com/2011/08/06/nyregion/planning-summer-breaks-with-eye-on-college-essays.html. For a leading purveyor of summer experiences geared to college essays, see everythingsummer.com/pre-college-and-beyond.

64. "parent, v." OED Online, Oxford University Press, December 2019, oed.com/view/Entry/137819. Accessed January 24, 2020; Claire Cain Miller, "The Relentlessness of Modern Parenting," *The New York Times*, December 25, 2018, nytimes.com/2018/12/25/upshot/the-relentlessness-of-modern-parenting.html.

65. Matthias Doepke and Fabrizio Zilibotti, *Love, Money & Parenting: How Economics Explains the Way We Raise Our Kids* (Princeton, NJ: Princeton University Press, 2019), p. 57.

66. Nancy Gibbs, "Can These Parents Be Saved?," *Time*, November 10, 2009.

67. Doepke and Zilibotti, *Love, Money & Parenting*, pp. 51, 54–58, 67–104.

68. Madeline Levine, *The Price of Privilege: How Parental Pressure and Material Advantage Are Creating a Generation of Disconnected and Unhappy Kids* (New York: HarperCollins, 2006), pp. 5–7.

69. Ibid., pp. 16–17.

70. Ibid., citing research by Suniya S. Luthar.

71. Suniya S. Luthar, Samuel H. Barkin, and Elizabeth J. Crossman, "'I Can, Therefore I Must': Fragility in the Upper Middle Classes," *Development & Psychopathology* 25, November 2013, pp. 1529–49, ncbi.nlm.nih.gov/pubmed/24342854.

72. Ibid. See also Levine, *The Price of Privilege*, pp. 21, 28–29.

73. Laura Krantz, "1-in-5 College Students Say They Thought of Suicide," *The Boston Globe*, September 7, 2018, reporting results from Cindy H. Liu, Courtney Stevens, Sylvia H. M. Wong, Miwa Yasui, and Justin A. Chen, "The Prevalence and Predictors of Mental Health Diagnoses and Suicide Among U.S. College Students: Implications for Addressing Disparities in Service Use," *Depression & Anxiety*, September 6, 2018, doi.org/10.1002/da.22830.

74. Sally C. Curtin and Melonie Heron, "Death Rates Due to Suicide and Homicide Among Persons Aged 10–24: United States, 2000–2017," NCHS Data Brief, No. 352, October 2019, cdc.gov/nchs/data/databriefs/db352-h.pdf.

75. Thomas Curran and Andrew P. Hill, "Perfectionism Is Increasing Over Time: A Meta-Analysis of Birth Cohort Differences from 1989 to 2016," *Psychological Bulletin* 145 (2019), pp. 410–29, apa.org/pubs/journals/releases/bul-bul0000138.pdf; Thomas Curran and Andrew P. Hill, "How Perfectionism Became a Hidden Epidemic Among Young People," *The Conversation*, January 3, 2018, theconversation.com/how-perfectionism-became-a-hidden-epidemic-among-young-people-89405; Sophie McBain, "The New Cult of Perfectionism," *New Statesman*, May 4–10, 2018.

76. Curran and Hill, "Perfectionism Is Increasing Over Time," p. 413.

77. college.harvard.edu/admissions/apply/first-year-applicants/considering-gap-year.

78. Lucy Wang, "Comping Harvard," *The Harvard Crimson*, November 2, 2017, thecrimson.com/article/2017/11/2/comping-harvard/; Jenna M. Wong, "Acing Rejection 10a," *The Harvard Crimson*, October 17, 2017, thecrimson.com/article/2017/10/17/wong-acing-rejection-10a.

79. Wang, "Comping Harvard."

80. Richard Pérez-Peña, "Students Disciplined in Harvard Scandal," *The New York Times*, February 1, 2013, nytimes.com/2013/02/02/education/harvard-forced-dozens-to-leave-in-cheating-scandal.html; Rebecca D. Robbins, "Harvard Investigates 'Unprecedented' Academic Dishonesty Case," *The Harvard Crimson*, August 30, 2012, thecrimson.com/article/2012/8/30/academic-dishonesty-ad-board.

81. Hannah Natanson, "More Than 60 Fall CS50 Enrollees Faced Academic Dishonesty Charges," *The Harvard Crimson*, May 3, 2017, thecrimson.com/article/2017/5/3/cs50-cheating-cases-2017.

82. Johns Hopkins eliminated legacy preferences in 2014. See Ronald J. Daniels, "Why We Ended Legacy Admissions at Johns Hopkins," *The Atlantic*, January 18, 2020, theatlantic.com/ideas/archive/2020/01/why-we-ended-legacy-admissions-johns-hopkins/605131.

83. Calculated from data presented in Desilver, "A Majority of U.S. Colleges Admit Most Students Who Apply," Pew Research Center.

84. Katharine T. Kinkead, *How an Ivy League College Decides on Admissions* (New York: W. W. Norton, 1961), p. 69.

85. Admissions lotteries have been proposed by a number of people in recent decades. One of the first was Robert Paul Wolff, who in 1964 proposed assigning high school students to colleges at random. Wolff, "The College as Rat-Race: Admissions and Anxieties," *Dissent*, Winter 1964; Barry Schwartz, "Top Colleges Should Select Randomly from a Pool of 'Good Enough,'" *The Chronicle of Higher Education*, February 25, 2005; Peter Stone, "Access to Higher Education by the Luck of the Draw," *Comparative Education Review* 57, August 2013; Lani Guinier, "Admissions Rituals as Political Acts: Guardians at the Gates of Our Democratic Ideals," *Harvard Law Review* 117 (November 2003), pp. 218–19; I am indebted to the discussion of random selection in Charles Petersen, "Meritocracy in America, 1930–2000" (PhD dissertation, Harvard University, 2020).

86. For the notion of merit as a threshold qualification, I am indebted to a conversation with Daniel Markovits and the students in my undergraduate seminar "Meritocracy and Its Critics."

87. Andrew Simon, "These Are the Best Late-Round Picks in Draft History," MLB News, June 8, 2016, mlb.com/news/best-late-round-picks-in-draft-history-c182980276.

88. National Football League draft, 2000, nfl.com/draft/history/fulldraft?season=2000.

89. An account, based on archival research, of the proposed Stanford experiment is presented in Petersen, "Meritocracy in America, 1930–2000."

90. Sarah Waldeck, "A New Tax on Big College and University Endowments Is Sending Higher Education a Message," *The Conversation*, August 27, 2019, theconversation.com/a-new-tax-on-big-college-and-university-endowments-is-sending-higher-education-a-message-120063.

91. As discussed above, Daniel Markovits proposes conditioning the tax-exempt status of private colleges' endowment income on increasing the class diversity of their student bodies, ideally by expanding enrollments. See Markovits, *The Meritocracy Trap* (New York: Penguin Press, 2019), pp. 277–78.

92. Michael Mitchell, Michael Leachman, and Matt Saenz, "State Higher Education Funding Cuts Have Pushed Costs to Students, Worsened Inequality," Center on Budget and Policy Priorities, October 24, 2019, cbpp.org/research/state-budget-and-tax/state-higher-education-funding-cuts-have-pushed-costs-to-students.

93. Jillian Berman, "State Colleges Receive the Same Amount of Funding from Tuition as from State Governments," *MarketWatch*, March 25, 2017, citing an analysis by Peter Hinrichs, an economist at the Federal Reserve Bank of Cleveland, marketwatch.com/story/state-colleges-receive-the-same-amount-of-funding-from-tuition-as-from-state-governments-2017-03-24.

94. See Andrew Delbanco, *College: What It Was, Is, and Should Be* (Princeton, NJ: Princeton University Press, 2012), p. 114.

95. Budget in Brief, Budget Report 2018–2019, University of Wisconsin–Madison, p. 3, budget.wisc.edu/content/uploads/Budget-in-Brief-2018-19-Revised_web_V2.pdf.

96. "The State of the University: Q&A with President Teresa Sullivan," *Virginia*, Summer 2011, uvamagazine.org/articles/the_state_of_the_university.

97. UT Tuition: Sources of Revenue, tuition.utexas.edu/learn-more/sources-of-revenue. The figures do not include income from an endowment that generates oil and gas revenues. The share from tuition and fees rose from 5 percent in 1984–85 to 22 percent in 2018–2019.

98. Nigel Chiwaya, "The Five Charts Show How Bad the Student Loan Debt Situation Is," NBC News, April 24, 2019, nbcnews.com/news/us-news/student-loan-statistics-2019-n997836; Zack Friedman, "Student Loan Debt Statistics in 2020: A Record $1.6 Trillion," *Forbes*, February 3, 2020, forbes.com/sites/zackfriedman/2020/02/03/student-loan-debt-statistics/#d164e05281fe.

99. Isabel Sawhill, *The Forgotten Americans: An Economic Agenda for a Divided Nation* (New Haven, CT: Yale University Press, 2018), p. 114.

100. Ibid.

101. Ibid., pp. 111–113. Data for OECD countries.

102. Ibid., p. 113.

103. Although this is a personal, impressionistic observation, I am hardly the first to make it. See, for example, Delbanco, *College: What It Was, Is, and Should Be*; Anthony T. Kronman, *Education's End: Why Our Colleges and Universities Have Given Up on the Meaning of Life* (New Haven, CT: Yale University Press, 2008); William Deresiewicz, *Excellent Sheep: The Miseducation of the American Elite and the Way to a Meaningful Life* (New York: Free Press, 2014).

104. Michael J. Sandel, *Democracy's Discontent: America in Search of a Public Philosophy* (Cambridge, MA: The Belknap Press of Harvard University Press, 1996), pp. 168–200.

105. Christopher Lasch, *The Revolt of the Elites and the Betrayal of Democracy* (New York: W. W. Norton & Company, 1995), pp. 59–60.

106. Ibid., pp. 55–79.

7. RECOGNIZING WORK

1. Anne Case and Angus Deaton, *Deaths of Despair and the Future of Capitalism* (Princeton, NJ: Princeton University Press, 2020), p. 51. See also Sawhill, *The Forgotten Americans*, p. 60; Oren Cass, *The Once and Future Worker* (New York: Encounter Books, 2018), pp. 103–4.

2. Case and Deaton, *Deaths of Despair and the Future of Capitalism*, p. 161; Sawhill, *The Forgotten Americans*, p. 86.

3. Sawhill, *The Forgotten Americans*, pp. 140–41; Case and Deaton, *Deaths of Despair and the Future of Capitalism*, p. 152.

4. Sawhill, *The Forgotten Americans*, p. 141.

5. Case and Deaton, *Deaths of Despair and the Future of Capitalism*, p. 7; Sawhill, *The Forgotten Americans*, p. 19.

6. Sawhill, *The Forgotten Americans*, p. 18; Case and Deaton, *Deaths of Despair and the Future of Capitalism*, p. 51. See also Nicholas Eberstadt, *Men Without Work: America's Invisible Crisis* (West Conshohocken, PA: Templeton Press, 2016).

7. Case and Deaton, *Deaths of Despair and the Future of Capitalism*, pp. 2, 37–46; Associated Press, "For 1st Time in 4 Years, U.S. Life Expectancy Rises—a Little," *The New York Times*, January 30, 2020, nytimes.com/aponline/2020/01/30/health/ap-us-med-us-life-expectancy-1st-ld-writethru.html; Nicholas D. Kristof and Sheryl WuDunn, *Tightrope: Americans Reaching for Hope* (New York: Alfred A. Knopf, 2020).

8. Case and Deaton, *Deaths of Despair and the Future of Capitalism*.

9. Ibid., pp. 40, 45.

10. Ibid., p. 143.

11. In 2016, 64,000 Americans died from drug overdose, according to the National Center for Health Statistics of the Centers for Disease Control and Prevention: cdc.gov/nchs/nvss/vsrr/drug-overdose-data.htm. 58,220 Americans lost their lives in the Vietnam War: "Vietnam War U.S. Military Fatal Casualty Statistics, National Archives": archives.gov/research/military/vietnam-war/casualty-statistics.

12. Nicholas Kristof, "The Hidden Depression Trump Isn't Helping," *The New York Times*, February 8, 2020, nytimes.com/2020/02/08/opinion/sunday/trump-economy.html. See also Kristof and WuDunn, *Tightrope*, p. 10.

13. Case and Deaton, *Deaths of Despair and the Future of Capitalism*, p. 3.

14. Ibid., p. 57.

15. Ibid., pp. 57–58.

16. Ibid., pp. 133, 146.

17. Ibid., p. 3.

18. Michael Young, "Down with Meritocracy," *The Guardian*, June 28, 2001, theguardian.com/politics/2001/jun/29/comment.

19. John W. Gardner, *Excellence: Can We Be Equal and Excellent Too?*, p. 66.

20. Jeff Guo, "Death Predicts Whether People Vote for Donald Trump," *The Washington Post*, March 4, 2016, washingtonpost.com/news/wonk/wp/2016/03/04/death-predicts-whether-people-vote-for-donald-trump.

21. Richard Butsch, "Ralph, Fred, Archie and Homer: Why Television Keeps Re-creating the White Male Working Class Buffoon," in Gail Dines and Jean Humez, eds., *Gender, Race and Class in Media: A Text-Reader*, 2nd ed. (Thousand Oaks, CA: Sage, 2003), pp. 575–85; Jessica Troilo, "Stay Tuned: Portrayals of Fatherhood to Come," *Psychology of Popular Media Culture* 6, no. 1 (2017), pp. 82–94; Erica Scharrer, "From Wise to Foolish: The Portrayal of the Sitcom Father, 1950s–1990s," *Journal of Broadcasting & Electronic Media* 45, no. 1 (2001), pp. 23–40.

22. Joan C. Williams, *White Working Class: Overcoming Class Cluelessness in America* (Boston: Harvard Business Review Press, 2017).

23. Joan C. Williams, "The Dumb Politics of Elite Condescension," *The New York Times*, May 27, 2017, nytimes.com/2017/05/27/opinion/sunday/the-dumb-politics-of-elite-condescension.html.

24. Joan C. Williams, "What So Many People Don't Get About the U.S. Working Class," *Harvard Business Review*, November 10, 2016, hbr.org/2016/11/what-so-many-people-dont-get-about-the-u-s-working-class.

25. Barbara Ehrenreich, "Dead, White, and Blue," TomDispatch.com, December 1, 2015, tom dispatch.com/post/176075/tomgram:_barbara_ehrenreich,_america_to_working_class _whites:_drop_dead!/; the W. E. B. Du Bois quote is from *Black Reconstruction in America* (1935).

26. Barbara Ehrenreich, "Dead, White, and Blue."

27. Katherine J. Cramer, *The Politics of Resentment: Rural Consciousness in Wisconsin and the Rise of Scott Walker* (Chicago: The University of Chicago Press, 2016).

28. Katherine J. Cramer, "For Years, I've Been Watching Anti-Elite Fury Build in Wisconsin. Then Came Trump," *Vox*, November 16, 2016, vox.com/the-big-idea/2016/11/16/13645116 /rural-resentment-elites-trump.

29. Arlie Russell Hochschild, *Strangers in Their Own Land: Anger and Mourning on the American Right* (New York: The New Press, 2016), p. 135.

30. Ibid., p. 141.

31. Ibid., pp. 136–40.

32. Ibid., p. 144.

33. Author's search of "dignity of labor" in online archive of the American Presidency Project, presidency.ucsb.edu/advanced-search.

34. Jenna Johnson, "The Trailer: Why Democrats Are Preaching About 'the Dignity of Work,'" *The Washington Post*, February 21, 2019, washingtonpost.com/politics/paloma/the-trailer /2019/02/21/the-trailer-why-democrats-are-preaching-about-the-dignity-of-work /5c6ed0181b326b71858c6bff/; Sarah Jones, "Joe Biden Should Retire the Phrase 'Dignity of Work,'" *New York*, May 1, 2019, nymag.com/intelligencer/2019/05/joe-biden-should-retire -the-phrase-dignity-of-work.html; Marco Rubio, "America Needs to Restore the Dignity of Work," *The Atlantic*, December 13, 2018, theatlantic.com/ideas/archive/2018/12/help -working-class-voters-us-must-value-work/578032/; Sherrod Brown, "When Work Loses Its Dignity," *The New York Times*, November 17, 2016, nytimes.com/2016/11/17/opinion/when -work-loses-its-dignity.html; Arthur Delaney and Maxwell Strachan, "Sherrod Brown Wants to Reclaim 'The Dignity of Work' from Republicans," *Huffington Post*, February 27, 2019, dignityofwork.com/news/in-the-news/huffpost-sherrod-brown-wants-to-reclaim-the -dignity-of-work-from-republicans/; Tal Axelrod, "Brown, Rubio Trade Barbs over 'Dignity of Work' as Brown Mulls Presidential Bid," *The Hill*, February 22, 2019, thehill.com /homenews/campaign/431152-brown-and-rubio-trade-barbs-over-dignity-of-work-as-brown -mulls.

35. Agriculture Secretary Sonny Perdue quoted in Johnson, "Why Democrats Are Preaching about 'The Dignity of Work'"; Donald J. Trump, "Remarks on Tax Reform Legislation," December 13, 2017, the American Presidency Project, presidency.ucsb.edu/node/331762; on distributional effect of tax cuts, see Danielle Kurtzleben, "Charts: See How Much of GOP Tax Cuts Will Go to the Middle Class," NPR, December 19, 2017, npr.org/2017/12/19 /571754894/charts-see-how-much-of-gop-tax-cuts-will-go-to-the-middle-class.

36. Robert F. Kennedy, Press Release, Los Angeles, May 19, 1968, in Edwin O. Guthman and C. Richard Allen, eds., *RFK: Collected Speeches* (New York: Viking, 1993), p. 385.

37. For discussions of "contributive justice," see Paul Gomberg, "Why Distributive Justice Is Impossible but Contributive Justice Would Work," *Science & Society* 80, no. 1 (January 2016), pp. 31–55; Andrew Sayer, "Contributive Justice and Meaningful Work," *Res Publica* 15, 2009, pp. 1–16; Cristian Timmermann, "Contributive Justice: An Exploration of a Wider Provision of Meaningful Work," *Social Justice Research* 31, no. 1, pp. 85–111; and United States Conference of Catholic Bishops, "Economic Justice for All: Pastoral Letter on Catholic Social Teaching and the U.S. Economy," 1986, p. 17, usccb.org/upload /economic_justice_for_all.pdf.

38. For a more detailed account of the contrast between a civic and consumerist conception of

politics, see Sandel, *Democracy's Discontent*, pp. 4–7, 124–67, 201–49; Sandel, *Justice: What's the Right Thing to Do?* (New York: Farrar, Straus and Giroux, 2009), pp. 192–99.

39. Adam Smith, *The Wealth of Nations*, Book IV, Chapter 8 (1776; reprint, New York: Modern Library, 1994), p. 715.
40. John Maynard Keynes, *The General Theory of Employment, Interest, and Money* (1936; reprint, London: Macmillan, St. Martin's Press, 1973), p. 104.
41. See Sandel, *Democracy's Discontent*, pp. 124–200.
42. I describe this shift in ibid., pp. 250–315.
43. Martin Luther King, Jr., March 18, 1968, Memphis, Tennessee, kinginstitute.stanford.edu/king-papers/publications/autobiography-martin-luther-king-jr-contents/chapter-31-poor-peoples.
44. John Paul II, *On Human Work* (Encyclical *Laborem Exercens*), September 14, 1981, vatican.va/content/john-paul-ii/en/encyclicals/documents/hf_jp-ii_enc_14091981_laborem-exercens.html, sections 9 and 10.
45. United States Conference of Catholic Bishops, "Economic Justice for All: Pastoral Letter on Catholic Social Teaching and the U.S. Economy," 1986, p. 17, usccb.org/upload/economic_justice_for_all.pdf.
46. Axel Honneth, "Recognition or Redistribution? Changing Perspectives on the Moral Order of Society," *Theory, Culture & Society* 18, issue 2–3 (2001), pp. 43–55.
47. Axel Honneth, "Work and Recognition: A Redefinition," in Hans-Christoph Schmidt am Busch and Christopher F. Zurn, eds., *The Philosophy of Recognition: Historical and Contemporary Perspectives* (Lanham, MD: Lexington Books, 2010), pp. 229–33. For the relevant passages in Hegel, see G. W. F. Hegel, *Elements of the Philosophy of Right*, edited by Allen W. Wood, translated by H. B. Nisbet (Cambridge: Cambridge University Press, 1991), paragraphs 199–201, 207, 235–56 (Wood edition, pp. 233–34, 238–39, 261–74). See also Nicholas H. Smith and Jean-Philippe Deranty, eds., *New Philosophies of Labour: Work and the Social Bond* (Leiden, NL: Brill, 2012), and Adam Adatto Sandel, "Putting Work in Its Place," *American Affairs* 1, no. 1 (Spring 2017), pp. 152–62, americanaffairsjournal.org/2017/02/putting-work-place. My understanding of Hegel's conception of work is indebted to discussions with Adam Sandel.
48. Axel Honneth, "Work and Recognition," pp. 234–36. See Émile Durkheim, *The Division of Labor in Society* (1902), edited by Steven Lukes, translated by W. D. Halls (New York: Free Press, 2014).
49. Robert F. Kennedy, Press Release, Los Angeles, May 19, 1968, in Guthman and Allen, eds., *RFK: Collected Speeches*, pp. 385–86.
50. Oren Cass, *The Once and Future Worker: A Vision for the Renewal of Work in America* (New York: Encounter Books, 2018).
51. Ibid., pp. 161–74. On the idea of a wage subsidy, see also Daniel Markovits, *The Meritocracy Trap*, pp. 282–83.
52. Peter S. Goodman, "The Nordic Way to Economic Rescue," *The New York Times*, March 28, 2020, nytimes.com/2020/03/28/business/nordic-way-economic-rescue-virus.html; Richard Partington, "UK Government to Pay 80% of Wages for Those Not Working in Coronavirus Crisis," *The Guardian*, March 20, 2020, theguardian.com/uk-news/2020/mar/20/government-pay-wages-jobs-coronavirus-rishi-sunak; Emmanuel Saez and Gabriel Zucman, "Jobs Aren't Being Destroyed This Fast Elsewhere. Why Is That?," *The New York Times*, March 30, 2020, nytimes.com/2020/03/30/opinion/coronavirus-economy-saez-zucman.html.
53. Oren Cass, *The Once and Future Worker*, pp. 79–99.
54. Ibid., pp. 115–39.
55. Ibid., pp. 25–28, 210–12.
56. Ibid., pp. 26, 211–12.
57. Robin Greenwood and David Scharfstein, "The Growth of Finance," *Journal of Economic*

Perspectives 27, no. 2 (Spring 2013), pp. 3–5, pubs.aeaweb.org/doi/pdfplus/10.1257/jep.27.2 .3, citing Thomas Philippon and Ariell Reshef, "Wages and Human Capital in the U.S. Financial Industry: 1909–2006," NBER Working Paper 14644 (2009) on financial service earnings; Adair Turner, *Between Debt and the Devil: Money, Credit, and Fixing Global Finance* (Princeton, NJ: Princeton University Press, 2016), pp. 1, 7, 19–21; See also Greta R. Krippner, *Capitalizing on Crisis: The Political Origins of the Rise of Finance* (Cambridge, MA: Harvard University Press, 2011), p. 28.

58. Rana Foroohar, *Makers and Takers: The Rise of Finance and the Fall of American Business* (New York: Crown Business, 2016); Adair Turner, *Economics After the Crisis: Objectives and Means* (Cambridge, MA: MIT Press, 2012), pp. 35–55; J. Bradford Delong, "Starving the Squid," Project Syndicate, June 28, 2013, project-syndicate.org/commentary/time-to-bypass -modern-finance-by-j-bradford-delong.

59. Adair Turner, "What Do Banks Do? Why Do Credit Booms and Busts Occur and What Can Public Policy Do About It?" in *The Future of Finance: The LSE Report*, London School of Economics (2010), harr123et.wordpress.com/download-version.

60. Michael Lewis, *Flash Boys: A Wall Street Revolt* (New York: W. W. Norton & Company, 2015), pp. 7–22.

61. James Tobin, "On the Efficiency of the Financial System," *Lloyds Bank Review*, July 1984, p. 14, cited in Foroohar, *Makers and Takers*, pp. 53–54.

62. Foroohar, *Makers and Takers*, p. 7.

63. Warren E. Buffett, "Stop Coddling the Super-Rich," *The New York Times*, August 14, 2011, nytimes.com/2011/08/15/opinion/stop-coddling-the-super-rich.html.

64. Ryan later qualified his statement. See Paul Ryan, "A Better Way Up from Poverty," *The Wall Street Journal*, August 15, 2014, wsj.com/articles/paul-ryan-a-better-way-up-from -poverty-1408141154?mod=article_inline; Greg Sargent, "Paul Ryan Regrets That 'Makers and Takers' Stuff. Sort of, Anyway," *The Washington Post*, March 23, 2016, washingtonpost .com/blogs/plum-line/wp/2016/03/23/paul-ryan-regrets-that-makers-and-takers-stuff-sort-of -anyway.

65. Rona Foroohar, *Makers and Takers*, p. 13.

66. Ibid., p. 277.

CONCLUSION: MERIT AND THE COMMON GOOD

1. Howard Bryant, *The Last Hero: A Life of Henry Aaron* (New York: Pantheon Books, 2010), pp. 23–27.

2. Ibid., p. 25.

3. R. H. Tawney, *Equality* (1931, reprint ed., London: Unwin Books, 1964).

4. Ibid.

5. James Truslow Adams, *The Epic of America* (Garden City, NY: Blue Ribbon Books, 1931), p. 404.

6. Ibid.

7. Ibid., pp. 414–15.

8. Ibid., p. 415.

9. I draw in this paragraph from Michael J. Sandel, *What Money Can't Buy: The Moral Limits of Markets* (New York: Farrar, Straus and Giroux, 2012), p. 203.

ACKNOWLEDGMENTS

I am grateful for having had the opportunity to try out some themes of this book with my colleagues on several occasions: in the Harvard University Department of Government's political theory colloquium, where I had the benefit of a searching critical commentary by Jonathan Gould; in the Harvard Law School's summer faculty workshop, which prompted challenging responses and follow-up exchanges with Richard Fallon, Terry Fisher, Yochai Benkler, and Ben Sachs; and in Art, Popular Culture, and Civic Life, the faculty seminar I co-chair with my wife, Kiku Adatto, at Harvard's Mahindra Humanities Center.

During the fall semester of 2019, I taught a seminar on Meritocracy and Its Critics with one of the most spirited and intellectually engaging groups of undergraduates I have encountered. I am indebted to all of them for deepening my understanding of the topics in this book. Daniel Markovits of the Yale Law School, whose recently published book on meritocracy we read in the seminar, joined us on one occasion for a memorable discussion, from which the students and I learned a great deal.

I had the good fortune to present portions of the book in lectures, followed by discussion, in a number of stimulating academic and public settings: the Niemeyer Lectures in Political Philosophy at the University of Notre Dame; the Garmendia Memorial Lecture at the University of Deusto in Bilbao, Spain; the Airbus Lecture at the American Academy in Berlin, Germany; the RSA (Royal Society for the Encouragement of Arts, Manufactures and Commerce) in London; the Institute for Human Sciences in Vienna, Austria; the Reset Dialogues on Civilization at the Giorgio Cini Foundation in Venice, Italy; the Marshall Institute at the London School of Economics and Political Science

(LSE) in London; the Democratic Agendas conference at Northwestern University; and the inaugural Day of France at Harvard University. I am grateful to the audiences and discussants on these occasions for their thoughtful engagement.

I would like to thank Elizabeth Anderson, Moshe Halbertal, Peter Hall, Daniel Markovits, Cullen Murphy, and Samuel Scheffler for helpful conversations or email exchanges on aspects of the book, Charles Petersen for sharing chapters of his PhD dissertation on meritocracy and college admissions, Aravind "Vinny" Byju for excellent research assistance, and Deborah Ghim at Farrar, Straus and Giroux for her thoughtful editorial support. I owe thanks to my agent, the redoubtable Esther Newberg at ICM Partners in New York, and to Karolina Sutton, Helen Manders, and Sarah Harvey at Curtis Brown in London.

Writing a book with FSG, now for the third time, is a joy, thanks to the generous intellectual and literary sensibilities of Jonathan Galassi, Mitzi Angel, Jeff Seroy, and Sheila O'Shea. I owe special thanks to Eric Chinski, a brilliant editor who understood what I hoped to achieve with this book before I wrote it and who offered wise advice at every point along the way. I am also deeply grateful to Stuart Proffitt, the rightly celebrated editor at Allen Lane/ Penguin, my British publisher, who, like Eric, gave each chapter a close critical reading. Receiving such editorial care from both sides of the Atlantic leaves me little excuse for whatever weaknesses remain.

Finally, and above all, I am grateful to the members of "writers' house." This is the name that my wife, Kiku Adatto, our sons, Adam Adatto Sandel and Aaron Adatto Sandel, and I have given to our practice of reading draft passages and chapters aloud to assembled family members, inviting and sharing critical commentary on our respective projects. Their attentiveness, advice, and love improved this book and me.

INDEX

ALLEN LANE
an imprint of
PENGUIN BOOKS

Justice: What's the Right Thing to Do?
by Michael J. Sandel

**Michael Sandel invites readers of all ages and political persuasions
on a journey of moral reflection, and shows how reasoned debate
can illuminate our lives**

Is it always wrong to lie?
Should there be limits to personal freedom?
Can killing sometimes be justified?
Is the free market fair?
What is the right thing to do?

Questions like these are at the heart of our lives. In this acclaimed book
Michael Sandel – BBC Reith Lecturer and the Harvard professor whose
'Justice' course has become world famous – reveals how an understanding
of philosophy can help to make sense of politics, religion, morality – and
our own convictions. Breaking down hotly contested issues, from abortion,
euthanasia and same-sex marriage, to patriotism, dissent and affirmative
action, Sandel shows how the biggest questions in our civic life can be
broken down and illuminated through reasoned debate.

Justice promises to take readers – of all ages and political persuasions – on
an exhilarating journey to confront today's political and moral controversies
in a fresh and enlightening way.

'One of the most popular teachers in the world' *Observer*

'Enormously refreshing ... Michael Sandel transforms moral
philosophy by putting it at the heart of civic debate' *New Statesman*

'One of the world's most interesting political philosophers' *Guardian*

'Spellbinding' *The Nation*

ALLEN LANE
an imprint of
PENGUIN BOOKS

What Money Can't Buy: The Moral Limits of Markets
by Michael J. Sandel

**The Top Ten *Sunday Times* Bestseller on how our culture is
mesmerised by the market**

Should we give children money to read books or to get good grades? Is it
ethical to pay people to test risky new drugs or to donate their organs? What
about hiring mercenaries to fight our wars, buying and selling the right to
pollute, auctioning admission to elite universities, or selling citizenship to
immigrants willing to pay? Isn't there something wrong with a world in which
everything is for sale?

In recent decades, market values have crowded out nonmarket norms in almost
every aspect of life – medicine, education, government, law, art, sports, even
family life and personal relations. Without quite realizing it, Sandel argues, we
have drifted from having a market economy to being a market society.

In *Justice*, an international bestseller, Michael Sandel showed himself to be
a master at illuminating with clarity and verve the hard moral questions we
confront in our everyday lives. Now, in *What Money Can't Buy*, he examines
one of the biggest ethical questions of our time and provokes a debate that's
been missing in our market-driven age: what is the proper role of markets in
a democratic society, and how can we protect the moral and civic goods that
markets do not honour and money cannot buy?

'Brilliant, easily readable, beautifully delivered and often funny ...
an indispensable book' David Aaronovitch, *The Times*

'Provocative and intellectually suggestive ... little less than a wake-up
call' Rowan Williams, *Prospect*

'A star philosopher ... entertaining and provocative' Diane Coyle,
Independent

'Let's hope that *What Money Can't Buy*, by being so patient and
accumulative in its argument and examples, marks a permanent shift
in these debates' John Lanchester, *Guardian*